Tall, dark, and i \ he owned the whole

He bestowed smiles on every female he encounte... From grandma to teenager, server to customer, they looked ready to fall into those long arms swathed in the charcoal gray sleeves of a well-tailored suit. Despite the smile, he moved like a predator. Even from a distance, Steffi's skin prickled beneath his power.

In a few long strides, he stood at her table. "Miss Anbruzzen?"

The flutters in her belly flipped like Olympic gymnasts. Close up, the man looked even better than he had at the bar. A wing of black hair swept over a broad forehead. His nose had taken a few punches, and thick werewolf brows brought out deep-set gray eyes. A generous mouth and a jaw like granite suggested an intriguing blend of soft and hard.

"Mister Montaigne? Or do you prefer *Monsieur* Montaigne?" According to Ellyn's message, he was French Canadian.

His eyes opened wider. She'd caught him off-guard. Good.

"I prefer Sawyer."

So he leaped to a first-name basis. Like a Mentor. At least he had better credentials. "Steffi."

"It's a pleasure to meet you, Steffi."

Huge hands but a comfortable grip. "You could have fooled me." Withdrawing her hand, she indicated not the seat he stood by, but the one on the opposite side of the small table.

Without breaking eye contact, he slipped into the chair he'd chosen. "What makes you say that?"

Praise for Zanna Archer

Finalist/Third Place
Speculative Category
2019 Heart-to-Heart Contest
San Francisco Area RWA

Shiftless in Sheboygan

by

Zanna Archer

Shapesisters, Book One

Shiftless in Sheboygan

Cover Art by *Debbie Taylor*

The Wild Rose Press, Inc.
PO Box 708
Adams Basin, NY 14410-0708
Visit us at www.thewildrosepress.com

Publishing History
First Edition, 2022
Trade Paperback ISBN 978-1-5092-4189-7
Digital ISBN 978-1-5092-4190-3

Shapesisters, Book One
Published in the United States of America

Dedication

To Sarah and Layla

Acknowledgments

Although I have always had the support of family, friends, and teachers with my writing, for this book, I would like to specifically acknowledge my editor, Callie Lynn Wolfe, for her thoughtful guidance in making this book the best it could be, and Debbie Taylor for designing a cover that captures the essence of the story. In the capricious business of publishing, Rhonda Penders, Co-founder and President of The Wild Rose Press; RJ Morris, Co-founder and Vice President; and Lisa Dawn MacDonald, Marketing Specialist, have made my vision reality. Throughout the editing process, the Wild Rose Press garden of associates, writers, and editors has been available for support and advice. Anonymous judges of various RWA contests provided useful suggestions and encouraging comments. From mangled draft to final revision, the members of my writer's group have been invaluable critique partners. Many thanks to our fearless leader Colleen Driscoll, Dustina Diane Davis, Nancy Hall, Pepper Hedden, Ron Knoblock, Lindsey Minardi, and R. Gene Turchin.

Chapter 1

As the speaker droned on, Steffi Anbruzzen clutched the handbag in her lap and muttered, "My name." *SAY MY NAME!*

"And last, but certainly not least—"

Finally! Steffi rested her hands on the table in the rear of the university banquet hall and prepared to stand when Dr. Tobias Underwood acknowledged her contribution to his award-winning research project.

"—and has graciously consented to become Mrs. Tobias Underwood."

What? Halfway to her feet, Steffi froze. The curvaceous blonde who trotted across the stage to join Dr. Underwood was one of the postdocs from the research team. *What about me?* The time and energy Steffi had devoted to his project flashed in her mind like calendar pages in an old movie. Without her preliminary observations, would he even have undertaken the study?

The white-haired professor beamed like a besotted boy when his fiancée flashed a diamond that triggered a standing ovation.

ENOUGH!

The room turned red. Rage thudded against the inside of Steffi's skull like lava inside a volcano. *CONTROL! CONTROL!* The voices of her OASIS Mentors thundered in her brain. *Control! Control! CHANNEL!*

1

She pushed the clawing monster deep into her gut and scrambled through the audience to the nearest exit. Outside the hall, she paused. *Control. Channel.* She had to shape-shift. And soon. But not here in the middle of campus where a Simple Human might see her.

Where then? She scanned for cover. *Trees! GO!* She ripped off her shoes and sprinted toward the tall trees on the opposite side of the parking lot.

Leaping over a low hedge, she plunged into the greenery.

Control. Control. Channel. Focus. LIONESS.

When she squeezed her eyes shut, the shape appeared, mighty and fierce. *Shift! NOW!*

She threw back her head and opened her mouth. Instead of a satisfying roar, no sound emerged. Weird. She tilted her head. An eerie blackness surrounded her. Her heartbeat pounded in her ears, and she peered into emptiness.

What's happened? Where is everything? Ever since she'd set fire to her crib during an infant tantrum, Mentors dispatched by the Organization to Assist, Support, and Inform Shape-shifters had trained her to manage the emotions that fueled her ability. Everyone at OASIS feared what she could do if she lost control as an adult.

I tried my best, but I couldn't... Instead of shape-shifting, she must have unleashed her rage with catastrophic results. Annihilation. A sob caught in her throat. Images of her family burned into her awareness. Libby's sweet smile. Dayzee's bright eyes. Mom's open arms. Dad's goofy grin.

Gone. And not simply family. *Everyone. Every living being.* A fresh torrent of grief mixed with guilt washed through her. Billions of lives. *Everyone and everything. I've destroyed it all.*

Tears filled her eyes. She rubbed her nose and blinked. Fuzzy nubs, not fingers. Pads, not a palm. When a claw dug into her nose, she hissed and set the paw down in front of her. Retractable claws. She'd felt none of the muscular and skeletal realignment that accompanied a shift—must have been too angry to notice—but she *had* shifted. *Thank God!*

Relief streamed into her muscles. The world, every thing and every being in it, still existed.

She stared into the darkness. Where, then, was she?

A long stretch disturbed a slight weight on her back. When she brushed her whiskers against the barrier, a familiar vanilla, citrus, and rose fragrance bombarded her brain, and she sneezed. Her feline sense of smell was much more sensitive than her human one.

She inched along a smooth, dark surface. Her toe pads bumped into something cold and hard. She pressed her nose against the object. Her tongue flicked out and tasted metal. Tiny edges. Zipper! In her human shape, she would have laughed.

Steffi sat back on her haunches, licked a paw, and washed her face. She'd been in too much of a rush to strip before shifting. Must be stuck in her dress. But her lioness was bigger than her human. Should have ripped her way out of the garment. Yet, when she stood, folds of loose fabric drooped on either side of her. Maybe this fabric had some sort of superstretch. No sense thinking about that now.

Get out! Follow...the...zipper-tooth road—aha!

She found an opening, pushed her head through, and wiggled her body free. The scents of spring grass and

3

early flowers soothed her frazzled nerves. A full moon floated above the trees. The chirping of spring peepers counterpointed human and automotive noises from the nearby parking lot.

Thank you, thank you, thank you!

If she'd had arms, she would have embraced the night and everything in it. She should return to her human shape and head back to the hotel, but first she would take a stroll and use the heightened senses of her lioness to enjoy this wonderful world.

The hedge that bordered the park looked higher than it had when she'd jumped over it. Moonlight revealed white mitts instead of big golden paws.

"Meow?"

She barely felt the soft sound emerge from her throat.

Steffi's brow lifted. Ohmigod! She wasn't a lion. She was a cat. She lifted one paw for inspection. Not even a full-grown cat. A *kitten.* Even worse.

She sniffed. If she walked in the park in this shape, she'd be a strolling snack for nocturnal predators.

Relax. Cat to lion. Nothing to it. Closing her eyes, she visualized a powerful beast—it helped to imagine sinking sharp teeth into Dr. Tobias Underhill's bony arm. That would wipe the smirk off his face.

Nothing happened.

No need to panic. She drew a few deep breaths. Under normal circumstances, she could shift directly from one animal shape to another, but controlling her anger must have taken a toll. All right. She would return to her primary shape—her human—slip into her clothes and drive back to the hotel. Definitely the smartest move. A lioness prowling in a public park might attract unwanted attention from Simple Humans. Resting her paws on the grass, she closed her eyes and focused on Steffi Anbruzzen: chin-length dark hair, longish face with two slashes of eyebrows, decent nose, mouth a bit too big, square jaw.

With every breath, muscle and bone should have lengthened into a skinny torso, strong arms, and long legs. But her chest did not expand into a generous bosom. Her pelvis did not drop and curve. Capable hands and big feet did not replace those stupid kitten paws.

Damn you, Tobias Underhill! Tonight's event had marked another celebration of Underhill's research. In his book and in his speech, he had mentioned everyone who had contributed to his academic achievements. Almost everyone.

Damn, damn, double damn you.

Cold fear trickled down her spine. Returning to the human that was her base shape should have been simple, but tonight, that fundamental skill had deserted her. If she kept trying and failing, she would worry more. Better rest now and try again in the morning when she was fresh.

She turned her paws. No thumbs to flex or fingers to wiggle. What if she never— *Don't think like that.* Other Shifters must have gotten stuck in their shapes. OASIS surely had a remedy. They were supposed to help Shifters. It was in their name: Assist, Support, and Inform. Of course, if a Shifter was far from family, colony, or pack, who besides that Shifter would know about the problem?

She hadn't told anyone about this trip, but Libby and Dayzee would worry if they didn't hear from her. Libby was a cop. She'd turn the whole country inside out if she had to. Fortunately, she wouldn't have to go that far. She could track the phone.

Steffi glanced toward the crumpled outfit that covered the purse that contained her phone. Safe now, but for how long? A kitten could guard the site, but not fend off a thief. More important, in every shadow of the moonlit park, predators lurked. Their heavy breaths rattled the air. How long could a lone kitten last?

Growling, Steffi unsheathed her claws. *Tiny* claws. She padded toward the sheltering base of a nearby tree. Without the protective warmth of a mother and littermates, she shivered. She would fix this shifting problem. But first...

****

"You took a *nap*?"

Steffi eyed her sister's shocked face on the phone. "That's what cats do. Plus, I was tired. Of course, I didn't get much sleep since I woke up whenever I heard a noise. You have no idea how loud the woods can be when you're little."

"Sounds scary." After inspecting her polished shoe, Libby placed it on her shoe-rack and started buffing its mate. Even though she no longer wore a police uniform, she kept her shoes shiny enough for her to see her reflection. Typical Lib.

"It was."

"What did you do to shift back to base?"

"That's the strangest part. I finally fell asleep. When I woke up, I ran over to check on my dress. It was still lying in the grass. Then I decided—I almost didn't try. I was so afraid I'd fail again, and I didn't know what I would do if..." She pressed her tongue against the roof of her mouth to relax her jaw. If she didn't stop gnashing her teeth, her next dental appointment would cost the moon.

Libby put down the shoe and gave the screen her full attention. "Easy, Steff." Her voice was soft, and the golden lights in her dark eyes sent warmth. "You're back. Everything's okay."

"You're right." Steffi hugged herself. "I've never appreciated being human so much." Her coffeemaker beeped. "I still don't know why it happened. I mean, I did get superpissed, but I controlled it. I channeled it." She poured her coffee and added milk.

"There's a first time for everything. Maybe this will be the last time, too." Libby offered an optimistic smile Steffi didn't feel comfortable returning. "Have you shifted since you got home?"

"Are you kidding? I feel so lucky to be human again I don't want to take any chances. Also, the OASIS rep said I shouldn't shift until my 'problem' is resolved." Steffi sipped her coffee. A comforting, *human* ritual. "I'm sure she thinks I am the problem. Along with you and Dayzee."

"Ah, yes. The Three Anomalies." Libby laughed. "Bubble, bubble…" She pantomimed stirring a cauldron while Steffi groaned at their official OASIS designation.

"Anyway, I called because there's this guy. Sawyer Montaigne."

Her sister sat up, suddenly alert. "You've been holding out on us! Is he as sexy as his name?"

"Put a sock in it, Lib. OASIS has assigned him to help me. I bet he's an ancient gnome. Will you ask Ellyn about him?"

"Why don't you ask your Mentor?"

"Because she hasn't been with OASIS as long as

Ellyn has. Ellyn knows everything about everybody who works there." Steffi clasped her hands. "I want to be sure this guy is competent."

Libby picked up her shoe and took a few more passes at it. "You're too suspicious. You should be the cop instead of me." She placed the second shoe on the rack. "I know you and your Mentors haven't always gotten along, but you should give OASIS credit. If they hadn't turned up after your first shift, who knows what would have happened to us?" She frowned. "There might not even have been an 'us' because Mom and Dad could have been too freaked out to have more kids after you."

Steffi lifted her hands in surrender. "You're right. OASIS has been helpful."

"Do you honestly think they would assign an incompetent?"

"I guess not." Steffi refilled her coffee cup. "But this Montaigne character will know all about me, and I don't know anything about him. Please ask Ellyn."

Libby smiled. "I'll do better than that. I'll send you her number so you can ask her yourself."

"Thanks."

"That's what sisters are for, right?" Libby paused. "I hope he can figure out what happened with your shifting and why. You need to know. We all do." The suggestion of fear skittered across her face. "Suppose this turns out to be something normal?"

Normal? Steffi gulped her coffee. "It will be the first thing in our lives that is."

The bad joke didn't even elicit a smile. "Seriously, Steff, suppose our ability has an expiration date. Don't you think Dayzee and I need to know?"

"Of course you do." Memories of her kitten

entrapment frosted Steffi's spine. "If I find out that you have any reason to worry, I'll tell you."

"Do that." Libby's eyes narrowed, and her jaw stiffened as the cop replaced the amiable sister. "And promise me that until this is fixed, you won't shift unless one of us is with you."

Steffi drew back her shoulders and lifted her chin. "That's not necessary. I already told you that OASIS recommends—"

"And I know how you handle OASIS recommendations." Libby blew a raspberry. "What if you hadn't been able to get back to your human base this time?"

"I was. I did."

"But if you hadn't?" Although her delicate features made her look like a pushover, the steel in Libby's gaze could wring a confession from The Pope. "You'd be stuck in Sheboygan. Locked up in animal control. Maybe even euthan—" She pressed her knuckles to her mouth.

"Don't be so melodramatic." Hard to believe this human jelly dealt with murder and mayhem on a regular basis. "I was an adorable kitten. Someone would have adopted me." Of course, if they hadn't— *Stop. You're fine.*

"That makes me feel so much better." Libby whipped a strand of caramel-colored hair back from her forehead. "In the meantime, I'd have filed a missing persons report, which wouldn't have been worth spit. What could Dayzee and I have told Mom and Dad?"

Libby's concern settled over Steffi like a comfortable quilt. "You're a great cop. You would have found me. If it makes you feel better, I won't shift without you. Unless shifting is part of my treatment."

"Promise me you won't do it alone. Please!"

"Okay, okay, but I think you're overreacting."

"Says the woman who spent the night as a kitten." The tension in Libby's mouth eased, but her expression remained serious. "I'm your sister, Steff. I love you."

"I love you, too." Steffi gripped her phone. Although she enjoyed seeing Libby when they talked, today she ached to hug and be hugged. "Thanks for listening."

"Any time. Keep me posted."

"Will do. Give my regards to Tommy and stay safe."

With a laugh, Libby brought her fingers to her forehead in a crisp salute. "You, too. Especially if Sawyer Montaigne is half as hot as his name." She blew a kiss and vanished.

Chapter 2

The smoky scotch at the hotel bar didn't erase the sour taste in Sawyer's mouth every time he reflected on his meeting with OASIS Director Richards, his uncle Mel. Upon learning that the Organization had assigned him to help the eldest of the Three Anomalies recover her shape-shifting ability, Sawyer had asked, "Why me?"

"Why not you?" Uncle Mel fiddled with the papers on his desk and spoke without looking him in the eye. "You've helped other Shifters recover their ability."

Sawyer had to move closer to hear him. "And?"

"Everyone knows how tough she's been on her Mentors." His uncle continued to organize his desk.

According to her file, a bitch to the nth degree. An incredible pain. He'd stood by the desk and waited for Uncle Mel to meet his gaze.

"We all agree that she needs a firm, experienced hand—*your* hand—to guide her." The older man's fingers lingered near his mouth, a sure sign he was hiding something.

"What else?"

His uncle cleared his throat. "That you can keep her occupied until her recovery window closes."

Sawyer stared at the tower of a man he'd always considered above reproach. "Let me get this clear. You don't want me to help her. You want me to—"

"To apply your highly publicized womanizing skills for the greater good." Every inch the Director, his uncle straightened his shoulders. "Charm her. Distract her. Do whatever it takes. Give us one fewer Anomaly to worry about."

One fewer Anomaly— Hello!

When Stefanie Anbruzzen entered the hotel lobby, the *loup-garou* within him stirred, and Sawyer left his stool at the hotel bar. The photos in her file didn't do her justice. Beneath the sconces, mahogany highlights shone in her hair. She had wide-set eyes, high cheekbones, a stubborn chin, and a mouth that would have been made for kissing if it ever relaxed. A bluish-green dress skimmed her torso and stopped above her knees. Shapely calves and ankles. When he'd made the appointment with her on the phone, her voice had been as warm as melted honey. As sticky, too, if a man wasn't careful.

At the entrance to the restaurant, she checked her watch. Then she scanned the lobby. When her gaze skimmed past, he cleared his throat with the rumble of a low growl. Most women would have paused long enough for him to reel them in with a smile.

Another glance at her watch. She tapped her toe and spoke with the maître d' before following him inside.

Sawyer left his drink, drew a deep breath, and approached the restaurant. She'd chosen a table in the far corner. Like most Shifters, she wanted to be inconspicuous. As if someone who looked like Stefanie Anbruzzen could ever fade into the background.

The sommelier presented the Châteauneuf-du-Pape Sawyer had ordered in advance. She accepted the choice and brought the glass to her lips, but set it down without tasting it. Too preoccupied? Too irritated? She checked her watch again, surveyed the restaurant, and shifted position as if preparing to leave.

He mentally rehearsed his opening remarks. He often began by emphasizing patience, but Uncle Mel's instructions nagged him. *Keep her occupied. Charm. Distract. One fewer Anomaly.*

Lyrics from an old Seventies song popped into Steffi's head when Sawyer Montaigne entered the restaurant. Tall, dark, and indecently handsome, he looked like he owned the whole damned hotel, restaurant included. He bestowed smiles on every female he encountered. From grandma to teenager, server to customer, they appeared ready to fall into those long arms swathed in the charcoal gray sleeves of a well-tailored suit. Despite the smile, he moved like a predator. Even from a distance, Steffi's skin prickled beneath his power.

In a few long strides, he stood at her table. "Miss Anbruzzen?"

The flutters in her belly flipped like Olympic gymnasts. Close up, the man looked even better than he had at the bar. A wing of black hair swept over a broad forehead. His nose had taken a few punches, and thick werewolf brows brought out deep-set gray eyes. A generous mouth and a jaw like granite suggested an intriguing blend of soft and hard.

"Mister Montaigne? Or do you prefer *Monsieur* Montaigne?" According to Ellyn's message, he was French Canadian.

His eyes opened wider. She'd caught him off-guard. Good.

"I prefer Sawyer."

So he leaped to a first-name basis. Like a Mentor.

At least he had better credentials. "Steffi."

"It's a pleasure to meet you, Steffi."

Huge hand but a comfortable grip. "You could have fooled me." Withdrawing her hand, she indicated not the seat he stood by, but the one on the opposite side of the small table.

Without breaking eye contact, he slipped into the chair he'd chosen. "What makes you say that?"

"You were standing at the bar when I arrived but made no effort to join me. In addition, your late arrival suggests a lack of enthusiasm for this job."

"I understand your reasoning, but you've drawn the wrong conclusion." He poured wine into the empty glass the server had provided, swirled the liquid, inhaled the aroma, and sipped. "I often learn a lot by watching clients move when they don't know they're being watched."

"Then you should improve your surveillance skills." When he did not react to the insult, she continued, "From the moment I entered, I felt your eyes on me."

"You didn't seem uncomfortable." He lifted his glass and drank again. "Some women in your situation have moved from the center of the room to a less exposed side. You made no effort to do that. Instead, you advanced in a forthright but cautious manner. You must be used to people looking at you."

"No, I'm not." When his brows lifted, the corners of her mouth twitched, but she stifled her smile. "In my work, I'm the observer, not the one being observed."

"Spoken like a true predator." He sounded approving. "So you were watching me while I was— perhaps we could split the difference and start over, eh?" He stood and offered his hand again. "It's a pleasure to meet you, Steffi."

She clasped his hand and let her gaze range from his head to his knees before returning to his face. "We should get to work."

He returned to his seat. "First, let's order."

She set the menu aside. "Let's go someplace more reasonable."

"Pardon?"

"I didn't expect my membership in OAS—" With a glance at the crowded restaurant, she substituted the public term. "—the Organization—to cover such extravagant meals."

Sawyer sat back. "We think you're worth the expense."

"Please! I can almost hear a collective groan whenever they see me or my sisters coming."

"Don't take it personally. They don't like dealing with the unknown. You and your sisters are Unknowns with a capital U. They respect your ability, but no one— not even the three of you—knows your limits. They also wonder how many more like you there could be that they don't know about."

Steffi brightened. "They've found others?"

"Not yet."

"Oh." She didn't hide her disappointment.

"Tradition and oral history suggest there were genetic mutations in earlier times. Many may have perished in infancy or in persecutions. Others might have been driven away…or gone off on their own…like the dragons guarding their treasure. Nowadays, with more women working in science and industry, others may have been exposed to the chemicals like the ones that affected your mother's eggs."

She shook her head. "Well, the Organization can stop worrying about my ability until I get it back."

Until, not if. Sawyer felt a twinge of pity at her confident word choice. Her desire to recover was almost palpable. "That's why I'm here." He waited for the server to leave with their order before asking, "What questions do you have?"

Her nostrils flared slightly as if she scented danger. "Do you really want to talk here?" She gestured at the occupied booths and tables, the staff weaving their way between narrow aisles.

"Why not? We have reasonable privacy. We're not going to say or do anything indiscreet." He grinned to counteract her somber expression. "Nobody will notice two people enjoying each other's company on a blind date." He paused. "We are enjoying each other's company, eh?"

She sat back. "I'm not enjoying much of anything these days."

So much for charm. "Of course not." He lifted his glass. "At least, the wine is good."

She sipped. "For the price, it should be."

"Are you going to worry about money all through the meal?"

"When I think about how much my sisters and I have paid the Org—"

As he leaned toward her, the scent of freshly mowed pasture after a summer rain made him catch his breath, and sudden heat passed through him with the force of a kick from one of *oncle* Jacques' mules. "You've gotten your money's worth."

Her dark eyes widened. "What do you mean?

"Do you have any idea how much the Organization

has invested in you?"

"About the same as they spend on everyone else."

"Hardly." He tapped his chest. "We—the rest of us—learn from our families and the Elders of—in my case, our pack, in others, their Family affiliations. You had no one. Keeping up with you and your sisters hasn't been easy. The Organization had to train your Mentors to teach you what you needed to know about your condition."

"I'm sorry." She looked down at the table. "I never realized…I always thought that Mentors were like regular teachers. Everyone had them."

Sawyer spied their server. "If I'm not mistaken, our food is here." His stomach growled as a rare filet appeared in front of him.

Steffi eyed her plate with a half smile that vanished in a heartbeat.

"Why don't you tell me what happened in Sheboygan?"

She gripped her knife handle. "If you'd read the report, you'd know."

Brr! "I have read the report. The facts are clear. As to why it happened and how you recover your full operating capacity—" *Zut.* He sounded like a technician trying to fix a computer, not one Shifter talking with another. "I'm here to help you." The lie rolled off his tongue with surprising ease.

She nibbled a bit of chanterelle mushroom. "That's supposed to reassure me…how?"

"Look, I'm sure you're feeling anxious. If I were in your shoes—"

"You're not." She put down her fork.

"True. But I've handled other cases like yours."

Her glance made him feel three feet tall. "Don't be offended, but I'm not sure you're up to the task."

It was his turn to come to attention. "I beg your pardon?"

"If the Organization really wanted to help me, they would have sent someone more experienced. Older."

He ate another chunk of filet. "I've worked with the Organization for almost ten years."

"Troubleshooting but nothing steady. You took bachelor's degrees in psychology and zoology with a smattering of business. You dropped out of vet school." She paused. "How am I doing so far?"

He brought his hands together in silent applause. "Want a gold star for your record?"

"Wouldn't hurt." The corners of her mouth tipped up, but once again, a full smile failed to appear. "Since you're so experienced, what's your plan?"

"Every case…every client…is unique. We start by looking for external causes. A physical explanation."

The possibility must have interested her because she looked ready to leap to her feet. "Like what?"

He shifted position as if preparing to catch her but kept his voice neutral. "Allergies."

She brushed off the suggestion. "None."

"Drug reactions."

She shook her head. "I haven't taken drugs since I was a teenager. Before then, everything was fine. I got all the standard vaccinations. Once my hormones kicked in, medicine started having weird side effects."

A chance to establish common ground! "I know what you mean. When I was fourteen, I took something to clear my skin, but it triggered sudden hair growth. Fur popped out everywhere." Steffi's solemn face made him suppress his smile.

"Must have been horrible."

Add ten points for empathy to her personality profile. "Not horrible. But embarrassing. I *did* miss my first school dance."

"That's too bad." Steffi sipped her wine. "When I was thirteen, I had tonsillitis, and the doctor wrote the usual prescription, which helped with the tonsils, but I threw up every time I tried to…use my ability. It was worse than being sick. I haven't taken any drugs since then. Unless you count caffeine. Or chocolate." She stroked the stem of her glass. "Alcohol, too, I suppose."

"Pharmaceuticals are the usual culprits. Since you've traveled to remote locations, you could have ingested a drug without knowing it."

"Maybe. Do they test for anything else?"

"Viral strains. Bacterial infections. Exotic parasites."

Steffi's pretty lip curled.

"Don't look so disgusted. With parasites, once you flush the bugs out of your system, everything goes back to normal."

"Just like that?" She snapped her fingers.

"Exactly." Sawyer imitated her motion. "Our medical facility here in Chicago can take the blood for the tests." *But not right away.*

"I hate needles." Steffi glanced at her upper arm, but the corners of her mouth softened. "Something medical. That could fix everything." She finished her entrée with a flourish.

"I wouldn't get my hopes up." As he uttered the warning, the sparkle in her eyes dimmed. "These problems often have more complicated, internal causes."

"Gee, thanks. Have any of your other clients told you you're a real killjoy?"

A muscle in his cheek twitched. "Not that I remember."

"Of course, I suppose it's not all bad from your point of view."

"Pardon?"

"The longer it takes to solve the client's problem, the longer you get to enjoy first-rate meals and five-star accommodations." She gestured toward the lobby. "I assume you're staying here."

He nearly choked with laughter. So that was why she treated the wine like poison and wanted a "more reasonable" meal. She thought he was padding his expense account. "Let me assure you, Steffi, the sooner we solve your problem the better. In fact, the longer it takes, the less likely—" The information he routinely provided slipped out before he could stop it.

Her eyes became huge. "The less likely what?"

He hesitated.

"Are you saying I only have a certain amount of time before I'm stuck like this?" Fear shimmered in her eyes.

"The sooner we start, the better. Please tell me your story. From the beginning."

"First, tell me about this time thing."

Damn. She wasn't going to let it go.

"How long do I have?"

He toyed with his tie. "That depends. Health and age can be factors. Older clients have a recovery window of about three months. Someone your age should have at least six—"

"Six months? That's all?" She stared at him.

He lifted a restraining hand. "There's no way of knowing with you and your sisters."

"So I might have less than six months."

"Or more."

Instead of whining or wailing, she tossed her serviette on the table. "We'd better get busy. I want those blood tests now."

"The lab is closed." No reason to mention the Emergency Unit.

"First thing tomorrow then."

"I'll see what I can do." He sipped his wine. "Now, tell me your story, Steffi."

"Since you've read my file, you already know—"

"What others have written about you."

Steffi crossed her arms. "Don't believe everything you read."

"That's why I want to hear your story from you. In your own words." With luck, the soothing tone that settled his nieces in for their bedtime stories would soften her defenses. "Tell me what happened in Sheboygan, Steffi."

Chapter 3

Steffi swallowed. "It wasn't so much what happened as what didn't. I became a cat instead of a lion. Then I couldn't shift from cat to lion. When I tried to return to base—" Although she began in a low voice, as her anxiety increased, so did her volume. "I couldn't do anything!" She slapped a hand over her mouth, drew a deep breath, and squeezed her eyes shut as if that would blot out the stunned faces of diners turned in their direction.

Dropping her hand to the table, she met Sawyer's steady gaze. "Oh, dear." She glanced at the Simple Humans. "We should leave."

"We're a momentary distraction. It'll be all right. Relax." When the power of his big hands surrounded her fists, her shoulders stiffened. "Breathe easy. Nice and slow."

His deep voice cooled her overheated brain. The concern in his eyes assured her that he wanted to help. Beneath his sheltering hands, her fingers uncurled. Inhale. Exhale. Inhale. Exhale. Like yoga practice.

"Better?"

"Much." Their fellow diners had returned to their own conversations. When Sawyer released her hands, a calming wave moved over them.

Over dessert and coffee, Sawyer watched her as if she were a puzzle he was trying to solve. "You do understand that you have two problems, not one."

She shrugged. "I always was an overachiever." When his expression didn't change, she added, "But not much of a joke-teller."

He flashed a quick grin. "That wasn't half bad. You surprised me."

She sat up. "So I have two problems instead of one."

"Right. Unexpected...misfires...occur more often than you might imagine, especially for younger and older...practitioners. Being unable to return to your base shape, however, is more serious."

"No kidding." Except for the twitch in his jaw, Sawyer seemed unruffled. Of course, he was unruffled. He'd never had shifting problems.

"Other clients have said that they felt as if their world turned upside down...or inside out. So I do understand—in a limited sense—the frustration you must have experienced." He cleared his throat. "The more you can tell me, the better I can identify the cause or causes and develop a treatment plan. You've told me how it ended. Could you start at the beginning?"

Did he really want her to regurgitate the whole sorry saga? She rested her coffee cup against the saucer with a clink. "That could take a while." Maybe he'd prefer to move on.

"I'm here to listen." Sawyer sat back. "Take as long as you like."

He had no idea what he was asking for. Delectable ganache mixed with ice cream slid down her throat. "Ever since I was a kid, I've been fascinated with how SH"—she supplied the OASIS abbreviation for Simple Humans—"behave in groups."

"Know thy enemy."

"Oh, no!" She bit back the exclamation. "I could never think of them that way." She brought a hand to her heart but returned it to the table so his eyes wouldn't linger on her bosom. "My parents are the best people I know, and they're SH."

"Most of the ones I've known have also been good." Sawyer's reassuring smile dimmed. "Of course, some of the talk that's circulating here in the States has made many of us worry."

"Like that Crispin Alexandros creep who wants to expose the 'shadow dwellers'?" The shudder moved through her before she could quiet it. "I know what you mean, but that wasn't why I—I liked watching people and trying to figure out why they behaved as they did. In college, I discovered sociology, anthropology, and ethnology. When I was accepted into a good doctoral program, I was over the moon." She paused, shoulders tensing as she prepared to ward off questions about why she'd left school without her degree.

"Too bad it didn't work out." Sawyer's voice reflected no judgment. Maybe people gave him a hard time for dropping out of vet school.

"While I was deciding what I could do, one of my favorite professors told me about a research project she was considering with a remote community that had no recorded contact with outsiders. The number of these groups is dwindling, and in some countries, you need official permission before you make that first contact. Gwen—Dr. Mallory—didn't want to jump through the bureaucratic hoops until she had a clear plan for making a successful first contact. She really liked the group observations I'd done for her classes. On the basis of those reports, I talked her into hiring me to do preliminary observations—watching, no contact. She would use my report to plan how to proceed with the project. She liked my work, recommended me to another scholar, who recommended me to someone else. Two years ago, Tobias Underhill hired me."

A forkful of carrot cake paused halfway to Sawyer's mouth. "Underhill? The guy who wrote that Zuntos book?" The light in Sawyer's eyes brightened. "I heard him on a podcast."

Steffi bit her lower lip. "That's him all right. He'll go anywhere, talk to anyone about *his* work. The Zuntos project attracted attention, especially after a company purchased mining rights to their region and wanted to relocate them. Then, Dr. Underwood became more than a respected scholar. He became a champion of the oppressed. Which, I'm sure, has also been great for book sales."

She paused. If she were talking with her sisters, by now, their eyes would have glazed. Sawyer still looked interested. Better pick up the pace before he started to fidget. But those big hands looked far too solid to fidget. Her eyes traveled from the hands up the long arms to shoulders broad enough to carry the weight of the world without straining. The elegant lines of his jacket emphasized a solid chest tapering to a thinner waist. After years of observing scantily clad men in less industrialized cultures, she easily envisioned the thick, corded muscles of his shoulders and back beneath the dark jacket and crisp white shirt.

"You were saying?" Sawyer's voice broke into her reverie.

"I should get to the point before I bore you to death." *Or tear off your shirt.*

"Don't worry."

When Sawyer chuckled, she wanted to hug him for his affability. Too bad a hug would bring them much too close together. She glanced down at the table so he wouldn't catch her staring.

"Take all the time you need."

Time. Six months. She drew back her shoulders. "I've never been an official member of the research teams, but the other PIs—Principal Investigators—have always acknowledged my contributions. Getting that sort of mention, along with a good reference, can be helpful. I worked harder for Tobias Underhill than I ever worked before. He demanded longer observations. Detailed reports. He used my notes in his book. Sometimes word for word."

"Is that legal?"

"He paid me, so he owns whatever I produced." She added cream to her coffee. "In the rush to publish, sometimes people get left out of the acknowledgments. When his book was published, I didn't see my name. I wrote him a note congratulating him and reminding him of my contribution. I asked him to acknowledge my work in future editions. When I heard that he was receiving an award in Sheboygan and promoting a new edition, I decided to attend because I hoped…" As the memory of Underhill's voice oozed into her brain, she squeezed her eyes shut and gritted her teeth. "All he had to do was mention my name."

"But he didn't."

Eyes still closed, Steffi nodded.

"Frustrating."

She opened her eyes. "I went from hurt to insulted to furious in two heartbeats." Sawyer's concerned face slowed her racing pulse. "I pushed the rage way down deep. The way Juliet—my first Mentor—taught me." She demonstrated with her hands. "I left the banquet hall before I blew the roof off. Got away from people as fast as I could. Found a safe spot."

"You did what you should have done. Good for you."

"Ha!" Her cry wiped the approving smile from Sawyer's face. "If I did everything right, why did it all go wrong?" Before he could spew more OASIS claptrap, she continued, "No. Everything didn't. Only me. It sounds silly now, but at first, I thought I'd annihilated the universe." She waited for the inevitable laughter.

Instead, the eyes that met hers were solemn. "That must have been horrifying."

"It was…until—" She shook her head. "In one minute, I went from destroyer of worlds to kitten."

"In some ways, that must have been even more frightening." Sawyer finished his coffee.

"Yes. Can you imagine being the rabbit instead of the wolf?"

"Sorry, no. I've never been anything but a predator. Rabbits are prey." He closed his eyes and smiled.

Steffi cleared her throat. "Don't look so damned happy. That could have been me."

Sawyer's lids opened slowly. "Your Shifter scent would have put me off."

She didn't know whether to feel pleased or insulted. "All right. So you werewolves wouldn't have gobbled me up."

"*Loups-garous*."

"Lewga-what?"

"What you call werewolves."

"Oh. Well, you *loups-garous*—" She liked the way the phrase rolled inside her mouth. "You might not have eaten me. Owls wouldn't have been that picky."

Sawyer interrupted their conversation to settle the bill. Outside the main entrance, he gestured toward a waiting cab.

Steffi looked up. "It's a nice night, and my apartment's not far. I can walk."

Instead of saying good night, Sawyer fell in step beside her. "When your return to your human failed, you decided to rest rather than push yourself to keep trying. Smart."

"I don't know about that." Steffi pushed a strand of misplaced hair behind her ear. "I felt ready to drop on the spot. Which could have been fatal." When her shoulders tensed, Sawyer's warm hand found her elbow. His musky male scent mingled with the tang of apples and sage.

"You survived the night." His deep voice rasped against her ear like a lupine tongue massaging bare skin. "The next morning, how many times did you try to return to your base shape?"

"Only once, thank God. If I'd failed, I don't know what I would have—" She stopped and turned to face him. "You have no idea how awful it feels to be trapped in a powerless form."

"Especially when you're used to being a predator."

"One of the first things our Mentors taught was to always choose our shapes from the top of the food chain."

They walked in companionable silence for a few minutes before Sawyer spoke. "I never felt powerless, but I have endured a few humiliations with shifting."

Steffi's gaze traveled from his eyes to his dark dress shoes and back. "I find that hard to believe."

"You and your sisters were shifting in the cradle.

The rest of us can't use our ability before puberty. Everyone says since our bodies are already going through so many changes at that time, shifting is simply one more. They don't tell us how painful that first reshaping of bones and muscles can be. I felt like I was being pulled to pieces from the inside out."

A hand seemed to squeeze her heart. "How awful!"

"It was. And I was part of a group. I knew that if I even whimpered, the other guys would never let me live it down. Didn't help that my grandfather was the pack alpha."

Steffi paused at a corner. "This is my street." They turned together.

"The first shift was bad, but the first hunt was worse."

"How so?"

"By then, I was feeling comfortable. Cocky, even. I was bigger and stronger than most of my peers. I was also young and stupid."

"What happened?" The closer they came to her door, the slower her steps became. She wanted to hear the whole story.

"I was so excited about the hunt that as soon as I shifted, I took off, tearing through the woods and howling my fool head off."

Easy to envision him as an exuberant young wolf. "You must have been a wild thing."

"I was. Then I realized I was all alone in the middle of the woods."

All alone. A freeze gripped her spine. She'd been there.

"Packs have a protocol for hunting. The alpha and the Elders lead, followed by the experienced hunters.

They make the first kills, claim the prime portions. Newcomers bring up the rear, along with the old and disabled. They get the remains, go after smaller prey. The Elders had taught us the order, but I was so full of myself that I forgot." He stopped.

When she looked up at him, she clasped her fingers to keep them from brushing the twitch in his jaw.

"Taking the lead was bad enough, but that wasn't the worst part." He scowled. "My noise spooked the prey. I ruined the hunt for the entire pack."

"Oh, no!"

"The Elders barred me from hunting for two seasons. During that time, the other pack members my age never let me forget what I was missing." The hint of a growl beneath his deep voice suggested the beast within. "Isn't this your building?"

Steffi blinked as if waking from a dream. "Yes. Yes, it is." The dark street added mysterious shadows to Sawyer's rugged face. She opened her mouth to invite him up for a nightcap or another cup of coffee, but he spoke first.

"What's on your schedule for tomorrow?"

"Since it's getting close to the end of the semester, I have papers and projects to look at, along with preps for the final. Tuesdays and Thursdays are full, but I can work with my online classes on my own time, and I have only one class tomorrow—an evening one—so my day is free."

"See you in the morning then." His hand clasped hers. "Good night, Steffi."

Steffi started toward her door but turned and aimed a finger at him. "Blood tests. Tomorrow."

"I'll do my best." Sawyer swallowed. What should

have been an empty statement rang with the sincerity of a promise.

With a crisp nod, Steffi disappeared through the open door beside a flower shop.

She knew what she wanted, and she didn't hesitate to ask for it. Hell, she didn't ask—she demanded. One of the traits that no doubt drove her Mentors crazy. Most of his clients were awed by OASIS, but Steffi regarded the Organization with a mixture of respect and distrust. His success at delaying her recovery would validate her worst suspicions.

Instead of calling for a ride, Sawyer walked back to the hotel. The memory of Steffi's honeyed voice and her open-air scent stayed with him. He was supposed to distract her, but she seemed to be doing the distracting. He laughed at the irony.

For the next few weeks, Steffi's teaching jobs would keep her busy. After that, they could travel. Rest and recreation helped his clients. Even if he prescribed exhausting triathlon training—his own muscles protested—Steffi's ability might return. Of course, for full recovery, the restored ability required stabilization. Sawyer stopped in the middle of a block and clenched his fists. If Steffi did recover, OASIS might supply a panacea instead of the medical stabilizer. That would go against everything they preached about caring for their clients.

Swearing beneath his breath, Sawyer stomped along the broad sidewalk. If his uncle thought the Anomalies were a problem now, wait until one of them was betrayed by OASIS. If Steffi exposed their existence to Simple Human society, she could make life miserable for Shifters everywhere.

Uncle Mel might be the Director of OASIS, but he hadn't thought this through. He might not even have gotten clearance from the board. Likely the board had approved, but with discussion that disguised their actual intent so they could have deniability if anyone ever confronted them. At the head of the table, Uncle Mel would have led the charge.

When Sawyer entered the hotel lobby, Steffi's image floated across the floor. An Anomaly, but more important, his OASIS client. A fellow Shifter with a serious problem. Three, actually. Two she knew about, while the third... He tugged at his shirt collar and took out his phone to report in. The demands of OASIS weighed on his shoulders. Like Uncle Mel and the board, he chose his words with care.

****

Steffi trudged the four flights up to her apartment, and a tornado of questions swirled around her. When they'd stood beneath the streetlight, a flash of interest had lit Sawyer's eyes, but his good night had been brusque, business-like. He'd spoken about their being on a date, but that had been a joke. They had a professional relationship, nothing more. She was his OASIS client, and he no doubt intended to maintain an appropriate distance.

Even if he did like her, Sawyer was a werewolf. No, wait. What was the Canadian? "*Loup-garou.*" The whispered word caressed the roof of her mouth. Why did everything sound so much more romantic in French? For the same reason everyone French— *Whoa, girl!* Sawyer was French Canadian. Big difference.

After taking off her shoes and slipping out of her dress, she picked up her phone and sat at her table. Too late to call, so she texted Libby.

—*Good meeting. Not a gnome!*—

Far from it. Then, she opened the earlier message from Libby's Mentor. She'd skimmed it before meeting Sawyer, but perhaps she'd missed something significant. Like whether he had a mate. Nothing about that in the message.

She put down her phone. What was she thinking? She'd asked for Sawyer's professional credentials, not the details of his personal life.

Leaving her phone on the table, she went into the bathroom. Would a *loup-garou* with a mate invite a female Shifter to dinner, let alone joke about their being on a blind date? Maybe. If OASIS had arranged the meeting. But a *loup-garou* with a mate would have been efficient, ending the dinner as soon as they concluded official business so he could get back to his family. Sawyer had ordered more wine and kept her talking through coffee and dessert. He'd also walked her home.

So likely no mate. Why not? According to his background, Sawyer was in his early thirties, certainly old enough. Even though he charmed every woman in the restaurant—almost every, she'd seen through him— he might be gay. Did *loups-garous* have same-sex mating? He padded his expense account, so he might not earn enough to attract a mate. Some *loup-garou* males could have the same difficulties as Simple Human males did when it came to females. Steffi paused in wiping off her makeup to stare into the mirror as if she could summon Sawyer's imposing figure. No physical impediments there.

With Sawyer's image hovering at the edge of her consciousness, Steffi turned on the water and stepped beneath the shower. Perhaps OASIS had saddled Sawyer with her case because his pack wished to avoid the disruption caused by his unharnessed sexual energy. They might want him out of their fur until he was ready to settle.

Under the shower glove that slipped down Steffi's arm, her skin tingled. How long had it been since she'd felt this...stimulated? No! Excited? Worse. Interested? Yes, that would serve. Interested. Bland and safe. The exact opposite of the emotions Sawyer triggered.

Steffi shut off the water, stepped out of the shower, and towel-dried her hair. Why waste time fantasizing about someone she could never have? OASIS Mentors had taught about the organization of Shifters into affiliated Families. Most mated with their own kind, but *loups-garous* were distinctive because they mated for life and only with their own kind. Different packs to keep their bloodlines strong, but always *loup-garou*.

When Steffi smoothed rose-scented skin cream from her ankles to her thighs, from her neck to her wrists, she felt Sawyer's big hands covering her fists. She'd met plenty of Shape-shifters who liked to flaunt the energy linked to their ability. In contrast, Sawyer's power surrounded him as naturally as the air he breathed. When she'd become upset at the restaurant, he could have hustled her out to avoid risking further exposure.

Instead, he'd made a protective gesture, something no other being had done. Although Mom and Dad had always shown their love, they'd also confided that, terrified by her first shift, they'd defended themselves and minimized damage to the apartments. Steffi's ability had been hell on security deposits. Growing up, she and her sisters had looked after each other, but as the oldest, she'd always had the most responsibility. Secure in her ability, she had never felt vulnerable.

Until Sheboygan.

Sawyer's touch had shielded her. Her hands warmed, and comfort rippled through her body.

Pulling down her foldaway bed, Steffi flopped onto the old mattress. Nothing posh, but serviceable. She lay on her back and stared at the ceiling. Caffeine from the after-dinner coffee buzzed in her brain.

She sat up, reached for her robe, and stopped. Before Sheboygan, when sleep eluded her, she went up to the roof, spread her arms, and shifted. In her owl shape, she glided through the velvet night of Chicago's parks. Tonight, if she stood on the roof, her human ears would hear only the traffic noise that shattered the midnight stillness; her human eyes would see only the city lights that blotted out the starry skies.

She took a deep breath and stretched her arms wide. Then she snapped her elbows back to her ribs. Every inch of her body yearned to fly, but she'd promised Libby. Maybe a small bird. A parakeet. She shouldn't do it. She might screw up again. When she'd aimed for a lion, she'd turned into a kitten. Instead of a parakeet, she might end up as a fly or a gnat. An excellent snack for a hungry spider.

More important, as Sawyer had pointed out, she had two problems. After a good shift, she might still fail to return to her human base. If Sawyer found her in bird form, he'd give her a disgusted glance before he dropped her in a box and shipped her to OASIS Central. If they failed to bring her back to her human base, she would spend the remainder of her brief life caged in Mom and Dad's sunroom.

If OASIS did return her to her human base, they might pump her full of that X-Ting drug they used to extinguish the ability of criminal Shifters. Assuring her they were acting in her best interest, they could reduce her to a Simple Human. Everyone in her family would do their best to help her, but no one would understand the depth of her loss.

No shifting, then, until Sawyer gave her the Go sign. *The sooner, the better*. Steffi marked her calendar. Almost a month gone. She slipped off her robe, groaned, and punched her pillow.

Look on the bright side. Chicago was always fun, especially with a fascinating man at her side. In reality, the handsome *loup-garou* might never be more than an OASIS-appointed advisor, but she could always dream. Wriggling with pleasure, she closed her eyes.

Chapter 4

Repeated buzzing yanked Steffi out of a delicious slumber. Grunting, she rolled out of bed. When she reached her front door, she punched the intercom.

"Good morning!" The cheerful voice rumbled in her ear, and one tantalizing image from her dreams skimmed past: Sawyer pulling off his shirt to expose abs that Michelangelo's David would have envied.

Steffi groaned. He'd said something about an early start. Should have set her alarm.

"I've brought breakfast. Why don't you buzz me up, eh?"

Her eyes made a quick circuit of the compact apartment that even her average-sized Simple Human friends called a matchbox. Sawyer would look like a giant in a kid's playhouse. Would his broad shoulders crack the door frame, his dark head punch a hole in the low ceiling? *"Let him in,"* the invisible imp on her shoulder prodded. *"No way!"* The voice of caution rang out. To the intercom, she said, "I'll be down in a few minutes."

She opened the drawers built into the wall and pulled out serviceable-looking tan garments. Someone knocked on the door.

"Sorry," Sawyer said as she opened the door. "One of your neighbors let me in."

Steffi looked as if she'd tumbled out of the unmade

bed a few steps behind her. Strands of dark hair feathered her forehead and cheekbones. Good thing he had his hands full because he itched to stroke her flushed skin. As it was, he fought the arousal caused by a brush with one sleeve of the wrap robe that hugged her curves and ended at midthigh. "Hope I didn't wake you. When I stopped by a coffee shop, I thought that we might talk over breakfast, eh?"

"What time does the lab open?" She tightened the knot on the sash of her satin robe as if adjusting her armor.

"We're scheduled at nine." He lifted the food. "Where should I put this?"

"Over there." When she indicated a small table close to an equally tiny stove and refrigerator, she bumped his shoulder, hopped back so fast she bounced off the edge of the bed, and popped up like a Jack-in-the-Box with her open hands spread against his chest. With a gasp, she pulled back. Because her gaze seemed glued to his torso, Sawyer drew a deep breath and tightened his abs.

"Sorry."

Steffi's eyes widened. "If anyone should apologize, it should be me."

"Force of habit." Sawyer smiled. "And a Canadian childhood."

The corners of her mouth twitched. "I've heard you folks are much more polite than we are. Still, I bumped you."

"Not really a bump. More of a brush."

She took the food and set it on the table. Then she turned to reach for the foot of the bed.

"I can do that."

"Thanks, but it's easier than it looks." She lifted the

bed and pushed it into storage. "I've gotten used to hauling it up and down." She paused. "Especially if I'm expecting company."

He scanned the room. Family photographs and a few large prints of stunning vistas covered the walls. A full-length mirror hung on the washroom door, and a built-in bookcase covered the wall beside a small window. Two chairs. One square table. "Entertain much?"

For the first time, he caught the flash of a real smile that vanished as quickly as it appeared. "Hardly. My sisters stay with me, and sometimes my book club... My friends and I meet at restaurants, theaters, wherever we're going."

What about dates? Lovers? His gut knotted. OASIS client! "How long have you lived here?"

"Since I left school. I did a favor for a fellow student whose grandfather owns this building. Good location, reasonable rent, and a great lease. When I'm away, I either sublet or Airbnb. While I'm getting dressed, you should start." She pointed at the table. "Your coffee's getting cold."

Something had better get cold. As Sawyer eased his leg around the edge of the table and took a seat, his hyperkeen hearing picked up the quick movements behind the washroom door. Running water to wash her face. Brushing her teeth with one of those motorized brushes. Did she take that on her research jaunts? Soft footpads on linoleum. Slinky robe slithering to the floor. Silence. When his imagination traveled up those long runner's legs to the dark triangle at their juncture, he shifted position and eased the pressure. OASIS client!

She emerged clad in tan cargo pants and a faded tan jersey. With a few quick strokes, she brushed her hair back from her face and took the seat opposite his. When she sampled the coffee, her eyebrows lifted. "It's the way I like it. How did you know?"

The pleasure in her voice was like a burst of sunshine in the small room. "You had coffee with dessert."

The corners of her mouth relaxed. "You are good."

He dipped his chin. "I aim to please."

"Mission accomplished." Steffi saluted him with her cup. "Thank you."

Her satisfied purr tickled his crotch.

"So you're from Canada. What part?"

Why was she asking? "Montreal in Quebec."

She folded a napkin as if she were doing origami. "Does your OASIS work take you away from home a lot?"

She seemed fascinated by that napkin. She hadn't asked him anything personal last night. Why the sudden curiosity? "I take assignments when I can fit them in with the family business."

She crossed her arms and rested her elbows on the table. "That's good."

He swallowed a bite of his breakfast. Good, eh? Spoken like someone who'd never sat through a board meeting. "I suppose."

"If you were gone a lot, you'd miss so much, don't you think? I mean, I don't have any children—"

Ah! "Nor do I." In case she missed the point, he held up his bare left hand.

A blush bloomed on her cheeks, and she focused on her breakfast. Under other circumstances, this conversation might have led right to that hidden bed, but not while she was his OASIS client. If she figured out his genuine assignment, she'd boot him without a word. The realization stung.

"This is tasty."

"I'm glad you like it. After all your travels. I thought you might have more exotic taste."

She swallowed. "In camp, I use packaged meals. When I'm observing, I eat whatever my shape eats. Plants, grubs, ants, sap."

Sawyer wrinkled his nose.

"Don't be a food snob. The people I observe eat bugs, too, sometimes because hunting is bad or crops fail, but basically because protein is protein, however you get it."

Sawyer stretched. "Thank God we *loups-garous* eat real food."

"And that would be?"

"Meat! And lots of it." He laughed.

"You like the hunt."

"Of course!" He spread his hands on the table. As her steady gaze softened, he dialed down his natural enthusiasm. "You're a predator. Don't you enjoy the chase? The kill?" At the thought, his heartbeat quickened.

When her lips tightened, the energy drained from the room. "My shapes hunt when they need to, and it's not a social event. Since I seldom inhabit a shape long enough to establish a long-term connection like yours, my human base doesn't recall much of the experience."

His *loup-garou* stirred in displeasure. "That's too bad."

"Not really. If I had strong bonds with every shape I've shifted to, I might have all sorts of creature awareness jumping around inside me." She pressed her fingertips to her forehead. "Trying to keep it all straight might make my mind go"—she made a circle with her hands and drew it out—"Pop!"

"Nothing like that is going to happen while we're working together."

She looked down at the table. "Especially now that all my shapes have vanished."

"They'll come back."

"You have great faith in OASIS."

"I have faith in you." The truth of his words triggered a flash of surprise.

She must have been less convinced because she pulled her hands free and stood. "I'm glad one of us does."

Sawyer's watch buzzed. "We should go."

When they stepped onto the sidewalk, he swung his arms. Good to be in the open air.

"Where's the lab?"

"Near Oak Park." Sawyer held up his phone. "I'll call for a ride." Georges had dropped him off minutes ago and parked nearby.

Steffi regarded the busy street. "The El is quicker. And cheaper."

His luxury sedan would add to her concerns that he was abusing his expense account. He sent a quick cancel and pocketed his phone. "After you." He followed her fast stride. "For someone who hates needles, you seem to be in a hurry to get stuck." Although he'd intended to joke, when she turned, her expression was grave.

"The sooner they take the blood, the sooner I'll have the results." She bounced. "If I'm lucky, these tests could solve everything."

"Here's hoping." When Steffi recovered, what

would happen to the captivating woman he'd glimpsed beneath her mask?

Squeezing into a crowded train, they stood side by side as if glued at the hips. His *loup-garou* distinguished her fresh scent from the odors of their fellow passengers, and her body seemed to hum, most likely from the vibration of the train but perhaps also from her optimism. When they reached their stop, she turned away and severed their connection.

The front rooms of the medical facility served Simple Humans. A nurse guided them into the private facility reserved for Shifters. While a lab tech prepared to draw her blood, Steffi gritted her teeth, and her jaw tensed.

"Take a deep breath, and don't look." Sawyer nested her icy free hand between both of his, a comfortable fit. "It will be all right."

"I know." The trust in her dark eyes was like a blow to his chest.

"All done!" the technician chirped.

"Wow! I didn't even feel it." Steffi turned to the technician. "Great job. Thanks." The other woman smiled. "When can I get the results?"

The technician organized the tubes. "We send this to the main lab in Minnesota. Should take about a week or two. Depending on their backlog."

"A week or two. That's not too—"

Steffi interrupted Sawyer by squeezing his hand. "I need these results as soon as possible." She regarded the technician. "Don't you have some sort of express...emergency service?"

The other woman hesitated. "Priority One." She sounded dubious.

Steffi's gaze drilled into him. Sawyer nodded at the technician. "Do it."

They stepped out of the facility and into the fresh spring air.

"That wasn't too bad." Steffi turned from the building to him. "Thanks for providing a diversion."

"My pleasure." *And my job.* As they walked, he shortened his stride. Steffi brushed the hand he'd held as if she were trying to wipe him off. Should have used the hand sanitizer.

"If they find something like a virus or a bug, I guess that means I'll be…you won't need to…we won't…"

"Yes. If you have a medical problem, the doctors will handle it." The hint of regret in her voice made his heart race, but he maintained a matter-of-fact tone. "Right now, you can get on with your end-of-the-semester business, and I…you can call me if you have any questions."

When he turned away, she said, "Wait. Suppose the results are no good?"

"My clients and I explore alternative possibilities."

"Can we do that now?"

"Yes, but you have a busy schedule for the next few weeks, and if the medical results—"

"You've already suggested that there might be—what did you call them?—'more complicated, internal causes'?"

Sawyer winced at her imitation—did he sound that hopelessly pedantic?—and nodded.

"The clock is ticking. I don't want to waste time waiting for useless information. I want to start exploring those 'alternative possibilities'."

Would she ever stop throwing his words back at

him? He took out his phone. "When would you like to meet?"

"I'm free until this evening." When he hesitated, she asked, "Are you busy with other clients?"

So easy to lie, and exactly what OASIS ordered. But hope shone in her face. "No. Where could we meet? I don't have an office here."

"Can't the Organization set you up?"

"That could take a few days." He scratched his chin. "What about your place?" *Charm. Distract.*

"I don't think so." Steffi gestured at his shoulders. "You need more room."

"Depends on the circumstances." He flashed a grin even though she was right. "What about my hotel?"

"No." She shook her head so vehemently that a dark wave of hair whipped across her face.

Without thinking, he reached out and started to brush the strands from her cheek, but the second he touched her smooth skin, his fingers stopped as if glued to the spot. Amber fire blazed in her widened eyes, and her lips parted slightly, in what might have been an invitation. A brown shutter eclipsed the glow. Dropping his hand, he stepped back. "I'm open to suggestions."

"The library."

Library, eh? Books, magazines, computers. A practical place for a professional exchange. "Sounds good."

Chapter 5

On the elevated train, they once again stood side by side. Although Sawyer pretended to watch the city whizzing past in the window, Steffi's presence occupied his mind. What captured his attention had nothing to do with her OASIS case and everything to do with her long, slender form and the lively gaze so at odds with her controlled mouth. In a few months, he would become the son his parents desired and take a mate. In the meantime, he wanted to see Steffi smile and hear her laugh. When incoming passengers jammed them against each other, heat rushed to his groin, and his grip on the strap tightened. Steffi Anbruzzen was not, would never be *loup-garou*.

Her facial expressions and voice might remain neutral, but her body betrayed her interest. Last evening, on the walk back to her apartment, she'd mirrored his posture. This morning, when she regarded him over her coffee, her pupils had dilated. She'd also tried to find out if he had a mate.

Her earthy scent floated above the Simple Human stench of the other passengers. When she tapped his arm, he almost jumped. "This is our stop." Watching the easy sway of her hips, he followed her down the stairs to the street level, where she turned toward a large red brick building with tall arched windows.

"Impressive."

"Wait till you see the inside."

Although he took a moment to admire the elegant but functional reception area, Steffi occupied his thoughts. OASIS trusted him to maintain confidentiality and not take advantage of his client. This time, however, they expected him to exploit a client's vulnerability. He massaged the tension in his neck and wished he could wipe away the stain of the assignment. If only Steffi weren't so damned appealing.

"What's wrong?"

He swore silently. "Soft pillow." She already distrusted OASIS. Did her suspicions extend to him? Could she, perhaps, detect the desires hidden behind his professional façade, right beside the gnawing guilt? Although OASIS had studied Steffi and her sisters for years, no one knew the full extent of their powers. If she could read his mind, she'd no doubt have terminated their contact already...unless she planned to get everything out of him she could. If so, good for her.

From now on, when they were together, he would concentrate on the most important attributes of their relationship and make them his mantra. The words danced beneath a bouncing ball on his mental screen: Sawyer Montaigne did not take advantage of his OASIS clients. Steffi Anbruzzen was not, would never be *loup-garou*. She was merely a lovely Shifter with a mouth the color of summer roses.

When Steffi found an isolated corner, he set his phone on the small table. "May I record our conversation? Purely for my use. To give me a verbatim record. I don't want to miss anything significant."

The corners of her lips twitched in one of those half smiles. "I'm sure you won't." She squared her shoulders and gestured at the recorder. "You may fire when ready."

"Please!" Sawyer laughed. "This is an interview, not an interrogation. If you feel uncomfortable, let me know, and I'll turn it off."

"Thank you. I will."

"From what you've already told me, I have the impression that your work demands a lot of your ability."

She straightened as if he were questioning her competence. "Nothing I can't handle."

Another silent swear. He didn't want to make her defensive. "I wasn't suggesting that. I am curious about your procedure. For instance, when you observe in a shape, you can't take notes. How do you put together your reports?"

"Now you're fishing for trade secrets." Although her voice remained serious, gold glints danced in her eyes. A hint of mischief, eh? "As a student, I developed mental mapping strategies for my classes. I applied that to my first observation. Time and place. People involved. Types of interaction. Words and gestures. Behavior patterns. I hid a recorder and returned to base a few times a day to make notes."

"So you shifted from your observation shape to your human base several times a day? That must have been exhausting."

"Mostly annoying because I had to shift in a secluded spot and the breaks interrupted the flow of my observation." Sitting back, she stretched. "My sister Dayzee works in films, and she knew a tech Shifter who solved the problem." She indicated a faint scar in the middle of her forehead. "Chips."

"Like the kind they put in pets?"

The corners of her lips turned up slightly. "More

sophisticated. Mine transmitted everything I saw or heard back to my computer. When I returned to camp, the notes were waiting for me. I could even include images and actual sound in my report."

"Clever! Your work sounds fascinating."

Steffi pressed her lips together. "Not everyone agrees. My sisters think it's really boring."

"They don't know how wrong they are. When you talk about your research, your face lights up and your voice has a passion." *Mon dieu*! Terrible word choice. Sawyer Montaigne did not take advantage of his OASIS clients. Steffi Anbruzzen would never be *loup-garou*.

"No kidding?" Her eyes widened. "My voice has passion?"

Sawyer cleared his throat. "Your love for your work comes through with every word."

"I do love it but don't know how much longer I'll be able to do it now that everyone is using drones. Faster and cheaper."

But no substitute for you. "How do you decide what shape to take?"

Steffi rested her elbow on the table and leaned toward him. "First, I research the local fauna. That's a fun part. I've spent hours here in the library. I use the Web, too, but I love being surrounded by all this knowledge." Her eyes glowed. "I choose several species that should get me close enough to observe the community without anyone—animal or human— noticing me. I start with the predators, but major predators can make lousy observers."

"If you get hungry, you might snack on the people you're supposed to be watching?"

She shook her head. "That never happened, but

predators can present other problems." Her gestures became more expansive. "Take green anacondas."

"Big floppy snakes? No thanks."

"In water, they rule. On land, they're huge and slow—like humongous slugs. Other predators are too conspicuous. If a jaguar lurks near a village, the humans may start hunting her." She bounced. "I did squeeze in some jaguar shifts in South America. You haven't run until you've been a jaguar."

When Steffi stretched, Sawyer envisioned her in that sleek, powerful shape. He could almost see her whiskers twitch. Sawyer Montaigne did not take advantage of his OASIS clients. Steffi Anbruzzen, who loved running as a jaguar, would never be *loup-garou*.

She drew in a sharp breath. "I'm sorry. I shouldn't talk as if you—I'm sure when wolves run, it feels wonderful, too."

"Yes," Sawyer agreed. *But not like a jaguar.*

"It's not always fun," she continued. "During my Zuntos observation, I almost got eaten."

Sawyer's heart skipped a beat. "What?" His question would have bounced off the high ceiling, but she lifted a restraining finger.

"Hush." Gold twinkling in her eyes, she pressed her finger against his lips.

Heat kindled in his belly, but before he could kiss her hand, it returned to the table. Sawyer Montaigne did not take advantage of his OASIS clients. Steffi Anbruzzen would never be *loup-garou*.

"I thought I'd found the best shape: a large lizard with great camouflage. Unfortunately, that turned out to be Zuntos filet mignon." She described her subsequent capture and escape as if summarizing an action movie.

When she finished, he laughed.

Steffi scowled. "You think it's funny?"

"Of course not. I'm sorry. I am...somewhat...amused...that you brush off almost perishing in a primitive stew-pot as a minor inconvenience, but shifting into a kitten terrified you."

Her lips formed a silent "o" before she spoke. "When the Zuntos captured me, I had full control of my ability. I never doubted that I could escape. In Sheboygan, I had...nothing." She held up her palm and spread her fingers as if to illustrate her ability slipping into oblivion. The unsteady movement of her chest suggested that she drew pain with every breath connected to that memory.

He wanted to wrap his arms around her and assure her that nothing bad would happen to her while he was at her side. If he followed instructions, however— *Stop!* Sawyer Montaigne did not take advantage of his OASIS clients. Steffi Anbruzzen could never be *loup-garou.*

He shifted position. Better move to a less sensitive topic. "Do you try out your possible observing shapes?"

"At first, I did."

Sawyer's jaw dropped. "Here in Chicago? In that apartment?"

Unfazed, she nodded. "My observer shapes haven't been large. For my first jobs, I practiced a lot, but with the Zuntos project, I waited until I was at my base camp. Then I visualized and shifted." She looked at him. "Isn't that what you do?"

Sawyer shook his head. "We already know our shapes. When we think about the change, it happens."

Her eyes widened. "Wow! That's so simple."

"Not quite. We still have to endure stretching and

contracting muscles, realigning tissues and organs, changing skeletons."

"Ellyn—Libby's Mentor—thinks that since we started so young, our bodies have more flexibility."

"You also have many more choices."

"I do like that. Of course, being different can be lonely. I mean, my sisters and I have each other, but that's about it." She looked at him. "Other Shifters have group affiliations, and you *loups-garous*—my God, you have packs everywhere. Plus, you have history, traditions, roots."

Sawyer turned off the recorder. "Traditions and roots have their value, but they can also trap you. You and your sisters don't have to answer to anyone else."

"Not true." She frowned. "We have to follow the laws of the Organization. Like that stupid Pack Covenant."

Sawyer rubbed his forehead in frustration. Any policy discussion with Shifters who weren't *loup-garou* inevitably led to complaints about the Pack Covenant. "The Covenant applies to all non-*loups-garous*, and it went into effect shortly after OASIS formed."

"I know, I know. Other canines wanted to become *loups-garous*. Big deal."

"It was. A very big deal. A few of the wannabes—mostly coyotes—made successful shifts, but some couldn't maintain their *loup-garou*. Others wanted to belong to their original communities but participate in our packs when the spirit moved them. Such divided loyalties weaken packs, and the crossbreeding would also weaken our bloodlines. That's why OASIS agreed to restrict other Shifters from becoming *loups-garous*."

"I understand the reasons, but did they have to

mandate such a severe punishment?"

When she shuddered, he wished he could correct her. Unfortunately, X-Ting not only extinguished shifting ability but also impaired intelligence. Most criminal Shifters lived in institutions and performed simple tasks under supervision. "The punishment is designed to make others think before they break the Covenant."

"Do you really believe that?"

Sawyer shifted in his chair. "The facts suggest that the threat of punishment has been an effective deterrent. No one has broken the Covenant since it went into effect."

"Maybe the Organization overestimated the number of Shifters who wanted to join you." She toyed with a strand of hair. "Maybe no one else wants to be *loup-garou*."

Steffi's comment hit him like a bucket of ice water. Centuries ago, when other types of Shape-shifters were scrambling to exist in a world dominated by Simple Humans, *loups-garous* had already organized into packs. As the network of packs expanded, *loups-garous* had helped other Shifters unite for their common survival. Everyone in the shifting world recognized and respected the power of the packs. They were wise, powerful, and handsome to behold. Who wouldn't want to be *loup-garou*?

"Don't get me wrong." Steffi's wide eyes seemed to appeal for his understanding. "I'm not dumping on the Organization. It's been a lifesaver." She turned on the recorder and repeated the statement in a louder voice. Despite his assurance of privacy, she must think he was sharing this conversation.

"What sort of routine do you follow during your observations?"

"I'm on the site before the real research team arrives."

Sawyer frowned. "Alone?"

She must have registered the alarm in his voice because the corners of her mouth softened. "My sisters always know my general location, and I check in regularly. If I ever missed a call, they'd contact the PI and mount a search."

"But by then—"

Her shoulders moved, and the hint of a laugh seemed to catch in her throat. "Now you sound like Libby. I don't take unnecessary risks. I follow a simple routine. In the base camp, I become a bird. I fly to the observation site, where I shift to my observer shape. When I'm finished, I return to my bird and fly back to the base camp."

He did a mental calculation. "Four shifts a day?"

"Sometimes more. Occasionally, somebody will be hanging out close to my base. Then I roost in a tree and wait for them to leave, but if they're taking too long, I might become a bat and swoop down to spook them."

"How long do you observe in a typical day?"

"Sunrise to sunset." She paused. "Sometimes longer because so much happens once the sun has gone down. After a good hunt, everyone feasts. They thank the gods for the food and eat the meat before it spoils. Often, they have ceremonies—weddings, funerals, initiations— along with religious services tied to the phases of the moon. I don't want to miss anything because I never know when I might witness an exchange that would either help or hurt the research team when it makes contact."

"Really?"

"Oh, yes. Facial expressions or hand gestures can be incredibly important. Fingers pointing in one direction might say 'Friend' and in any other direction—" With a grim expression, she ran her forefinger across her neck.

Sawyer frowned at the thought of Steffi beyond the edge of the civilized world without protection. "What's the longest shift you've sustained?"

"I'm not sure." She moved her fingers as if calculating.

"Can you give me an estimate?"

"Three…maybe four…days." She tossed out the number as if it were nothing special.

"*Sacrébleu!*" The curse popped like a firecracker. Several browsers paused to stare. Sawyer coughed and lowered his voice. "Do you know—do you have any idea of—the longest shift on record?"

"One of my Mentors may have told me, but I don't remember."

"Forty-eight hours." He held up two fingers. "Two days. Under laboratory conditions. The poor subject took four days in the hospital to recover from the strain." Yet here was Steffi, who could contemplate days alone in the wilderness without so much as fluttering those long, dark eyelashes. "Four days. Unbelievable."

Her eyes sparkled. "I could be off a bit. I follow the schedule of my shape. Sleep when it's safe, eat when I can, and watch as long as possible. I lose track of time."

"How much base time do you take between shifts?"

"Sometimes a night. Sometimes a whole day." She paused. "Sometimes, I don't have an opportunity for base time. If I run into an unexpected predator, for example, I either get bigger or get gone."

He stared at her. "Let me get this straight. You can shift from one shape to the next with no rest in your human shape?" When Steffi put her finger to her lips and indicated the phone, Sawyer turned it off. "That's not in your record." He sat back to regard this amazing woman.

"The Organization was interested in the range of our ability. We returned to our base after each shift."

Sawyer looked deep into her eyes. "I've never heard of anyone moving from shape to shape without pausing to rest as a human. Aside from you, that is. Can your sisters—"

"No. I'm the only one who doesn't need a base return, but my sisters have abilities I don't have."

"Do you plan to tell the Organization?"

"Someday maybe."

OASIS should stop treating Steffi and her sisters as inconvenient freaks. Their extraordinary talents might prove useful. "So you're doing four shifts a day. Sometimes spending three or four days with no return to your human base." When Sawyer reached toward his phone, Steffi moved a hand as if to stop him. He sat back. He'd never forget this conversation. She made her work sound effortless, but such long shifts exacted a heavy physical and mental toll. "You're remarkable."

"I was."

The small catch in her breathing tugged at his heart. Spying the glint of tears in her eyes, Sawyer covered her hand with his. "You are."

Suddenly all business, Steffi lifted her chin, reclaimed her hand, and sat up. "I will be again." The determination that blazed in her eyes softened. "With your help."

"That's why I'm here." He almost choked on the lie. Sawyer Montaigne did not take advantage of his OASIS clients. Steffi Anbruzzen would never be *loup-garou*.

Chapter 6

"Dayzee Anbruzzen." When the phone identified her caller, Steffi's finger hesitated above the "Accept" button. Libby had no doubt passed along news of her mishap, and Dayzee wouldn't be satisfied until she had all the details. Might as well get it over with. Her sister's photogenic face appeared. "Hey there, Day."

"How's it going?"

"All right."

"Are you shifting again?"

"Not yet."

"What are you doing with *Sawyer Montaigne?*" Dayzee seemed to roll the name around in her mouth.

"Talking."

"That's it?"

"We've had a few meals together."

"Drinking?"

"A little wine."

"Be careful."

Steffi frowned. "You sound like Mom when I was sixteen." Since when had her baby sister issued warnings?

"You're going out with *Sawyer Montaigne.*"

Again, that strange emphasis on Sawyer's name. "We're not dating. OASIS assigned him to help me recover my ability."

"Steffi!" Dayzee slapped a palm against her

forehead. "I Googled him. He's one of the ten sexiest men in Canada. Major wow factor. Wow in all caps with a zillion exclamation points."

Only a well-placed hand kept Steffi's jaw from hitting the floor.

"You've hooked up with one gorgeous hunk."

One gorgeous hunk. Dayzee had that right. "Slow down. No one has hooked up with anyone."

"You do think he's cute, don't you?"

That raven's wing hair, wicked grin, and strong jaw? "I wouldn't say that."

"Okay, not cute. But sexy as all get-out. You can't deny it."

"I can't—that is, I don't know. He's...attractive." She pressed her nose to keep it from pulling a Pinocchio at her understatement.

"You're glowing like you did after Tony Wilson kissed you for the first time." Dayzee's waving index finger sparkled. "Something's up."

"No. Not at all." Steffi did her best to sound sensible. "Neither of us has—even if we wanted to, nothing could happen."

"He's taking you under his wing, isn't he?"

Steffi almost laughed at her sister's tone. Trust Dayzee to give a protective image an X-rated flair. "OASIS has assigned him to help me. Beginning and end of story."

"But you do like him."

Steffi groaned. Middle sister Libby always knew when to back off. Baby sis Dayzee could have medaled for the Spanish Inquisition. "Yes. He's a nice guy." With gray-velvet eyes and protective hands. Above all, *loup-garou*. A fist squeezed Steffi's heart.

"Don't let him get too nice." Dayzee dropped her voice to a near whisper. "His father is like the Godfather of Canada."

Steffi drew back. "More Google gossip?"

"Nope. I had it straight from the horse's—in this case, the wolf's—mouth. A wolf tech I know from Vancouver. He said the Montaigne pack controls most of eastern Canada. Sawyer's father is the pack alpha, and Sawyer is the oldest son." She hugged herself. "You know what that means."

Ridiculous! Steffi put her hands to her ears. "No, no, no! Sawyer's father is not the Godfather, and Sawyer is not a criminal. He's…" She fumbled for the right word. No female would describe Sawyer as ordinary. "He's intelligent and attractive. You're being silly."

"You're being dumb. Or playing dumb. Which is it?"

"Neither. I do not, cannot, will not have anything other than a professional relationship with Sawyer Montaigne." The sounds of his name snuggled in the contours of her mouth.

"Sometimes you're too stubborn for your own good, Steff."

"And you're the annoying little sister you've always been."

Dayzee's gleaming smile winged over the ether. "That's because I'm always right."

"You wish." Steffi groaned. "You're lucky I love you anyway."

"I love you, too. That's why I'm worried about you. So is Libby."

"It's only been a few days, Day."

"We're going to check in at least once a week."

"Please don't."

"But—"

"I appreciate your concern. I will call when I have something to report." Dayzee's lips parted, but Steffi cut her off. "Not *that*. I'll call you when I can shift again."

"Suit yourself." Dayzee composed her mobile features into a solemn mask. "Remember to sleep with the wolf, not the fishes."

Chapter 7

Over the next few weeks, Steffi and Sawyer sandwiched meetings between her classes and finals. One afternoon as they lunched, he said, "Being able to choose your shape is an extraordinary gift. How do you decide?"

Perhaps she heard the longing in his voice because the firm corners of her mouth softened. Sawyer sat back rather than attempt to arouse her sympathy. He had a job to do. Sawyer Montaigne did not take advantage of his OASIS clients. Why would Steffi Anbruzzen, who could shift to any shape she chose, ever violate the Covenant by becoming *loup-garou*?

She mirrored his posture. "In the beginning, it simply happened. The first time, for instance. One minute, I was wailing in my crib. The next, I was floating above it."

"That's a nice understatement." His other clients' histories tended to blend in his memory. He'd never forget Steffi's. "Your father claimed you took the shape of the dragons in the mobile that flew over your crib. Good thing they were small."

"I'll say. When I opened my mouth, this hot light rushed out. At the time, I didn't know it was fire. I only knew that the room got brighter, and the light changed shape when I made different sounds. I hovered above my crib. Frightened but fascinated." She paused. "Mom and

Dad were in their room getting ready for bed when the smoke alarms went off." She brought her fingers to her ears. "My poor parents!"

"How do you know what they were doing?"

"They never let me forget it. On my birthday, Mom tells the story with every fiery detail."

"You must have been a handful."

If she opened her eyes any wider, he might fall into them. "I think I scared myself as much as I scared them. Dad smothered the mattress fire while Mom swaddled me in a blanket."

"You were still a dragon?"

Steffi nodded.

"That took courage."

"Mostly love. Mom always says that we are her babies, no matter what shapes we take. While Dad tore down the mobile and threw out the stuffed animals in case I got ideas about lions and bears, Mom cuddled me until I went to sleep. When I woke up, I was a baby again. Must've returned to my human base in my sleep. By the next time it happened, OASIS had given me a Mentor."

"So you and your parents get along well?"

"Yes."

"What about you and your sisters?"

She looked at him. "You know how it is with siblings. We love each other when we're not making each other crazy. Like when we played Dragon Tag. Did you ever—since you don't shift until you're teenagers, I guess you didn't have wolf games."

Playing Hide and Seek as pups would have been fun. "What happened in Dragon Tag?"

"We had a great time chasing each other over open fields. Until Dayzee pissed me off, and I burned her wing." Steffi tapped her upper arm. "She has a scar, I got scolded, and we were all grounded for the rest of that summer. No more Dragon Tag. Ever."

"Just as well…before you accidentally started a wildfire."

She offered a half smile. "You sound like my dad."

"Wise man." Her compliment stuck in his throat. If she saw him as a father figure so much the better. Sawyer Montaigne did not take advantage of his OASIS clients. Steffi Anbruzzen would never be *loup-garou*. "You have a good family life and friends here in Chicago. Any other significant relationships?" He tried to make the question sound casual.

"I've lost contact with most of my Maryland relatives. I had friends in school but was never close to any of them. I've had a few…relationships…with SH men. Nothing serious."

"What about other Shifters?"

"I've met a few I liked, but they're like *loups-garous*. They prefer their own kind. There may be male Shifters like my sisters and me, but they're not looking for us."

Her clear voice ran through his mind like the ripples in a brook. *They should be.*

Steffi fingered the edge of the table. "In graduate school, my studies kept me occupied. Now, I'm so busy working or looking for work I don't have much time for a social life."

Or for relaxation. Despite her extraordinary ability, the elements of her problem had a familiar pattern.

"What does this have to do with my situation?"

"Family and friends can either support or interfere with recovery. In your case, they seem to have a positive influence. As far as the other...maintaining secrecy in intimate relationships often increases a client's stress levels, which can block recovery. You don't seem to have any worries there."

"Lucky me. What if I were with someone I could trust?" Her eyes seemed to peer into his soul.

His pulse skipped a beat, and his mantra pounded between his temples. Sawyer Montaigne did not take advantage of his OASIS clients. Steffi Anbruzzen would never be *loup-garou. Don't trust me.*

"Wouldn't that kind of relationship be helpful?" she asked.

"I suppose so."

"Good." She played with her silverware. "I have a dinner date tomorrow. Maybe he'll be the one."

More like pairing an ocean with a cup of cold tea. Sawyer's lip curled. A new admirer might provide what OASIS ordered—an excellent distraction—but that was *his* job. "Until you've recovered, it might be wise not to become too involved."

Gold sparkled in her dark eyes. "I'll keep that in mind." Although her mouth remained solemn, her voice was light. Was she teasing him? She stood. "I should go." She started to leave but turned back. "You should call the Organization and find out why I haven't gotten my test results."

Clearing his throat, he pulled a plain white business envelope from the inside pocket of his sports jacket.

She almost tore the envelope from his grasp. "They sent this to you?"

"Standard operating procedure. So we can prepare a client if the news is bad."

She brandished the envelope. "I don't know how

you do things in Canada, but in this country, we have privacy laws, and you had no right to open it."

He lifted a shoulder as if to counter her attack. "Actually, I did. Organization employees can access members' records when necessary. In addition, when you requested help, you signed a waiver, giving us access to any relevant accounts."

When she scanned the report, her frown deepened until it threatened to bisect the bridge of her nose. "It doesn't matter. This is worthless." She squeezed the paper in her fist and dropped it into the remains of her salad.

"You don't want to do that." Sawyer wrapped his pocket-handkerchief around his hand and retrieved the report.

"I do. You don't want me to."

He folded the handkerchief around the dressing-encrusted paper and eased it into his breast pocket. "I want to protect your privacy and minimize our exposure."

"*Our* exposure." Her gaze sliced through him. "That's really why they assigned you, isn't it?"

"Pardon?" Hoping to show more innocence than he felt, he widened his eyes.

"You're supposed to be helping me, but really all they care about—all you care about—is protecting the Organization."

"Steffi—"

When Sawyer reached toward her, she gestured at his pocket. "When did you get this?"

"A…few…it's been a while." A muscle in Sawyer's jaw twitched. "I was meaning to give it to you but put it off because…I thought it would upset you. Of course, now that the tests have ruled out external causes, we can address the internal ones."

"Stop." She brought her hands to her temples. "I am upset. With you."

"Pardon?"

She pointed at him. "It's been almost two months since Sheboygan. At best, I have four months left. Maybe less."

"Or more. We don't really know."

"The clock is running, and you—I should have known." Her voice was dangerously calm, like the sea before a storm. "You don't have a plan. You never did."

"I wouldn't say that." He signaled the server. "Let's go somewhere and talk."

"No." She placed her hands on her hips. "Talking hasn't gotten me anywhere. You've helped others recover, but not once have you suggested anything I could try. All you want me to do is keep talking."

The charge felt like an uppercut across his jaw. He looked down at the table. "I'm sorry."

"You should be. You said you wanted to help me, but you've done nothing. It's almost as if—" Her eyes narrowed. "You're keeping me busy until my time runs out. You don't work for me. You work for OASIS." She slapped her forehead. "I should have known. Well, I'm done with the lot of you." She whirled on her heel and stormed out.

The loathing in Steffi's gaze complemented the disgust churning in Sawyer's stomach at OASIS, at Uncle Mel, and at himself for going along with their plan. He hadn't really attempted to delay Steffi's recovery. In fact, the more he'd watched and listened to her, the more he'd come to believe that OASIS was wrong. If he told them he'd lost her, they'd replace him with someone who would do everything possible to block her recovery. He didn't want that to happen. He wanted Steffi to regain her amazing ability.

Impatient clients sometimes tried to speed up the recovery process. A few succeeded, but those who failed often became more cooperative clients. Steffi might succeed—he hoped she would—but determination might make her foolhardy. Blotting the sweat from his forehead with a clean section of his handkerchief, he texted several Chicago-based OASIS operatives to begin surveillance. They should be discreet but stay alert.

Sawyer pushed away his coffee, which had lost its flavor. Moments ago, he'd witnessed the first emotional cracks in Steffi's meticulously controlled façade. Steffi hid her smiles and stifled her laughter, but anger made her eyes blaze and her nostrils flare until she looked ready to exhale tongues of fire. Dragon Tag indeed. This new Steffi both challenged and enticed. *No, no, no.* He signaled for the bill. Sawyer Montaigne did not take advantage of his clients. Steffi Anbruzzen would never be *loup-garou.*

He glanced at his watch. When would he see her again?

Righteous exhilaration fueled Steffi for the rest of the day. As soon as she got back to her apartment, she wrote a text to Dayzee about how one of Canada's ten sexiest men was also a Class A creep. On the Send button, she paused. Announcing that she'd dumped OASIS would only worry Dayzee and, by extension, Libby. After she recovered her ability, she'd share the full story, and they could all have a good laugh. Deleting the message, she set her phone on the table.

The test results danced in her mind: No parasites, bacterial infections, or viruses. Normal. Normal. Normal. If her problem had an internal cause, the solution must lie within her as well. She stripped and sat cross-legged on the thin carpet. *Sorry, Lib. I know I promised, but I have to do this on my own.*

Where to begin? Maybe recall the shapes she'd enjoyed most. Land-based. Real. Mammals. And birds. Definitely birds. Closing her eyes, she slowed her breathing. Predators paraded across her mind. Her body quivered with longing.

Jaguar!

As her mind traced each sleek curve, elegant paws seemed to reach toward her. She waited for the skeletal shift from biped to quadruped, for the realignment of muscles and fascia.

Nothing.

She grunted. At least, she hadn't become a kitten or, worse, gotten stuck in midshift. OASIS would have loved that!

Jaguar might be too ambitious. It wasn't one of her regular shifts, and she hadn't done it in almost a year. Maybe start with something smaller. More domesticated. Cat or dog? A husky, perhaps. The closest she would ever come to *loup-garou.*

Damn Sawyer! Broad shoulders. Thoughtful gray eyes. Always ready with a smile or a sympathetic word. *"I'm here to help you."* Yeah, right. Dayzee worried that he would break her heart, but he'd done worse: betrayed her trust. She shook her head as if that could erase his image.

Steffi took a deep breath. Time was too precious to waste on Sawyer Montaigne. Better to focus on regaining her ability. Try again tomorrow when she was fresh. This time, she'd choose a familiar shape. A bird!

The next morning, after meditation, she eyed the middle of the room. Her falcon would hate this enclosed space, but she wouldn't keep the shape for more than a few minutes. She stood, brought her hands together beneath her chin, and closed her eyes. Images circled in her awareness. Her skin opened to release the feathers. *Yes!* Dropping her arms to her sides, she waited for the bones to hollow and bend into wings.

Nothing. She wiggled her fingers.

"Damn, damn, damn." Two tries. Two misses. She paced. *Slow down.* She could be trying too hard. Once again, she sat on the floor, closed her eyes, and inhaled. Focus on the breath. In. Out. In. Out. Like the ticking clock. Every exhale a minute lost. She tried to let the thought drift through her mind, but the sound remained. In. Tick. Out. Tick. Time. Time. Time!

She opened her eyes and stood. She needed to move. Cleaning forced her attention on something other than her problem, but when she dusted the pottery on the shelves, every piece evoked the shape she'd held for that observation site.

Housekeeping finished, she wandered to the kitchen area. Thin pickings in her cupboards and refrigerator. Too many restaurant meals with Sawyer. The way the tip of his tongue brushed his upper lip when he sampled his coffee. The light in his eyes when she said something he liked. His charm was addictive. She'd get him out of her system in time.

Time! The numbers on the kitchen clock kept moving. Minute by minute, her ability might be fading.

She made a grocery run and then went to a yoga

class. After the practice, she toasted goat cheese on half a bagel and added Boston lettuce to the other half. No dessert. She checked online for any new research opportunities. Grant money tighter than ever, and competition stiffer. Time to make contacts for adjunct teaching in the fall.

After washing dishes and putting them up to dry, she tried to read or stream videos but soon gave up. Through her small window, the night sky beckoned. No wonder her earlier shift had failed. No self-respecting falcon would emerge in such a tiny space. Her owl liked the roof. When the bird shape stirred within her, her pulse raced.

She sprinted up the stairs to the roof and stuck a cinder block against the heavy door so no one could interrupt her. Then she slipped off her robe and closed her eyes. *Owl!* Instead of emerging, the shape seemed to shrink.

Steffi opened her eyes and swore. She pulled on her robe and knotted the tie. She couldn't count the times her owl had flown from this site, but not tonight. Something was off. She walked to the parapet. The city below throbbed with light and movement. Traffic sounds mocked her.

When she glanced at the neighboring rooftops, one silhouette sent shivers down her spine. An eagle! The filthy scavenger might be waiting for roadkill or fish remains at low tide, but he would definitely have snapped up her tasty owl before she could give a hoot. Her inner owl must have sensed the danger. *Good bird!*

No shifting on the roof with an eagle nearby. She would find another, more natural environment. She checked the time. By now, all the city parks had closed.

Sliding into her bed, Steffi closed her eyes and smiled. *Sleep, little bird. Tomorrow we fly!*

Steffi filled the next day with routine tasks: paying bills and submitting applications for teaching and research positions. When sunshine gave way to city lights, she set off for her favorite park. She would shift to her owl and return to base before the park closed at eleven. In a few hours, she'd be sharing her triumph with Libby and Dayzee!

A few Simple Humans lingered on the well-lit paths, but she danced with delight along an isolated trail that led to a private thicket she'd used before. The deep green curtain embraced her. Much better than the roof. No hawks or eagles. She peeled off her human clothing, closed her eyes, and envisioned her bird. *Owl. OWL. OWL!*

She opened her eyes and flapped her floppy human arms. The right place. The right time. One of her favorite shapes. Hope sank like a stone in her gut.

If she kept trying, something might happen, but the more she tried and failed, the more likely that her window for recovery would close, and she'd become human. "Simple Human," she muttered, kicking at a nearby stone. The owl had stirred within her. Why couldn't it emerge? How long before the familiar flutter grew fainter and stilled?

She couldn't do this alone. Who could help? Sawyer had given her his number, but she couldn't trust him or anyone else OASIS might send. Better get dressed. When she reached down to pick up her underwear, twigs snapped behind her. She turned.

A bulky forearm slammed across her neck, and a big hand mashed one breast. She opened her mouth to scream, but no sound emerged. She gulped and locked her lips together.

The arm tightened.

She burrowed her chin into her neck to create a breathing space and rammed both elbows into her attacker's body.

"Hey!"

The choke hold loosened enough for her to free her head. Gasping, she started to move away, but he grabbed her arm. Agony. Whirring. Growling. Shrieking. Darkness.

Chapter 8

Steffi squinted. Someone had taken a meat cleaver to her skull. When she tried to speak, her throat felt as if she were gargling gravel.

"Easy, Steffi."

The deep voice wrapped around her like a blanket, and the tension in her muscles eased. A steady gray gaze blocked the bright light. His hair was mussed, and stubble covered his jaw. He'd lost his jacket, and his rumpled shirt bore dark spatters. She rasped his name.

"Don't try to talk." He held a cup to her mouth. "Here." Honey in the tea settled into sore spots. "Better?"

She nodded and opened her mouth.

"No talking." He pulled a small notebook from one pocket. "Write it down if you like."

Long scratches scored her forearm. She and her sisters healed quickly. Had her shifting problems affected her human base?

"You had a mild concussion along with a few cuts and scrapes, but you'll be all right."

All right? Fragments of the attack sliced into her awareness. Iron arm against windpipe. *Breathe! Breathe!* That excruciating pain when—holding her breath, she reached across her chest to find her shoulder, which protested when she tried to move it. She eased her fingers down and inhaled in relief. Her arm was still attached.

"Dislocated shoulder. You'll need to keep it in a sling for a few days, and it will feel stiff for a while. Even as a human, you are tough."

Despite the admiration in Sawyer's voice, she frowned. Tough? She'd tried, but she hadn't escaped. She pulled the sheet up and held it with her chin while her free hand moved toward one breast. No shower could burn away that vile... Her head throbbed, her breath came in short bursts, and chills raced across her skin. What else had he done?

"Steffi."

When Sawyer moved his hand, she pulled back. If anyone laid a finger—her stomach churned. Although he stepped away from the bed, his eyes remained on her.

She pushed the call button and scrawled a quick list for the nurse. When the nurse shook her head, Steffi bit her lip so hard she tasted blood. What kind of a hospital was this? She punched a finger at the list. "Need!"

When Sawyer reached over the nurse's shoulder and took the page, Steffi repeated the word in the loudest croak she could manage.

"No, you don't." Sawyer dismissed the nurse with a thank-you.

Steffi glared at him. She could be infected with an STD...with HIV, for God's sake. She could be pregnant. Bile scalded her throat. She needed that morning-after pill.

"We got there right after he threw you against a tree."

Relief flowed into her muscles, and she lay back against the pillows. A frown required too much effort. She wrote in huge capitals: *WE?*

"I hired some local associates to keep an eye on you in case you ran into any trouble with your self-help healing."

The eagle on the rooftop. She should have guessed.

"I told them to keep their distance. If they'd been closer—" Sawyer punched one of his hands. "—he would never have gotten near you. I'm sorry."

Stupid Simple Human. Steffi's grip on the neck of the hospital gown tightened. She hadn't seen his face or heard more than a grunt. She scribbled another note: *Not your fault. I can't ID.*

"You won't have to. My associates took care of him."

The grim finality in Sawyer's voice and the strong set of his jaw chilled her. The growls echoed in her brain. That ghastly screech would haunt her nightmares, yet if Sawyer and his crew hadn't appeared—she shuddered. "Thank you," she whispered.

"You're welcome." He scratched his jaw. "You *were* my client."

Of course. The protective haze faded. He'd have done the same for any of his OASIS charges. He might have done more for those he actually wanted to help. He'd let her walk away, but then he'd rescued her. Why?

"Try to relax. We brought you in last night around ten. They're keeping you a day for observation." Sawyer stood. "I'll come back when you're feeling better, and we can talk."

Talk? What else was there to say? Why was he here? Throbbing confusion overheated her brain. She gestured at the room and croaked, "Where? What?"

"This is the OASIS emergency unit attached to the clinic."

OASIS! She shot up so quickly she pulled at the wounded shoulder and fell back with a groan.

"Easy." Sawyer arranged her pillows. "I checked the medication. They're not giving you anything that will affect your ability."

Why should I believe you?

"There's something I want to clear up." He indicated the chair. "May I stay for a few minutes?"

He looked flustered. She dipped her chin.

"I'm sorry about what happened in the—" He shook his head. "No, I'm sorry about everything. I should never have agreed to take your case. It was wrong. I was wrong."

When she didn't move, his shoulders stiffened. Did he really expect her to pat him on the shoulder and say he was a good boy? She filled a page with large capitals and passed it to him.

"Despicable? I don't know if that—" He tapped the paper. "Yes, that is the word. OASIS was despicable to make the plan, and I...I was despicable for going along with it." He crumpled the paper and tossed it in a nearby wastebasket. "But that's over. For me, at least."

Steffi blinked. *Don't leave me.*

"When I took this assignment, I had reservations. The more you told me, the more I knew..." He dropped his voice so low she could barely hear it. "I don't think they have this place bugged." He scanned the room. "But if they do..." He wrote a paragraph and passed it to her.

He'd written that he'd been wrong and was sorry. Although he'd have to let OASIS think he was following their plan, he wanted to help her, this time for real.

She hesitated.

"If you don't want to, I understand. OASIS can

appoint someone else, or you can tell them you want to go it alone."

Alone. That horrible moment of darkness yawned inside her. She shook her head. "Need help."

"Maybe not. Rest and relaxation seem to be the best treatment."

She scrawled a question and turned the notebook so he could read it.

"I diagnose possible causes, develop a plan, and provide support."

She wrote another question and passed the notebook to him.

Sawyer's brows knitted as he regarded the message. "Let's talk about my plan when you get your voice back. In the meantime, you should rest." He glanced at his watch. "Elizabeth should be here soon."

Eliz—Libby! Steffi sat up as if he'd sent an electric jolt racing up her spine. *No, no, no!* She shook her head so hard it should have flown off her wounded neck.

Sawyer hovered. "Slow down." When he reached for the button to call the nurse, she pushed his hand away. "They notified her because she's listed as your next of kin. They won't let you go home alone. If you have someone else you want me to call, I will do it, but since she's already on her way…"

Steffi slumped against the pillows. She'd made a mess of everything, she couldn't even talk, and now she had to face Libby.

Sawyer stood with arms crossed and mouth set in a straight line. "What's wrong? You said you all got along well."

She reached for the notebook.

Sawyer read her comment. "So you promised you

wouldn't shift. She doesn't have to know."

Steffi grabbed the notebook.

"She may be a cop, but she's also your sister. She cares about you. You promised not to shift. You didn't promise not wanting to shift, eh?"

She nodded.

"In fact, you didn't shift."

She bit her lower lip. *I tried.*

"So technically, you didn't break your promise."

She rolled her eyes. Did he really think that hairsplitting would satisfy Libby?

"Someone attacked you in the park. That's all your sister needs to know. Let me do the talking."

As if she could do anything but croak or scribble. When Sawyer patted her shoulder, she drew back. Sawyer seemed sincere. She'd take what she could use but stay on guard. *Fool me once…*

When Steffi pulled away, Sawyer's hands dropped to his sides. What was he thinking? She'd just survived an assault…could have been… His associates deserved a bonus. "Sorry." Steffi looked down at the bed.

He checked his watch. "Her plane should be landing soon. If you'd prefer that I not be here—"

Steffi lifted a finger and wrote another note.

"Yes, I did offer to do the talking, but only if you want me to."

"Please," she mouthed. She wrote again.

Two days ago, she'd never wanted to see him again. Now, she wanted to know his thoughts on her problem, or maybe she wanted company. Either way, he'd oblige. He settled into the chair beside her bed. "From what you've said, I think you've been under a great deal of stress for a long time. Years, in fact. You've done far too much for far too long without taking care of yourself."

She printed another message: *Overachiever*.

"Whatever you call it, you've overextended. You need time off."

Steffi's dissatisfaction was etched on her face. *Off since Sheboygan.*

Sawyer scanned the note. "Technically, that's true, but you've spent much of your time since the incident worrying about it, eh?"

A reluctant nod.

"Plus your ability and your work have a close connection, so I'd guess you're also worried about your next job."

She gave him another note: *Don't have $$$. Need to work.*

He winced. *Touché.* "Still, worrying never helps. You have extraordinary ability, but you've pushed yourself too hard for too long." When she rested her hands on her generous bosom, he glanced down and recalled her lying naked at the foot of that tree. Paler than moonlight, with one arm warped at a strange angle, and unnaturally still. He'd muttered a prayer of thanks when her pulse fluttered against his fingers.

"Broken," she rasped.

"Injured." He jammed his hands into his pockets to keep from wiping away the tears that threatened to spill from her eyes. "But as I've told you, you're not the first to have this problem, and you won't be the last. Others have recovered."

A turn of her lower lip indicated her skepticism.

"Everyone worries. The less time you spend worrying, the better. The first thing I want you to do is stop thinking about shifting."

She stared at him as if he'd suggested she grow a second head. She wrote one word and tore off a page she thrust at him.

IMPOSSIBLE!!!

"I understand." He tapped the paper. "It's never easy—all my clients hate it—but they learned to do it, and so can you." When she prepared to write again, he covered the notebook page. "Hold off on the blazing pencil, eh? Our ability is as much a part of us as an arm, a leg, or a lung. We don't think about them until something goes wrong. We get a cold, pull a muscle, get an ache, or have a shifting problem. When that happens, we do what we can to make things right. Worrying increases stress, and stress blocks recovery."

He could almost feel her solemn gaze ranging across his face in search of a lie.

Evidently satisfied, she lay back.

"You need a holiday—what you call a vacation. Go somewhere and enjoy being you."

The hint of a smile played across Steffi's lips.

A slim figure clad in a dark suit burst into the room. "Steffi!" The newcomer clapped a hand across her mouth, but momentum propelled her forward. Sawyer stepped back so she wouldn't bump into him.

She stopped at the edge of the bed. "Oh, Steff." Her voice melted as she brushed the hair back from Steffi's forehead. "How are you? What happened?"

Steffi poked her throat.

Sawyer spoke. "She shouldn't try to talk for a while. The attacker used a choke hold."

"Attacker?" The blaze in Elizabeth Anbruzzen's eyes, dark like her sister's, overwhelmed the delicacy of her face, shaped like a Valentine heart. Her head swiveled toward her sister, and she gripped Steffi's hands. "Have you talked with a counselor yet? Did they do an exam?" She swallowed. "Use a rape kit?" She held out one of Steffi's hands and studied her fingernails. "Check for DNA?"

Sawyer cleared his throat. "That wasn't necessary."

Elizabeth's gaze threatened to nail him to the far wall. "What do you mean? In these cases, we—" She eyed the room. "This isn't a *real* hospital, is it?"

"OASIS health facilities meet necessary licensing requirements."

"Tell me they at least did an examination."

"The attacker didn't—your sister didn't let him get that far."

"Oh. Good." For a moment, Steffi's sister seemed chastened. Then she planted her hands on her hips. "Who the hell are you?"

Sawyer drew himself up to his full height, but Elizabeth didn't look impressed. "Sawyer Montaigne."

"The OASIS guy, right? How could you let this happen? Where were you?"

Sawyer crossed his arms. "I was assigned to help your sister recover her ability, not serve as her full-time bodyguard."

Bouncing in her bed and grunting, Steffi waved a note. After reading it, the other woman took a deep breath. "I see." When she didn't look as if she were ready to boil you in oil, Steffi's sister might be pretty. Smaller than Steffi, with caramel-colored hair in a short, no-nonsense cut. She held up the note. "She says you rescued her. Guess I owe you an apology."

"Your sister exaggerates. I had help. You must be Elizabeth."

She extended a hand. "Libby."

No-nonsense grip. "Sawyer."

Elizabeth—Libby—stroked Steffi's tangled hair. "How are you doing?"

Steffi wrote on the notepad.

Libby read the note. "That's good." She gestured at the wounds on Steffi's arms. "Because you look like you've been through a king-sized grater." Then she regarded Sawyer. "And you're not much better. I'm guessing you haven't slept since you brought her in here." She pointed at the door. "Go home and get some rest. I'll stay with Steff." She started to sit but stopped. In the time it took her to stand and turn, Sawyer retrieved her small bag from the doorway. "Thanks."

"You're welcome. Suitcase?" He pulled out his phone. Georges would deliver any luggage she'd left in the car.

Libby gave a small laugh. "Not for such a short stay." Keeping her eyes on Steffi, she returned to the chair. As a police officer, she no doubt spent hours in hospitals waiting to interview suspects and victims. The scene must be more painful when the victim was your sister.

"They'll bring in a bed for you. Are you hungry?"

"Food?" Libby uttered a short laugh. "Since the hospital called, I've been so busy that I never thought— Food would be good." She glanced at Steffi. "For both of us."

When she pulled her wallet from a jacket pocket, Sawyer waved it off. "I'll handle it."

"Thank you."

He turned to go.

Steffi croaked his name.

He spun. "Yes?" He took her note.

Glad she's here. Thanx!

For the first time since he'd cradled her in his arms in the park, he smiled. "My pleasure. I'll see you in the morning. Rest." He pointed at Steffi. "Dream about holidays."

As soon as he left, Libby turned to Steffi. "Holidays?"

Steffi described Sawyer's plan in a few sentences and passed the notebook to her sister.

"I need my glasses for this one." Libby took rimless specs from an inside pocket and peered at the paper. "Your handwriting's worse than mine." She reached into her bag and pulled out a tablet which she placed on Steffi's overbed table. "This should keep me from getting more squint lines and save you from writer's cramp." She returned to the message. "Worry less. Relax more. And don't think about shifting. Good luck with that one." She glanced toward the door. "Seems like a nice guy."

Seems.

"Not to mention easy on the eyes. Lives up to his name."

Steffi remained silent.

"Don't pretend you haven't noticed."

Had Libby and Dayzee been talking about her? Steffi's cheeks heated, and she avoided Libby's probing gaze by rearranging the items on her table.

"When I got the call, I thought about texting the rest of the family."

Steffi gasped.

Libby laughed. "I decided to wait until I saw you." She mimed zipping her lip.

Steffi patted her heart.

"Excuse me." A young man dressed like a restaurant server stood in the doorway. "Ms Anbruzzen?"

Steffi pointed at her sister, whose mouth had dropped open. Libby, who was never at a loss for words! If Sawyer had been here, Steffi might have hugged him.

The young man pushed a room-service table filled with boxes into the room near the foot of the bed. With a flourish, he uncovered a full-course dinner that included wine. Libby offered a tip, but he shook his head. "Enjoy your meal, ladies."

When they were alone again, Libby studied the table as if it were a crime scene. "I was expecting pizza. Maybe Chinese. Nothing like this." She moved a bowl and spoon to Steffi's table. "Soup for you!"

The aroma of well-seasoned corn chowder made Steffi's taste buds tingle.

Libby picked up a card that the server had left on the table. "No wine for you because of your meds. And we have to share the ice cream."

She flipped the card to Steffi, who noted the hotel insignia and the huge S that slashed across the bottom like a lightning bolt.

After demolishing the salad and sampling the wine, Libby took a bite of the small filet mignon. "Oh, my God! I think I've died and gone to heaven." She chewed as if she wanted the meal to last forever.

The ice cream dessert coated Steffi's throat like cold velvet.

Libby stood and stretched. "That was amazing!"

Steffi typed a few words—much faster than scribbling on paper and definitely easier to read.

"Sawyer likes good food? Who doesn't?" Libby

gestured at the crumbs and scraps. "But a meal like this would wipe out half of my weekly grocery budget, and that's for Tommy and me."

Steffi uttered a rasping laugh and supplied another message.

"Family money. That explains a lot." Libby tapped her chin. "When I called the department to see about release time, someone had already arranged it and booked my flight. At the airport, I almost got into a shouting match when they gave me a seat in first class. I thought they wanted to stick me for an upgrade, but it was a real first-class ticket." She laughed. "Way better than the cheap seats, even on a two-hour flight. At O'Hare, a driver was waiting for me the way they do in movies. He whisked me out of the airport and into a big, beautiful car." She hugged herself. "Pretty spiffy. I was surprised that OASIS was going to so much trouble for us."

OASIS? Steffi would have laughed if her throat had allowed it.

"Looks like it wasn't OASIS at all. It was your Mister Montaigne."

Not mine. Libby had had a hellacious day. She'd had to change any plans she and Tommy had as well as finagle time off. Through it all, she'd have been worried sick. Sawyer had done everything in his power to make her trip as comfortable as possible. The next time Steffi saw him, she'd have to thank him.

"Does he do this for all his clients?"

Steffi tapped a note:

—Only the ones who end up in the ER—

When Libby read the screen, she clicked her tongue behind her teeth. "No need to get snarky. Maybe he feels guilty since he wasn't—"

Steffi waved her free hand and shook her head.

"I know you like him, Steff."

When Libby hesitated, Steffi could almost see the "But" hanging in the air.

"Situations like this…with serious power inequities…can get messy." Libby held up her index finger. "Sawyer is in charge of your case, so he's your link with OASIS." The middle finger joined the first one. "Plus, he has lots more money than we do."

Steffi lay back. Her subconscious had flashed similar warning signs, but she'd tried to ignore them because in some ways, Sawyer was different. His sense of duty—honor, even—had evidently trumped his orders from OASIS. When she fired him, he could have left town, but he'd stuck around and protected her.

"Be careful."

Easy enough. Steffi flashed an okay sign and yawned.

Libby stood. "Let me get rid of this food and have them bring in my bed." She pushed the cart toward the door but paused on the threshold. "Do you want me to go to your place and get it ready for you?"

After the day Libby'd had, the last thing she needed to do was clean house. Steffi patted the bed. "Stay."

Chapter 9

The next morning, Steffi lay back, and Libby grunted when the nurse left the room. "Now, this feels like a hospital." Libby shook her head. "Waking people up at all hours."

Steffi glanced out the window at the rose-tinted sky. "Sun's up."

"A voice!" Libby clapped once.

"Not much of one." Steffi swallowed. "Throat's still sore." She moved the injured arm. "Shoulder aches, but that should go away soon." She pulled off the sheet and sat up. "I want to go away now."

"Slow down. First, you need the doctor's okay. Then, you should take it easy for a few days."

Steffi tilted her head.

Libby frowned. "What are you staring at?"

"Do I sound like that?"

"Hell, no!" Libby bounced on her mattress. "You're much bossier...or you were when we were kids."

"I had to watch out for you and Dayzee."

Libby patted Steffi's free arm. "Now, it's my turn to watch out for you. For today, at least. Wish I could stay longer, but—"

"I'm glad you could get here at all." Steffi squeezed her sister's hand. "Hope I didn't cause too many problems."

"Nothing I can't handle. I'm relieved that you're all

right." Stripping the sheets from her small bed, Libby sat on the bare mattress. "In my job, I see so much pain...families destroyed...lives lost. This could have been so much worse."

"I was lucky." *Thanks to Sawyer and his crew. Sneaky bastards. My heroes.*

Libby's fingers curled. "That son of a bitch still hurt you."

"Roughed me up a little. I'll be fine." Once again the big sister, Steffi gave Libby a one-armed hug. Sitting back, she gestured at the far side of the room. "I think they put my stuff in that closet. Could you get my clothes?"

Instead of moving, Libby frowned. "You shouldn't—your things—the arresting officers should have bagged what you were wearing and stored it as evidence."

Arresting officers? One of Steffi's teeth bit into her lower lip. The police might have arrived after she passed out, but what had Sawyer said? *"My associates took care of him."*

Libby opened the closet door and pulled out a bulging plastic bag she set on the foot of the bed. When she opened the bag, she drew a sharp breath. "Interesting."

Steffi stiffened. Caring Sister had become Curious Cop.

Libby extended the sleeve of a pale green jersey top. "You look like hell, but this isn't pulled or torn." She flipped the garment. "Not even a grass stain."

Oh, shit. Steffi stared at her hands. Sawyer had promised to do all the talking. Where was he?

Libby spread the other items at the foot of the bed.

"Everything neatly folded and stacked so that someone could put it on in a hurry after a shift." She riffled the garments. "Juliet would be proud of you."

Steffi's fingers worried the blanket. This must be how a trapped mouse felt beneath the cat's merciless eye.

"You promised."

When she met her sister's disappointed gaze, Steffi's heart seemed to crumple. "I know. I didn't mean to…I shouldn't have, but I had to try." Disappointment was almost as sharp as the ache in her shoulder. "I couldn't."

Libby rested her hands on her hips. "Why were you alone? Where the hell was Sawyer?"

"We had a disagreement. I sort of fired him."

Libby addressed the ceiling. "I should have guessed." Her gaze returned to Steffi. "You're damn lucky he stuck around."

"I know. He says he's had other clients like me."

"I seriously doubt that."

"I am sorry, Lib." She blinked back tears.

Libby sat beside her but not too close. "You let me down, Sis. Of course, after what you've gone through…"

"It wouldn't have happened if I'd listened to you. I learned my lesson." Steffi fingered the scab on her cheek. *The hard way.* "I promise—" She lifted one hand, but Libby pushed it down.

"No more promises. Whatever you do—what are you always telling me?—stay safe."

When he entered the room, Sawyer's breath caught in his throat. Libby sat beside an empty bed. Yesterday evening, when he'd left, Steffi had looked good, but concussions…internal bleeding… He dropped the bags he was carrying. "Where's Steffi? What's happened?"

"Chill." Libby put down her tablet. "She's in the bathroom."

Sawyer lifted his chin and listened. Running water. His pulse steadied. "She's all right?"

"Good to go. As soon as they bring the release form." Libby pointed at the items on the floor. "You've been shopping?"

Sawyer retrieved the scattered purchases and placed them on the bed. "I bought her some clothes because I didn't know if she'd want to wear what she had on."

Libby hooked an arm over the back of her chair. "Stop right there. Steffi's already admitted she tried to shift, so you don't have to lie for her." Sawyer opened his mouth, but she continued, "The police should have taken her clothes as evidence." The light in her eyes was as sharp as a laser beam. "Funny thing, though."

When Libby stood, Sawyer planted his feet.

"While Steff was with the doctors, I checked on the case. Guess what?" Libby tapped the screen of her device. "No one was arrested for an assault in any of the parks last night."

Sawyer drew a steady breath. "I'm sure the police department in a city this big has a lot to handle. They could be running behind with their reports."

"Reports maybe, but booking is fast. If there's been an arrest."

Sawyer shifted position so her penetrating gaze would miss his backbone.

"Steffi said you rescued her. You said she got loose on her own." Libby clasped her hands. "What really happened?"

She was determined to ferret out the whole story, eh? Best stick as close to the truth as possible. "I was too busy looking after your sister to pay attention to anything else."

"Good of you to be so concerned since she'd dumped you."

His jaw tightened. Steffi's sister wanted to goad him into saying something stupid. At least, this part was easy. "She's not the first. Clients who go out on their own either regain their ability or return after they've had a few failures. Disappointment or frustration can make them reckless, so I call for support when I feel it's warranted. And, yes, I did think it was warranted in your sister's case. I hired some local OASIS operatives to keep an eye on her."

"So one of your trackers was following her?"

She hung on like a dog with a bone. "Yes."

"Why didn't he prevent the attack?"

"He lost her in the park. I'd given them strict instructions to keep their distance so they wouldn't invade Steffi's privacy." Also, Steffi would have been pissed if she'd known she was being watched.

"After Jake texted, I contacted the others. We met at the entrance. Everyone took a different path." He raked a hand through his hair. "Felt like we searched forever, but in reality I suppose it was only a few minutes before one of my guys sent the emergency alert. She was in an out-of-the-way copse. A good spot for shifting."

"What happened next?"

He stopped moving. "I don't—that is, I didn't see anything except…Steffi." *Motionless on the grass.* "I called OASIS Emergency. Found a pulse." Strong and steady, but her body…as limp as a rag doll. "I covered her with my jacket, tried to keep her comfortable."

"Did you call the police?"

"I guess not. I don't remember."

"You kept your human shape?"

"Yes."

"What about your friends? When did they shift?"

His jaw twitched. "Not in the presence of a Simple Human."

Libby folded her arms. "Do you really expect me to believe that they didn't shift?"

Be still. Don't look away. Stick to the truth. "They're all ex-military. Even in human shape, they make a formidable team." Still, no one could have missed the startled panting and panicked pleas of a Simple Human, the deep growls of the bears, and the eagle's screech.

"Doesn't sound like the attacker was armed. If your guys were as strong as you say, they could have detained him until the police arrived."

Sawyer brought his knuckles to his jaw but maintained eye contact. "Most of my associates are not white. From what I've read and seen in local news, there's tension between police and men of color, a tendency to shoot first and ask questions later. In any shape, my associates avoid Simple Human authorities."

"What did they do?"

"I don't know for sure. I was too focused—"

"On Steffi. Right. Did they attack him?"

"Of course not. They know the Rules. Never harm a Simple Human." Sawyer flexed his fingers. Rules be damned, he would have used every ounce of his *loup-garou* strength to eviscerate that monster.

"That's the Second Rule."

"The attacker must have run. By the time the medical team arrived, he was gone."

"They let him escape."

93

"They followed the First Rule: Protect our own. Once Steffi was safe, they saw no need for further action."

"He's free to strike again. Police would have searched the area."

"By the time they arrived, he would have been long gone."

"Possibly." Libby tapped her pointed chin. "Or maybe having investigators on the scene would have been inconvenient."

Sawyer's spine stiffened. "What are you implying?"

"In one moment, you...and your friends...are confronting Steffi's attacker. In the next, he's gone." She snapped her fingers. "Simple Humans don't disappear that quickly."

"He was big, maybe a Djinn. They can vanish in a blink."

Libby's brow wrinkled. "They also use seduction instead of physical force. Humans are messy. Wherever they go, they leave a trail. They also have connections. Families, coworkers, drinking buddies. Someone may already be looking for this man."

"Good luck with that. I'm sure the police have better things to do than trying to find traces of a guy who liked to prey on women." When Libby's eyes narrowed, Sawyer bit his tongue. *Liked. Damn.* Should have kept the present tense. Libby already thought his team had punished the assailant. He'd confirmed her suspicion. "For all I know, he was a rogue Shifter."

"Perhaps Steffi can—"

"Steffi has been through hell." He jammed his fists into his pockets to keep from grabbing the interrogator's shoulders. "Stop."

"Are you threatening me, Mister Montaigne?" Although he loomed over her, Libby looked ready to crush him with the finger resting on her phone. One call, and he'd be stuck in a holding cell.

He pulled back. "Not at all. I want what's best for your sister. We both do. Right now, her body is using energy that could help her regain her shifting ability to mend her physical wounds. The longer her physical and psychological healing takes, the more it could delay her recovery. The longer the delay, the less likely the recovery." When Libby gasped, he nodded. "She needs to get away, go somewhere she can relax."

"And take you with her?"

The hairs on his nape rose at the disapproval in Libby's voice. Sawyer Montaigne did not take advantage of his OASIS clients. Steffi Anbruzzen would never be a *loup-garou*. "I often travel with my clients in case they need me. Of course, if you have your fellow officers take me in for questioning—"

"Who's getting questioned?" Wrapped in a couple of towels, Steffi popped out of the washroom and looked from Sawyer to her sister. The bruises on her neck were fading, but the scratches on her arm stood out in dark relief.

"Your sister thinks I'm withholding information about what happened in the park."

Steffi glanced at her sister. "Back off, Lib." She turned to Sawyer. "Occupational hazard." She gestured at the bags on the bed. "What's this?"

"Clothes. I thought you might not…"

"Sawyer." Her husky voice caressed his name as if he'd dusted the bed with diamonds. "That's so sweet of you. You shouldn't have." She gestured at her stacked garments. "Those will be fine."

He swallowed. "I'll wait outside while you dress."

Minutes later, Libby opened the door on a pleasant surprise. The new rust-colored top brought out deep red highlights in Steffi's hair, and the tan skirt showed off her legs, shapely despite the scabs.

"I decided you were right. Better to make a fresh start. Also, since I can't lift my arm, it's good to have a top I can slip into." Steffi traced the diagonal line of the blouse that fastened at her waist. The pleasure on her face brightened the bland room.

A doctor appeared and peppered Steffi with instructions. When he finished, Libby folded the release forms and put them in one of her pockets. "Now, you're good to go."

"Whoopee." Steffi made a lazy circle with the index finger of her free hand.

Sawyer texted Georges to bring the car around. "Would you like to stop for lunch?"

"Yes!" Steffi started to bounce to her feet, sat for a moment on the edge of her bed, and stood.

When Libby drew herself up to her full height, she and Steffi were almost eye to eye. "You should rest."

"I've been in bed more than a day. I'm hungry." Steffi appealed to Sawyer. "Dinner last night was delicious, but breakfast this morning?" She turned one thumb down. "Institutional to the max. I'd die for a cup of real coffee."

Libby's jaw clenched, and Sawyer tensed.

Steffi looked from Sawyer to her sister. "Lighten up. I'm exaggerating." She nudged her sister with her free elbow. "We should eat something good now because we'll be nuking leftovers at my place." She turned to

Sawyer. "Did Libby tell you how much she enjoyed her dinner?"

Libby squared her shoulders. "The steak was a delicious surprise. Thank you."

"You're welcome." He reached for Libby's carry-on, but when she latched onto it, he offered his arm to Steffi. "May I join you?" He'd planned to spend his day preparing for the next Montaigne Enterprises board meeting, but the less time the sisters spent together, the better. Good thing inquisitive Libby was taking the red-eye home.

Steffi's fingers nestled in the crook of his elbow, and her lips parted in a soft curve—another almost smile. "Please do."

The blood sang in his veins.

Chapter 10

When Steffi slapped the table, Sawyer swallowed the bite of burger he'd been gnawing, and Libby stopped picking at her salad. They both looked at her. *Good.* They didn't have to have anything to do with each other, but they *would* listen to her. "I've been thinking about vacations."

Libby pointed her fork at Steffi. "First, you have physical therapy."

Steffi gestured at the fork, which Libby returned to her plate. "The doctor gave me a handout with the exercises. They're simple. I can do them anywhere." She appealed to Sawyer. "The sooner we leave, the better, right?"

"Sounds good to me." A smile flirted with the corners of his mouth. "What do you have in mind?"

"Going home." She turned to Libby. "I haven't seen Mom and Dad in ages."

Libby's jaw relaxed. "They'd like that."

"Montana is beautiful."

The grudging admission in Sawyer's voice tempted Steffi to smile. "You've been there?"

"I have property in Alberta, so I've visited some of your parks."

Libby spoke up. "You'll keep busy at home. Hiking. Riding."

Steffi's heart leaped at the memories evoked by her

sister's words. Hiking. Riding. Fly—she started to open her arms, but her aching shoulder wrenched her back to reality. Hiking and riding would make her focus on the moment, but the open skies would only make her yearn... The doctors said her dislocated shoulder might always be weaker. If—when—she regained her ability, how would changes in her human shape affect her wings? Her pulse thudded in her throat. What if she couldn't fly?

"Steffi." Sawyer's soft voice brought her back to the table.

She drew a deep breath. *Don't think about shifting.*

"Are you all right, Steff?" Worry darkened Libby's eyes.

"I'm fine. I was...thinking."

"If you turn up unannounced, Mom and Dad will wonder why. I mean, it's not like you live around the corner. They could guess something's wrong, and you know how they are."

"You're right." Steffi looked to Sawyer. "They're both scientists. Love solving problems and puzzles." Almost as much as they loved their family. "Is there any way they could help?"

Sawyer's serious gaze punctured the flash of hope. "Providing love and support. That's about it."

Libby's fingers tapped the table. "Don't sell them short. They may be Simple Humans, but they're damn smart."

"I'm not disputing that, but even Shifter families can't help much." Sawyer turned to Steffi. "Learning about your problem might create a conflict for your parents."

Libby stared at him. "What do you mean?"

"They're Simple Humans with three amazing children. They might welcome having a Simple Human daughter."

"That is a vile suggestion." When Libby's fingers fisted as if she were getting ready to punch, Sawyer drew back slightly. "Mom and Dad would never do anything to change us, and they will do whatever they can to help Steffi. Don't you agree, Steff?"

Steffi nodded. "Lib's right. Mom told me once that when we were small, OASIS offered them drugs that could make us Simple Human."

Libby sat up. "They were going to give us X-Ting?"

"That was before anyone knew about the side effects, but Mom and Dad still said no. They wanted us to be who we were."

Sawyer cleared his throat. "Even with your parents' support, Montana might not be good because it holds so many memories."

Bird shifts and Dragon Tag. Steffi wiggled in her seat. "Lib, do you remember the first time we were wildcats?"

"You bet. The Wicklow kids threw rocks at us to chase us away. As if we'd go after their skinny sheep." Libby's smile faded. "Sawyer may have a point. It might be hard not to think about shifting in Montana."

Not hard. Impossible. Steffi's spirits sank.

The tines of Libby's fork played upon the shredded lettuce she'd barely eaten. "I bet he thinks you'll have the same problem if you visit me."

Steffi eyed the center of the table, where Libby's words seemed to rest like a challenge. "I'm sure he—you don't think that, do you, Sawyer?" Her sisters were her staunchest allies.

"Depends." He drank his water. "When you're together, how much do you talk about shifting?"

"We do a lot of shifting. As far as talking about it—not until Sheboygan. Since then, of course…"

"I'm guessing your sisters share your worries." He didn't look at Libby. "Spending time with them might make you focus more on your problem, not less."

Libby's eyes narrowed. "Let me get this straight. Steffi should relax, but not in familiar places with people who love her. She shouldn't go anywhere or do anything that makes her think about shifting. Sounds like you want to shut her in a box. How's that supposed to help?"

"Libby's right. Where will I go? What will I do?"

When she waved her hand, Sawyer grasped it. His inscrutable expression might have masked anger or frustration. Then a smile stole across his rugged features like sunrise on a mountain, and the brightness stunned her heart. "Don't worry. I have a few ideas."

****

"Whew!" Libby threw the deadbolt and rested her back against the apartment door. "I thought he was never going to leave!"

Steffi smiled. Sometimes Libby could be as dramatic as Dayzee. Poor Sawyer! When he'd accompanied them to the apartment, Libby had done everything she could to get rid of him, short of pushing him out the door and down the stairs.

Libby pulled down the bed. "You should rest." As Steffi stretched out, Libby perched on the edge of the bed. "That man could talk the ears off an elephant."

Steffi regarded her sister. "He wasn't that bad."

"Maybe not. But he asked so many questions about places you've been, places you'd like to go, things you like to do." Libby shook her head.

Steffi's laughter bubbled. "He wants us to leave as soon as I have the doctor's okay."

Libby took off her shoes, put her feet up, and sat against the wall that served as a headboard. "I suppose."

Steffi rolled onto her good side. "You sound suspicious."

"I don't mean to, but…"

Steffi sat up. "Out with it, Lib. What's bugging you?"

"I think he stuck around because he doesn't want us talking about what happened in the park."

"That makes two of us. I wish I could forget…" Steffi bit her lower lip. "I can't believe I was so stupid."

"No, no, no!" Libby moved until she and Steffi were face to face. "As far as the attack is concerned, please remember one thing: what happened was *not* your fault." She paused. "What worries me…some of what Sawyer says doesn't add up. One minute, he and his friends have the assailant surrounded, and the next, the guy disappears. Poof! Like a magic trick."

"My associates took care of him." Nothing magic about it. Steffi pressed her tongue against the roof of her mouth. "Everything happened so fast. I don't remember much. Mostly pain." She patted the sling. "And noises." That horrid screech. She brought her hands to her ears as if she could shut it out.

Libby sat up. "Really? What kind of noises?"

"I don't…a big jumble." Steffi covered her eyes. "I hurt so bad I could have been screaming inside my head."

"Then you lost consciousness."

Steffi nodded. "I don't—wait a minute!" Her sister

looked ready to pounce. "I *do* remember something." She brought her fingers to her face. "A touch." Incredibly gentle. "A voice." Breath brushing her cheek. *"Steffi, stay with me!"*

"Must have been Sawyer. He says he watched you until the medical squad arrived." Libby shifted position. "Are you sure that's all—"

"Yes. That's it." Steffi brushed away the half-uttered question. "Sawyer and his OASIS guys may have saved my life." She stood and walked to the wall with the built-in dresser.

Libby joined her. "I know that, and I am grateful." She reached for Steffi, but Steffi stepped back.

"Then why do you keep poking around, trying to turn over every rock to see what's underneath?"

The corners of Libby's mouth turned down. "That's how I am, Sis. I swore to enforce the law, and I take that seriously. I don't like vigilantes. Simple Human *or* Shape-shifter."

"Understandable." Steffi faced her sister. "As a cop, what would *you* have done?"

"Good question." Libby straightened her shoulders.

"He was big. You'd have needed backup. I don't think he'd have let anyone—" She broke off, that screech vibrating in her ears.

"I like to think that I would still have acted professionally. But if I'd seen *you,* I don't—" The color drained from Libby's face. "No. I do know." She reached to her shoulder as if she were wearing a holster. "I would have taken the son-of-a-bitch out, no questions asked."

Steffi gave her a one-armed hug. "Thank you, Lib." *I rest my case.* Releasing her sister, Steffi pulled the top drawer from the wall.

"What are you doing?"

"Deciding what to pack."

Libby frowned. "You don't know where you're going yet."

"I know it will be someplace relaxing. Maybe a beach. Blazing sunlight. White sand. Blue water." And Sawyer in a swimsuit. "Heaven!" She closed her eyes and sighed.

"Better check with your tour guide. Otherwise, you could end up in the mountains with a suitcase full of swimwear."

"I don't have many clothes to begin with, so my choices are limited. And you heard him. If I need anything, we'll pick it up."

"True." Libby smiled. "I do like the way he takes care of you."

"My associates took care of him." Steffi bit her lower lip. "He's serious about his OASIS assignments."

"Whatever." Libby hugged her. "There's something to be said for someone who'll do anything to protect you."

Steffi met her sister's knowing gaze. "I couldn't agree more."

Chapter 11

Sawyer eyed the suitcase sitting by the door. "This all you're taking?" Steffi's solemn nod triggered alarms in his brain. "I'm not complaining. I admire your efficiency." The tension in her mouth eased, and he relaxed. "My sisters pack enough for an invading army."

When he reached for his phone, she said, "Not yet. I have to make one last check." She scanned the apartment. "Trash out. Dishes done and put away. Refrigerator cleaned out. I hate coming home to moldy food. Kitchen water off. Bathroom, too. Once I left the toilet running. Outrageous water bill! Thermostat adjusted." She brought her hands together. "Now you can call."

She retrieved a dark green jacket from a hook that hung over her washroom door and slipped it on. When she straightened the big photo of her with her sisters, Sawyer pressed his fingers, curved to ease the longing on her face, to his sides. He could look all he wanted but keep his hands to himself. Sawyer Montaigne did not take advantage of his clients. Steffi Anbruzzen would never be *loup-garou*. "Cheer up. This is a holiday, not an exile. Relax. Let yourself go."

Her throaty noise might have been a smothered laugh. "I can't remember the last time I did that."

Good thing he'd reviewed her record. "Before your fifth birthday. You wanted a pony."

"Me and every other five-year-old in the country."

"Your parents alerted OASIS that you were going to be disappointed."

Steffi snapped her fingers. "That's why Juliet showed up. I must have had a major meltdown, but I don't remember it."

"That's because it didn't happen."

"I must have been angry."

"No doubt. But you kept control."

Fragments of memory merged. "I was ready to blow, but I didn't. Instead, I told them what I was feeling. I felt so powerful...by not exerting power. Ironic, isn't it?" Although the corners of her mouth refused to release a smile, her radiant face rivaled the noon sun. "After that, I never had another unplanned shift. In fact, I never had any shifting problems." The light dimmed. "Not until..."

"Your control may have put the brakes on your ability."

She frowned. "How so?"

"Your emotions trigger your shifting."

"But if I didn't control—"

"Once in a while, you'd blow up. Big deal."

"No one knows how much damage I could do."

"OASIS may have exaggerated your power because you make them nervous, and your Mentors wanted you to learn control. No one realized how rigorously you would apply their teaching. You've imprisoned your emotions."

She lifted her chin. "I've never—"

"Sure you have. You don't allow yourself to smile or laugh or even shout." He gazed deep into her eyes. "Right now, for instance, you're irritated with me, but the only evidence is the little gold sparks in your irises.

They no sooner appear than they vanish into the darkness, and you pretend that everything is fine. That you've functioned so well for so long is a testimony to the strength of your ability. You should get in touch with your emotions again."

"I appreciate your concern, but I am in touch with my emotions." She crossed her arms and covered her lovely bosom.

Don't shut me out. "You don't have to be afraid."

She took a step back. "I'm not." She turned slightly as if checking for the exit.

"When was the last time you laughed?"

"I like a good joke as much as anyone else."

She sounded so damned defensive. "How long has it been since you laughed down deep in your belly so hard that your eyes water?"

"Not everyone laughs like that."

"Everyone should."

"You really can be annoying." She almost smiled.

"It's part of my charm."

Steffi scoffed.

"By the time this is over, I hope to see a real smile and hear a genuine laugh, not a lady-like titter."

A shadow crossed her face. "Sounds as if I have a lot of work to do."

He reached out, but she backed off before he could brush her cheek. Good move. He'd respect her limits. "And I mean to see that you enjoy as much of it as you can." He pulled out his phone. "We're ready," he told Georges. Then he straightened his cuffs the way the actor did in his favorite spy thrillers, and he picked up Steffi's luggage.

The car was waiting in front of her building. As

Sawyer helped her into the backseat, Steffi stroked the upholstery, her admiration increasing the value of the insanely expensive leather.

When Georges pulled onto the Stevenson Expressway, Steffi sat up. "We're not going to O'Hare?"

"Not today."

She uttered a breathy "oh" and sank back into her seat. The sparkle in her eyes dimmed, but by the time they reached the private airfield, she was looking around with renewed interest.

"This way." Taking her arm, Sawyer led her toward the jet, where Isabeau greeted them.

"*Monsieur Montaigne*." Daniel popped out of the cockpit to pump Sawyer's free hand. "Good to see you again."

"Thanks, Daniel."

"Will you be at the controls today?"

Sawyer's fingers flexed, and his pulse bumped up.

Steffi tilted her head. "You fly?"

"Not today." Maybe before they left Montreal—what in God's name was he thinking? He had a pilot's license, but Steffi—she could really fly.

"This way, *mademoiselle*." Isabeau led Steffi into the first cabin, where she chose a window seat on one side of the broad aisle instead of the couch that folded out into a bed. Sawyer took the seat across from hers. His knees brushed hers. Good thing they both wore long pants.

"*Champagne, monsieur*?"

"*Mais oui*." Isabeau pulled out the small table that separated him from Steffi and stepped away. "Why the frown?"

"It's early for champagne."

"Someone once said that it's always eight in the evening somewhere." He grinned. "Pretend we're there."

"I'll try." She accepted the glass with a reserved *"merci"* but made no move to drink.

"This comes from a family vineyard in France." When he lifted his glass, Steffi brought her drink up to meet his. She looked as if she were preparing to swallow poison. "May you find what you seek." The rim of his glass grazed the lip of hers.

"Thank you. I'd wish the same for you." Her dark eyes sparkled when she looked from him to the interior of the plane. "But I can't imagine what you would want that you can't have."

Perhaps a smile to accompany her melted-honey voice? "You'd be surprised." Sawyer Montaigne did not take advantage of his OASIS clients. Steffi Anbruzzen would never be *loup-garou*. Yet the longer he knew her, the fainter both of those warnings seemed to become.

When the plane lifted off, she pressed her face against the window. Her arms curved and moved away from her sides. With a muttered curse, she slapped them against her ribs as if she were slamming a barn door. She turned away from the window. A tooth dug into her lower lip.

How could he have been such a fool? "Steffi, I'm sorry. When I made these arrangements, I was thinking about efficiency, not about how you might feel."

"I should get used to it. Even if—when—I recover, I may have problems with my left side." She patted her weak shoulder. When Sawyer started to refill her glass, she waved him off. "If I drink any more, you'll have to carry me off the plane."

His cock stood on full alert. "That wouldn't be so

109

terrible. Try not to york on my shoes, eh?" Holding her in his arms again would be well worth the clean-up.

"York? Oh, you mean, vomit." Steffi pushed the wine away. "That's a distinct possibility."

"Are you hungry? The larder is well stocked, and Isabeau's an excellent cook."

"No, no, I'm fine. A bit overwhelmed." She gestured at the cabin. "I've never even flown first class, let alone on a private plane. I like that wolf's paw with the huge 'M' on the rudder."

"The Montaigne Enterprises logo."

"Is your father really the Godfather of Canada?" She clapped a hand across her mouth.

"Pardon?" Sawyer sputtered champagne across the table. His laughter boomed throughout the cabin. "Where did you hear such nonsense?"

"My sister Dayzee." Steffi did that fake origami thing with her napkin. "A *loup-garou* she works with told her."

"No doubt an O'Shaugnessy *beau cave* from Vancouver. They can never forgive the Montaignes for arriving in North America two centuries before they did, so they cast aspersions on us whenever possible."

"Dayzee meant well."

"Indeed."

"She was worried. Warned me to be careful."

Setting his glass aside, he rested his forearms on the narrow table. "What else did she tell you?"

"Not much." Steffi could stifle smiles and laughter but not the deep blush that bloomed on her cheeks. Clearly, her sister had shared more than O'Shaugnessy gossip. "That your family has lots of money."

Sawyer laughed again. "That's why you stopped

worrying about me cheating on my expense account, eh?"

Steffi nodded. "You do like expensive things."

"We were taught to accept nothing but the best, and I like my clients to be comfortable. For the record, Montaignes settled in Québec in the mid-1700s shortly after the HBC—Hudson's Bay Company—was established. A small but diligent pack with good instincts for business."

"*Loups-garous*?"

"Always. They left France to escape persecution. In The New World, they could run free, and they got on well with the First Nations. Today, Montaigne Enterprises reaches around the world. All legitimate business interests." When he extended his arms, pleasure in his family's achievement warmed him.

"You're obviously quite proud of them. As the oldest son, why are you working for OASIS instead of learning the family business?"

Sawyer chuckled. "You sound like my parents. They want me to come home and settle down."

"Sorry. I know it's none of my business."

"We're getting to know each other better. Nothing wrong with that. In fact, the more we know, the more smoothly we should be able to work together. You love your family. Why did you choose work that takes you away for weeks, sometimes months at a stretch? Why do you live in Chicago?"

Steffi sat up. "You're supposed to answer me, not ask other questions."

He smiled. "Be patient. I'm getting there. Why didn't you stay in Montana?"

Steffi rested her hands on the table. "My sisters and

I don't live near Mom and Dad because we've already disrupted their lives enough."

"All offspring do that."

"Not like we did. I mean, they're Simple Humans. All their friends are Simple Humans, and their children are…not like us. We did our best to fit in, but it was hard. When I got older, there was no reason for me to stay. We don't have a family business. If we did, I would have done my share."

"Do you plan to move back or live closer to them when you have a home and family of your own?"

"I haven't thought about that for years. When I was a kid, I dreamed about Prince Charming and all that. Now, I know the world is short on Prince Charmings, and I'm no princess."

Maybe not, but Steffi possessed far more power. Swathe that creamy skin in silk or satin, sprinkle orchids in that dark hair, circle that long neck with diamonds, and she would outshine any storybook princess.

"You think I should connect more with my emotions, but when I do, bad things happen. Like when I zapped Dayzee at Dragon Tag. Some of us aren't made for happy endings." Her lips twisted. "I don't even believe in once upon a time."

"That's one of the dumbest things I've ever heard."

Steffi's chin came up.

"Don't look so insulted. Your emotions are important for your ability, hell, Steffi, not only for your ability, but for your life. Your real life apart from shifting." When he touched one of her hands, electricity stung his palm. *Back off! Got it.* Pulling back, he cleared his throat. Steffi looked altogether too smug. "You've learned to control your emotions. Now, you need to learn how to channel them more effectively."

"And you're going to teach me to do that?"

"I'll certainly try."

"I answered your question." She pointed at him. "Now, it's your turn. Why are you working for OASIS instead of Montaigne Enterprises?"

"I work for both. I've spent much of my life learning about the family business, but a few years ago, I wanted to do something where I could see concrete results without making a five-year plan." He sipped his champagne. "One of my uncles serves on the OASIS Directorate. He agreed to hire me as a troubleshooter. I take cases when I can fit them into my schedule. I enjoy solving problems that don't focus on profit and loss. I also like having the opportunity to serve other Shifters." He cocked his head. "Does that answer your question?"

"Yes, indeed."

The respect in her voice made him feel ten feet tall. "I should apologize, by the way. I was planning to take you to Costa Rica, but I have to take care of business at home, so we'll be spending a few days in Montreal before your true holiday begins."

Steffi's dark eyebrows dipped in a frown. "How can I not think about shifting if we're with your pack?"

"Don't worry." Sawyer laughed. "I have a board meeting, not a pack activity. Technically, the pack gathers monthly for the full moon, but everyone's so busy that we now require attendance only at quarterly meetings and cotillions. Spring and fall."

"Sounds elegant."

"Oh, they are. That's when we choose our mates." The wine in his mouth turned sour.

One of Steffi's eyebrows lifted like a facial question

mark. "You haven't done it yet, have you?"

"No, but my parents started nagging when I turned eighteen."

"So young!"

"Packs have always encouraged early mating. Females are entering their prime breeding years, and young males without mates often get into trouble."

"From the pack perspective, that makes sense, but…" Steffi's fingers went to the notch between her collarbones, which drew his gaze to the curve of her neck. "At eighteen, I wanted to explore the world outside Montana. If I'd been you, I'd have felt as if my life was ending before it began."

"My sentiments exactly. I'd been shifting for about four years, had barely begun to understand what it meant to be a *loup-garou* in a Simple Human world."

"How did you get out of it?"

"I didn't. I procrastinated—much to my mother's distress. I went to university and stayed in school as long as I could. In the meantime, my siblings dutifully mated and produced offspring, which eased the pressure on me until I turned thirty. Then the countdown clock started running again. Many packs, including mine, ostracize males who haven't mated for the first time by thirty-five."

"How strange!"

"Not really. Younger unmated males can cause problems in the Simple Human world; older unmated males often create dissension in the pack. Now, *Maman* fills my inbox with photos of candidates, and *Papa* reminds me that he is ageing. He's not yet sixty but begins every conversation with 'I'm not going to live forever.'"

Steffi's gaze glided across his face. "With all that pressure, I'm surprised you waited so long."

"First, I wanted my freedom. The same way you did. Then, I discovered—let me put it tactfully—the attractions of Simple Human females. Now, I understand how important it is not merely to mate but to find the right mate."

"True love?"

She looked so skeptical he hesitated to continue. "It may sound silly, but I've attended more cotillions than I can count, and I've seen something happen—some spark—when true mates connect. My brothers would never admit it, but each of my sisters swears she and her mate shared a moment when they *knew*."

Her features softened. "Must be nice."

He nodded. "I've done my best, especially in the past few years, but I've never felt—" He shook his head. "I'm sure it's all foolishness." He stood and stretched in the aisle. "We'll spend a few days in Montreal. If you'd like to see more of Canada, on our way to the beach, we can visit Nova Scotia and Prince Edward Island."

Steffi bounced as if she'd sat on a spring. "I read wonderful books set there!" Disarmed by surprise or delight, the barriers at the corners of her mouth failed to rise, and her true smile slammed like a two by four across his chest.

Inside Sawyer, his *loup-garou* pounced.

Hands with claws at their tips gripped Steffi's head like a vise, and a fierce mouth locked on hers. She froze. This couldn't be happening again. Not with Sawyer. She inhaled. No problem breathing. Wiggling her fingers and toes, she reviewed what she'd learned in self-defense class. *Kick in the groin.* But she was sitting down.

When she dug her fingers into his shoulders, the painful burst in her injured arm redoubled her determination. *Go for the eyes.* She liked Sawyer's rugged features, but if she had to gouge that feral gaze to gain her freedom, so be it. She couldn't move her lips, but his name filled her mouth. One last chance. She drew a deep breath and shouted. "Sawyer! Stop!"

He blinked. Gray smoke quenched the yellow that ringed his irises. The aroma of sage laced with Sawyer's distinctive scent surrounded her. The hands against her cheeks gentled.

This was the touch she remembered from the park.

His lips softened against hers. When his shoulders drew back as if he were retreating, she reached behind his head with her good hand and slid her fingers into his thick hair. Whisper-soft kisses covered her face before he returned to her mouth and kissed her in earnest. He tasted dark and mysterious, like the deep wood at midnight. Longing stirred within her, and she parted her lips to welcome him.

He uttered a strangled cry and staggered back. With his covered mouth, wide eyes, and disheveled hair, he looked as if he'd encountered a monster. Or an Anomaly.

Sinking onto the couch, he buried his face in his hands.

Oh, no! When Steffi closed her eyes, she saw sixteen-year-old Mickey Moorman's face, his swollen tongue pushed against his blistered lips. What had she done this time? *Not Sawyer. Please, not Sawyer.* She ventured from her chair to stand beside him. "Are you all right?"

His hands muffled his reply. Had she scarred him so badly he couldn't bear to show his face? "Sorry."

She nearly choked. "What?"

In a louder voice, he said, "I'm sorry."

When he lifted his head, relief leached the strength from her legs. She dropped onto the far edge of the couch and stared at his perfect face.

"I don't know what or how, but—" He pulled his phone from his jacket pocket. "You can have a new advisor waiting at the airport."

"No." She slid toward him and rested a hand on the phone. "OASIS doesn't want to help me. You do. We agreed—"

Standing, Sawyer strode to the rear of the cabin. "I know, but that was before—" He shot a tortured glance in her direction.

"I'm fine." Unless you counted the persistent hum in her blood and the kiss that lingered on her lips. She held up her palms. "No harm, no foul."

"Kind of you to say, but not true. I don't know how or why it happened. One minute, I was looking at your beautiful smile, and the next, my *loup-garou* seized control."

"You didn't shift."

"I know, but his awareness pushed into my human shape. That's never happened before, and I'll never let it happen again. I must have frightened you."

"Your *loup-garou* is fierce."

"And determined."

She went to him. "But he listened. When I cried out to your human, your *loup-garou* backed off." Her pulse shifted into overdrive at the memory. "Didn't you feel the difference?"

"Yes." He pulled away. "That doesn't erase what I did." He studied her face. "Are you sure you're all right?"

"Relax. First of all, you—Sawyer—weren't in control. Your *loup-garou* was, and he behaved…like a beast. Which he is. Second, you've apologized. I accept your apology."

"I could have hurt you."

"You didn't. You may not believe it after that thing in the park, but I can take care of myself. The first boy who tried to stick his tongue down my throat ended up in the ER. Poor kid."

Sawyer scratched his jaw. "The loss of shifting ability can affect other powers. You may be more vulnerable than you realize."

"I've taken Simple Human self-defense classes." Steffi flexed the hands she'd rested on those iron shoulders. "I could have hurt you if I had to. I'm glad I didn't." She started to bring a finger to her mouth but pushed her hand into a pocket instead. "I'd really like to see Prince Edward Island."

"Of course." He did the sexy thing with straightening his cuffs. "Once I'm finished in Montreal, we will go anywhere you like, stay as long you like, and do whatever you like."

Whatever she liked? Maybe a bit more of the post-*loup-garou* kissing that had awakened an ache to melt into Sawyer until nothing else mattered? Not having full power might offer unexpected benefits. For the first time since Sheboygan, her world seemed brighter.

Chapter 12

"Welcome to *l'Auberge Montaigne*. The Montaigne Inn."

Steffi eyed the massive stone building that looked as if it had been erected when this ancient section of Montreal was new. While porters whisked their luggage away and the bellman summoned the manager, Sawyer responded with polite indifference. He'd never had to wrestle suitcases in an endless check-in line or, worse, arrived only to learn that something had gone awry with his reservation. The manager's effusive welcome made it clear that neither Montaignes nor their guests required reservations. Discoursing in animated French, the small man escorted them past the registration desk to a private elevator.

Sawyer cut off the manager's speech. "*Plus tarde, Henri, s'il vous plaît.*"

The manager brought his heels together and dipped his chin slightly. "*Merci, monsieur.*"

When the elevator door closed, Sawyer moved to the other side of the small enclosure. Since the incident on the plane, he hadn't come near her. Saying he had reports to read, he'd spent the remainder of the flight in the back cabin. On the drive from the airport, he'd kept his eyes on the road ahead even as he pointed out landmarks. Now, he seemed to commune with the blank door.

"What was that all about?"

He looked at her. "I thought you spoke French."

"I can read it fairly well, but natives speak too fast for me to catch everything."

"There's a problem with the laundry service."

"He expects you to take care of the laundry? Isn't that his job?"

"Yes, but services sometimes need a push from upper management. A phone call should set everything right." He lifted a warning finger. "Not muscle."

Steffi sighed. Would she ever live down that Godfather question? *Thanks a bunch, Day.* "If you can fix everything with a phone call, why do you want to talk with him?"

His smile flashed. "Ah, you did catch that part. Be patient." A slight movement of his head directed her attention to the small camera mounted in one corner.

Eyes and ears everywhere. When she shot Sawyer a skeptical glance, he said, "Better to be secure than sorry." The elevator door opened into a small foyer outside a huge sitting room.

Steffi stared up, up, up at the high ceiling and its elegant molding. She slipped off her shoes, partly to show respect, but mostly to feel the Persian carpet beneath her feet. She stroked leather upholstery as smooth as silk. *Loups-garous* seemed to have a thing for leather.

"You approve?" Beaming, Sawyer watched from the foyer.

"Oh, yes!" She scanned the big room. "No cameras?"

"Not here. And not in any of the guest rooms."

"Good." She wouldn't have to undress in the closet. She approached huge windows that looked over the old city. "What a spectacular view!"

"It does take one's breath away."

She turned to catch Sawyer looking at her, not the city. Her cheeks heated, but he took two quick steps back and gestured toward doors on opposite sides of the parlor. "They put my bags in my usual room, but please choose the room you prefer."

The one with him in it? Dream on. He seemed determined to restore their professional relationship. "I'm sure they're equally comfortable."

Sawyer's lips parted in a tense smile. "They'd better be, or Henri's ass is grass."

"Tough talk."

He opened the door beside the small kitchen and breakfast nook. "What do you think of this one?"

Steffi brought her hand to her mouth to keep from gaping at a room twice as large as her Chicago apartment. The king-sized bed had wrought-iron backstop and footer. The scent of lavender floated in the air. "It's the nicest bedroom I've ever seen, and I've been to Louis XIV's bedchamber in the Palace of Versailles." She wrinkled her nose. "Too much gold." She peeked into the private bathroom. "And Louis didn't have a hot tub." She could almost feel the bubbles against her skin.

"Would you like to see the other room?"

She stopped stroking one arm of the white bathrobe that hung in the closet and met his amused gaze. "Oh, no." She scanned the room. "This is great."

"Good. Now, I should talk with Henri. Please make yourself comfortable." He gestured toward the phone. "We have a masseuse on call, and the private pool is one floor down. If you want to explore, you'll find shops below the lobby."

She rummaged through her pockets for her wallet, but Sawyer lifted a hand.

"Charge everything to the room." He whipped through the number in French and jotted the numeral on a pad. Then he placed a computer card on top of the pad. "Use this in the elevator. I'll meet you in the brasserie after I finish with Henri."

"Finish with?" The set of Sawyer's jaw punctuated his words. She followed him into the sitting room. "That sounds unpleasant for your manager."

"He may be complaining about the laundry service to distract us from money he has 'borrowed' to pay off his gambling debts."

"What?"

"*Papa* has heard gossip for several months, but this is the first opportunity anyone has had to make an unannounced check of the books."

Steffi followed him to the elevator. "Sawyer."

He turned.

"Be careful."

He studied her face and shifted his shoulders into a slight slouch. "Don't worry, babe." His exaggerated, tough-guy voice made her cringe. "I stashed my gun in the washroom."

She planted her feet on the fine carpet. "Sawyer!"

With a full-throated laugh, he disappeared.

****

Eyeing the graceful arches and polished wood framing of the intimate restaurant, Steffi sipped the Montrachet that Sawyer had reserved. Scents of tarragon, sage, and garlic filled the air. The butter on the crusty bread melted in her mouth, and the brie kissed her taste buds. She could become comfortable with this life far too easily. *Enjoy it now, but remember that all things must end.* When Sawyer appeared, her heartbeat stuttered, and she set the wineglass on the table with her trembling fingers. No matter how much she longed to trust him, he might still be loyal to OASIS.

"May I join you, *mademoiselle?*" Although he purred the question, the confident lift of his chin suggested he already knew the answer.

"Please do."

A server materialized with a slight bow. Sawyer rattled off a few items.

Steffi glanced at the server's back and returned to Sawyer. "No menu? What is *méchoui à la Montaigne?* The specialty of the house?"

"The specialty of the family. Grilled lamb. If you don't like lamb, I can call for a menu."

"I'll give it a try." She leaned toward him. "How did your meeting go?"

His thick brows met. "Let's not talk business." He poured a bit of wine into his goblet, swirled it slightly to appraise the color, then sniffed and tasted.

"All right." She sat back. "Tell me about Montreal."

"One of my favorite cities. Ah!" He lifted his glass. "Three true smiles in less than twenty-four hours."

And one unforgettable kiss. "Your enthusiasm must be contagious."

"Good. Montreal offers a tantalizing blend of the very old and the very new."

The rich wine bloomed on her tongue. "Tantalizing, eh?"

One corner of his mouth quirked. "Practicing your Canadian, eh?"

"Guilty as charged. Please continue."

"The more you come to know her, the more you want to know." The intensity in his gaze suggested he was no longer talking about the city.

She focused on her wine. "Did you grow up here?"

"Oh, no. We have a house in the country."

She looked up. "Oh?"

He skewered her with his gaze. "A country house, not a guarded compound."

She lifted her hands and shook her head. "Sorry."

"Don't be—especially since you're smiling again." He broke off a piece of bread. "How was your afternoon?"

"Relaxing. Although I did worry about you."

"No need. Everything has been resolved."

"Too bad we can't fix my problem so easily."

Dark clouds appeared in his eyes. "I'm sorry I had to change our plans."

"Please don't be. I understand. You have so many other obligations that you can't spend as much time on my case—"

He cut her off with a lifted hand. "I intend to spend as much time as it takes to help you. Frankly, after reading your record and talking with your former Mentors—don't roll your eyes!—I thought working with you would be something of a chore." The flash of a grin drew the sting from his words. "Instead, it's been a pleasant surprise."

"Glad to hear it. Thank you."

"Except, of course, for my—"

"Sawyer!" A long-legged woman with artfully tousled hair of an unnatural platinum shade dropped a professionally manicured hand on one of Sawyer's shoulders. Huge green eyes in a face that belonged on a

124

Renaissance portrait. Dramatic cleavage drawing attention to breasts that looked too good to be true. Sawyer opened his mouth, but before he could speak, the stranger loosed a barrage of French punctuated by smiles, pouts, and enough eyelash flutters to start a tsunami.

When she finally paused, Sawyer looked across the table. "Steffi, I'd like to you to meet Nicole Chasseur. Nicole, this is Steffi Anbruzzen. She's visiting from the States."

Steffi's lips twitched in the approximation of a smile. "Nice to meet you."

"The pleasure is mine." The other woman's blindingly white smile didn't reach her eyes. Stroking Sawyer's sleeve—she couldn't keep her hands off him— she continued her recital. Eyes fixed on her fabulous face, Sawyer provided a rapt audience.

"Oui, oui." When Sawyer stood, the Chasseur woman wound her hands around his arm. "I'll be back in a minute," he told Steffi.

The other woman's smile bordered on a sneer. She drew Sawyer across the room to a table where another impossibly beautiful blonde sat. As the three people talked, the Chasseur woman stood close enough to crawl into Sawyer's pocket. Beneath the table, Steffi gripped her hands to keep from ripping those long fingers off Sawyer's arm.

As the two women laughed and gesticulated, Sawyer smiled and inserted occasional remarks. They looked so cozy they might have been arranging a threesome for later in the evening once Sawyer dumped his American baggage.

Trying not to feel abandoned, Steffi sipped her wine

and feigned fascination with the restaurant décor.

The Chasseur woman followed Sawyer back to the table. "Good to see you again, Nicole. I'll be in touch."

She rested one hand on his cheek. "*Écoute-moi*."

"*Listen to me.*" The intimate command crawled down Steffi's spine. The other woman sashayed back to her friend.

Looking unruffled, Sawyer reclaimed his seat.

"You do know she's a witch?"

Sawyer smiled. "C-level sorceress."

"Oh." One step above Simple Human. "So she doesn't know…"

"She lacks the ability to recognize anyone of a different class or above her level, and I never told her." Sawyer cleared his throat. "Sorry about the interruption. She wanted to introduce me to her aunt."

Aunt?

Sawyer poured himself more wine. "Nicole covers business for one of the local papers. A few years ago, she interviewed me about a project I was working on. One thing led to another." He took a drink. "I haven't seen her in a while."

When he glanced at the two women, they wiggled their fingers at him. Steffi's stomach rolled over.

"Are you all right?"

"I did some of those shoulder exercises before I came down, and I am a little tired. I'll be fine."

"Are you sure?" He put his hands on the edge of the table. "We can have the meal sent up."

"No, no." She sipped some water. "I'm all right." This was Sawyer's city. Better get used to running into his old girl friends.

"Someone on the hotel staff must have told her I was

here. She's heard that the board is meeting to discuss tar-sands oil and wants an exclusive on our plans."

So, pumping him for information required her to stick like flypaper and flaunt her cleavage with every breath? Steffi bit her tongue. In fairness, being sexy might be one element of Nicole Chasseur's success. "What did you tell her?"

"That she has better sources than I do. Of course, you can't keep a good dog off your leg."

"What?"

"Some people can be annoyingly persistent." He turned slightly. "Ah!" A fragrant dish of lamb accompanied by a salad appeared in front of her. "Taste. If you don't like—"

Chewing, she silenced him with a raised hand and swallowed the first morsel. "You were right. This is incredible."

Sawyer nodded to the server, who departed.

When she took another bite, the subtle seasoning filled her mouth until she thought she might burst from sheer delight.

They both concentrated on eating. Would they ever regain the easy companionship that had begun to develop before the incident on the plane?

"Earth to Steffi! Come in, please."

She blinked. "Yes?"

"You look as if you have a live lobster dancing a jig in your stomach."

"Oh." She moved the remains of her meal around with her fork. "A little heartburn." As accurate a diagnosis as any.

Sawyer sat back and stretched as if he owned the place, which, in a sense, he did. "You've had a long day.

We should call it a night."

Put the cat away, and the mice can play. Although her weary muscles welcomed the suggestion, her stomach clenched at the notion of Sawyer in a lascivious tangle with the Chasseur witch and her companion.

"…fresh start tomorrow."

"Sounds good." At least, while they strolled through Montreal tomorrow, she could force her attention on something other than Sawyer, but she already suspected that his figure would dominate any local sights.

Chapter 13

When they returned to the apartment, Sawyer paused in the sitting room. "Good night, Steffi. Perhaps tomorrow will rate five smiles?"

"Perhaps." Without the possibility of another kiss, why bother?

"Sleep well."

With Sawyer so close? Not likely.

He sat on the couch and pulled a file from his briefcase.

"What are you doing?"

He spread papers on the coffee table. "Business."

So he wasn't heading off to bed the delectable duo. Steffi's heart gave a happy-bunny hop. "Want company?"

"Thanks, but you should rest, and I concentrate better alone. See you in the morning." The smile that warmed her toes vanished. "Lock your door."

Closing the door behind her, she paused with her hand on the lever. Sawyer had sounded deathly serious. Perhaps he feared another *loup-garou* eruption, this time more violent. She shook her head. That made no sense. If Sawyer's *loup-garou* had wanted to harm her, he would have taken his own shape. If she had to face him again, she wouldn't be as scared. Nevertheless, she turned the deadbolt.

A bath full of bubbles soon relaxed muscles stiff

from standing at attention whenever Sawyer looked her way.

After drying off, she pulled on the short satin nightgown she'd bought several years earlier during a long layover in the Hong Kong airport. She'd never worn it before, but it was her only suitable nightwear for such an impressive bed. She played with the settings until the mattress felt most comfortable. All that was missing... *Don't think about him.*

Despite her intentions, when she closed her eyes, she relived that amazing moment when Sawyer replaced his *loup-garou*. His big hands cradled her head like something precious. Her face still tingled from his quick kisses, and the taste of his mouth lingered beneath the flavors of the excellent dinner.

After prepping for the big meeting, what would Sawyer do?

She rolled over. Enough fantasizing about a man who charmed as effortlessly as he breathed. Wanting a man like—no, not a man like him—wanting Sawyer himself was a waste of time and energy. He'd all but told her so. If the Chasseur witch was a good example, he liked females who were smart, sexy, and effervescent. She could check off the first category, but that was about it. As a Simple Human, she'd never make the grade. As a Shifter...his *loup-garou* needed a mate. Another *loup-garou*, not an Anomaly.

Yet something extraordinary had happened between them. She'd experienced both the power of his *loup-garou* and the tenderness of his human, something none of his Simple Human honeys or his C-level sorceress would ever know. Running the tip of her tongue across her lips to recover the sweetness of his kiss, she closed her eyes.

In the sitting room, Sawyer read the same sentence for the sixth time, put the papers down, and closed his eyes. Two days until the meeting. Plenty of time for review. Nicole thought she'd put him under a spell to renew their relationship. After the meeting, he'd satisfy her with a few inconsequential nuggets of information. *Papa* liked to keep the media happy.

When he stood and flexed his biceps, his body protested spending most of the day in tight spaces. The enforced intimacy of the plane and cars might have contributed... Tomorrow, he'd have to spend time in the gym.

Steffi had closed her door. He'd told her to lock it but hadn't heard the click. He should check.

He reached out but, instead of moving toward the door, took three steps back. If she hadn't thrown the bolt, the door would open. Even if he couldn't see her slumbering form, the susurrus of her breath would lure him into the room. Toward the bed where she slept. Alone. He stuffed his hands in his pants pockets and turned away. He'd done enough damage.

Every time he thought of his actions on the plane, a miasma of disgust crawled up his throat. In a heartbeat, he'd gone from basking in Steffi's glorious smile to destroying the fragile framework of their relationship. His ribs still ached from the pounding of his heart. The thunder of his *loup-garou*'s mental howl had obliterated his human thoughts until only a single word remained. *MINE!*

When he bedded Simple Human females, his *loup-garou* seldom stirred. His *loup-garou* knew that even in her Simple Human shape, Steffi was a Shifter. His parents were right: his *loup-garou* needed a mate.

He shut the door to his room behind him. When he closed his eyes, he could still hear Steffi calling his name. Her voice had seemed to come from far away, and he'd raced toward it, shoving the darkness out of his way until he was standing over her with her head between his hands and his mouth on hers.

As soon as he drew a breath, the lips his *loup-garou* had tried to plunder blossomed. Bending his neck to relieve stiffness, he felt again the gentle tug of Steffi's fingers threading through his hair. *Mon dieu*, she hadn't merely refused to let him go—she'd pulled him toward her. Her bosom melted against his chest. He'd kissed her temples, her eyes, her cheekbones, the tip of her nose, and the unguarded corners of her mouth before returning to those luscious lips. Despite his *loup-garou*'s behavior, she wanted him, and the stiffness in his groin had made it achingly clear that the desire was mutual.

Her invitation to explore the rising passion had jolted him back to reality. He would not take advantage of his clients, and Steffi Anbruzzen would never be *loup-garou*. He lay down on the big bed but tossed and turned for what felt like hours. Finally, he stood and began to move around the room. The slow rhythm of his steps soothed his jangled nerves. *Walk*. Yes, he would walk. He preferred the open air, but not tonight. Not with Steffi here. His bones and muscles began to stretch.

With a gasp, Steffi shook off her dream and sat up. Someone in the outer room!

Moving like a shadow, she slipped out of the bed, pulled on the thick bathrobe, and knotted the tie. She checked the lock on her door—*Merci*, Sawyer, for the reminder!—and pressed her ear against the thick wood.

Someone seemed to be bumping into things. An intruder, unfamiliar with the layout of the sitting room?

She frowned. Maybe Montaigne Enterprises wasn't the squeaky-clean business Sawyer claimed. The disgruntled manager might have decided to go out with a real bang. Henri did have access to the private elevator.

Where was Sawyer? He might have rewarded himself for surviving a hard day of OASIS duty by hooking up with that Chasseur witch. Or he might be one of those people who could sleep through a bomb blast.

She glanced at the phone she'd left charging on the nightstand. *Damn*. What did Canadians call for 911?

She rested her hand on the door and continued to listen to the intruder's shuffling. If Sawyer was here, he should have easily overpowered the smaller manager, and she'd have heard the scuffle. Henri might be armed. If he'd surprised Sawyer in his sleep, Sawyer might be wounded or... She took a deep breath and lifted her chin. Sawyer had rescued her in the park. She would not cower in her room if he needed her.

Relieved that staff dutifully oiled the hinges, she unlocked the door. She visualized shifting to a grizzly bear, but nothing happened. *Damn*. What would a Simple Human do? Catch the invader off-guard. Weapons? She scanned her room. The bed lamp would serve. Whacking him on the head with the heavy base should knock him out. If that failed, she could stab him with the decorative point at the top. Taking a deep breath, she opened her door.

The darkness in the sitting room explained the intruder's clumsiness. A faint light spilled through the window and out of Sawyer's room. A shadow crouched near his door. Henri! He was either trying to hide or waiting to ambush her when she went to Sawyer's aid. She listened for moans or sounds of movement from the other bedroom but heard only a deep, rolling inhalation and exhalation from the lurker in the shadows. Heart hammering in her throat, Steffi lifted the lamp above her stronger shoulder and moved forward.

When the shadow turned, she nearly choked. The hand carrying the lamp dropped to her side, and the would-be weapon thumped against the carpet. She clapped and turned on the overhead lighting.

A huge gray wolf stalked into the middle of the room. His fangs gleamed. His body jostled an end table. That was the sound she'd heard.

Sawyer halted in front of her. With one hand, she clutched the lapels of her bathrobe. He watched her but mercifully did not growl. If he had, she might have wet herself, and God only knew how *loups-garous* responded to the scent of human urine. Her Mentors had taught that werewolves were like dogs. *Let them know you're not a threat*. Dropping to her knees, she wished she'd paid more attention to those long-ago lectures. She steadied her breath, fixed her eyes on the rug, and waited.

Something like wet sandpaper brushed across her forehead. Dear God, he wasn't attacking—he was licking! Ugh! Her stomach revolted at the thought, but her heart leaped into her throat at the reality. She'd expected doggy smells, but his breath had a minty scent as if he'd come from the dentist's office. Mouthwash. When his tongue flicked down the side of her face, she giggled.

He stopped.

"That tickles." She should get to her feet and return to her room. She opened her mouth to wish him a good night. Instead, she said, "Slow down."

He gave a low growl, and then his muzzle brushed her cheek. Moving slowly, his tongue caressed every inch of her outer ear. Upon completing the circle, he reversed direction to make a new path along the inner, more intimate curve.

"Nice." The word slipped out before she could stop it, but she was too giddy to care. When his tongue meandered down her neck to the base of her throat, her skin tingled as if awakened from a long sleep. Closing her eyes, she envisioned every detail of her *loup-garou* shape but remained human. Which was just as well.

The rasping against the curve of her breast exposed in the opening of her bathrobe yanked her back to the present. "Sawyer!" She clutched her robe shut and sat up.

A querulous rumble sounded deep in his throat. She pressed her nose against his cold, wet one. "No." Poor *loup-garou*! He needed a mate. One of his own kind. Something she would never be.

Her gaze wandered from *loup-garou* nose to familiar gray eyes. With another rumble, he buried his snout in her hair. When his nose pushed at the curve of her neck, she plopped down on the carpet. So much for making a graceful exit.

Smiling, she lifted one hand to stroke his thick fur, the coarse hairs on the top growing finer as she neared the skin. "You are a fierce and handsome *loup-garou*, and I am honored to make your acquaintance." If she'd been standing, she would have curtsied. When his heavy head rested upon her shoulder, she wrapped her arms around his neck and purred his name.

Chapter 14

When Steffi's door opened, Sawyer nearly snapped off the handle of his coffee cup. Taking a deep breath, he stood. "Good morning."

Her thick white robe completely hid her body, but the more he tried to forget the purple concoction of satin and lace that passed for a nightgown as well as the curves it covered, the harder he got. His mouth felt as if he'd swallowed the Sahara. He finished his coffee in a gulp. "Sleep well?"

An enchanting blush colored her cheeks. "Yes." She hesitated. "But I had the strangest dreams. About your *loup-garou*."

"Indeed?" So she thought it had been a dream. "Hope he didn't create any problems."

"Oh, no." The corners of her lips curved up. "He was rather...sweet."

"Sweet?" He pretended to scowl. "Don't tell my pack, or I'll never live it down. Male *loups-garous* are fierce." He thumped his chest. "Strong." Another thump. "Powerful." This time, he thumped so hard he coughed. "But sweet?" He threw up his hands. "Never!"

"Don't get all bent out of shape or whatever you Canadians say. Strength and power may be important to *loups-garous*, but sweetness has its virtues." Steffi rested her hands on her hips. "I dreamed you were playing with your pups."

He snorted. "Since we can't shift until adolescence, we are never pups."

"Too bad." When she brushed the front of her robe, her hand stopped near a lapel. "What's this?"

"Allow me."

Ignoring his offer, she retrieved the item caught in the nap of her robe. His breath stalled in the back of his throat when she held up a long, silver hair. "Is it yours?"

"Yes."

She frowned and stretched the strand between her hands. "It wasn't a dream."

"Some of it was. The pups part. But not all."

He grasped her hands loosely. Her palms turning to rest against his awakened a fierce protectiveness. "I sometimes shift when I can't sleep. I should have warned you."

Golden specks sparkled in her eyes. "That might have helped." When she described her suspicions about an intruder, Sawyer regarded her with growing admiration. "It sounds silly now," she finished.

"Not at all. You exposed yourself to an unknown threat to help me. That took courage."

She smiled. "You've done more than that for me."

"I wasn't alone, and as your OASIS advisor—"

Her smile vanished. Pulling her hands away, she stepped back. "Stop saying that. Whenever you connect yourself with OASIS, it chips away at the trust I want to feel for you."

"I'm sorry. Force of habit. I am working for you."

"And that's why you rescued me. Professional responsibility." A trace of sadness edged her matter-of-fact statement.

He dragged a hand through his hair as if mining for

the right answer. She'd offered him an out. All he had to do was agree, and their relationship—their arrangement—could return to a purely professional basis. "Of course not." Where had that come from? He waited for her to respond, but only the light in her eyes signaled distress. "I...in my..." *Mon dieu!* He hadn't fumbled so much since he'd stumbled into Brigitte Menton's bosom in grade six. He cleared his throat. "*Loups-garous* are taught that males protect females." The fire in her eyes blazed brighter. In her dragon shape, she'd have turned him to toast. Time for a diplomatic retreat. "I know you don't think that way. Thank you for coming to my rescue."

"You're welcome." The coolness in her voice suggested she was having second thoughts.

"I'm sure you would have done the same for anyone you thought was in trouble."

Her stony expression didn't change, but she did nod. Maybe she appreciated the compliment.

"Creative choice of weapon." He gestured at the lamp, which he'd set on a nearby side table.

"I couldn't shift, so I had to improvise."

Touching the sharp tip, he winced. "I'm glad you didn't use it."

"Once I saw you, I knew that everything was all right."

"After what happened on the plane, I'm surprised you didn't return to your room."

"I was curious. I've seen ordinary wolves, but I've never seen a *loup-garou.* You're different." Her gaze moved across his frame as if she were making mental measurements. "Size, for instance. Wolves are smaller and leaner. *Loups-garous* are massive, and the power…rolls off you in waves." When he threw back his shoulders to show off the pecs he'd developed at the gym, she shot him down. "Strong but not overwhelming. Very similar to the power of your human shape." She lifted a finger. "Don't get me wrong. Your *loup-garou* is intimidating, but he seemed quite friendly." Her features softened as she tugged her earlobe. Then she drew the neck of her bathrobe closer. "Sometimes a bit too friendly."

The sweetness of the curve of her breast was unforgettable. Honey in her skin as well as her voice.

Her fingers fumbled with the knot of her robe sash. "The last thing I remember is curling up with you out here. Then I woke up—" She gestured at her door. "I don't know what…how…or whether we—we didn't do anything, did we?" Her question ended in a squeak.

He pressed his lips together and tried to look forlorn. "Am I that forgettable?"

Steffi slapped her cheeks. "Oh, Sawyer, I didn't mean…but I…I…"

He laughed so hard he had to wipe his eyes. "Now that is a beauty of a blush." He cleared his throat. "Don't worry. We couple as *loups-garous* only with our mates."

With fingers still shielding her lower face, Steffi regarded him. "But you weren't always— I suppose your *loup-garou* could have rolled me into the bedroom, but he couldn't have put me in the bed."

Sawyer swallowed. "Near dawn, my phone woke me, and I returned to my human base to answer it. You were sleeping so soundly that I didn't want to disturb you, but I also didn't want to leave you lying on the carpet without a cushion. I suppose I could have put you on the couch, but I thought you'd be more comfortable in your own bed." *And the less I looked at you, the better. For both of us.*

She gripped the robe at her neck. "You took off my robe."

"You were using it like a blanket." His fur had kept them from skin-to-skin contact, but the pressure of her body stretched against his had made sleep damn near impossible. His groin heated at the memory. "I wrapped it around you to carry you to your room and unwrapped you when I rolled you into bed." Like an early Christmas gift.

"I didn't turn on the lights." No need to mention his human shared his *loup-garou*'s night vision. He'd memorized the way the fabric hugged her curves and her long, lovely legs extended from the bottom fringe of the short gown. Covering her with the sheet, he'd done his best not to let his hand brush against the swell of her lovely breast. When she'd murmured something, he'd frozen, waiting for her next move. Steffi had smiled, but her eyes remained closed.

He'd edged toward the door. Hearing movement in the bed, he paused on the threshold but didn't dare look back in case she'd kicked off the sheet.

Cutting into his reflections, Steffi offered him a tight smile. "Thank you for not taking advantage of me."

"I like my partners willing, aware, and awake." He paused. "Mutual comfort…does have its own pleasures."

"Especially in a strange place." Steffi's hands moved toward his face until she looked at them and put them behind her back.

"What's wrong?"

She avoided his gaze. "I rubbed your ears last night, and I almost did it again." She kept her hands behind her.

"That wouldn't have been so terrible." Although he was careful to use a neutral tone, heat radiated from the crown of his head to his toes. No one had treated his *loup-garou* with such tenderness since that first agonizing shift. After his *loup-garou* finally emerged, he'd made a silent vow never to shift again. Then *Maman,* watching in human shape, had stroked his ears and told him how proud he'd made her. The pain didn't go away, but he could shift and survive.

"They're incredibly soft."

And hers were delectable. If he captured her earlobe between his human lips... Would she prefer his *loup-garou* to his human? She'd certainly encouraged his attention. He'd even made her laugh. A giggle, no less. Silly girly noises set his teeth on edge, but with Steffi, everything was different. Desirable. He picked up the empty cup. "Coffee?"

"I'll dress first. Won't take long." She pursed her lips as a faint line appeared above the bridge of her nose. "Most of what I brought is casual." She indicated his suit. "I didn't know Canadians had such a business-like attitude toward sightseeing."

"We don't. I've had to change plans yet again. Board meeting has been rescheduled for this morning."

Her gaze traveled along his jaw as if she were evaluating his shave. "Worrying about the tar-sands vote?"

How could he think about company business when she was this close? "It is the major item on the agenda."

"From what I've read, it's a dirty way to get oil."

"I'm sure that will come up during the discussion. Before the vote, *Papa* will no doubt point out that someone will develop the properties and that no one will attend to the environmental issues more scrupulously than Montaigne Enterprises. We do, after all, have a stronger connection with the natural world than Simple Humans have." As Steffi opened her mouth, he cut her off. "Don't be too impressed. He's used versions of the same speech to support cutting timber, mining ore, and harvesting fish. All legitimate enterprises, but even the best-managed leave scars."

He slipped several thick files into his briefcase and then included his laptop. "I'd hoped to meet you for lunch, but *Papa* has 'requested' my company." He gritted his teeth.

"You look as if you're planning to chew on his leg. You might want to take a few deep breaths before you join him."

He smiled at her earnest face. "I'll keep that in mind. We will vote after lunch, so I won't be free until this afternoon at the earliest."

"No problem." She crossed to the big window and looked out. "Yesterday, while you were checking on the manager, I did some online research, and the concierge helped me put together an itinerary."

Disappointment sat like a boulder in his throat. "That was very…enterprising. But you're my guest. I don't want you wandering around on your own." In his city, he wanted to wander with her. He checked his watch. "My cousin Yvette should be here soon. I think you'll like her."

Steffi turned with her hands on her hips. "Sawyer, I do not need a sitter."

"She's not a sitter. She's a companion, and you'll have more fun if you see the city with someone who knows it well." He winked. "Yvette also loves to shop."

Steffi's lips twitched. "I hate shopping, do it mostly online."

That and her limited income from teaching and research no doubt accounted for her practical wardrobe.

"You and Yvette can look at what you've brought and list anything you need. She knows where to find the best bargains."

"Do I have a say in this?"

He shook his head. "Pretend you're doing an observation. You can report to me this evening."

"Report?" Steffi crossed her arms. "This is supposed to be a vacation."

"Then forget about observing. Relax and have a good time with Yvette." Sawyer lifted a hand toward her chin but then plunged it into a pocket. One fleeting stroke, and he'd never leave. "I'll call as soon as I'm free." He gestured at the porridge in the bowl that occupied the center of the small table. "Try the *cretons* on toast. I think you'll like it."

Chapter 15

Sawyer departed, taking most of the energy in the apartment with him. Steffi sank onto the couch. Dreams and reality swirled in her mind. Sawyer covering her like a furry shield. His broad chest moving with each rumble of his deep breath. His heartbeat thudding against her ear. Comfort, sensuality, and safety in a handsome package, wolf and human. Would Sawyer's mate appreciate how lucky she was?

She stood and headed for the coffeemaker. Her body welcomed the familiar caffeine jolt. Following Sawyer's instructions, she spread the lumpy porridge on a slice of toast. When the unexpected spices of the pork pâté—cretons—coated her tongue, she sat up. "Wow!"

After scraping the last of the amazing breakfast from the bowl, she washed her face and moisturized in the bathroom. Dark green cargo pants and a long-sleeved tan jersey should work with the mild June air. She was finishing her second cup of coffee when the elevator door opened to reveal a pretty redhead who looked close to Dayzee's age.

"*Bon jour, bon jour*, you must be Steffi." The newcomer grabbed her hands. "I—"

"Cousin Yvette." Steffi returned the squeeze and released the hands. "Sawyer told me he'd commandeered you to show me around town."

A booming laugh burst from the other woman's

compact frame. The kind of laugh Sawyer liked. "I told him I would be delighted to substitute for him. Not that anyone could ever substitute for Antoine, *n'est-ce pas*?" Her neat eyebrows gave a faint wiggle. "Don't you agree?"

Steffi frowned. "Antoine? He told me to call him Sawyer."

Yvette laughed again. "Antoine is the name the family uses. Antoine Sawyer Montaigne is his full name. *Tante* Jeanette is from the Sawyer pack in Michigan."

So half of Sawyer's heritage came from the United States. No wonder he chafed against ancient pack restrictions.

Yvette tapped a freshly polished fingernail against her chin. "You and my cousin are friends." Her voice held the hint of a question.

Steffi gathered her breakfast dishes and carried them to the sink. "Not quite."

"Oh!"

Yvette's blush suggested that she was drawing a salacious conclusion. Better set her straight. "I'm his client. OASIS." Steffi almost spat the word.

"I'm sorry. I meant no offense." Yvette seemed to weigh her speech. "But your height, your hair," as her eyes went to Steffi's bosom, her voice dropped, "your endowment."

Steffi crossed her arms. "I beg your pardon."

"My cousin likes statuesque brunettes."

Steffi fingered a strand of hair near her chin. "That's odd. We ran into one of his friends last night. A blonde."

"Occasionally, I suppose he may vary—"

"Platinum dye."

"Oh, dear! He must hate that!" Yvette brought her

palms together and laughed. "Of course, he's too much of a gentleman to show it. Not that it matters. She is a Simple Human, *n'est-ce pas*? Isn't that so?"

"No. A C-level sorceress."

"But not *loup-garou*." Yvette smiled. "My cousin will take a mate this year. Since you are his type, I thought you might be a candidate."

Steffi's shoulders stiffened. "Sorry to disappoint you." She bit back the regret that shaded her words. "I'm an Anomaly."

Yvette's eyes widened. "Antoine said you were from the States but he never—*mon dieu*! I've heard about you, of course. Everyone has. Is it true that you can take any shape?"

"Any biological shape. I could." No reason to keep this secret. "But something went wrong. Your cousin's trying to help me recover my ability."

One of Yvette's arms drew Steffi close. "If anyone can do it, it's Antoine." Yvette consulted her phone. "He sent me his plan for the day. All those museums!" She opened a blank screen. "I have some other ideas."

As the other woman planned a new itinerary, Steffi admired her appearance—every auburn strand that curved around her head, the blue and white pattern of the jaunty scarf that complemented the well-cut shirt, the tailored dove-gray slacks, and pristine walking shoes. Steffi flattened her hair at her nape and tugged at one of her sleeves that was starting to fray. She felt like a beggar at the castle gate.

Yvette showed her a split screen. "The choice is yours. Would you rather look at history or make it?"

Steffi hesitated. She'd spent so many years—too many years—watching other people live. "Make it."

Beaming, Yvette waved her phone. "Marcel has squeezed you in. *Allons*! Let's go!" With her determined stride, Sawyer's small cousin looked less like a sugarplum fairy and more like a female Napoleon.

When they strolled down the street, the spirit of the ancient buildings seemed to seep into Steffi's bones. They stopped outside an imposing edifice. The Palace of Beauty? As Steffi mentally translated the legend on the arched doorway, Yvette gestured for her to enter a hall filled with displays of more cosmetics than Steffi had ever seen.

"*Madame* Grillant!" At the reception desk, a young woman with an air of casual elegance greeted them. After she exchanged rapid-fire French with Yvette, the girl's beautifully framed gaze swept over Steffi's face. Steffi's throat tightened, but Yvette blocked the exit.

They followed the girl down another long corridor. "Marcel is a marvel with hair," Yvette confided.

Scissors flying in all directions? Steffi shielded her shaggy head. She kept her hair short for convenience, had it styled when necessary. Since Sheboygan, she'd been too distracted to think about hair. She must look as if she'd been dragged in from the wild.

"A little trim." Yvette nudged her into an immaculate room that looked like a laboratory from a science fiction movie. A skeletal silver-haired man clad in surgical white awaited them. No scissor hands, thank God. Yvette gestured at the swivel chair. "Sit and enjoy."

While Steffi eyed them in the mirror, Yvette and the marvelous Marcel circled her and conferred in French. From the way Yvette deferred to the stylist, this was Marcel's world. Although he listened politely to her suggestions and requests, his decision was law.

"Marcel says your hair is very thick and well cared for," Yvette cooed.

Steffi unclenched her jaw. "I do my best."

The stylist worked with swift precision. Yvette assured her that he would do nothing radical. "*A little trim.*" As scissors and combs flew about her like mechanical creatures, Yvette's comforting refrain ran through her brain.

"*Voilà!*"

Amazing! When she turned her head from side to side, the strands fell in perfect alignment. The short wave of dark hair that dipped slightly across her forehead made her eyes look bigger, and the curves at her chin softened her jaw. She smiled at Marcel. "*Merci bien.*"

"My pleasure."

When she got home, she'd dine on grilled cheese for a month or more, but this haircut was worth the sacrifice. She took a few selfies so her regular stylist could attempt Marcel's cut. Steffi hugged a glowing Yvette. "Where do I pay?"

Yvette dismissed her question with another hearty laugh. "Don't worry. It's all taken care of."

Steffi's cheeks heated as she stuffed her wallet back in one of her vest pockets. Was there anything in this city in which Montaigne Enterprises didn't have an interest?

Blue eyes sparkling, Yvette took her arm. "Marcel has given you the perfect frame. Now, Marie-Louise will give you the perfect face." Clutching Steffi's chin, Yvette turned her head from side to side. "Don't frown."

"I've never used much makeup."

"It's time you began. You have beautiful skin, and you should show it off. Marie-Louise can add a hint of mystery to your gaze and give you a mouth men will ache to kiss."

Sawyer? Steffi pressed her lips together. "Sounds more like magic than makeup."

"A bit of both, I think. But Marie-Louise will make *you* the enchantress."

How could anyone refuse such an invitation?

An hour later, Steffi paused before dispatching the delivery to the auberge. "I feel like I ordered a whole chemistry lab." She riffled through the instructions that accompanied the bottles, tubes, vials, and brushes. "I used fewer notes for my doctoral exams." She regarded the woman in the mirror, a slightly unfamiliar version of herself. "This looks fantastic, but I'll never be able to reproduce it."

"Practice." Yvette's smile gleamed. "Isn't that right, Marie-Louise?"

"*Mais oui.*" The cosmetologist responded with an emphatic nod. "Of course, you must practice."

Steffi drew a wary breath. From the crown of her head to the curve of her chin, the Palace of Beauty had transformed her. The face in the mirror had a sparkle she'd never seen. The eyes seemed to smolder, and even at rest, her mouth had a seductive glow. Was it powerful enough to make Sawyer kiss her again? *I'm his OASIS client, nothing more.*

"And now," Yvette crowed as she hooked an arm through Steffi's, "we shop!"

They rolled through the old city like a conquering army. They began at the Marché Bonsecours, a modern bazaar that had once housed the Canadian Parliament. "Your history lesson for the day," Yvette announced. Then, they stormed the boutiques. At every stop, Yvette bargained with good-natured ferocity.

Finally, Yvette declared, "Let's eat." When they settled into their chairs in a crowded family restaurant— "the best in town for *la poutine,*" according to Yvette— Steffi relaxed with an unguarded smile.

"Something amuses you?"

"I was imagining how overwhelmed the hotel porters will be when all those packages descend upon them." She stirred mushrooms and onions into the basic mixture of French fries and cheese curds smothered in gravy. "Sawyer will be surprised, too. I told him I wasn't much of a shopper." They'd work out a plan so she could reimburse him.

Yvette paused to swallow. "I don't think he will complain when he sees you in the rose silk or the black lace." Her hearty laugh rang out. "Are you blushing?"

"No. A bit." Sawyer would see the dress. But the fancy lingerie? "May I ask you a personal question?"

"You may ask." The lifted eyebrow suggested that Yvette reserved the right to not respond.

"Everyone calls you *Madame* Grillant. You're married?"

"Widowed."

How clumsy of me! Steffi swallowed. "I'm sorry."

"Don't be. When I came of age—" Yvette looked around and lowered her voice. "What do you know about our mating practices?"

"That your pa—family—wants you to do it at eighteen."

Yvette nodded. "And my family circumstances were not the best."

"You're a Montaigne."

"Montaigne blood, but little Montaigne money. I was the oldest of five, and my father wanted me to mate

150

as early as possible. We made a bargain." She pursed her lips. "I would attend the cotillion, but if no one chose me, I could postpone mating and go to university."

Steffi stared at her new friend in disbelief. "How could anyone not choose you? You're pretty and smart. And so well connected." Yvette's wince sent a frisson through Steffi's shoulders.

"I wasn't that pretty then. I wasn't that smart, either, else I would have known that the most desirable quality of a mate is often the bloodline."

"And yours is one of the most important in Canada."

"Canada? In the world." Yvette sipped her cider. "Jean-Paul was a widower from Nova Scotia. A kind man and not much over forty, but at eighteen, I thought him ancient. He died two years after we mated."

"How sad. For him. You did gain your freedom."

"Yes, but he left me with nothing."

"Surely your family—"

Yvette shook her head. "Once mated, I was no longer their responsibility. Fortunately, *oncle* César and *tante* Jeannette—Antoine's parents—took an interest in me."

Steffi studied Yvette's serious face. "Did they help you get to college?"

"That was my dream when I was eighteen. Now I am too old."

"Nonsense." Steffi set her drink on the table so quickly the liquid sloshed over the rim of her glass. "Many American—college students in the States are older than you."

"*Vraiment?*"

"Yes. Truly. Some return to school to upgrade their skills so they can move ahead in their work. Others have lost their jobs and want to learn skills that will lead to new professions. Many women are like you. Their lives have changed because of death or divorce. The situation might be similar in Canada. While I'm here, we can go online to find schools that offer programs you might like."

"That sounds exciting, but university is expensive."

When Steffi tapped her fingers on the small table, the fresh manicure flashed. "We have community colleges, much cheaper than universities, and I'm sure you have something like that. We can check out scholarships and other financial aid as well as programs."

"That would be wonderful!" Yvette's animated features stilled. "But Antoine wants me to entertain you. He will be unhappy if I put you to work."

"Then we won't tell him. You're not forcing me to do something. In fact, I can't think of a better way to use my time."

A mischievous smile brightened Yvette's countenance. "I'm sure Antoine can."

"You don't understand. Your cousin and I do not…are not…" While Yvette's smile broadened, Steffi tried to cool the mounting heat in her cheeks by finishing her drink. "Let's go back to the hotel and start our research."

"All in good time." One of Yvette's hands rested on Steffi's arm. "First, let's talk about you and Antoine."

Chapter 16

While the slender, matronly woman droned on, images of Steffi displaced the speaker's slide presentation in Sawyer's mind. She'd looped her arms around his *loup-garou* neck. Her soft breath had ruffled the fur at his throat. She'd nestled against him with absolute trust. This morning, it had taken every ounce of willpower not to reestablish that connection in his human shape.

When the man sitting near the head of the table cleared his throat, Sawyer shifted position to ease the tightening in his groin. *Sacrébleu!* Had *Papa* caught him smiling? Pressing his lips together, Sawyer forced his attention back to the presentation. His father demanded that the board members treat even the most mind-numbing speakers like oracles from the gods. Today's presentation had done nothing to change the vote he could have submitted online. Hell, if *Papa* hadn't demanded his presence, he and Steffi would be on the beach.

The speaker sped through her conclusion with a tremulous smile. After *Papa* thanked her, she remained on her feet while the other board members pelted her with questions, some germane, some—like his brother Roland's—purely to gain their father's attention. The speaker answered each question with respect. She'd learned how to handle hostility. When César Montaigne smiled at her, her jaw softened.

"*Bien fait, madame.*"

"*Merci.*"

Papa closed his folder, and the others at the table mimicked his move. When he stood, so did everyone else except Sawyer, who took his time. No need to rush.

Murmuring among themselves, the other board members filed from the room like a school of navy-suited fish swimming toward their food. Over lunch, all the keeners on the board would plot their strategies for brownnosing his father prior to the vote. Most would make their points succinctly, but Germont's lengthy disquisitions could cure insomnia. If he couldn't cut off the old windbag before he started, Sawyer wouldn't get back before midnight. To the auberge. To Steffi.

"Antoine. *Viens.*"

When his father uttered his name, Sawyer's spine stiffened. Did *Papa* truly think he might try to escape? Near the main door, Roland paused, clearly wanting to join them. *Papa's* failure to extend an invitation changed his brother's hopeful-puppy expression to a scowl directed at Sawyer as if he were responsible for the exclusion. While Roland scurried to catch up with his fellow board members, Sawyer held the door for their father.

Papa acknowledged the gesture of respect with a nod.

Sawyer followed the older man to his office, where he again held the door, this time a heavy wooden one with the Montaigne crest carved slightly above eye level. The smaller room adjoining the expansive office had a table set for two and servers awaiting his father's commands. Immaculate white linens and gleaming porcelain also bore the ubiquitous crest.

Sitting across from his father, Sawyer regarded his plate while *Papa* intoned a brief grace. Servers brought in salad, soup, fish, and a stew with a scent that made Sawyer's mouth water.

"Your mother knows you are in Montreal. She wonders why you chose to stay in the city instead of your home."

"I don't expect to be here long, and the auberge is more convenient."

"You've been gone for months." *Papa*'s eyes narrowed. "Make time to see her."

"I have an OASIS client with me."

"Mel told me you were dealing with that…creature."

Sawyer's jaw clenched. "She is not a creature."

"Creature. Anomaly." His father shrugged.

"Steffi and her sisters are Shape-shifters with extraordinary gifts. They also have a human base like ours." A quick sip of ice water almost dampened his arousal when he thought of her sensuous human shape. "Most important, she is an OASIS client and my guest. I will send *Maman* my regrets, along with a few of her favorite pearls. The same type you give her."

"*Pardon?*" The question emerged as a snarl, and César Montaigne's graying hair bristled as if his *loup-garou* were about to emerge. "A child should not show such disrespect for his parents." His father wielded his spoon like a scepter. "You have delayed your duty to your family and your pack long enough. If you fail to mate this fall, you will lose all pack rights and privileges your status has given you." His father spoke, not in anger, but in simple resignation. "The Elders may even vote to expel you."

Sawyer sat back. "I have every intention of doing what I must."

"See that you do." César Montaigne's gaze seemed to bore into Sawyer's eyes. "It would break your mother's heart to lose you."

The sorrow that crept into his father's commanding voice moved Sawyer's own heart. *Papa*'s slumped shoulders suggested the toll his work as leader of Montaigne Enterprises and alpha of the Montagne pack had taken.

Papa swallowed his first bite of small-mouth bass. "You did little this morning to make your presence known."

Sawyer returned his spoon to the plate. "I speak when I have something to say."

"People are questioning your ability to lead." His father laid an open newspaper on the table.

When he saw the photo above the business column byline, the tasty stew in Sawyer's mouth turned to dust and pebbles.

"I thought you and *Mademoiselle* Chasseur had an amicable parting."

Sawyer cleared his throat. "So did I. I haven't seen her in more than a year."

"She has noted your absence from our meetings."

"I stay involved, *Papa*. You know that. So do the other board members."

"Public perception matters. Rumors make potential investors nervous."

Sawyer slapped the paper. "This has nothing to do with business. I ran into—no, that's not what happened. Nicole accosted me last night while Steffi and I were dining."

"Steffi, eh?" His father's fork paused midway to his mouth. "Dining together. Sharing accommodations. Perhaps your interest in this client is…more than professional?" He returned the fork to his plate.

"Now I know why you don't discharge that thieving manager."

"Henri has his uses."

"Yes, Steffi—*Mademoiselle* Anbruzzen—and I dined together. I often dine with my clients." He paused. "And, yes, we are sharing the Montaigne suite. You would have preferred that we stay elsewhere?"

"Of course not."

"No eyes in other hotels, eh? So this OASIS client and I dine together and occupy the same suite. As I do with my other clients. But Henri can't answer the question that truly interests you. Not that it's any of your business, but Steffi and I have a purely professional relationship. She is my client, not my lover." His groin ached at the memory of her curves snuggled against his fur.

"She must be rather attractive to incite Chasseur's jealousy."

Rather attractive? To say the least. "She's tall and slender with dark, curling hair." And a bosom his fingers itched to explore. "Like your Angelique."

His father glared at him.

"You're not the only one with spies, *Papa*."

The older man drew himself up. "Do you challenge your pack alpha?"

Sawyer bit the edge of his mouth to keep from smiling. "Not at all. You taught us that knowledge is power." Before his father could respond, he continued,

"As my client, *Mademoiselle* Anbruzzen is under my protection."

"Very well. But she is not under you, and Nicole Chasseur should be. Soon."

"*Papa!*"

His father actually laughed. "Don't look shocked. You've bedded her before." He tapped the paper. "You created this problem. Fix it." He cleared his throat. "This evening, you will take Chasseur to dinner at the casino. Enjoy the meal, gamble a bit, get a room, and win her over."

Sawyer winced. "What is Steffi supposed to do while I'm seducing Nicole?"

His father thought for a moment. "I'll arrange a theater ticket. Better yet, two. I'll send Yvette."

"What should I tell Steffi?"

"You're a clever lad. You'll think of something. If all goes well, in her next column, Chasseur will be singing your praises instead of casting doubt on the future of Montaigne Enterprises." He checked his watch. "Eat."

Sawyer put his serviette on the table. "I feel like a whore."

"Eating a delicious dinner and having sex with a beautiful woman are sacrifices we would all gladly make."

Not if it meant turning your back on Steffi. "May I be excused?" He started to rise.

"Not yet."

Sawyer sank back in his chair. What now?

"I've sent you several messages about The Snow Angel."

"That lodge near Mont Tremblant? I thought Michel

was looking into it."

"He has problems in Halifax." He pointed at Sawyer. "I want you to go. See if it's worth an offer."

"Why don't you send Roland?"

"I want you."

"*Papa*, I came for the board meeting because you demanded my presence, but I'm in the middle—"

"I know, I know. Another of your OASIS projects."

"This case is complicated."

His father smiled. "Mel said he gave you special instructions. All the more reason you should take the Anom—your client—with you." *Papa* unfolded his plan in brisk sentences. "She could be useful, and it will keep her...occupied."

"I don't know if Steffi will agree. I'll talk to her about it and get back to you."

"No. Don't talk about it." His father aimed his index finger like a gun. "Talk her into it."

"That won't be easy after I've spent the night with another woman."

His father regarded him with renewed interest. "So, there is something between you."

"No." Not yet. Probably not ever if he fucked Nicole. "Engaging in this Snow Angel masquerade could affect our relationship."

"All the more reason to convince her. I know you, son. The sooner you bed this cr...client, the sooner she'll be out of your system." He stood to signal the end of the meal. "Visit your mother."

Sawyer watched the older man stride from the small room into his office. *Papa* might know him, but he didn't know Steffi.

****

Sawyer was on his way! When Steffi regarded her reflection in the mirror on the back of the closet door, her fingers fluttered over the rose silk bodice. Yvette had told her to save the prettiest dress for last, but her hair and face would never look this good again. They deserved the best. The waistband of the lace bikini panties tickled the skin below her navel, and the new bra made her breasts look ready to launch into the stratosphere. Maybe this strange new Steffi was too much. Maybe she should slip into a cotton tunic and a nice pair of—

"Steffi?"

Oh, God, he was here! Too late to change now. She gritted her teeth. *Smile, dammit!*

He stood by the small dining table and picked up the wine bottle. She'd accepted the sommelier's recommendation, but Sawyer put down the bottle with no comment. His tie hung loose, and he'd unbuttoned the top buttons of his shirt. His hair looked as if he'd been caught in a wind tunnel. His shoulders sagged. The meeting had taken a lot out of him.

"Someone from your office called. We have seats for a play, so I thought we could eat here before—but if you're not hungry or if you want to cancel—" She covered her mouth to stop her babbling. For the first time, Sawyer looked at her. The grim set of his jaw and the tense line of his mouth made her wish the floor would open up and swallow her. "Rough day?" *Or do I look that bad?*

"You might say that." He sniffed. "New perfume?"

New hair, new face, new clothes, and all he noticed was a scent? Of course. *Loups-garous* had a keen sense of smell. She showed her teeth and uttered the provocative name of the fragrance, a word that wrapped around her tongue the same way the scent seemed to encircle her body.

"Sultry."

He hated it. *Damn!*

"Did you have a good day with Yvette?"

Her "yes" sounded like air escaping from a balloon.

His gaze crawled from the top of her head to her feet. She curled her toes to hide the silly pedicure that peeked out of the open-toed stilettos. "You look different."

Her fingers tightened on the neckline of her dress. "Different good or different bad?"

"Trick question." He gave her a slow smile. "If I say 'good' you'll think I'm saying that you needed improvement, that you were somehow…lacking." He shook his head. "Nothing is farther from the truth. But saying 'bad' suggests that you look worse than you did, and that's not true, either. I think you look amazing. Still you. But different. More polished."

She threw back her head and uttered a throaty laugh. "Yvette said you would finesse that question, and you did!"

A grin flashed across his face. "I also made you laugh."

"That calls for a drink." She had a slightly unsteady step in these unfamiliar shoes. He opened his arms as if he expected her to fall into them.

"I'd love to, but I can't stay."

She set the wine back in the holder. "I thought you'd be free after the board meeting."

"So did I." He stuffed his hands in his pockets. "Something has come up."

"The kitchen can hold our order until you get back."

"You and Yvette should eat it. She's going to the theater with you."

"That wasn't…I don't want to…can you cancel…"

When Steffi started to brush back her hair, he reached out to stop her. "Don't muss it."

The concern in his voice made her smile. "I couldn't if I tried." She shook her head to demonstrate. "See?" Every strand returned to its appropriate place.

"Marcel, eh?"

Steffi gave an enthusiastic nod. "He was wonderful!"

"You gave him good material to work with. Your hair's like midnight silk."

When Sawyer's fingers brushed her temple, a ribbon of heat shot to the crown of her head, and her breath caught in her throat. Did he use that line with all the dark-haired women he knew?

"Every woman in my family swears by Marcel."

"I'm glad I'm not the only one." When Steffi put her hands behind her, the rose fabric tightened across her chest.

Sawyer glanced toward his room but didn't move. "It looks as if you had a good time with Yvette."

"I can see why you like her. She adores you."

"We've always gotten along well, but I don't know if I'd go that far." He seemed to be looking over her shoulder as if he found something in the corner of the room far more interesting. He must not like the way she looked but was too polite to say so.

"You're her favorite family member."

"Because I let her use my credit cards." He gestured at the bags piled outside her bedroom door. "Which she seems to have done quite freely."

"You and I can work out a payment plan for what I want to keep." She moved toward the pile. "I'm sending these back."

Sawyer frowned. "No. Don't."

When he took a step toward the items, Steffi blocked him. "Why not?"

"You would insult my cousin."

Her silver-tipped toes nudged one of the shocking pink bags. "She doesn't need to know."

"Yvette works as a personal shopper for some of my sisters' friends. She has spent years building good relationships with their favorite merchants. Returning such a large purchase might damage that."

"Oh, dear. I didn't know." She could never do anything to hurt Yvette.

"Why return it?" Sawyer regarded the bags. "Everyone needs underwear."

"This isn't underwear. It's lingerie." She scooped a handful of fabric from the nearest bag. Dear God, did she have to pull out something so transparent?

Sawyer looked from the item in her hand to her overheated face. "All the better. Don't you like wearing clothes that make you feel good?"

"Yes. Of course." The filmy fabric nestled in her palm like a baby bird. "But this isn't designed to make *me* feel good." She stuffed the piece in her hand back into its bag.

"Why did you buy it?"

For the same reason she was wearing those itchy lace panties and that supersonic bra. "Yvette said I needed it. She called it *myseductionkit*." Steffi ran the last three words together as if they were one. Then she clapped a hand over her mouth. Had she really said that?

"Pardon?" Sawyer reached for one of the bags, but she put out her hand.

"Please don't." She turned away. "This is embarrassing enough."

He followed her. "Is this an all-purpose seduction, or do you have a specific target in mind?"

When her eyes met his, the five-alarm fire on her face could have set off the sprinkler system.

"You want to seduce me?" He gestured at the table. "That's the reason for the fancy dinner?"

"Yvette says that before you choose a mate, you deserve one last fling."

He stepped back. "A fling? With you?"

His incredulous questions slapped her. She dropped her gaze to the carpet. She would not let him know how much his words hurt. "It's a joke." She forced a laugh. "I told Yvette it was a silly idea, but she can be so determined that I said I would give it a try." She tossed the words out as if they were bubbles.

"Sounds like Yvette." He cleared his throat. "I'm sorry I've ruined tonight."

She waved off his apology. "Like I said, it's a joke. That special dinner was burgers and fries." When he grasped her hands, she swallowed a gasp.

"What's your Plan B?"

"I don't…" She pulled away and walked toward the window. "I've never…I mean, with Simple Human men…I never…they never…no seduction."

Sawyer stared at her as if she'd crawled out from under a rock. "Must have been rather boring."

Steffi folded her arms. "Not at all. It's always been quite…good. Of course, to someone like you—"

"Pardon?"

"My sister Dayzee says you're one of the ten sexiest men in Canada."

"She's the one who told you my father was the Godfather, right?" He laughed. "A girlfriend wrote that article."

"Not…"

"No. Not her." Stepping back, he spoke in a casual voice. "It's been a while since anyone tried to seduce me, but as I recall, it's not that hard to put me—any man, for that matter—in the right mood." His eyes met hers. "Sometimes all you have to do is smile."

He was an expert at this game, but she didn't leap to the bait. After all, hadn't he made it painfully clear that she wasn't up to the job? Steffi opened her mouth to tell him the joke was done, but his fingers brushed her cheek.

"I'm sorry, but I have to go. Have fun with Yvette."

"Do they provide English titles above the stage?"

"Better. It's an English-language theater." On the threshold of his room, he turned. "Don't wait up. I'll see you in the morning."

Before Sawyer's door shut her out, she wanted to grab his arm and ask him what was wrong. This morning, she'd felt his human warmth as surely as she'd felt it beneath the thick fur of his *loup-garou*. This afternoon, everything had changed even before she'd blurted that asinine seduction plan. Montaigne Enterprises seemed to be making more demands on his time than he expected or desired. Maybe that was why he seemed so edgy.

She turned up the lights, blew out the candles, and put away the dishes. Then she called the kitchen to cancel the dinner. She should never have mentioned that stupid seduction kit. Yvette had made playing the seductress sound like fun. For Yvette, no doubt it was.

But for a Shape-shifter who'd grown up on a ranch in Montana, the fancy haircut and cosmetics makeover were pathetic attempts at disguise. Like wrapping practical cotton underwear in glitzy paper, sprinkling it with glitter, and adding a humongous bow.

"A fling? With you?"

Steffi eyed the lingerie bags. None of these purchases would fit her sisters, but the women at the domestic violence shelter could use them. What they didn't want to wear, they could sell in the consignment shop. In the meantime—she grabbed the packages—better to stash this stuff in the darkest corner of her room than have a constant reminder of her failure front and center.

Chapter 17

Bodies crowded the dance floor at the small club. Everyone seemed to be drinking, laughing, smiling, hugging, and kissing. Sweat, alcohol, and a perfume store's collection of scents assailed Steffi, whose feet tapped the salsa rhythms of maracas, marimba, and trumpet. The zippy music bounced around her hollow core.

She and Yvette settled into their seats in an out-of-the-way corner. "Talk to me, Steffi."

Steffi stared at the tiny woman with the imperious gaze.

"You didn't even smile during the play, and now you look as if you're at a funeral." She gestured at Steffi. "You wore that dress to spend the evening with me?" Yvette shook her head. "I don't think so. What happened?"

"Nothing." Unless you counted making an ass of yourself in front of the most attractive man you'd ever known. "I had everything set up, and I did try to seduce him, but...he...he laughed at me."

Yvette frowned. "That doesn't sound like Antoine."

"Maybe you don't know him as well as you think you do. I am not his type."

Yvette sat up. "Nonsense."

"He made it quite clear that if he has a last fling, it will not be with me." Steffi sipped the cocktail that she wished would sweep her shame away in a wash of tiny bubbles.

"Pains me to say this about my favorite cousin, but sometimes that man can be as sharp as a beach ball." Yvette reached out. "I'm sorry."

Steffi waved off the apology. "I should have known better." The Palace of Beauty transformation might make her feel incredibly sexy, but underneath the paint and powder, she was still Steffi Anbruzzen. She'd been a fool to think Sawyer would see anything more.

A distinguished-looking, silver-haired man stopped by their table. "*Bonsoir, mesdames.* May I join you?"

Yvette beamed. "Of course, *oncle César.* Please do."

Uncle—oh my God, Sawyer's father! Just what she needed to make a miserable evening worse. Steffi took another drink.

"Steffi, I would like to present—"

"César Montaigne. It is a pleasure to meet you, *Mademoiselle* Anbruzzen"

When he took her hand with a courtly bow, Steffi caught her breath at the aura of power that surrounded him. His eyes, darker and more calculating than his son's, lingered on the modest cleavage of her new dress. Steffi's spine stiffened, and she lifted her chin. "The pleasure is mine." She retrieved her hand. "Please call me Steffi."

He rested one hand over his heart as he took the seat beside her. "César."

"I've heard a great deal about you from Sawyer."

The older man frowned.

Damn! She'd screwed up right away by not using the family name. *Antoine.*

"I trust that at least some of my son's remarks have been favorable."

"Of course." She spoke as if Sawyer had programmed her.

"Did you ladies enjoy the play?"

Yvette clapped. "It was delightful."

Steffi pasted on a smile. "Very funny." If someone hadn't stomped on your heart. "Our seats were excellent."

He had a controlled smile. "Good seats are not easy to obtain at such short notice, but my assistant has exceptional skills."

So he, not Sawyer, had arranged the theater outing. "Thank you, and please extend my gratitude to your assistant as well."

The smile deepened. "My pleasure, Steffi."

When he uttered her name, he lowered his voice, and the word lingered in her ear like an unexpected caress. Beneath his scrutiny, she bit her inner lip and maintained a steady gaze. A server set a drink before him.

"I hope your meeting went well." Would Sawyer be joining them? After what he'd said, she should never want to see him again, but she did, damn it.

With the glass halfway to his mouth, Sawyer's father paused. "The board had a rather heated debate. We often do in these matters, but in the end, we made the right decision." He drank slowly, clearly relishing the taste.

No late meeting for Sawyer? Steffi managed a tepid smile. A predator like César Montaigne would interpret distress as weakness.

"Are you enjoying Montreal?"

"Very much."

"Good. While you are here, I shall arrange for you to sample our Canadian cuisine at our finest restaurant."

"Yes!" Yvette's murmur sounded like a prayer.

"*Haute cuisine* has its place," César lowered his voice to a husky near whisper, "but nothing compares with the fresh kill of the hunt." He snapped the word as if he were attacking prey. When Steffi didn't respond, he said, "Pardon me. I should not extol a pleasure you've not experienced."

She favored him with a cool gaze. "On the contrary, sir, I've done my share of hunting. As a girl in Montana, I flew as an owl or a bat."

"Vermin and rodents." The words wriggled with his scorn.

Steffi sat up. César Montaigne might be head of the biggest pack in Canada and one of the most important businessmen in the world, but two could play this game. "As a lioness, I've brought down gazelle and okapi…and a wildebeest or two. Too stringy for my taste, but I was hungry, and they are big. As a bear, I've devoured everything that moves."

"Quite…impressive." His eyes seemed to calculate her value. "My son told me that you are an extraordinary creature."

Creature? Steffi's drink curdled in her mouth.

Apparently oblivious to his insult, César Montaigne flashed a grin so like his son's that for an instant Steffi thought she might be seeing a future Sawyer. But Sawyer was taller, with broader chest and shoulders. He also had a more generous mouth.

"You will accompany Antoine to The Snow Angel."

Steffi blinked. Did they have year-round winter festivals? "Snow Angel? Like…?" She made a discreet up and down movement with her arms.

"No, no." He dismissed her demonstration with a sharp motion. "My son said he would talk with you."

"We didn't have much time together before he left. He was in a hurry."

"I'm sure he was." A strange smile played across his father's mouth. "It seems he has left the task to me." He gave a small grunt. "Not the first time and not the last, I'm sure." The server brought a fresh drink and removed his empty glass. "The Snow Angel is a resort. I've asked Antoine to make an informal inspection. It should take only a few days."

So Sawyer would be leaving her alone in Montreal again, this time for days? Everything in this city seemed to conspire against their being together. Steffi's spirits sank, but she forced another smile.

"The owners would turn themselves inside out to please a Montaigne. My son will pose as a businessman from the States so he can experience the resort as if he were a guest."

Steffi stared at the older man. "His face is so well-known. Won't they recognize him?"

César gestured at Yvette. "That's where she comes in. From working with local theater productions, my niece has developed skill with makeup and costume. When she finishes with Antoine, *you* won't recognize him."

Yet another reason to leave now.

"...a woman's perspective on the property." Sawyer's father was still speaking. "A couple draws less attention than a single traveler." César cleared his throat. "For those reasons, I hope you will agree to pose as Antoine's wife." Ignoring Steffi's gasp, he lifted his glass to her. "He's led me to believe that the two of you get on well enough for a plausible masquerade."

"That may be, but—" Pretend to be married to a man who'd sneered at her? She shook her head.

"You will have the opportunity to experience a beautiful part of our province, and you will also perform a valuable service for Montaigne Enterprises." He dipped his chin. "I will be in your debt."

Steffi was about to explain her objection when a loud giggle rattled the air. She looked toward the source of the noise. Her eyes widened, and she clutched her jaw to keep it from hitting the table. The Chasseur witch had squeezed her voluptuous body into a short, tight dress the color of shelled pistachio nuts. The V-neckline dipped almost to her navel. Her heels were so high she must have trained for altitude sickness. Smiling beside her and stroking the hand that grasped his jacket sleeve...Sawyer!

Steffi's drink threatened to erupt from her throat.

The headwaiter guided the newcomers to a center table on the edge of the dance floor. When Sawyer held the other woman's chair, she reached up and pawed his cheek. He actually smiled down at her. Then he kissed her palm and took a seat so close they could have been glued together. They talked and laughed as if no one else existed. *Like lovers.* Steffi's heart crumpled.

Chasseur traced her plunging neckline to lead Sawyer's eyes down the front of her dress. He patted her cheek, her neck, her shoulder. She fawned over him as if he really were the sexiest man in Canada, and Sawyer, damn it, lapped up every bit of attention as if he deserved it. Some business meeting. More like a public seminar in Sexology 101.

Steffi glanced across the table for Yvette's reaction, but her friend's chair was empty. "Yvette?" She looked around.

César Montaigne offered a feral smile. "She has other work to attend to."

Steffi blinked. She'd never thought of herself as work. Neither Sawyer nor Yvette made her feel like a burden. But Sawyer had never looked at her the way he looked at that damned reporter.

When a strong hand grasped hers, she stiffened.

"Let us conclude our business." A document lay on the table. With his free hand, Sawyer's father pulled a dark pen from his inner pocket. "Please sign here. And here."

He thought she would pretend to be married to a man who was clearly obsessed with another woman? Her gaze strayed again to Sawyer and his companion as the witch took a selfie of them.

Beside her, César Montaigne cleared his throat.

Tearing her gaze from Sawyer's table, Steffi pushed the paper away. "No, no. I'm sorry, but I can't."

"Yes, you can." The pen tapped the empty line on the page.

"I should never have come here." If she stayed until she was ninety, she'd never relax enough to recover her ability. By then, it would be too late. "I'm leaving." She started to rise, but César Montaigne's curved fingers dug into her arm and kept her in her place.

"Would that your situation were so simple."

She frowned. "What do you mean?"

"Montaigne Enterprises will pay you—rather generously—for your assistance at The Snow Angel."

"I'm not interested. Perhaps you should ask her."

She gestured at the Chasseur witch.

"Nonsense. She is far too well-known. More important, she and Antoine would spend the whole time in bed."

"A fling? With you?" Sawyer's jeer struck again. "There must be someone else."

Sawyer's father cleared his throat. "Before refusing my offer, you should consider the expenses you have accrued during your stay in Montreal."

She stared at him. "What?"

"Montaigne Enterprises has always supported OASIS, and the board approves the use of company resources for my son's OASIS projects. However, when they learn that you took advantage of our hospitality but refused to assist us, the board will expect some compensation for company services rendered. Let me see now. The plane that brought you from Chicago to Montreal. The penthouse apartment. Meals. Theater tickets. Wine." As he spoke, he scrawled numbers on the back of the document, slashed a line below the final item, and supplied a total.

The numbers swam before Steffi's eyes. "I don't have that kind of money."

"All the more reason you should accompany Antoine to The Snow Angel." César Montaigne's smile didn't connect with his eyes. "Consider the benefits, *ma chère*." His voice dropped so she had to draw closer to hear him. "The resort may be enjoyable, but even if it's terrible, the mountains are alive with summer. In addition, while you are earning a handsome sum, you can also make my son miserable. Should you shift to a formidable shape, you may wound him. A few scars might build character. But please don't eat him. After all, he is my eldest son."

When he dangled the pen in front of her, she snatched it and scrawled her name on the line.

"*Très bien.*" He photographed the document with his phone and smiled at her. "Let us seal our agreement with a toast." With a wave of his hand, champagne appeared.

Steffi gathered her skirt. "It's late. I should be going."

"Nonsense. The night is young, and you've signed a lucrative contract with Montaigne Enterprises." He lifted his glass. "To your sweetness and your strength."

As she acknowledged the toast, another giggle drew her eyes to Sawyer's table.

"May this mark the beginning of a fruitful relationship," the older man murmured.

The champagne bubbled down her throat. Sawyer and his companion stepped onto the dance floor. Sawyer moved with seductive grace through an intimate samba, and his partner was with him, grinding her hips against his on every beat. C-level sorceress, ha! She was working him like a succubus.

A rustle drew Steffi's eyes away from Sawyer and his date. Sawyer's father had moved closer. A few millimeters, perhaps, but closer. She might stink at seduction, but she could flirt. She took another sip of her drink. Then she widened her eyes as she smiled at Sawyer's father. *César.* His power glowed like a flame daring her to approach.

"My son has a great deal of charm." The older man dropped his voice to a near growl. "Some say he changes his ladies as often as they change their shoes."

She laughed.

"I thought he was exaggerating about you. Now, I can see that if anything, he underestimated you."

"Really?"

"You are extraordinary. In every way." His voice deepened, and his dark eyes exercised a strange, hypnotic pull. "You deserve more than he can ever offer. Much, much more."

Steffi took a deep breath and tried to blow the champagne fuzz from her brain. Was this how Eve felt when she met the serpent in the Garden of Eden? "*Monsieur* Montaigne—"

"César, please." He seemed to be enjoying her distress because he moved a bit closer. Toying with his prey like a cat, not a wolf. "A beautiful, desirable woman like you should not waste her charms on a pup."

Recalling Sawyer's majestic *loup-garou*, Steffi swallowed. *Some pup.* "If you think that, why are you sending us away together?"

"Why indeed? I'm now asking myself the same question." His gaze traveled past her. He must be watching his son with that witch. "Antoine will go alone as originally planned. You, however…" He tapped the table.

Deep in her core, resistance stirred. "I beg your pardon?"

"I would like to know you better, Steffi Anbruzzen." His voice purred against her ear like velvet.

When his hand covered hers, Steffi's brain buzzed, but she silenced the warning. "What would you like to know?"

"Everything. Especially what gives you pleasure."

The slow circles that his thumb traced on her palm sent tiny ripples up her arm. A blend of repulsion and attraction rose in her throat. "I'm a simple person. I don't need much."

"I'm not talking about needs. I am talking about desires."

He drew out the word as if he were wrapping it around her, trapping her. Distrust churned in her core.

"Do you have any idea what I can do for you?"

Her mouth ached from her forced smile, but if Sawyer was watching, she would not let him see her back down. "What do you have in mind?"

The older man's hand sliding up to grasp her elbow felt like a bug crawling up her arm. She pressed her lips together. She was supposed to be flirting with him, but damned if he wasn't making the moves on her.

"Let us go someplace more private."

She edged her arm away from him. "The auberge…"

"No." He shook his head. "I have other accommodations."

She looked at him. "Really? *Vraiment?*"

"You sound shocked."

"Surprised. We were taught that *loups-garous* mate for life, and you do have a mate."

"The mating bond within the pack is sacred, but our human males have needs. My mate understands."

"I'm sorry to hear that." She regarded him with genuine sympathy. "My parents have always been faithful."

César looked skeptical. "Come now, *ma chère*, children have no way of knowing about their parents' union so long as the adults exercise discretion, *n'est-ce pas?*" When she didn't respond, he asked, "Wouldn't you agree?"

"I suppose that's possible."

"Of course, it is. And if your parents do practice fidelity, what else can one expect of Simple Humans?"

Steffi sat up. "What do you mean by that?"

He reached for her hand, but she hid it beneath the table. "Our lives are more intense; our hungers, deeper."

His words recalled the dark caress of the ocean depths against her whale skin and the glorious spring breeze between her feathers. "That may be true."

"You know that even more than I do because of your ability." The crisp lemon scent of his aftershave almost masked the stench of rutting dog. "We needn't stay in Montreal. Where would you like to go? We can be on our way in under an hour." He pulled out his phone. "Anywhere in the world. Name it."

She lifted her chin. "My work has already taken me all over the world."

"That was work. This will be pleasure."

The hunger in his gaze communicated whose pleasure he was considering. She looked down at the table. "It's a generous offer, but I can't accept."

"I don't think you understand what I can do for you." His cajoling voice was pleasant, and far more dangerous. "I can give you anything your heart desires."

Get real. A smile tugged the corners of her lips as she thought of her lost shifting ability. "I doubt that."

He sat back and crossed his arms. "You seem quite certain."

Steffi mirrored his posture. "I am."

"My son said you were attractive. He didn't warn me that you were also a coquette."

Steffi blinked. "I'm sorry. I never—"

"Don't try to play innocent with me, *mademoiselle*. I've seen it all before. Fluttering those long, dark lashes."

He looked at her bosom. "Tempting me with the promise of paradise beneath the silk."

She wanted to glance at Sawyer but why bother? He was too smitten with his reporter friend to notice what was happening at his father's table. César Montaigne's dark eyes burned like coal. He could not only tempt but also destroy.

Strength swirled in Steffi's belly.

One of his hands dropped beneath the table. "The time for games has passed." His hand rested on her thigh.

Power spiraled into her heart. "Take. Your. Hand. Off. Me." Her voice was soft but strong.

His fingers dipped beneath the hem of her dress to grasp her knee, and he laughed.

"*Now*." Steffi snarled.

César Montaigne's sharp cry rang out. He almost overturned his chair when he sprang to his feet. Eyes wide with horror met Steffi's. Cradling one hand against his breast, he fled.

Chapter 18

Another annoying giggle exploded from Nicole. "Your father looks as if someone stuck a lit firecracker up his bum!"

Sawyer leaped to his feet and pulled her up. "Go to him. Please!"

"Sawyer!" Nicole's whine rose above the boom of the band. Once, he'd found her pout alluring.

"Please, Nicole. He'll do far better with a beautiful woman like you than he will with me, and I—" He needed to check on Steffi. The last time he'd looked, she was guzzling champagne with *Papa*.

Now, he took a deep breath and approached the table where Steffi still sat. Slowly, as if she feared something might be missing, she brought her fingers to her eyes, her nose, her mouth. Her hands dropped to the table, but her stunned expression remained. Questions whirled in Sawyer's brain, but only one emerged. "Are you all right?"

Without changing expression, Steffi looked up at him. Golden light flickered around her. "Yes, thanks. I'm fine." Tension tugged at the corners of her mouth, and darkness eclipsed the gold and green lights of her eyes.

"No, you're not."

Her teeth bit down on her lower lip. "I didn't... I never..."

"We'll talk later. Let's get out of here." He pushed

her purse into her hand and stepped behind her to hold her chair, but she didn't move. "Can you walk?"

"Of course." She rose as if she felt an ache deep in her bones. One hand rested over a spot in her skirt. Her expression shifted from confusion to distress to resignation. "I ruined my dress."

"The cleaning service can handle it." When her fingers opened to expose a ring of burned fabric, his heart crashed against his ribs. "You sure you're all right?"

She gave an absent-minded nod, and her contrite face looked up at him. "I didn't know...I never meant to—" She grasped one hand to her heart in imitation of his father.

Sawyer's pulse resumed its normal rhythm. *Papa* might be hurt, but Steffi was unharmed.

"Sawyer!"

Zut alors. When Nicole grabbed his arm, lightning flashed in Steffi's gaze. Sawyer patted Nicole's hand before detaching it. "How's my father?"

"Stunned, but no serious injury. They're taking him to the hospital to be sure." Nicole pointed at the damaged skirt. "What happened?"

Steffi cleared her throat, but Sawyer spoke first. "Accident." He gestured at the light in the middle of the table. "Steffi wanted a closer look at the candle but was a bit clumsy from the champagne. Must have dropped it in her lap. My father snuffed it."

Nicole's mouth flew open. "How terrible!" She glanced toward the door through which *Papa* had fled. "And how brave of your father!"

"Yes." Sawyer crossed his arms and clenched his teeth to keep from laughing. "He's quite the hero, eh?"

When Steffi coughed, he shot her a warning scowl. With luck, a few admiring inches in Nicole's column would redeem the evening and soothe his father's wounded pride.

"Management should do something to improve patron safety." Nicole's critical eye traveled from the offending candle to Steffi's dress. "That's a Eustace Pelliter, isn't it?" She brought both hands to her bosom. "*Quelle dommage!* What a pity! That's what happens when one overindulges, eh?" She looped an arm through Sawyer's. "We can drop your friend off on our way to the auberge."

A shadow clouded Steffi's features.

Sawyer gave a faint shake of his head. *No more accidents tonight, please!* He wrestled his arm from Nicole's grip. She'd been working out. "I don't think so. Steffi's had a bit of a shock, and I'm going to stay with her. You can ride with us if you like."

Nicole lifted her chin. "That won't be necessary." Turning on her heel, she sashayed out of the club. Her hips kept time with the music, no doubt to remind him of the delights he could have enjoyed.

"I'm sorry." Although Steffi offered an innocent smile, her tone conveyed no regret. "I didn't mean to spoil your date."

"It wasn't—never mind. It doesn't matter." Sawyer took her arm. "*Allons.*"

During the brief ride to the auberge, they sat side by side, but the inches that separated them yawned like a continent. Outside the car windows, the multicolored brilliance of the city flickered past. Inside, darkness wrapped them in individual cells of solitude. The regular rhythm of Steffi's breath stirred the air, but she sat, immobile, with her hands folded in her lap.

What was she thinking? What was she feeling? What was she doing in that club, at that table, alone with *Papa*? He should have kept a better eye on her, but when she'd given his father that special smile—the one that made you feel like the most wonderful man in the universe—he'd had to look away. The memory turned Sawyer's stomach inside out. It was good he hadn't yielded to the attraction he felt for her. Why did he feel so bad?

Uncomfortable silence accompanied them through the lobby and into the express elevator.

As soon as they entered the apartment, Steffi sank into the couch and buried her face in her hands. Sawyer loomed over her. "I did my best to come up with a story. What really happened?"

"I warned him."

Sawyer had to kneel in front of her to hear her.

Her fingers brushed the scorched skirt.

The hole could have come from a laser beam, destroying layers of fabric until it reached her skin. "We should have this looked at. You could be burned."

"Oh, no." She regarded him with an awkward smile. "The heat came from me and went into—I'm so sorry. I didn't know…" She opened her palm and used the index finger of her other hand to make a ring in the center. "All he had to do…I told him, but he didn't move his hand."

An emotional whirlwind filled Sawyer's chest. Anger. Embarrassment. Shame. He got to his feet. "Are you saying that my father groped you?"

"Not quite." Steffi drew a ragged breath. "He had more…panache."

Steffi's flirting no doubt encouraged *Papa*'s

advances, and he'd grown up in a time when men often ignored a woman's protests. Once he knew what he wanted, *Papa* never gave up. Not until tonight.

Sawyer stepped back. "I thought you and Yvette were going to the theater. How the devil did you end up at the club with him?"

"After the play, Yvette suggested we stop for a drink." The golden light in Steffi's eyes blazed. "And then your father—Yvette must have known. She wasn't surprised when he appeared." She hugged herself. "I liked her. I trusted her."

"Yvette was with you?" He'd been so surprised to see Steffi with his father that he hadn't noticed anyone else.

"For a while. I looked for her right after you arrived, but she was gone." Steffi waved her hand.

"It's not like her to leave without saying goodbye."

A flush colored Steffi's cheeks. "She might have. I was distracted by your date's... distinctive...laugh."

More like a dentist's drill. Sawyer winced. "It wasn't really a date."

"It didn't look like a business meeting."

"It was all about business." He described the damned newspaper column. "I was trying to make things right."

"And that's why you were there...with her?"

His chest swelled with pleasure at the hint of jealousy. "When we were dating, the club was always our last stop before...you know."

One of Steffi's newly sculpted eyebrows arched. "You thought having sex with her would fix your problem?"

He shrugged. "It's worked before. This time, I've

only made things worse." He turned toward the window.

"Maybe not." Steffi joined him. "It might be harder for her to write something nasty about you after everyone saw you together tonight. You were obviously enjoying each other's company. Until I messed everything up."

He regarded her. "You didn't mess up. My father did."

"Ah, yes. The hero of the evening." She smiled. "That was an inspired story. I wish you hadn't made me sound like a drunken klutz."

"Best I could do on short notice. I'm sorry you've had such a lousy evening."

"And I'm sorry that I hurt your father. On the bright side, I think my recovery has begun." Her face glowed.

"Fantastic!" He moved toward her, but she backed away with her palms up.

"Careful. This power is stronger than anything I've ever felt." She regarded her ruined skirt. "I didn't even know what I'd done until I smelled the burning fabric. Your poor father—" She clutched her hand to her heart.

"That'll teach him to play with fire. You scared the shit out of César Montaigne!" Sawyer threw back his head and howled with laughter. "Do you know how many people in this province would erect a monument to you?" His eyes met Steffi's, and he clapped. "*Brava*, Steffi! And congratulations!" He dipped his head toward her. "Do you want to shape-shift?"

Her smile grew more thoughtful. "Not yet."

"It won't be long before you do. Those of us who are Family specific shift to our familiar shapes. I'd recommend that you choose an animal comparable to your human shape and size. Puts less stress on your bones and muscles. A primate maybe."

She pressed her lips together and nodded. "Makes sense."

"Above all, take your time. Now that recovery has begun, you don't need to rush. When you're ready, you'll know."

Her gaze danced toward the window as if she were already planning to fly away. The notion struck him like a bullet.

She rested one hand against his jaw. "What's wrong?"

The warmth of her palm permeated his skin as it had when she'd stroked his *loup-garou* muzzle. Had that happened less than twenty-four hours ago? He patted her hand. "I'm glad your power has returned. I was sure you would recover. I didn't expect it to be so soon."

"Soon?" She hooted. "It's felt like an eternity to me. All the uncertainty…never knowing when or if… Don't get me wrong. I like my human base." She eyed her manicured fingers. "Especially when people fuss over it the way they did today. But—"

"But you are much more than human. Even those of us with only one other shape can understand that feeling."

Steffi pulled a folded paper from her bag. "I guess I can tear this up."

"What is it?"

"My contract to accompany you to that resort."

Sawyer frowned. "Contract?"

"That's why your father came to the club."

"I doubt it. I think he was curious…wanted to see you." He opened the document and studied it as if it were an archaeological artifact. "This is ridiculous. You're doing us a favor."

"Not from your father's perspective. For him, it was strictly business. Now, I suppose he will bill me for this trip instead." Steffi placed the contract on an end table.

"Pardon?"

She flipped the document. "He did the calculations down to the penny."

Sawyer's anger grew as the numbers mounted. "Son of a—if he tries anything, we'll trash his heroic image. Don't worry about the money. I can cover it." He pushed the contract to the floor. "So much for The Snow Angel."

She looked at him as if she could peer into his soul. "You're disappointed?"

"As a boy, I had wonderful times in *les Laurentides*—the Laurentians, to English speakers. I was looking forward to sharing that region with you."

"Then we should go. We agreed to make the trip. Your father has no scruples, but that doesn't mean we— we should keep our word." Steffi sat on the couch and patted the spot beside her. "Tell me about *les Laurentides*."

Relaxing for the first time since he'd awakened with her snuggled beside his *loup-garou*, he joined her. As he related tales of skiing, hiking, and roaming, first with his siblings and later with pack members, joy rushed through him.

When he finished, Steffi smiled at him. "I love how you and Roland used to give your brother and sisters *loup-garou* rides through the dark woods. Must have been fun."

"Except when Lucie got excited and kicked whoever she was riding in the ribs—and Lucie always got excited. She rode with me most of the time because I was the oldest." One of his hands went to his side.

"Ouch!"

"I survived, and now Lucie has her own wild ones. The region has become more developed, but much of it is still wild and beautiful. Like you." She blushed. "Sorry. I didn't mean to embarrass—you know, I was in such a rush to get through this evening, I don't think I told you how beautiful you look."

"Thank you." She glowed. "This is the nicest dress I've ever worn." She examined the hole. "I ruined it."

He covered her hand with his own. "I'll buy you a new one. Hell, I'll buy you a dozen. In a dozen different colors."

"Now you sound like your father."

The words hit him like an Arctic blast. Releasing her hand, he stood. "Well, you know what they say." He opened his arms. "I guess this apple settled right beneath the tree."

"Sawyer—"

"I thought…since you like the dress, and you look so good in it…you'd look fantastic in every one they had."

"I wouldn't be so sure." Her husky laugh tickled his ear. "Yvette said I looked like a pumpkin in the orange one."

"I doubt that." She would be radiant. "Pumpkins are round, and so are you. Not all over, but in all the right places."

Her blush complemented the color of her dress. "Thank you." She moved her hands as if she were washing them. "What I said…I'm sorry. You're not like your father."

"I have neither his vast resources nor his magnetic power, but I've inherited my share of his vices and a few

188

of his virtues. He does have some, eh?"

"If you say so. But you're different. You care about other people."

"So does *Papa*. He takes responsibility for the pack and the company, so his concern for them is paramount."

"And for himself."

"Well, yes. Though some would say he's earned it." Sawyer scratched his chin. How had *Papa* become the center of a conversation that should have been about them?

"You admire him."

He took a few steps toward the dining area while he considered the comment. The wine she'd ordered earlier was still sitting out. Alcohol might dull the turn this discussion had taken. "Not as much as I did before he— before tonight. I still respect his power but not as much. I know he's...but I never saw anything like...and not with...someone I..." *Not with* you. He poured two glasses and put them on the table in front of the couch. The wine turned to vinegar on his tongue.

"Did you really tell him I was 'an extraordinary creature'?"

"No!" He slammed his glass down on the table as his denial ricocheted off the walls. "Is that what he—I don't remember everything I said, but I would never have said that about any Shifter, especially not—I may have used the word *extraordinary* in describing your range of ability. But I never..." The shame of his father's behavior stung his chest like a botched tattoo. He wanted to sling the wine bottle at the wall, but there wasn't enough booze in the world to staunch this anger.

"It's all right." Steffi left the couch and stood in front of him. "I didn't believe it when he said it."

"Then why did you ask me?"

"I wanted to be sure, and I knew you wouldn't lie."

His pulse gave a joyful thump. "You trust me."

Her eyes widened. "Yes. I guess I do."

"What else did my father tell you?"

She nibbled her lower lip for a few seconds. "That you were fickle and weak. In contrast to him, although I don't know why he thought a *loup-garou* who cheats on his mate would be preferable to a bachelor. An older man at that."

"But richer. Much richer."

"He thought that was a big selling point. He said he could satisfy my heart's desire."

"Sounds tempting."

"It would have been if I—oh my God!" Peals of laughter burst from her. "That's one claim your father actually made good on! I'm regaining my power. Because of him." She laughed until tears ran down her cheeks.

"So *Papa* satisfied your heart's desire." *Not me.* Why couldn't he have given her this prize? Sawyer handed her his handkerchief.

"And he'll never know." Wiping away the tears, she looked up at him. "Don't you love the irony?"

"Not as much as I love seeing you smile or hearing you laugh."

"And I have you to thank for it." She tapped his chest, too quickly for him to hold her hand against his heart. "None of this would have happened if you hadn't brought me here."

He threw up his hands. Best to keep his distance. "You would have recovered on your own."

"I doubt it. I was so obsessed with the problem that

I kept picking at it like a scab. You took my mind off it long enough to begin the healing process." As she spoke, the golden aura of her rejuvenated power intensified. Soon, she would shift, and then she would leave. Emptiness yawned within him.

"Sawyer. Relax." When she rested her fingers against his jaw, he realized he'd been grinding his teeth. Golden flickers gave her dark eyes the warmth of firelight. Her lips parted slightly, an offer he felt powerless to refuse. His hands cupped her face. His fingers traced the line of her eyebrows, caressed the smooth ridges of her cheekbones. Her mouth softened beneath his, and her breath brushed the back of his teeth.

Desire hummed in his veins. She tasted like mint and honey with a *soupçon* of cinnamon. Their tongues met, then tangled in a slow, intimate dance. As he explored the hidden hollows in the roof of her mouth, her shy probing echoed his movements. The pressure in his groin grew so unbearable he had to draw back.

Steffi regarded him with an unfocused gaze. "What was that?"

Did she really have to ask? "Something I've wanted to do since the first time I saw you."

Her dazed expression gave way to a minx-like smile. "Took you long enough."

"You were an OASIS client. My OASIS client."

Laughter bubbled from between her slightly swollen lips.

His fingers rested lightly on the fabric covering her shoulders while his thumbs stroked the warm skin at the edge of the neckline. He nuzzled the soft curve of her neck. He ached to continue kissing her all the way into his bed.

She turned her head and looked at him. "What happens next?"

"You have a couple buttons back here." He loosened them. "I could kiss you here. And here" His mouth softened against the freshly exposed skin below her neck.

She whimpered. "That feels so good."

Tastes even better. "Then I could unzip the back and kiss every other inch as it comes into view."

She stepped away. "So now you think I'd make a satisfactory fling?"

"What?" He stared at her. Where had that come from? "I don't…" When he hesitated, her body stiffened. "A fling sounds…ephemeral…tawdry. Why don't we see what happens?"

"You already have a deadline. When fall comes, you're choosing a mate."

He bit back a compendium of curses while emotions tangled in his chest like scouting knots. "By then, you'll be shifting up a storm. Who knows where you'll be or what you'll be doing?" *Or who you'll be doing it with.* When he stepped into the cotillion, she might be half a world away. He cleared his throat. "After The Snow Angel, let's make your Prince Edward Island pilgrimage. Then I'd like to double back a bit—take you to my property in Alberta."

"I'd love that." The light in her face dimmed. "Alberta's so close to Montana that it will be convenient when the time comes…"

She could soar across the endless prairie. Fly into freedom. He silenced her with a soft kiss. "Let's not get too far ahead of ourselves."

"Right." Her lips turned up, but her gaze was

solemn. "*Carpe diem*. We'll seize the day." When she wrapped her arms around his neck, the new perfume stirred the fire in his loins. "And the night."

He looked down at her lovely face, filled with a longing he'd never seen in her before. "If this is Plan B, it's definitely working."

Her heavy-lidded eyes popped open. "Oh, God!" Her hands covered her cheeks, but couldn't hide the bewitching blush.

He drew her to his chest and rested her head on his shoulder while he stroked her hair. "I told you it wouldn't take much." His lips fluttered at the corner of her eye and continued down the side of her face to her ear.

Instead of melting against him, she pulled back and stood. "Did you think that I—I mean, I'm not...but you—" Her eyes narrowed as she regarded him.

Merde. He felt lower than a garden worm. "I was teasing. I know you're not trying to seduce me. Though it would have been flattering."

"I'm not so sure about that. I don't...I do want to be with you." She drew a deep breath and surveyed the sitting room. "But not here. Could we go somewhere else? Someplace that doesn't belong to your family?"

He nodded. "Easy enough." He pulled out his phone.

"I should change my clothes, too."

He frowned when she squeezed the damaged fabric. His father's disgusting behavior had destroyed her enjoyment in the pretty dress along with her respect for anything Montaigne. Thank God, she still wanted him. "It's been a rough evening. Perhaps we should wait until tomorrow." When her gaze traveled the full length of his body, he rested a hand on his swollen crotch. "Won't be the first time I've gone to bed alone." He gave her a half smile.

Her lips brushed his. "I appreciate your thoughtfulness, but I don't want to tiptoe around because of—" Her fingers seized the fabric of his shirt. Fierce determination blazed in her eyes. "We will not let him win."

"*Magnifique*. You are magnificent." His mouth met hers in a kiss that superheated his groin.

"*Bonsoir*!" Yvette's cheerful voice rang out. "*Mon dieu*!"

Steffi and Sawyer leaped apart. Steffi's cheeks flamed with embarrassment. Sawyer clapped to turn up the lights. He glared at his cousin.

The hotel porter departed like a shadow. Yvette stood beside the boxes and satchels heaped on a bellman's cart. As the elevator doors closed, Sawyer broke into an explosive French tirade that required no translation.

Eyes swimming in tears, Yvette brought her hands to her mouth. She looked ready to collapse.

"Sawyer." Steffi gripped an arm that felt like a girder. "Stop. Please!"

He broke off and turned to face her. Storm clouds swirled in his gray gaze. He pointed at his terrified cousin. "She left you. With him."

Sniffling, Yvette patted her face with a handkerchief. "I was dismissed." She spoke in a low voice. She regarded Steffi. "You seemed to be getting on well."

Steffi frowned up at Sawyer. "What did you say? Your father didn't—"

"He would have if you hadn't fought back. And she

let it happen."

Dismissed. "He ordered her to leave."

Sawyer's lower lip curled. "Did you hear him?"

She shook her head. "I was too busy watching you." When Sawyer grimaced, she smiled. "Your father strikes me as a man who can issue commands without saying a word." She moved closer and spoke in a voice that only Sawyer would hear. "Your cousin feels indebted to your parents. She would never question their orders. Especially his."

As Sawyer nodded, his jaw relaxed. He turned to his cousin, who was backing toward the elevator. "I'm sorry, Yvette." He started toward her, but Steffi kept her hand on his arm. "What the devil are you doing here at this hour?" He gestured at the cart. "And what's all this?"

Yvette clasped her hands and lifted her chin. "Your father called. He said that because you will make an early departure, I needed to be here *tout de suite*. Right away," she translated for Steffi. "I've brought everything necessary for your disguises." She buttoned her jacket. "I didn't mean to interrupt you."

"I suspect that's what *Papa* wanted." Sawyer winked at Steffi. "Sore loser." Draping an arm across her shoulders, he drew her close. His lips grazed her temple, and she had to clench her fists at her sides to keep from throwing her arms around his neck and surrendering to another of those soul-baring kisses. She drew a deep breath to slow the blood that thundered in her ears.

Yvette cleared her throat. "I can return near dawn, or would you prefer a later hour?"

"Nonsense." Sawyer's deep voice was firm. "By the time you reach your apartment, you'll have to turn around and come back. The couch folds out. You can sleep there." He crossed to a closet near the elevator and pulled out bedding.

Moving closer to Steffi, Yvette frowned as she pointed at the ruined skirt. "What happened to your dress?"

"An accident." Sawyer paused in making the bed. "With any luck, you'll see the story in tomorrow's paper."

With César Montaigne in the hero's role. Oh, well. Steffi bit back her objection. If a little lie got Nicole Chasseur off Sawyer's back, so be it.

"In the meantime, Steffi's seduction is progressing quite nicely, *n'est-ce pas*, *chérie*?"

"Sawyer!" She rested her hands on his broad shoulders and inhaled his masculine scent. Much more intoxicating than champagne. "Must we discuss this in front of your cousin?"

"Why not? She's the one who put you up to it. Isn't that right, Yvette?"

Steffi shook her head and gestured toward her room. "While he finishes with the bed, let's get you something to sleep in."

As soon as Steffi closed the bedroom door, Yvette said, "I'm sorry I interrupted you. If I had known—but from what you said at the club—"

"It's all right." Steffi laughed. "I'm as surprised as you are."

Yvette applauded. "I knew you could do it!"

Steffi paused in opening a drawer. "No one is seducing anyone. It's like a game."

The other woman beamed. "And you are playing like a champion."

"Hardly." Steffi avoided Yvette's eyes by

196

rummaging through her nightclothes. All games ended, and this one would end when Sawyer found his mate. All other females he'd known—herself included—would fade away. In the meantime, she'd bring her A game even though she could never win.

"This should fit you." When she offered Yvette a short cotton nightgown, the other woman muttered a soft "*merci*" and fingered the fabric as if it were soiled. "If you want something more womanly, check out the lingerie bags, and take your time in the bathroom. I want to say good night to Sawyer."

When she joined Sawyer in the sitting room, he held her close. "You look exhausted."

She rested her head on his shoulder. "I hate to admit it, but I am. If you got us a room at another hotel, you should cancel. By the time we get there, I'll be asleep." Although she ached to explore the uncharted territory of his strong body, she wanted to be awake enough to savor the experience. "That's not how I want to spend our first night together."

"Agreed. If we're going to make an early start, we should sleep." His lips brushed the top of her head. "Tomorrow."

Steffi nodded. "Tomorrow." Beyond the shadows of César Montaigne and Montaigne Enterprises.

His mouth met hers in a long, slow kiss that almost turned her bones to jelly.

Still embracing her, he whispered in her ear, "Don't forget to pack that seduction kit."

She locked her hands behind his neck and looked up at him. "We won't be there long enough for me to wear it all."

"If I have my way, you won't wear any of it for

197

long."

She laughed. "Promises, promises."

"I do my best." His soft gray gaze caressed her features, and he kissed her forehead. "Sleep well, *chérie*."

Chapter 19

Yvette asked a question in French as she gave the mirror to the stocky man with the vivid scar above his salt-and-pepper beard. Pursing his lips, Sawyer studied his reflection. When he shook his head, a few ragged strands fell across his broad forehead and refused to return when he flicked them. "Damn, Yvette. Did you have to demolish a five-hundred-dollar haircut?"

Yvette shrugged. "*Il faut.*"

Sawyer appealed to Steffi, who had witnessed the transformation from a nearby armchair. "What do you think?"

"Amazing." She stood and circled the new—rather, the old—Sawyer. Disconcerting blue contact lenses covered his smoky irises, and his dark hair was almost silver. "You look so different. No one would know who you really are."

"That's the point." He grinned. "We'll see how the owners of The Snow Angel treat Mr. and Mrs. Sawyer from International Falls, Minnesota."

Steffi eyed Yvette with fresh respect. "My sister Dayzee works in films. She can always use people with your talents."

Sawyer's cousin twirled an auburn curl. "*Vraiment?*"

"Absolutely," Steffi said. "If you're interested, I'll set up a call when we get back."

The small woman gave her a quick hug.

Steffi smoothed the bottom edge of the dark cap of hair that Marcel's clever scissors had found beneath her split ends. She hoped Yvette's plans wouldn't include wrecking *her* hair.

Sawyer scanned her from head to toe. "Don't change Steffi too much. I like her the way she is."

"You may." Yvette poked his padded gut. "But Mister Sawyer from Minnesota likes *la belle potiche*, eh? Come along, Steffi." In the bedroom, she held up an off-white dress topped with a small bolero.

Staring at the keyhole neckline, Steffi splayed one hand across her chest. "I can't wear that."

"Of course, you can. First, we'll do your face." Yvette sat her in front of the dressing table.

"That dress is—"

"Exactly what you need. Don't frown." Yvette's meticulous hands created a more dramatic effect than Marie-Louise's subtle hues. Steffi's cheekbones looked higher, and the hollows seemed deeper. Two-toned shadow and more liner enlarged her eyes.

"I hate this new lip color. My mouth looks like it's bleeding."

Yvette laughed. "Trust me. It is perfect."

When Yvette squeezed her into the dress, the tight skirt ended with a small flutter above her knees. Steffi frowned at the bodice that offered a generous view of her cleavage, highlighted by one of those uplift bras.

"Shoes!" While Steffi moaned, Yvette strapped her into a pair of impossible stilettos and hustled her into the sitting room where Sawyer was waiting. "*Voilà!*"

Yvette gestured for Steffi to turn.

"No way." Steffi planted her feet on the rug. "I can

barely walk in these things." She looked at Sawyer. "Some women move so gracefully…like your friend."

Sawyer waved off the comment. "Nicole charms her shoes."

"What? Are you serious?"

Sawyer nodded. "I watched her once. Sprinkled some dark powder on the shoe. Stuck what looked like a chicken bone in the toe. Waved a crystal around and muttered a few words."

"That makes me feel better." With a glance at Yvette, Steffi executed a clumsy spin and managed to remain upright.

Yvette applauded. "*La belle potiche*!"

Hands on hips, Steffi regarded the other woman. "Okay. *Belle* is beautiful. What's a *potiche*?"

"A piece of porcelain."

"That's the technical definition." Sawyer cleared his throat. "In the States, you call it a trophy wife."

Steffi's mouth dropped open. So that was the reason for this outrageous costume.

"Trophy wife." Yvette grinned.

Steffi turned to Sawyer. "If that's what you want, you should take Yvette instead of me. She's a real beauty, and she can even keep your disguise looking good."

When Sawyer pushed the silver hair back from his forehead, the waves stood at a funny angle, and Steffi's fingers itched to smooth them. "Someone might recognize Yvette. No one will know you."

"Trophy wife." Steffi pressed her lips together. *Potiche* might sound classier, but the meaning remained. She fingered the revealing neckline.

"Look on the bright side." When Sawyer's hand

brushed hers, a happy tingle scurried up her arm. "Trophy wives don't get snatched by hawks or filleted by hungry villagers."

"How comforting."

After they said goodbye to Yvette in the lobby, Sawyer directed the porters, who packed their matching luggage in the back of a bright red sports car. A brown tweed jacket and ready-to-wear trousers added bulk to his padded frame and slowed his confident movements. When he joined her beside the passenger door, Steffi pointed at the broad red suspenders setting off his white cotton shirt. "Don't you think you're overdoing it?"

"The more distractions the better." Hooking his thumbs through the suspender webbing, he peered through wire-rimmed glasses. "And you, Mrs. Sawyer, will be the biggest distraction."

Steffi tugged at her skirt. "This dress is so tight I can barely breathe." When Sawyer's gaze took in the contours of her dress, the fabric seemed to melt into her skin.

"You look terrific. I almost forgot." Instead of closing the car door, he reached for her left hand and slipped a pair of rings on her third finger. "Now it's official." He patted her hand.

Steffi looked from the garish engagement ring and the thin platinum band with small diamonds and emeralds to Sawyer's face. "The wedding ring is gorgeous, but the diamond's a bit much."

"It belonged to Great-aunt Louise. She liked to stand out in a crowd." His real smile surfaced beneath the makeup. "The emeralds match the green in your eyes."

She reached out and squeezed his hand. If she could ever figure out how to breathe, this excursion might be fun. When they pulled away from the auberge, she intoned, "*Au revoir*, Montreal."

"We'll be back. We'll stop here before PEI—Prince Edward Island—so you can set up the conversation between Yvette and your sister." When she opened her mouth, he held up a finger. "You choose the hotel."

She studied his strong profile. "Won't your father give you something else to do as soon as he knows you're back?"

A muscle in his cheek twitched. "I doubt it. I'm hardly a favorite son at the moment."

"That's not fair." She sat up. "You weren't responsible for what happened at the club."

"True. But I'm guessing Nicole made sure he knew I was taking care of you instead of tending to his needs. And I voted against him on the tar-sands proposal."

"You did what you thought was right."

"Irrelevant. *Papa* believes family should maintain a united front. I've managed to disappoint him twice in one visit."

"By taking me to The Snow Angel, you could have a trifecta."

He laughed. With his eyes watching the road, he reached over and patted her knee.

Where his palm rested, warmth penetrated the sheer stocking and flowed into her veins. How different he was from his father! Power hummed around Sawyer, but she felt only comfort and protection. "Shouldn't you keep both hands on the wheel?"

"Right." He pulled back. "I hope I didn't—"

"Not at all."

"I'm hoping this trip will be a win for everyone. We'll enjoy a few restful days in the country and provide information my father can use. We'll even find isolated spots where you can practice shifting."

"Sounds good." She hugged herself. With every passing hour, her confidence grew. When they reached The Snow Angel, she'd be ready to test her skill. By the time their masquerade ended, she might be fully recovered and able to return to her real life. She stole a glance at Sawyer. The longer they were together, the more the reality of that other life faded like the turned page in a book that she had little desire to continue reading. In contrast, every day with Sawyer felt like an exciting new chapter in a story they were writing together. A story that would end when he met his mate.

Sawyer's thumb brushed the bridge of her nose.

"What are you doing?"

"Relax." He pulled off the expressway and found a parking spot. "Why the frown?"

She flipped the vanity mirror on the visor to be sure he hadn't left a thumb print on her face. "I was thinking." She repaired the spot.

"Thinking is good. Worrying isn't. *Potiches* don't have frown lines." He grinned. "Most have had so much work done they don't have any lines."

"I'll try to remember that." Observing her reflection, she arranged her features into an indifferent mask with wide eyes and lifted lips. "This what you're looking for?"

"No." He closed the mirror. "I like you the way you are."

Her heart gave a happy flutter. "And how is that?"

"Fishing for compliments, eh?" He looked at her for a minute. "Smart. Strong." His breath tickled her ear. "And sexy as hell."

When Sawyer turned onto another secondary road, Steffi asked, "Is this a short cut?"

"No. I need to pay my respects to my mother."

"What?" Feeling as if he'd rammed a steel rod up her spine, Steffi sat up, tugged at the flared hem of her skirt, and rested one hand on her exposed chest. "I can't meet your mother looking like *this*." She slipped on the bolero that accompanied the dress. The front pieces failed to cover the revealing bodice.

"You look gorgeous, Steffi."

She lifted one shoulder and tried to draw the front of the jacket over her heart. Gorgeous? Ha! If she tried to avoid indecent exposure, she'd look like the Hunchback of Notre Dame. "I can wait in the car while you visit." She held up her phone. "Check my mail. Read a bit."

Sawyer shook his grizzled head. "If you don't come in with me, it will be harder for me to get away. I always plan to be in and out as fast as I can, but it never works that way."

"I know what you mean." Steffi smiled. "No such thing as a quick family visit, is there?"

"Probably not. Anyway, *Maman* knows you're with me, and she will want to see you."

"To check out whether I have two heads or three arms on one side?"

"I'm sure *Papa* has disabused her of such notions."

Steffi wiggled in her seat. "I hope she doesn't expect…this sounds weird, I know, and it doesn't happen often, but sometimes other Shifters have asked us to shift. It makes me feel like a freak."

"I can assure you that my mother will not want any demonstrations unless, of course, you choose to be a she-wolf."

Steffi's breath stalled in her throat. "You can't be serious."

"I'm not."

"Violating the Covenant is nothing to joke about."

"Sorry." They rode for a few miles in companionable silence.

"How long is the drive?"

"Not nearly long enough." The artfully applied scar on Sawyer's left jaw twitched. "Why don't you do a little research on The Snow Angel? There's a folder in the side pocket."

While Steffi tried to bury herself in the report, Sawyer turned on some heavy metal music. When she stuffed the papers back in the folder, Sawyer lowered the volume. "That was fast. Learn anything interesting?"

"That your music shreds my concentration."

He laughed and pumped up the volume. "That's why I like it!" he shouted. "Keeps me from thinking. All I have to do is drive!"

Watching him zip past the other cars, Steffi smiled. In the city, he spent little time behind the wheel. When they returned to Montreal, perhaps they could take a day to stroll the boulevards, use the Metro, and behave like a Simple Human couple. Her heart thudded in her throat as she recalled the sweet pressure of his mouth.

Chapter 20

Sawyer braked and swiped a card that opened ornate metal gates.

"This is your idea of a simple country home?" Steffi eyed the strong fence and the battery of cameras. "Looks more like an armed camp."

"They've added security. Must not like what they've heard about anti-Shifter factions in the States."

"No one pays any attention to those weirdos."

"I hope you're right. Throughout history, *loups-garous* have suffered persecution. If troubles come, the Montaigne pack will be prepared." He drove down an avenue with stately oaks on either side. "*Voici!*"

When they rounded a long curve, Steffi caught her breath. Extensions, turrets, arches, even a small geodesic dome seemed to erupt from the massive stone building with tall, narrow casement windows. "Unusual architecture."

"How tactful of you!" Sawyer laughed. "I've heard it called eclectic, bizarre, and totally unhinged. My parents added a new room for every child after the first two."

Steffi silently counted the additions. "How many of you are there?"

"Seven altogether. Roland and I protested the additions for the twins, so we got new rooms to keep the peace." His smile faded. "That may be the first and last time he and I ever joined forces."

"That's too bad."

"Sibling rivalry." Sawyer pulled into a car lot. The garage was the size of a small bus station.

"Your family has so much that there should be more than enough to share."

"The key words are 'should be.' That's certainly true for Michel and me. Of course, all he's ever wanted is to oversee our maritime interests. Roland's only a year younger than I am, and he's always felt cheated. Can't say I blame him. After all, while I've pushed boundaries in every direction, he has been the dutiful son. Never misses a board meeting. Always votes with *Papa*. Mated at eighteen and, much to *Maman*'s delight, has sired not one, but two, pairs of twins. Yet the older son still takes precedence." He got out of the car and opened her door. "Don't slouch. You look lovely."

"Thank you. You—"

"Look old and fat, and this padding itches."

She rested a hand against his fake beard. "What you look like doesn't matter. Whether it's padding and makeup or *loup-garou* fur, you're still Sawyer." *My Sawyer*.

"Thank you, *chérie*. I think." After ringing the bell, he leaned down and brushed her cheek with his lips. "Whatever happens, keep smiling. You'll either light up her day or drive her round the bend."

"That sounds ominous." Steffi nibbled on her lower lip until Sawyer's finger pressed against it.

"Don't worry. We'll all survive." One lid dropped in a partial wink. "*Zut alors!*" He covered his eye with one hand.

"What's wrong?"

"I dislocated a lense." One gray eye, one blue.

"Antoine, *mon—mon dieu!*" When she opened the door, Sawyer's mother nearly fell out of the purple designer pumps that matched the sweeping skirt of her silk dress. The lady received her children in grand fashion. She rested perfectly manicured fingers against Sawyer's shaggy beard, and her rose lips trembled as if they might shatter. "What has happened to you?" Instead of French, she spoke in English.

"Relax, *Maman*. Yvette disguised me so I could inspect The Snow Angel—the resort Michel was supposed to visit—without betraying our interest." Sawyer patted her hand and deposited a kiss on her forehead. Opening his arms wide, he made a large circle. "What do you think?"

"Our Yvette is a very clever girl." His mother shook her head, crisp ash blonde curls in a Marcel cut. Her smile suggested she was used to surprises from this child. "I have not seen you in so long that such changes are alarming." She brought her hands to her ample bosom. "You nearly frightened me to death."

Sawyer scratched the edge of the fake beard. "Don't try to make me feel guilty, *Maman*. The disguise was *Papa*'s idea." He turned to Steffi and put an arm around her shoulders. "And this is my partner in crime, Steffi Anbruzzen. Steffi, this is my mother."

"*Madame* Montaigne. It is a pleasure—"

The other woman barely touched the offered hand. "Miss Anbruzzen." Her visual examination began at the crown of Steffi's head, took a leisurely scan of her face, and halted at the keyhole neckline before traveling to the flirty hem. Steffi's face felt as if she were roasting over a campfire.

Madame Montaigne looked at her son and spoke in rapid French.

"*Not at all what I expected.*" Steffi managed to translate a bit. *I agree*. She should have stayed in the car.

Before his mother could continue, Sawyer said, "*Papa* insisted that I say hello." He drew himself up and began to run a hand through his hair but then dropped the hand to his side. "Now, we must be on our way." Grasping Steffi's elbow, he started to leave.

"No, Antoine! Not yet!" When he turned back to face his mother, one of her hands came to his cheek, and she looked up at him. "I haven't seen or heard from you in months, my son."

Steffi bit back a smile at the familiar plaint. Parents!

"I want to know what is happening in your life. Are you well?" Her eyes focused on a spot over Steffi's shoulder. "Are you happy?"

Sawyer flashed a quick smile. "Yes and yes." He glanced at Steffi. "I'm also busy."

Sawyer's mother pursed lips shaped like her son's. "When your father told me you would stop today, I had Annette prepare one of your favorite lunches. You need to eat." Her eyes, the same fathomless gray as her son's, moved in Steffi's direction. "She can set an extra place for your…*friend*."

Her imperial nod sent a chill across Steffi's shoulders. Still, it felt better than that initial scowl. Perhaps things were looking up. At least, the food would be good. Steffi's stomach rumbled with premature appreciation. They'd skimped on breakfast, and the skintight skirt would force her to nibble. The more small meals, the better. The minibar at The Snow Angel had better be filled with popcorn and chocolates.

"Thank you, *Maman.*"

When Sawyer leaned down to kiss the small woman's cheek, her face lit up. Sawyer started to offer Steffi a steadying hand, but his mother wrapped her arm possessively around his and drew him into the big house. Steffi tried to keep up with them in those stupid stilettos that made her feel as if she were wearing stilts.

"OASIS keeps you so busy that it leaves you little time for your other responsibilities."

"*Papa* exaggerates. We talk almost every day."

His mother paused to regard Steffi. "Is *she* the OASIS—"

Steffi answered. "Yes. I'm Sawyer's—Antoine's—client."

His mother sniffed and resumed their march down a long hall. "I don't know why they assigned you. I know you've had success with *loups-garous,* and I suppose you can help *normal* Shifters. But an Anomaly?"

"Steffi and her sisters aren't all that different from us. They do have far more ability than we have, and their problems tend to be more complicated, *n'est-ce-pas,* Steffi?"

"I suppose." She bit her lip and concentrated on not wobbling.

Madame Montaigne launched into another French ramble that had something to do with women, but Sawyer cut her off. "I should warn you, *Maman.* Although Steffi is reluctant to speak French, she understands it quite well."

Please don't ask me to translate!

"I meant no insult." But her disparaging glance in Steffi's direction belied the not-quite apology. She tightened her grip on her son's arm. "Has Lucie told you about Barbara?" Without waiting for Sawyer's response, she addressed Steffi's shoulder. "She is charming."

"Charming, eh?" Sawyer growled. "Does that mean ugly or simply plain?"

"Antoine!" His mother slapped his arm. "She doesn't flaunt her attributes like some women."

Her steely gaze hit Steffi like a spear. Steffi's face heated, and she gripped the bottom edges of the bolero in a vain effort to shield her chest.

"Maybe she has nothing to flaunt." Sawyer's wink made her smile.

"She's from British Columbia." His mother continued to describe the other woman.

"Not an O'Shaugnessy, I hope." Sawyer laughed. "They're still spreading terrible stories about us."

His mother sighed. "All the more reason for an alliance between our packs."

Sawyer scoffed. "We're not the royal houses of Europe, *Maman*. Lucie may have been happy to take an alpha from the First Nations as her mate, but I'm not going to choose mine to satisfy *Papa*'s political strategies."

"My dear boy, we're aware of that." *Madame* Montaigne patted him on the cheek and frowned at seeing the makeup on her fingers.

Sawyer would need a touch-up when they got back to the car. Dear God, let it be soon!

"But if you like Barbara—and I think you will once you've gotten to know her—I've met her, and she is, as I said, charming—quite charming—there's all the more reason to choose her. Wouldn't you agree, Miss Anbruzzen?"

Steffi blinked. "The choice is your son's, *madame*. I

have no opinion."

"That's not how you look at him." The older woman's eyes narrowed. "I suppose that is one of the skills you learn in your profession."

"I beg your—"

"*Maman!*"

"*Pardon?*"

The confusion on *Madame* Montaigne's face sent laughter bubbling into the back of Steffi's throat, and she coughed to stifle it.

"She looks like—"

When the older woman flung an arm in her direction, Steffi hopped back and stumbled. Sawyer seized her elbow, and she latched onto his arm.

When he drew her arm into his side and stroked it, she wanted to purr. If Sawyer hadn't caught her, the back seam of her dress would probably have popped when her butt hit the hardwood floor. "Steffi and I are both in disguise. In real life, she is a college professor from Chicago. For our visit to The Snow Angel, she is my *potiche.*" He lifted her left hand to display the rings.

Madame Montaigne's eyebrows almost grazed her hairline. "You're using Louise's ring?" She looked ready to rip it off Steffi's finger.

Smiling, Sawyer wrapped his hand around Steffi's. "All in the service of Montaigne Enterprises, *Maman.* Steffi is a beautiful distraction."

Steffi tugged at the bolero. "Who feels like a sausage stuffed into its casing."

"I see." *Madame* Montaigne's puzzled expression made it clear that she wasn't sure if the distraction was for her son or others.

The exquisitely furnished dining room offered an

excellent opportunity to change the subject. "My goodness!" Steffi approached the photos lining the walls. "What an impressive collection!" Her spontaneous smile seemed to relax the older woman's stern mouth.

"Careful," Sawyer warned, "or she'll give you the grand tour."

"I would love it." The words were scarcely out of her mouth before the older woman's fingers encircled her wrist. When Steffi shot her a cool glance, the claws retreated.

"Let us begin at the beginning."

Ignoring her son's muttered "Let's not," Sawyer's mother drew Steffi toward the far wall, which held a series of old, formally posed family portraits. "Montaignes have lived in Quebec for centuries. They were here when the British took control in *La Bataille des Plaines d'Abraham* in 1759. In fact, one of my husband's ancestors served as an aide-de-camp to General Montcalm and died in the battle."

Sawyer rested an arm across his mother's shoulders. "*Maman*, we don't have time for the complete, annotated history. Can you introduce the immediate family before the soup cools?"

Madame Montaigne regarded her son with a sniff. "You've always been an impatient child."

Sawyer chuckled. "I've always preferred my food at the proper temperature."

Men! The exasperated expression that Sawyer's mother sent in Steffi's direction required no translation, and Steffi almost burst out laughing.

The older woman drew Steffi's attention to the photo of an infant clad in a long, lacy christening gown. A distinctive frown registered the baby's displeasure.

"As you can see, Antoine has never had much respect for tradition."

Sawyer snorted. "At least I did not spew my breakfast into the baptismal font."

"Poor Lucie." Dismissing any possibility of sympathy from her son, *Madame* Montaigne regarded her guest. "Projectile vomiting. We went straight from the *basilique* to the hospital."

Steffi leaned toward Sawyer. "Is that the sister who used to kick you in the ribs?"

"One and the same." Sawyer grinned. "On the plus side, Lucie permanently retired that ugly dress."

His mother held up three fingers. "Three generations had worn it."

"Move along, *Maman*." Sawyer touched his mother's shoulder. "The soup is cooling."

"Very well." As the older woman swept through the newer pictures, Steffi tried to fit the faces with the family members Sawyer had mentioned. The tall, serious man surrounded by a large, dutifully composed family must be Roland, the next in line. His wife's vacant gaze above her smile revealed her exhaustion, and a corner of Roland's thin mouth bent down. Dissatisfaction? Perhaps she was reading too much into that. Michel stood among his brood on a sailboat. In contrast to Roland, he had a broad, happy face like Sawyer's, and his young wife clearly adored him. Each of the four sisters had a handsome mate and at least two children. The litany of names, ages, and achievements blurred in Steffi's mind, but the importance of family and pack remained paramount.

At the end of the tour, Steffi smiled at Sawyer's mother. "Thank you so much for sharing this." She couldn't resist a glance at Sawyer. "You must be very proud."

"I have been blessed." The older woman's gaze chilled Steffi's bones.

I get it, lady! You don't want me here anymore than I want to be here. Steffi glared at Sawyer. The hint of his sexy smile softened the tension in her spine. He held the chairs, first for his mother and then for her. Was he pleased that she was here with him or amused by her discomfort?

"Yvette must be keeping busy." *Madame* Montaigne gestured at Sawyer's transformed face. "How is she?"

"Doing well." Sawyer's bread pierced the thick cheese crust and dipped into the fragrant soup.

"Good. I haven't seen her in months, and I miss her. Such a delight!" She clasped her hands.

Steffi frowned. Sawyer's mother used the tone some women used when they spoke of their pet poodles. "Yvette has so many talents. It's a shame she hasn't had a chance to develop them."

"Pardon?"

Steffi finished a bite of bread she had slathered with what looked like fresh creamery butter. The Montaignes must have their own dairy. Score one in their favor for that and the delectable leek soup, which melted in her mouth. "She would like to do more with her life."

Madame Montaigne tapped her spoon against the rim of her bowl. "My husband and I have never restricted her, and we have offered her opportunities to develop her talents. I find it hard to believe that she would insult us by sharing her discontent with a stranger. After all we have done for her." *Madame* Montaigne's lips became a severe line of disappointment.

Steffi's spoon clinked on the plate beneath the bowl. "Oh, no, please! Yvette did not complain to me. She is very grateful and speaks of you and your husband with the greatest respect and love." She paused before pushing on. "In fact, those feelings create a major source of conflict for her. Her devotion to you pulls her in one direction while her desire to make her own life pulls her in another."

Sawyer cleared his throat. "Steffi thinks Yvette could work in films in California."

"Ridiculous!" When *Madame* Montaigne spoke, every inch of her, from chin to backbone, stiffened. "Yvette should mate again. Managing a household and caring for a family would require all her talents."

Steffi opened her mouth to protest, but Sawyer's sharp glance made her jaw snap shut. Why continue a doomed argument? Yvette could succeed without the support of Sawyer's parents.

Steffi indicated the garden beyond the terrace doors. "What beautiful flowers! The explosion of colors reminds me of Monet's home in Giverny."

Madame Montaigne accepted the compliment with a slight dip of her chin. "My daughter Adrienne has a gift for making things grow. Perhaps you think she should be working as a gardener instead of making a home for her mate and their offspring." The older woman's scornful gaze dared Steffi to deny the charge.

"Of course not." The meal continued in uncomfortable silence, and the succulent baby vegetables dropped into Steffi's stomach like bullets. If she'd waited for Sawyer in the car, she could have lunched on a protein bar and finished the latest novel by her favorite Canadian writer.

She stole a glance at Sawyer as the conversation turned to his property in Alberta. Evidently, he'd bought the land because he hoped to manage the company's interests in western Canada, but the board had given the job to his sister Lucie and her husband. Throughout their discussion, his mother urged him to sell. His future was here in Montreal.

Sawyer deflected her appeals with that heart-stopping smile no makeup could disguise. He loved his mother—that much was clear even to an outsider—and he wanted to please his parents, but he also wanted his own life. Why couldn't they understand that?

"Steffi?"

Hearing Sawyer's deep voice, Steffi looked up into his mismatched eyes.

"Are you finished?" Sawyer indicated the maid waiting at her elbow, signaling the end of this disaster of a meal.

"Oh. Yes. *Oui*." Steffi sat back so the young woman could remove her dishes. "*Merci*," she murmured, uncertain whether one was supposed to thank the household staff.

Standing, Sawyer tapped the corner of his gray eye. "I need to fix my lenses."

He was leaving her alone with his barracuda of a mother? Oh, no!

As if reading her mind, he rested one hand on her shoulder. The touch of his fingers and the ease of his smile relaxed her muscles. "I'll only be a minute."

"We will meet you in the foyer, my son."

With one last caress of Steffi's shoulder, Sawyer disappeared.

"Come along, Miss Anbruzzen." When one of *Madame* Montaigne's cold hands seized Steffi's forearm, she fought the temptation to pull away. Sawyer's mother was merely a *loup-garou*, not an ice giant.

They marched in silence down the long hallway toward the front door. *Madame* Montaigne directed her to an anteroom adjoining the foyer. With a show of strength remarkable for her size, the older woman pulled the heavy wooden door shut.

When *Madame* Montaigne turned, Steffi caught her breath at the ferocity stretching the bones of the older woman's human features. Her *loup-garou* was struggling to come to the surface much as Sawyer's had on the plane, but unlike Sawyer, his mother wanted not to possess, but to destroy. The older woman took a deep breath, and her *loup-garou* subsided. One did not attack one's guests, especially when the guest in question arrived with one's son.

Her gaze traveled from Steffi's head to her feet, with another pause at her cleavage. "Like father, like son." She sighed and looked toward the door. "My son may fancy you, but it will not last. It never does. His destiny is with us. His family. His pack." Her gray gaze frosted Steffi. "Not with you."

As Sawyer's mother circled her, Steffi held her ground but looked down as a gesture of respect. Although she probed, her new power did not respond. Had she moved too fast with Sawyer's father? Had she drained a limited reserve?

"Do you understand?" The fingertip that pointed at her resembled a dagger.

"*Oui, madame.* But you should be having this

conversation with—"

"Silence!"

The command whipped across Steffi's face.

When *Madame* Montaigne stepped closer, a disconcerting blend of lavender and wolfish musk enveloped Steffi. "I came to Quebec when I mated, but I still have family in the UP, and we Sawyers are fierce. If you interfere in my son's future, I will summon my brothers to deal with you. Before you suffer an agonizing death, they will make you curse the day you were born." When she snarled, her sharp canines glittered before receding.

As quickly as it had appeared, the wolf receded into the elegant woman. She stepped back and folded her hands as if she'd been discussing seating arrangements for a garden party. "Do I make myself clear?"

Steffi intended to spit out a terse "Quite," but when she locked gazes with *Madame* Montaigne, the frisson of horror in her throat almost became a giggle. Sawyer's mother didn't know about Dragon Tag or the Halloween when velociraptor "costumes" caused a local panic. The Sawyer Pack might be formidable, but they were no match for the Three Anomalies. "I understand."

"Good." The smile that played at the corners of the other woman's rosy lips did not warm her gaze. She moved toward the heavy door, but Steffi put her hand on the wood.

"Your son is a good man. Trust him." Steffi opened the door.

Chapter 21

"What were you two doing in there?" Sawyer glanced at his mother and lingered on Steffi. She bore no visible wounds, but the sparkle had left her eyes.

"I thought your friend might like to see the painting of Georges at the Battle of Quebec."

Sawyer frowned. "You lent that to the museum years ago."

"So we did!" His mother gave an unconvincing trill. "As one grows older, one sometimes forgets."

Forget the star-studded celebration at the museum and the fawning media? Not likely. When Sawyer embraced his mother, her eyes remained fixed on Steffi. *Maman* seemed to be daring Steffi to contradict her. Steffi's face betrayed no emotion. Taking Steffi's arm, he drew her toward the front door.

"It was good to see you." Although *Maman* spoke in a subdued voice, she gripped Sawyer's free hand so tightly he grimaced.

"You too, *Maman*." His lips grazed her chemically enhanced cheek. Pleasantly plump to look at but not as soft as Steffi's.

"Have a safe journey, my son. Miss Anbruzzen." She dipped her chin in Steffi's direction.

"Thank you for your hospitality, *madame*."

Maman turned again to face him. "I'll send you Barbara's address so you can—"

"No. Not yet." Maybe not ever, but no need to alarm her. Steffi stood beside him with her hands clasped and her eyes lowered. A study in decorum except for that dress glued to her curves. The thought of peeling it off made his cock stiffen. They needed to get to The Snow Angel. ASAP. "We should go."

Instead of releasing him, *Maman* tightened her grip and gazed up at him. "You are a good man."

With a hard-on that was driving him crazy.

"A good son."

The surprise in her voice made him regard her more closely. Was she having health problems? "I do my best, *Maman*. I'll see you soon." The necessary lie left a sour taste in his mouth.

He didn't speak again until he and Steffi were in the car. "That didn't go too badly."

"On what planet?" If he'd been a sheet of paper, Steffi's glare would have sliced him in half.

"My mother can be a bit hard to take."

"Does she bare her claws at every woman you bring home?"

"Hard to say." His laugh died in his throat. "You're the first." *The only*.

Steffi stared out the side window as the heavy gates opened, and they zoomed past a stand of evergreens. She didn't speak again until Sawyer turned onto a public road. "Why did you throw me under the bus for suggesting Yvette might work in California?"

"Throw you under—oh, I get it."

"I could almost see steam coming out of your mother's ears."

Sawyer grinned. "Her face did turn an amazing shade of red."

"More like puce."

"If you say so. I'm sorry if I embarrassed you. That wasn't my intent."

"You knew she'd be upset."

"I thought it was likely, but since you introduced the subject, I decided to use it. *Maman* believes that Yvette doesn't know what she wants. She doesn't believe that Yvette—that anyone—can have a rewarding life outside the pack."

Steffi sat up. "You've never told your mother that?"

"More times than I care to count. Unfortunately, she easily dismisses disagreeable advice that comes from her children. You showed her how someone outside the family perceives Yvette."

Steffi rocked in her seat. "I don't think my opinion matters much. She doesn't want your cousin to leave."

"Would you? It's convenient to have an Yvette jumping every time you snap your fingers." He lifted a hand to block her objection. "Yvette knows that leaving the pack means making a clean break."

"Exile."

"Only for those who are ejected from a pack. As a rule, female mates join the male's pack. After Yvette's husband died, my parents had to get permission from the Elders of both packs to bring her back to ours."

"That would make it doubly hard for her to leave."

"Perhaps. But a *loup-garou* who chooses to leave may also feel like he's throwing off shackles." *Gaining the freedom to pursue the life he wants, not the one everyone else dictates.*

"I don't think your cousin wants to leave the pack, but no one seems willing to help her do anything aside from mate, and that's not fair." Steffi sat back. "She did what was expected of her the first time but ended up with nothing. She lives on the generosity of your family."

"True."

Steffi drew a deep breath. "You think she owes—"

"No. I don't. *Maman* and *Papa* and other pack members do see some obligation. Especially since she is still young enough to have a successful mating." He paused. "If she were older, the Elders would apply less pressure."

"So it's more than your family or your pack that pushes this mating business."

"Oh, yes. For centuries, the Guardians of the Pack have operated across the globe. Each pack has Elders, who are their local voices."

She groaned. "Medieval sexists."

"Once that was true. Now, Guardians and Elders are not exclusively male. Their primary mission remains the same: to help *loups-garous* thrive in a hostile world."

"Don't forget preserving the bloodlines."

"That is a pack concern."

"Doesn't it bother you?" She turned in her seat and sat closer.

He leaned toward her. "That new perfume packs a punch."

"Are you trying to distract me?"

He drew a deep breath. "You're the one with the sexy perfume."

She sat back. "For most of us—Simple Humans and even many Shifters—falling in love, mating, marrying—whatever you want to call it—it's a private matter. But you *loups-garous* have family members and Elders staring over your shoulder from the day you're born and pointing you in the direction they want you to take."

He laughed.

"What's so funny?"

"We're not the only ones, Steffi. Centuries ago and even today, some Simple Human cultures have arranged marriages. In the States, you still have to cope with expectations from parents, family, clan, teachers, Elders—you name it. Not even you and your sisters are immune. What would happen if you brought home someone your parents didn't like?"

"I don't…I can't imagine my parents—no, that's not true. When I was in high school, I had a thing for this boy. Mickey Moorman."

"The kid who ended up in the ER when he got fresh?"

Her eyebrows lifted. "That's the one. He was tall, thin, brooding. I thought he looked like the hero in the vampire series I liked."

Sawyer frowned and drew near the bumper of a sleek gray sedan "What is it about teen-aged girls and vampires?" He settled them comfortably in the faster car's wake. "A couple of my sisters thought they were hot until *Papa* introduced them to some real bloodsuckers. Fangs and blood." He chuckled. "Grossed them out."

"Ugh." Steffi wrinkled her nose. "I'm glad my folks aren't that dramatic. Anyway, Mickey didn't look that much like my vampire hero, but in the right light, the resemblance was close enough."

"You can skip the details." Sawyer's low growl punctuated the remark.

Jealous maybe? Over poor Mickey Moorman. Steffi looked out the side window so he wouldn't see her smile. "When we started dating, I was thrilled. Mom and Dad, not as much. Even so, they went out of their way to be nice…more than nice…*gracious*. No matter how much they disliked Mickey, they did their best not to show it." She paused. "Like your mother."

Sawyer frowned. "My mother doesn't *hate* you, Steffi. She wasn't ready. You're the first girl—woman—female—I've ever brought home."

"A professor who looks like she earned her degree from Hookers R Us."

"Don't be silly." He gripped the wheel as if he could throttle it. "You're in costume." He touched his padded ribs with one hand. "Like me, eh?"

"Not at all. I feel as if I should have a neon sign on my collarbone that says, 'LOOK' with an arrow flashing at my breasts." She crossed her arms in a futile attempt to cover her bosom.

"The more attention you attract, the less people will look at me. They won't be able to take their eyes off you. I know I can't."

When his warm hand settled on her knee, sparks of longing zipped up her spine. "Sawyer! Please don't do that while you're driving." She made no effort to push him away.

"Sorry." He didn't sound sorry at all. Not for a second. With one final pat, he withdrew.

"I'm glad your mother was so busy fussing over you that she barely noticed me."

"Oh, she noticed. We all know about you and your sisters, and I'm sure *Maman* sensed your power."

"I doubt that." She extended her hands with her fingers pointed toward the windshield.

"No lightning bolts in the car, please. It's a rental."

"Don't worry." Her hands dropped to her lap. "I

couldn't if I tried. Earlier, I tried to summon a bit of what I felt last night—to feel the comfort—but nothing happened. Nothing." Thinking about the failure summoned that empty ache from Sheboygan.

"Relax. You'll be all right."

"Have your other clients had this experience?"

"Not that I recall, but every case is—"

"Yeah, yeah, individual." She uttered the word as if it were obscene. "I think that's your way of saying you don't really know what's going on." When he winced, she felt a twinge for giving him such a hard time. He was doing the best he could, and she wasn't an easy client.

"I don't think you should worry."

"That's easy for you to say. Last night you had the same ability you have today, but I had a new power. Today, I've got nothing." She bounced in her seat as her frustration mounted. "What if I've lost everything again? What if it keeps coming and going? I can't spend my life playing peekaboo with my ability. One minute I could be flying high, and the next, dropping out of the sky like a stone." She demonstrated with a sweeping arm.

"That shouldn't happen. Relax and stay in touch with your emotions. Full healing takes time."

"All right." She tried to focus on her breathing but shredded the tissue in her hands.

"Last night, when this new power emerged, you were responding to a threat, eh?"

Her hands dropped to her lap. "It wasn't really a threat. I mean, I knew your father wasn't—that is, I didn't think he would throw me on the table or tie me to railroad tracks or do anything like that."

"He touched you."

She shuddered.

"My mother, on the other hand, posed no threat."

She bit her lower lip. "She thinks I have designs on you."

Sawyer shot her a wicked grin that sent her pulse racing. "Don't you?"

"The more I learn about your family, the more I think—"

He held up a big hand. "Stop thinking so damn much. That's part of what got you into this mess to begin with. The second you get near your feelings, you back off."

She straightened her spine and lifted her chin. "You don't have to snap at me."

"Sorry. I'm tired of talking about my family." He cleared his throat. "If I promise not to play anything too loud, will you go back to that Snow Angel folder and let me know what we're looking at?" He found some classic rock. "How's that?"

"Better." She retrieved the folder. By the time she finished reading, they were whizzing down the main expressway. "The place looks beautiful."

"I'm sure." Sawyer gestured at the glossy prints in her lap. "No one selling property shows the plumbing leaks or the peeling wallpaper. Those pictures have been edited to make everything flawless."

Steffi read the promotional copy, "*Your cozy getaway in the shadow of Mont Tremblant.*"

"Cozy, eh?" Sawyer laughed. "Must be tiny."

"So Mr. and Mrs. Sawyer could be in for a tight squeeze."

"Tempting."

She giggled at his exaggerated leer.

"We have the honeymoon suite. It's not a good sign

that we were able to book it on such short notice. Business must be slow."

"That's good for Montaigne Enterprises, right?"

"We may be able to get it for a good price, especially if we make our offer before it goes on the market or anyone else knows about our interest. How's the title?"

Steffi shuffled the papers. "Mortgage paid off. No liens."

"Anything else?"

"A short but rather intriguing history."

"Intriguing, eh? Like spies on skis with nuclear launch codes?"

"Hardly. The main lodge dates back to the 1970s and this family from the States, somewhere in Maryland."

"Immigrants."

Steffi nodded. "The oldest son came to Canada during Vietnam, to evade the draft. When his parents visited, they liked it so much that the whole family emigrated. They started out farming but eventually bought the land and built the resort."

"*Loups-garous?*"

"Simple Humans. No Shifter connections."

"Still in the family?"

"Yes, but no one wants to take it over. They sound like nice people. I hope your father won't drive too hard a bargain."

"That's like hoping the sun won't rise in the East or set in the West. My father likes to win."

And you don't? Steffi shot a glance at the man beside her.

"Anything else?"

She summarized the information on rooms, services,

and activities. When she finished, she turned to Sawyer. "We should pull our story together before we arrive."

Chapter 22

"That's simple. We're newlyweds. Me and my trophy wife." He sounded altogether too pleased with himself.

Steffi eyed him with exasperation. "That's not what you call me. That's what others say behind your back to make fun of you. A middle-aged codger—"

"—with a hot babe warming my bed."

Steffi sat back and folded her arms. "Get serious. We should have some history, in case people ask." She paused. "Mr. Sawyer has obviously done well. You have enough money to consider buying The Snow Angel."

"No, no, no. We're not here on business. We're honeymooners." Sawyer gave her an exaggerated grin.

"Look at me like that, and they'll think you're having a stroke."

"How should I look at you? As if I can't wait to get you upstairs in bed?"

Although laughter lurked beneath the question, she approached it seriously. "Something like that, but I think we're both experienced."

"Really?"

"You're older, and I'm no teenager. We've been around. Maybe you've been married before, or maybe I'm the latest in a long line—"

"No. I'm a widower. No children. Wife #1 died five or six years ago."

"What was her name?"

"I don't know." He kept his eyes on the road. "She was about my age."

Steffi thought for a minute. "My aunt Debra turned sixty last year."

"Debra." Sawyer nodded. "That will work."

"So, you and Debra met in college, fell in love—"

"I'm not so sure about that. Maybe our families were friends. We did what was expected. She was a good person. A good wife. Not the prettiest girl in the room, but she always looked right. Good at entertaining. Everyone enjoyed her parties and dinners. Smart. Cultured. Good housekeeper."

"Must have been hard living with all that perfection."

"I wouldn't go that far. We had a good life together, but there was always something missing."

Steffi's eyes narrowed. "That's what you told yourself when you cheated?"

"Don't look at me like that, Steffi. We're telling a story. I didn't do it often, and I tried to make it up to her."

"How thoughtful. Dear, dead Debra." She didn't soften her sarcasm. "How did she die? Boredom?"

"Cancer. She was a fighter until the end."

"You didn't know how much she meant to you until she was gone."

"Oh, no. I knew well before that. I never loved her the way you're supposed to, but I always appreciated her."

"Okay, Wife #1 has been gone for four or five years. You'll need to decide on the year. When did we meet?"

"Not until after Debra—"

"Good. I didn't want you cheating with me while

232

she was dying."

"Give me a break." He shot her an agitated glance. "I'm not a bad guy. Just...human. Simple Human."

"Don't look so worried. Like you said, none of this is real. Let's say we got together three years after she died. How did we meet?"

"I would have been dating a lot. I had time and money to spare."

"Total babe magnet."

"I don't know if I'd put it that way, but yeah, the ladies liked me, and I liked them."

"Story of your life, eh?"

"I suppose. But there was always something missing." His voice deepened.

"Until you met me."

"Yes." Sawyer didn't speak for a moment. "Then everything changed." He cleared his throat. "What's your story, Mrs. Sawyer?"

Steffi sat back in her seat. "After high school, I went to California. Wanted to be an actress. I got a couple small jobs, did a little modeling, got involved with a few men who only wanted sex. I was in a big downward spiral, but before I hit bottom, I got out. I'd made such a mess of my life I didn't want to go home, so I worked my way across the country. Waiting tables. Working in convenience stores. Temping. The sort of thing I'd been doing in California between acting jobs. Maybe I worked for you."

"I'd have noticed someone like you."

"I could have been a temp. What if your assistant took maternity leave?"

"Then it would make medical history since my assistant's name is Simon."

"Not your real assistant!" Steffi swatted his arm.

Sawyer laughed. "Sorry. I couldn't resist." He drove without speaking for a moment. "So, you're sitting at the desk right in front of my office. I walk in one morning and sweep you off your feet."

Steffi shook her head. "I don't think I was that much of a pushover. I'd already run into a lot of romantic dead ends."

"But you were tired of bouncing around, and let's face it, I was a great catch."

"I don't know…"

"Okay, you held out until you sealed the deal with the ring." He pointed at the flashy diamond.

"You married me for the sex."

"You married me for the money."

"Sounds like Mr. and Mrs. Sawyer are heading from the honeymoon suite to divorce court." Steffi nibbled on her lower lip. She'd repair her lipstick before they entered the resort. "I wish we could come up with something better than sex and money."

"If you think of anything, let me know."

"You're—what's your first name, by the way?"

"Whatever it says on the reservation."

Steffi fished a paper from the folder. "Thomas." She stared at Sawyer. "You've got to be kidding. Tom Sawyer?"

"To my friends and, of course, my dear wife."

Steffi checked the reservation and screeched. "Abigail! Abigail Sawyer. Sounds like an ugly little farm girl in the middle of the eighteenth century. Abigail." She waved the reservation. "What were you thinking?"

"I used a list of names. Closed my eyes and pointed a pen. If I'd known it was going to matter so much to you, I'd have asked your preferences. What name would you like?"

"I don't know."

"See. It's not important. You can be Abigail Sawyer for a few days."

Steffi shook her head. "Abigail doesn't sound right for a trophy wife."

Sawyer drove for a few minutes without speaking. "The name might be part of the reason you are a trophy wife."

"What do you mean?"

"You hate your name. Perhaps it's for someone in your family you didn't know or never liked."

"Aunt Abigail, whose husband left her a ton of money?"

"Yes! Your parents gave you the name because they thought that would make the aunt more generous."

"But it didn't. She left everything to her dogs, and I got stuck with the name."

"So you had to grow up with this name you hated."

"And without much money."

Sawyer nodded. "You've been insecure about everything."

"Including my appearance." Steffi looked out the side window as she spoke. "Eyes too far apart. Long nose. Square chin. Big mouth."

After a silence, Sawyer spoke. "And then you met Tom Sawyer."

"Tom Sawyer!" Steffi burst out laughing.

Sawyer left the highway at the next interchange and pulled onto the shoulder, where he shut off the engine and set the brake. "I love it when you laugh. I love it even more when I make you laugh." He wrapped his arms around her.

His mouth found hers, and although the fake beard tickled her chin, the kiss made every centimeter of her skin quiver as if caught in a private earthquake. All her hesitations and misgivings dissolved in the heat that connected her with Sawyer.

The contours of his lips fitted against hers like one piece of a sensuous puzzle falling into place. His tongue entered her mouth and toyed with hers before she slipped into his mouth to caress the back of each tooth.

When his hands skimmed her neck to stroke the skin at the edge of the keyhole neckline, she deepened the kiss. With her hands on his lapels, she drew him closer, closer, as close as he could possibly be with that stupid floor shift between them. Her fingers pushed the rough tweed of his jacket aside so her hands could move across his chest. Even through the padding, the steady pounding of his heart provided a counterpoint to her own racing pulse.

When they finally separated, they each drew a long breath. She stared into the unfamiliar blue eyes. As soon as they reached the honeymoon suite, he had to dump those damned contacts so she could see his soft gray gaze. One of his fingers traced the outline of her lips and sent tremors of longing down the back of her throat. "I like kissing you." His deep voice was husky with passion.

"Me, too. I like kissing you." With a smile, she sucked the finger that rested on her lower lip into her mouth and held it lightly between her teeth as her tongue rasped against his skin.

He nibbled on the part of her earlobe that held no earring. "And you said you didn't know anything about seduction. Ha!" His breath tickled her ear before he made a trail of tiny kisses along her jaw to her chin. She released his finger to welcome his generous mouth.

Unlike the first kiss, which had the pulse-pounding intensity of a roller coaster ride, this one was as slow and sensuous as a tango. Like the one he'd dance at that damned cotillion. With. His. Mate. When the image flared in her brain, anger, disappointment, and sorrow swirled within her until the hungry fire at her core consumed them.

She drew back to find the rugged planes of Sawyer's handsome face beneath the clever disguise. *He's mine now. That's all that matters.*

Sawyer cupped her chin. "If we want to be convincing as honeymooners, we should practice, eh?"

Steffi threw her arms around his neck. *Mine now.* "By all means."

He traced the curve of her upper lip. "By the way, your mouth isn't too big. It's like the rest of you. Perfect." His lips locked with hers.

Chapter 23

The mountains behind the rustic-looking inn blazed with the orange and red of the setting sun. "Look!" Steffi sat up as if she'd never seen a sunset before. Watching her, Sawyer grinned. With lightly mussed hair and blooming mouth, she shone like a beacon. Some lucky bastard would see that glorious smile every day for the rest of his life. Sawyer's heartbeat slowed.

Steffi glanced at him. "What's wrong?"

He pulled into the reception area to park. "I'm sorry we ran out of exits." After that first stop, they'd left the AutoRoute at every opportunity for additional "practice." His index finger stroked the elegant line of her cheekbone. "But I'm definitely looking forward to the honeymoon suite."

In reply, she gripped the collar of his shirt and kissed him soundly.

"Mrs. Sawyer!" Sawyer regarded her in mock shock. "Control yourself."

Gold and green mischief flickered in her eyes. "Isn't that what you've been telling me not to do?"

"*Touché*." He caught her earlobe between his lips.

"Mr. Sawyer!" She giggled. "Your beard tickles."

He did his best to look wounded as he dropped a light kiss on her smooth cheek and inhaled her sexy perfume mingled with a musky passion. "Let's check in and get settled."

She lowered the visor mirror. "I have to fix my face."

With the intensity she must have brought to her scholarly observations, she applied a fresh crimson slash to her mouth and a dab of shadow to the hollows beneath her cheekbones. Perhaps required for Abigail Sawyer but totally unnecessary for Steffi Anbruzzen.

He'd met his share of attractive Simple Human women as well as *loups-garous*. Lord knew *Maman*, in particular, hurled potential mates with the speed of a professional baseball pitcher. Thus far, none had merited a swing.

But with Steffi, everything felt different. When she stepped in front of him with an easy sway of her beautiful hips, pleasure tickled his groin. He enjoyed watching her move, listening to her speak, and feeling her mouth on his. What would she be like as a *loup-garou*? As obstinate as her human base, no doubt, and even more ferocious. Too bad she would never find satisfaction in being only a *loup-garou*.

"Tom, dear," Steffi spoke as she slipped her hand through the curve of his arm, where it fitted as if it belonged, "what's bothering you?"

When they entered the lodge with its overabundance of colonial decorations and furniture, Sawyer gripped his suspenders and moved into his character. "Thinking about the business, honeybun."

"I hope you don't plan to call me that for the whole visit. It makes 'Abigail' sound good."

He kissed her cheek. "Point taken."

"Try not to look so serious." She brushed back a few strands of chopped-off hair that had fallen across his forehead. "This is our honeymoon, remember?" A nip at his earlobe made him laugh.

"Who could forget?" Sliding an arm around her slender waist, he drew her close.

The second they reached the honeymoon suite, Steffi broke away and hurled herself into the nearest armchair, an uncomfortable-looking quilted lump. *Cheap colonial.*

"Did you have to lay it on that thick?"

Sawyer stared at the scowling woman. What had become of his soft, smiling partner? He'd kissed and caressed her throughout the check-in, and he'd been looking forward to touching her a lot more now that they were alone. The erection that had almost been shifting the gears for the past fifty miles started to wane. "Pardon?"

"You were all over me." She kicked off her shoes and massaged her toes.

"I thought…we agreed that an older man…and his *potiche*… I'm supposed to be solicitous."

"Solicitous, yes. Obsessed, no."

"I wanted to make a memorable first impression. Sorry if I overdid it." He smiled at her. "First time I've ever been on a honeymoon."

"No, it's not." Steffi lifted a finger. "Don't forget Wife #1."

"Right. What was her name?"

"Debra."

"Ah, yes. Dear, dead Debra, who ruined me for all other women." His teasing tone vanished as he caressed her cheek. "Until I met amorous Abigail."

She flushed a becoming pink. "You looked at me as if you wanted to undress me right there in the lobby." One of her hands covered her keyhole neckline and blocked the enticing swell of her breasts.

When his imagination took charge, his flagging arousal returned to full alert. "Might have been fun."

"Not with all those people watching." The smile that played at the edges of her mouth belied her serious tone.

He stuck his thumbs in the handy suspenders. "Every man in the lobby was checking you out. I think you kind of liked it."

"It was flattering." When she stood and stretched, her dress clung to every curve. "My sisters have always attracted attention. I've stayed in the background."

"For the next few days, you're the star attraction." He circled the large sitting room and tried to avoid the small occasional tables. One held a bottle of champagne in an ice bucket and two glasses. He read the accompanying note. *With best wishes for a happy life together*. Nice welcome." When he took Steffi's hand, she didn't pull back. "Let's see what else we have here."

A crimson-covered, heart-shaped bed filled most of the bedroom. Steffi craned her neck and looked at the huge mirror mounted on the ceiling above the bed. She flipped one nearby switch. "Oh my God! It lights up."

They both laughed.

A second control made the bed rotate. "We'd better go easy on the champagne, or we'll get sick."

"At least it's not a waterbed." Sawyer pulled out a drawer in the nightstand. "No meds for motion sickness, but enough condoms to fuel an orgy."

Steffi's gaze traveled back to the mirror. "I bet there's a camera." She put her hands on her hips. "No videos."

He saluted. "No videos." At least they were back on track to do something worth recording. "Could use some redecorating." He made a note on his phone.

Steffi gestured at the bed. "Starting here."

Sawyer followed her into the sitting room. "Are you hungry?"

"Starving." Steffi tugged at her waist. "But it's almost impossible to eat in this dress."

"Why don't you slip into something more comfortable?" He read from one of the cards on the desk near the window. "Then we can *feast in the down-home dining hall.*"

"Are you kidding?" One corner of her mouth drooped. "I can't show my face in that lobby until we leave."

"If we're going to check this place out, you can't hide." Better not mention that the men wouldn't be ogling her face. "Remember you're playing a part. The beautiful wife of a rich, old fool."

She rested a hand on his chest. "My rich, old fool."

He grinned. "That sounds about right."

She stared at him for a minute but then turned away to rummage through the material on the desk. "Don't they have room service?"

"Here." Sawyer extended a page of stiff paper included in the menu.

Steffi examined the selections as if she were planning a mission to Mars. "Looks like basic meat and potatoes, with a little seafood thrown in. On the positive side, everything is local. It might be good for us as well as taste good."

"We can have champagne while we wait for our order." His arms encircled her waist and drew her close. "Honeymooners, remember?" When he rested his chin against her temple, he thought she might bolt, but her back softened into his torso, and her round rump nestled against his groin. His cock returned to full alert. The rosemary perfume of her hair stole into his nostrils as his lips grazed the inviting curve of her neck. A tremor moved through her frame.

When Steffi turned to the terrace window, he followed her. Beyond the trees rose the rounded peaks of the Laurentians.

"Good view."

"Great view," she corrected.

He took her hands. "I'd rather look at you."

"Sawyer—"

Still grasping her hands, he drew back. "Please don't tell me you've been thinking."

She laughed. "I have, but that's not what I was going to say."

"Good. Because something bad always follows."

"Not always."

"Often enough."

She freed a hand and moved it to her cheek. "I want to take off this…face…before we…"

His lips brushed her forehead. "Whatever makes you comfortable." He pulled back to regard her. "Can you re-create it?"

"I think so. I have notes from Marie-Louise. Yvette did everything she did, but more dramatic."

"Maybe you could use a different color here?" His thumb caressed her lower lip. "That pretty pink?"

"Yvette would say pink's too mousy for a *potiche*."

"Not for my *potiche*." He dropped a kiss on the tip of her straight nose. "While we're waiting for our meal, you can try out that fancy tub."

"Sounds great. Care to join me?"

"I'd love to." He envisioned them kissing their way toward the bedroom and discarding garments with every step. *Not so fast.* "But we'd never make it to the tub. I should report in to my father, and you can put Abigail away for the evening. Stretch out in the bubbles with another glass of champagne and relax."

While the water ran, he organized his notes. Fussy décor. Great views. Good location. Not too far from the slopes but not so close that the inn was likely to be buried beneath an avalanche. Friendly staff, a few with ties to the original owners. Solid construction, although the roof would need replacing in another five years. He'd have to invent a reason to examine the heating and plumbing. Few guests, perhaps because it was the off-season and they did little advertising. Montaigne Marketing would change that. He hoped they could expand the guest list without ruining the quiet intimacy.

He peeled back the red cover of the bed, smelled fresh air in the sheets, and tested the mattress. He liked firm, but Steffi might prefer something softer, more like her skin. A mattress with variable settings in the honeymoon suite might help couples get off to a better start. The condoms earned a plus for quantity, but a double minus for the tiny red hearts that adorned them.

An unexpected sound interrupted his concentration. From the bathroom, a smoky alto voiced a medley of old movie tunes. Sending his text, he put his phone aside. In the cheerful music, Steffi's joy was almost palpable. As soon as it emerged, however, the emotion vanished, like water slipping through his fingers.

By the time they finished here, Steffi's recovery would be complete. She would be ready to leave. She could take a plane from Ottawa. She might prefer to rent a car and drive back to Chicago. What the hell. Once she started shifting, she could pack her clothes and send them ahead so they'd be waiting in her apartment. Then, she'd spread her wings and fly.

Sawyer frowned. When Steffi disappeared, his life would go on, but his world would never be the same.

"Sawyer! Can you please bring me a towel?"

She was sitting with her back to him in the steam-filled washroom. He captured her wrist and kissed her damp palm. Lured by her softness and her scent, he drew the underside of her forearm to his lips and nibbled on the inner elbow.

"Sawyer." She turned and stroked his nape, where every hair stood at attention for her.

Her movement made it easier for his mouth to explore the curve of her neck.

"Your beard is scratchy."

"Sorry." The stupid beard itched, too. "I should take it off."

She drew back. "Can you do that?"

"Yvette gave me instructions. She said I should keep it on as long as I could because taking it off and cementing it back on will be rough on my skin."

"Wouldn't want that." Steffi toyed with the hairs on his nape. "Too bad you can't 'shave' it off because your new wife asked you to." She tickled his upper lip. "You could keep the mustache." She slid down until bubbles covered her shoulders. "The water's great, and there's plenty of room."

"My mustache is wilting from the humidity."

Her gaze traveled from his upper lip to his crotch. "No wilting there."

"Never when you're around." Someone knocked on

their door. "That must be our supper." He set her towel on the edge of the tub. "Don't take too long." He ached to kiss her, but if he did, he'd likely end up in the tub with her, and his disguise would go down the drain.

Chapter 24

Sawyer pushed his empty plate to the center of the small table and played with his suspenders. "Damn fine meal."

Steffi lifted an eyebrow at his exaggerated Midwestern accent. "Is that what you think I sound like?"

"Good God, no, but I've spent time at the OASIS offices in Minnesota. I thought I did a good job…a humdinger, if I do say—" He broke off as Steffi covered her ears with her hands. "All right, all right."

"If you start talking like that now, everyone on the staff will know we're phonies. If you were going to use an accent, you should have practiced before we got here."

"We had more interesting things to practice." The seductive rumble of his voice enthralled her.

She looked down at the table as her cheeks heated. "Be yourself, Sawyer. At least when we're not in public."

Sawyer lifted his glass. "Here's to being ourselves."

"I'll drink to that." The lip of her glass chimed against his. She took a sip. "Not as good as your cousin's champagne, I'm sure. But not bad."

"Better than I expected." Sawyer took a second taste.

"I liked the food, too."

Sawyer stood and patted his padded belly. "Mine was excellent. I don't know where they got him or what it will cost to keep him, but they have a first-class chef."

Steffi shot him a sharp glance. "It might be a woman, you know."

"Ouch!" He paused while making another note on his phone. "Fair enough." Returning to his message, he walked until he stood behind her.

Steffi drained her wineglass. "So, meals go in the plus column."

"At the—I was going say, 'At the top.'" His fingers resting against her neck sent happy pulses down her spine. "But that's where you are." When he stroked the shoulder of the short satin robe, she wanted to purr.

He pulled his hand away. "*Zut alors*! Steffi, are you shifting?"

"I might—I *was* feeling like a happy lion." Excitement hummed in her veins. *I'm ready!*

"I felt fur—"

She rubbed her neck. Nothing but skin. "It's gone."

"Do you want to shift before we go any further?"

After all those practice sessions kissing and cuddling, another delay? "No." Steffi stood. "I can keep everything under control."

"No." Sawyer rested his hands on her shoulders and fixed his blue gaze on her. "I'm not one of your Simple Human lovers. You have nothing to hide. I don't want you thinking about anything except...hell, I don't want you thinking at all. I want you to be with me."

Her pelvic muscles did an elated shimmy. "That will be a lot easier if you take out those contact lenses so I can see your real eyes."

He saluted her with a kiss. "Your wish is my

command."

When he started toward the bedroom, she gripped some of his padded chest. "Wait." Within her, twin desires warred. "I think you're right. While you're taking care of your eyes, I'm going to stay out here and try a shift. After all this time, I can't resist the urge."

"I'd probably feel the same. Take your time and enjoy your shift. If you need me, call." Sawyer closed the bedroom door.

In the silence of the sitting room, Steffi slipped off her robe, unhooked the barely there bra, and stepped out of the satin panties. Good grief, the crotch was already damp. Closing her eyes, she surrendered to the emotions Sawyer's touch had triggered: contentment, yes, but also hunger. As she visualized her lioness, her bones and muscles began to pull and turn as if awakening from a long sleep. She sniffed with a sense of smell keener than any human's. This was the strength she should have felt in Sheboygan. She shook as if she could throw off the memory and reveled in the fullness of her lioness.

Padding about the room, she paused to bury her nose in Tom Sawyer's boxy jacket. Beneath the sandalwood of the cologne, her Sawyer's masculine aroma invaded her head. An unexpected noise made her stiffen. She bared her fangs. On a field, she could flee. Here, she would fight.

But it was only tapping on the other side of the closed door. *Sawyer!*

She lifted her head and opened her mouth. The sound rolled through her body like a soothing hand.

The door cracked, but Sawyer didn't appear. "You've a beauty of a roar, *chérie*, but let's not frighten our neighbors." He laughed. "I suppose we could say we've been watching nature films. Or that you bring out the beast in me."

She padded toward his amused voice and nudged the door open. Sawyer stepped back. His thoughtful gaze studied her. "You are superb."

And he was a sexy devil. He'd peeled off his beard but kept the mustache. He smelled like baby oil. He'd also doffed his shirt and his silly padding. Mom would have called him "a long drink of water," one Steffi was thirsting to taste. Her blood bubbled as she appreciated his muscular shoulders. Silver speckled the arrow of dark fur that spread across his chest and narrowed as it moved down well-defined abs to his navel. She gave a happy growl, but Sawyer's expression remained solemn. She wanted to knock him over, drag her tongue across his beautiful torso, and caress his taut belly with her paws.

When she flexed her paws, her claws slipped out. Long, sharp claws designed to draw blood. That would definitely destroy the mood. *Blood.* Her tongue flicked out. Good thing she'd eaten before the shift. Not that she would ever attack Sawyer. Even if she didn't have human feelings for him, he didn't have enough fat to be tasty.

When he looked at her, she sat on her haunches and did her best to appear docile. *It's me, Sawyer. A new shape but still Steffi.*

He winked at her. "Enjoy your lioness. When you return to base, I'll be here."

He closed the door, and she uttered a low growl. Round doorknobs. Scratching the thick wood would damage her claws. She extended and retracted them several times. Every time, satisfaction rushed through her. Real claws, not kitten claws.

She prowled the room. Her lioness felt like a comfortable glove she hadn't worn in a long time. She hated to take it off but rejoiced in the knowledge that she could return to this shape whenever she wished. She was healed. She was whole.

More important, on the other side of that door, Sawyer was waiting for her human. Her heartbeat quickened. Rising like a whirlwind, her desire to join him swept away all other thoughts or sensations.

Moments later, she opened the door. "Hey there."

Sawyer lay on his back in the big red bed with his arms beneath his head. Her gaze roamed across the sculpted planes of his chest. He rolled onto his side and got to his feet. "Welcome back."

She waited for him to approach, but he stayed by the bed.

"How are you feeling?"

"Great!" Although she flung out her arms to embrace the world, a twinge on her left side made her drop that arm to her side. "Complete."

"How's your shoulder?"

She rolled it slowly. "A little stiff but otherwise okay."

"Good."

He didn't sound excited, and he barely smiled. He wouldn't be as thrilled as she was. He'd seen so many clients regain their ability that her recovery was no big deal. But wasn't she more than a client? Had something changed because of her shift?

He stood by the bed and regarded her through narrowed eyes. Did he want her to come to him? All right. When she stepped forward, he moved back. A muscle in his cheek twitched, and his shoulders stiffened.

Her heart threatened to snap in half. She checked to be certain she had returned to her human. "Are you afraid of me?"

His hesitation revealed the answer.

"I would never hurt you."

"I know that you wouldn't. But your lioness…"

She rested her hands on her hips. "My lioness is me, and your *loup-garou* is you. You would never hurt me, and I will never hurt you, no matter what shape I take."

His lips curved in a wistful smile. "I know you believe that. I want to believe it, but there's a hunger in your eyes."

"Oh! That." She threw back her head and laughed. "I am hungry." Her eyes made another appreciative tour of his upper body. The lava in her blood pooled in her belly. "But not for food."

He grinned. "That's a relief."

In two long strides, he was with her. Floating in his gray gaze, she gripped his nape and dipped his head so she could kiss his eyes. "So much better without those contacts."

His lips quirked in a smile. "If I'd known you were going to do that, I'd have taken them out as soon as we got here. Look all you like, wherever you like." He wrapped his arms around her and nuzzled her neck, each kiss igniting tiny fireworks beneath her skin.

She lifted her mouth so her whisper would graze his ear. "Dance with me. The way you danced at that club with her." She ground her hips against his.

Instead of following her lead, Sawyer rested his hands on her shoulders. Sweat beaded his forehead. "I don't think so. Not unless you want me to throw you on the bed and fuck you until you can barely walk." He drew a ragged breath. "That's not—is that what you want?"

"No. I was only…you seemed to like it."

"The key word there is *seemed*."

"You were excited."

His eyes widened in exaggerated shock. "Were you checking me out?"

"It was hard to miss." She paused. "Pun intended."

He laughed. "I'm a man. As I've told you before, it doesn't take much." He brushed the hair back from her forehead, and his cheek warmed her temple. "What do you want, Steffi?"

She pulled back and let her gaze range across his strong features. "You." She kissed the dip between his collarbones. "I want to feel your skin against mine." She kissed his fingers. "I want you to touch me." Her lips brushed his. "Taste me."

He cleared his throat. "You're ignoring a key part of my anatomy."

She gave a throaty giggle. "Saving the best for last. I want to touch you…taste you…and—"

One hand traveled slowly down his solid chest to his belt. He groaned. "Let's slow down so we can enjoy it all, eh?"

Chapter 25

Her enticing laugh magnified the tension in Sawyer's groin. He pulled her to him for a long, deep kiss that made desire wrap more tightly around his erection. Although she claimed she wanted skin to skin, her satin robe slipped against his chest in a silent tease.

He smoothed fabric over the pleasing roundness of her bum but caught his breath at the hum in her throat, halfway between a purr and a growl. Her stately lioness was bigger than his wolf. If they ever hunted together when game was scarce, she could eat him. Not that she would, of course. No matter what shape she assumed, she would always be Steffi, and Steffi would never—

"Sawyer."

When she nipped his ear, he snapped, "What?"

Her dark, human gaze scanned his face. "Is something wrong?"

"Sorry, *chérie*." He smiled and kissed her frown. "I'm still…adjusting. I'm not used to being the weaker partner."

"Don't be silly." Her fingers traveled across his shoulders in a massage that both soothed and stimulated. "When we're human, you will always be taller and stronger than I am."

He grunted. "Good."

Her feathery kisses caressing his chest made his breath flow faster, freer. With one hand, he cradled the

254

back of her head and lifted her mouth to his while his other hand freed her shoulder from the robe. Her skin was softer and smoother than the fabric, and her breasts crushed against him. His free hand slipped beneath the bottom of her short robe, where it encountered not silk or lace but glorious flesh. "You're not wearing any underwear."

Laughter danced in her eyes and her voice. "I had to strip to shift, and when I returned to base, I knew you were waiting, so I threw on my robe and left the lacy stuff on the sofa. Sorry to disappoint you."

When one of her buttocks settled in his palm, he grinned. "Surprise me, yes. Disappoint me? Never." He kissed her. "I can't tell you how good it feels to be here with you."

Her hands slid down his chest to play with his belt. "Maybe you could show me."

His pulse lurching into overdrive, he scooped her up in his arms, and she gasped his name. He mentally blessed the many hours he'd spent at the weight bench. "Hold on, and don't wiggle." She snuggled into a delectable package, her long legs dangling from his arms.

When he lay her on the bed, her hair spilled behind her in a dark cloud, and her scent flooded his senses. He'd been with more beautiful women, more voluptuous women, but he'd never wanted any of them as much as he desired Steffi. He reached to undo the tie of the robe, but she caught his hand.

"I'm down to one layer." She slipped a finger inside his waistband. "You still have two." When she probed enough to fondle him, he thought he might jump out of his skin along with his pants.

He covered her hand. "Keep doing that, and I won't have anything."

She stretched. "Don't forget the condoms."

"You're not using anything?"

"No drugs, remember? I had an IUD once but didn't realize that shifting could relocate the device. Damn near killed me when I had to pee."

Sawyer grimaced.

"I bet I set a record for returning to my human. I do have a diaphragm, but it's in my bag. If you want, I'll find it, unpack it, lube it—" She started to sit up.

Sawyer rested a hand on her shoulder. "Stay right where you are." Wet with essence of Steffi, not spermicide. He pulled a handful of condoms from the drawer. "We can avail ourselves of yet another honeymoon suite service."

Steffi glanced over his shoulder at the packets that filled the tabletop. "Can you do it that often?"

He grinned. "Hope springs eternal." He fitted his mouth to hers in what began as a soft, sweet kiss. Then his tongue deepened, and his mouth pressed more intensely against Steffi's. When Steffi initiated her own probing, every thrust seemed to stroke his erection.

They paused to breathe. Steffi pushed herself up on her elbow. "I'd be happy to help you take off your pants." When he unzipped and stepped out of his trousers, her jaw dropped. "Wow!" Her next comment punctured his sudden rush of pride. She fingered the edge of his boxer shorts. "Silk?"

"Yes."

"They're beautiful. I love the peacock color and that abstract print." She lay back. "I would have pegged Tom Sawyer for practical white-cotton briefs."

"That's what Yvette thinks I'm wearing, but I'd like to think Tom has a more sensuous side. After all, I—he—married you."

"The shorts are good to look at, but you're pretty impressive, too."

"Glad you finally noticed. If I'd known you'd spend so much time admiring my underwear, I would have used the white cotton."

"Oh, no!" Her fingers inched toward him.

When she lifted her face, he wrapped his arms around her, and his mouth found hers in an explosive kiss that rattled him to his core. *Mon dieu*, she was holding him as if she were playing an instrument. It took every ounce of control not to indulge his *loup-garou* instincts. He wanted to make this a night she'd remember for all the right reasons. He knew he'd never forget it.

Fortunately, her robe opened easily. As his hand caressed the stiff tip of one nipple, a whimper bubbled from her lips.

"You have beautiful breasts."

She sniffed. "I bet you say that to all the girls."

He met her teasing gaze with a smile. "I guess I do. Did." Steffi would be the last. His eyes moved down as his fingers worshipped her glorious curves. "Breasts are beautiful." *Especially yours*. The tip stiffened beneath his tongue. His other hand glided down her side. "I like this sweet curve at your waist." He paid tribute with a kiss. "Your round hips." His lips grazed the taut skin as his hand slid around to cup her buttock. "The way your bum fits my hand. Such soft, smooth skin." He tasted the valley between her breasts. Sweetness mixed with the bite of spice. The musk of passion nearly buried her fresh meadow scent.

His kisses meandered from her collarbone to her belly. When he rested his cheek beside her navel, she twitched. He lifted his head to grin at her. "Soft, smooth, and sensitive." When he brushed his fake mustache against her, she giggled.

He eased up to her head.

"Yvette wanted me to get waxed," Steffi told him. "Had I known you like smooth—"

"Don't be silly." His lips silenced her as one hand brushed the feathery hair on her mound. "You have a beautiful body. Power sings beneath your skin."

Her eyes widened. "You can feel it?"

"Definitely. It sings within you." He glanced over her shoulder. "You have a golden aura."

Locking her hands behind his neck, she brought her mouth to his. Her kisses made his vision blur, his blood blaze, and his groin ache in sweet agony.

He caught her face between his hands and buried his tongue in her willing mouth. He wanted her here. He wanted her now. He wanted—as their lips parted, he took a deep breath. He wanted to love her as she'd never been loved before.

"I'm going to kiss every glorious inch of you." He sucked an earlobe and grazed down her neck to her collarbone. "Here, for instance." He nuzzled the hollow between her breasts.

Her breath heated his shoulders. "Leave something for me to do."

"Don't worry." He smiled as his lips followed his fingers to her taut nipple. He loved the feel of her in his mouth, the taste of her swollen skin. She moaned and moved beneath him so he could suck deeper. If he'd had any doubt about the level of her desire, her quick, instinctive responses soon put it to rest. His lips and fingers skimmed the surface of her belly.

She caressed his shoulders, his chest, and one hand slipped toward his groin.

He kissed her as he caught her hand. "Easy."

She gripped his hair. "Don't get me too excited."

He lifted his head from her silky inner thigh. "Steffi, my love, I plan to get you *very* excited."

"No," she said. "Don't. I can't…I don't want to hurt you."

"You won't." He smiled. "Lie back and relax. Just let go." Resting his cheek on her thigh, he slid one hand between her legs and began to stroke the hidden folds. She was already wet. Good. His mouth fastened on her center while one finger slipped inside her. Wet and hot.

She moaned and moved against him.

Not yet, chérie. Not yet. His tongue made a lazy lap around her lower lips.

With a low moan, she opened to his questing fingers and busy tongue. Her skin heated, and her breath moved faster as if she were sprinting toward an invisible finish line.

Let go. Let go. Her slick, quivering muscles tightened around his tongue when it followed his fingers inside her. Every cell in her gorgeous body vibrated around him.

She grabbed his shoulder. "Now, Sawyer, please!" He needed no second urging.

As she rose to join him, he moved inside her. She was hot, wet, and ready. With every racing breath, she drew him deeper and deeper, her eyes squeezed shut and her lips locked together.

The radiance of her quivering body urged him to

release, and a starry shimmer surrounded them.

When he could feel his own body again, he kissed the glow of her lips and slipped away to dispose of the used condom. He returned to the bed and relaxed.

Beside him, something stirred. Steffi. Every splendid inch of her human flesh.

"Don't leave." She threw an arm across his chest.

"I'm not going anywhere." He stroked her cheek. "How are you doing?"

In response, she stretched and pushed up on one elbow. "Are you all right?" Her anxious gaze ranged from his face to his torso and below.

He kissed her forehead. "Never better. Though I did wonder if you were going to disappear."

"What are you talking about?"

"You went through the most amazing transformation. One minute, you were flesh and blood. The next, you were…still you…but the golden aura that signals your power deepened. We both ended up surrounded by this star-glow."

Her eyes widened. "Wow!"

"To say the least. So I guess that means everything was okay, eh?"

"Way better than that, and you know it." Smiling, she snuggled against him.

He felt a familiar stirring in his groin. "So good it bears repeating?"

Her smile was like a breath of summer sunshine. "Oh, yes!"

Chapter 26

Steffi opened her eyes and spread her fingers in front of her face. Normal, except for the ding in the middle finger on her left hand, where Libby had once slammed the car door. Human fingers. Human hands.

"Keep the rings." Sawyer's voice rumbled in her ear.

"I can't. They're much too expensive." When she wiggled her ring finger, the glitter from the engagement ring nearly blinded her. "And your aunt's diamond is too flashy for me."

"Your smile makes it look like paste." He nuzzled her shoulder. "You never cease to amaze me."

She stretched, relishing the feel of his legs against her, the strength of his arms, the muscles of his torso, and the stirring of his cock. "Glad I could offer something new. After so many females—"

"None like you." When he lifted his head, his intense gaze seemed to penetrate her soul. "I suspect you are much more than a Shifter."

"I don't know about that."

"You have powers that aren't connected to your shifting."

"Like what happened with your father?"

Sawyer nodded.

"That's not new, but I haven't…not in a long time. A couple of kissing disasters taught me to be very careful

261

with Simple Human partners and with other Shifters. I never lost control."

"Must have been frustrating."

"No." She sat up and pulled the sheet over her breasts. "It felt good."

"But not like this." He spoke in a matter-of-fact voice, not as if he were angling for compliments.

"No. This is different." Like the difference between catching a bus and lifting off in a spaceship. Amazing. Mind blowing. Wonderful beyond words. "I've never felt so free...so safe. You know who...what...I am."

"You're spectacular." One of Sawyer's long fingers traced the bones of her spinal column and ignited a fresh current of desire.

"With you, I can let go." She wrapped her arms around his neck and pressed her body against him. "Breakfast?"

"Starting here." He brought his mouth down on hers.

She trembled as his lips moved over her skin, and his tongue teased her nipple.

He flashed a delighted grin. "Then I'll move to this one." One hand cupped her other breast.

"Oh, no, you don't." Steffi's fingers encircled his erection. "My turn to sample the buffet."

Sawyer lay back with a satisfied growl. "Be my guest, but don't expect any fancy fireworks."

"I'll be the judge of that." She blew him a kiss and shimmied the length of his torso.

Later—no one was watching the clock—they lay back in satisfaction.

Sawyer looked up at the ceiling. "We may have to learn how to dial things down... or else go outside."

She rose on one elbow to regard him. "Are you

complaining?"

"Not at all. Being surrounded by stardust is splendid, but I think we shook the building."

"You're projecting. We were shaking, but it didn't go beyond...at least, I don't think it did." She sat up to study the walls. "I don't see any cracks."

"We might have gotten away lucky this time. I hate to think of what might happen if you ever went volcanic." He threw up his hands. "Fire flashing in the chimneys. Lava rolling down the stairs."

She rolled over to face him. "Don't be so dramatic. I could never do that. I would never want to do that." She smiled. "But it would definitely be hot!"

Sawyer embraced her. "Steffi, my love, if you get any hotter, you'll need fireproof underwear."

"Guess we'll have to stick with stardust."

"You'll get no complaints from me." He kissed her soundly and rolled out of bed. "I should visit the fitness center before we eat." He unrolled his padding on the bed.

"Don't forget the blue eyes."

"Thanks for the reminder." He turned toward the bathroom.

"Wait." She kicked off her bedding and joined him. Her hands glided slowly down his chest, and she kissed his shoulders. "I hate to see you hide this beautiful body."

He winked at her. "Think of it as a secret solely for you."

Watching him saunter toward the bathroom made every muscle in her body vibrate. While Sawyer covered up, she'd be exposing as much as legal. But first— "How long do you plan to work out?"

"About an hour. Then I'll come back to shower, and we can go down to breakfast. Why don't you try the pool?"

"I'd rather shift."

"Return to your lioness?"

"Not today. I thought I might do some observing."

He stared at her. "Pardon?"

"Might as well get my skills up to speed. Thought I'd do a lizard shift. That's always fun. I can hook on to the bottom of the housekeeper's cart, check out the other rooms, and evaluate how housekeeping works."

His eyebrows made a skeptical arch. "You're really going to work?"

"I signed a contract. I may as well contribute something."

Sawyer frowned. "What if you get caught?"

"My lizard is fast and great at camouflage."

"That may be, but if you're traveling around with the housekeeper, how will you get back here?"

"I hadn't thought it through. What if I find you at the fitness center? They always need fresh towels."

Sawyer shook his head. "You don't know who's assigned to that facility or when they bring towels. Housekeeping goes all over. You could end up in the basement, the loading dock, or the laundry."

"I can climb the walls."

"I don't like it. You'll be small. Vulnerable. Getting back here could be like climbing Mont Tremblant. Even if you do get back, you can't open doors."

"You'd be surprised how agile a determined lizard can be." She snapped her fingers. "I know! The women's locker room will have a dressing room and a few toilet stalls. I'll return to my human base there, wrap a towel around me, and have someone at the pool call you because—silly me!—I forgot my clothes."

"You won't have a bathing suit on."

"I'll pretend it's so skimpy I'm hiding it under the towel. I'll bat my eyelashes and play *potiche* to the max."

"That might work."

When Sawyer regarded her with a grudging admiration, her heart beat faster. "It will. You bring me clothes, we'll go to breakfast, and I'll give you my report."

"No way I can talk you out of this, eh?"

She arched an eyebrow. "You could pop out your contacts, take off your clothes, roll out of your padding, and hop back into bed with me." She tickled his padded ribcage. "I'll be happy to help."

He grinned. "I'm sure you would, but if I'm going to maintain this body to your standards, I need to work out. The fitness center is another service we need to explore. So I will wait for your call, and I'll come to the pool with your clothes."

"That sounds like a plan."

He kissed her. "Be careful."

"I will. If my lizard can't get into the pool area, I'll wait for you outside our room." She pointed up. "Above the door." She wrapped her arms around his neck and drew him closer for a flurry of kisses. Then she pulled back, and her lips curved in a slow smile. "Take good care of that dynamite bod."

****

On his way back to the honeymoon suite, Sawyer's pulse raced. Where was Steffi? The young lifeguard on duty at the pool assured him he hadn't seen his wife. He moved slowly, partly to maintain his disguise, primarily to search every spot along the way. Corners. Walls. Even the patterns in the carpet. No Steffi. He looked above the door to their suite. Nothing. He wanted to throw back his head and howl.

When he entered the suite, a low murmur from the bedroom slithered into his ears. Steffi!

"Oh, Alex!" Her voice sliced through his relief like a razor blade. He hadn't been gone more than an hour, and she was talking to a man? In their room? Their bed?

"That would be wonderful." The throaty laugh that had turned him on a few hours earlier now made his stomach heave.

Oh-Alex. Sawyer's hands fisted. He was ready to storm into the room and tear her companion to pieces. But Steffi wouldn't—not after… He returned to the entry and retraced his path to the bedroom, this time with deliberately heavy steps.

On the threshold of the bedroom, he paused. Relief ratcheted through his system, and his face heated with a trace of shame. Wearing a pair of shorts and a scoop-necked tank top, Steffi sat alone on the bed with her phone in front of her. She glanced up at him but then returned to her caller. "Gotta go. Keep me posted." She flashed an incandescent smile at the screen and put the phone on the night table. "How was your workout?"

"Good. What happened to your plans to go exploring?"

She swung her legs around and stood. "I shifted and literally crawled the walls for a while. When no one from housekeeping showed up, I returned to base." She hooked her arms around his neck. "They must figure honeymooners want extra time in the morning."

"Could be. The shift went well?"

"Absolutely. I couldn't stay a lizard too long, though. The pesticides they use are nauseating. More than a few whiffs, and I'd have spent the rest of the day barf—what do you call it?—yorking in the bathroom. Washroom." She shook her head. "Nasty stuff. You might want to mention it in your report."

"I will, but everyone has to keep bugs at bay."

"Not with such toxic compounds."

"I'll point that out." He added her complaint to the list on his phone. "You know, your ability gives you a perspective on worlds beyond the one either humans or *loups-garous* perceive. If drones do put you out of the academic observation business, you could find work with a Shifter-owned corporation. Montaigne Enterprises would hire you in a heartbeat."

Steffi laughed. "That's because I'm sleeping with the boss's son, but I'll keep it in mind. Fortunately, I don't need to worry yet." Radiant, she hugged herself. "I got the most amazing call."

He didn't trust himself to comment, but she didn't seem to notice.

"Someone I worked with a few years ago is putting together a proposal for a study in the Australian Outback—Australia!—and he wants me on his team."

Australia? A day from Montreal by air. Perhaps he could find an industry or service that would attract Montaigne Enterprises. *Papa* was always interested in expansion. "That's exciting. When will you leave?"

"Alex still needs funding, but he's really good. He should hear about his applications in the next month or two."

"How long will you be gone?"

"Four to six months."

"That's a long time."

"It goes by quickly." She waved off his objection. "Know what the best part is?"

"Better than spending six months in Australia?" *With Oh-Alex?*

"He wants me on the actual research team. No shifting."

"That's great." Sawyer swallowed the bile that rose in the back of his throat. Oh-Alex wanted her, all right. "He must have liked your work, to remember you after…how long has it been?"

Her brow furrowed. "About three years. Since then we've run into each other occasionally at professional conferences."

Work and conferences. *Was that all?* When he bit his tongue, the metallic taste of blood filled his mouth.

She wrapped her arms around his waist. "How was your workout?"

"Good." He moved away. "Although the guy who works there treated me like I was ninety going on a hundred."

Steffi laughed. "That's a great testimony to your disguise. You'll have to tell Yvette."

"I suppose. Right now, I need a shower." He pulled off his sweaty shirt and started to unwind his padding, but she rested a hand on top of his.

"Want some company?"

An hour ago, her invitation, coupled with the twinkle in her eyes, would have made him ready for action. After overhearing her conversation with Oh-Alex, not so much. He hesitated.

She studied his face. "What's wrong?"

He moved his forearm. "May have worked out

harder than I meant to."

"Are you all right? Would you like a massage? If you don't want me to do it, I'm sure they have a professional here."

"No, no." He covered her hand to keep her close. "I'm all right. I'm feeling strange. This morning, everything seemed so...we were...together. I'm gone for an hour, and when I come back, you're on the phone with this other guy." *Oh-Alex.*

Steffi's eyes widened. "Are you jealous?"

"Maybe a little."

"Sawyer!" Her embrace smothered her chiding. "I'm here with *you.*"

"But you and he—"

"We did have a thing." Her grip tightened. "Years ago, and it was nothing like what you and I—Alex is a great guy, but he's Simple Human."

Yet she was planning to return to him.

"Sawyer, we agreed that this would be our time, right?" When she massaged his nape, the tightness in his chest eased.

Her face was so open, so free from guile. She didn't dwell on his past. He should give her the same respect. Of course, his past wasn't going to be part of his future while hers... *Our time.* "Right."

"Let's not think about tomorrow. Let's make the most of today." She kissed him so soundly he thought he heard chimes.

Yes, yes. Let's. Her tempting aromas surrounded him, and desire rose within him. He reached under her top to unhook her bra. "I would very much like your company in the shower."

Chapter 27

The next morning, as they lay in the big red bed, Sawyer stretched. "What's your plan for today's shift?"

Steffi's smile dimmed. "Those pesticides spooked me. I want to shift outside."

"That makes sense. The area map shows a ridge beyond the eighteenth hole of the golf course. Forest borders the developed area, and it looks isolated. I thought we might picnic there tomorrow after we finish golfing, but we could hike out there this morning if you'd like."

"Yes!" The air around her sparkled. She rolled toward him and dropped her voice to a near whisper as if she feared the Fates might intercept the message. "I want to fly."

So soon? Her confidence struck his heart like the point of dagger. He thought he'd been preparing for this since the night he met her, but he'd been lying to himself. He'd pretended this day would never come.

She stroked his jaw. "You don't think I should?"

"I don't—how's your shoulder feeling?"

She rolled it. "It's still a bit stiff. If I do start to tire, I'll find a spot to land and rest before I come back." She hugged herself. "Flying is the most wonderful sensation!" She opened her arms to include him. "Maybe not the most. But definitely wonderful."

"Nice save." Sawyer kissed her. "Fly!"

After breakfast, they hiked to the far side of the property. "Practice time!" Sawyer stood by a tree near the entrance to the secluded thicket. "I'll stand guard while you shift." He caught her face between his hands and brushed his lips against hers. "Have fun, but be careful."

Her glowing eyes met his. The air around her vibrated. "I'll bring you a present."

"Come back to me." That would be present enough.

Although Sawyer assumed his sentry post on the edge of the thicket, his protective presence surrounded Steffi as she prepared to shift. Trees and shrubs blocked the sun. She shivered. Closing her eyes, she visualized her falcon. She drew in a long breath to welcome the fragrant forest air. Her arms curved slightly. *Yes!* As her bone structure changed, her frame grew lighter. The feathers that pierced her skin warmed her. *Oh, yes!* Her nose drooped, and her chin lifted to shape a beak. Her falcon had vision much sharper than her human base, but she took a few minutes to practice seeing from side to side rather than straight ahead as humans did. With a cry, she spread her wings and lifted from the leafy darkness into the light.

Below her, Sawyer stood. She tried to alter her flight path for a flyover—maybe she could even give him a little show—but the wind drove her up and away. Buoyed by the air passing over and under her wings, she let the currents carry her. Newly awakened strength surged through her. Power coupled with grace, she angled into a crosswind near The Snow Angel and soared toward the mountains. The warmth of the sun and the freedom of the air filled her heart. She felt as if she could fly forever.

Yet for the first time in all her years of flying, something was missing. No, not something. Someone. In other transformations, she'd left her lovers behind as easily as her human base, but the thought of Sawyer kept pulling her back.

She circled into a leisurely kettle. How Sawyer would enjoy this freedom! OASIS had many drugs. Surely, they could tweak their medications so a Shifter could move outside his genetic range. But OASIS also believed everyone should stay in his or her slot in the Shifter hierarchy. More important, broadening Sawyer's shifting range might weaken his connection with his *loup-garou*. Sawyer would never want that.

In a nearby tree, something glittered in an empty crow's nest. Gold chain. She'd promised to return with a gift. When she neared the nest, however, a loud squawk sounded off to the side. With a mental shrug, Steffi flew off. She was bigger and stronger than the nester, but crows could be feisty, especially when crossed. The bauble wasn't worth a fight. Not real gold anyway. Crows were suckers for costume jewelry. Her left wing began to ache.

****

While Steffi prepared for her bird shift, Sawyer opened his messages. Sounds of zippers unzipping and clothes settling in the grass interfered with his concentration. A feathered bullet shot into the sky. Speckled wings expanded, and the wind drew Steffi's bird up and away. When she dived and swooped above him, pleasure radiated from her form. Soaring across the field and out of sight, she took her exhilaration with her. Along with his heart.

His torso felt like a hollow shell. "Best get used to

it," he muttered. Like a robot, he submitted his final OASIS report. Everyone expressed surprise at the speed of Steffi's recovery, which he credited to her Anomaly status. No one expressed disappointment, but Uncle Mel reminded him that he wasn't done yet. Rereading his uncle's message, Sawyer shook his head. When assuring OASIS that he'd done his best, he'd thought of Steffi, not the Organization. He put his phone away.

A noise drew his eyes back to the sky. Steffi's plumage sparkled in the sun. With a cry, she swooped toward him. She circled closer and closer as she chattered. He watched for a moment in puzzlement before he understood. She was a falcon. She wanted to perch. Hoping she wouldn't dig too deep, he took off his shirt, wrapped it around his wrist, and extended his arm.

When her talons took hold, she opened her elegant beak and cawed. Her eyes, now a deep brown brimming with joy, met his. The heart in his chest beat once more. "Welcome back." He stroked her feathers and smiled at this amazing creature. With a breath of wind, she lifted from his arm and flew into the thicket. Her left wing looked a bit lower than the right. Movements in the underbrush. Had she crashed? He stormed into the thicket.

Fully human, Steffi stood with her back to him, her backbone moving in a sensuous stretch as she reached toward the sky she had left moments ago. With a groan, she dropped her left arm and lifted her shoulder. "Damn."

"Everything still there?" When he rested his hands on her lovely hips, she gasped. He would have moved, but she placed her hands on top of his, pressing them against the flesh recently covered by feathers. "Sorry. I didn't mean to startle you."

"You did, but it's okay." She rested her dark head against his chest. "Better than okay." She rolled her left shoulder. "I overdid it."

"You and every other recovered Shifter I've known. Take it easy, and don't worry." He nuzzled her neck.

"How can I worry when you're doing that?" She turned to face him. "This is the best return I've ever had. Bar none." She gave him a long, lazy smile. "Miss me?"

She was giving him the cue to begin talking about goodbyes, but all he could say was "More than you know."

Framing his face between her hands, she stood on tiptoe and kissed him with undisguised hunger. Perhaps a bit of her bird of prey lingered in her human tissue. He answered with the longing that thundered from his core. The kiss was a long union of lips and tongues, touches and tastes, whimpers and moans. Steffi's body warmed his while he stroked her bum. Finally, Sawyer found his voice. "You should get dressed."

With a mischievous smile, she tapped his collarbone. "You should get undressed." She began to loosen his padding.

He covered her hand. "Don't."

"Seriously?"

When she moved her hips against the swelling in his groin, he groaned. "Someone could see us."

"You said this was the most undeveloped part of the property."

"It is, but someone might still—"

"So?" She lifted the hand with the rings. "Honeymooners, remember? Can't keep our hands off each other." As if to illustrate, her other hand traveled down his front to the tenting at his fly.

He surrendered with a deep kiss as she freed his torso. While she ran her fingers across his bare shoulders, he dropped to the grass with her and kicked off his shoes. He fumbled in his wallet for a condom. Her lips followed her hands, and she pushed him back as she liberated him from the constraints of his trousers. Her fingers fluttered over him as her mouth traveled down his arm. With a gasp, she pulled back, cooling the heat within him.

"What is it?"

She kissed the abrasions on his wrist. "I hurt you."

"It's a scratch. Don't worry." He captured the dark cloud of her hair in his hands.

"When I was training, my Mentor and my father used gloves, but today I didn't think—"

"I heal quickly."

"Next time we'll use a glove."

"Next time." Even as he kissed and caressed her until the golden glow surrounded them, he wondered if there would be a next time. Her heat welcomed him as her inner muscles tightened and their bodies joined everywhere, except in that most intimate space where the damned condom separated them. If only they could have enjoyed a total union once, but the risk was too great. Also, after a taste of freedom, they'd never have returned to restraint. Her muscles drew him deeper and closer until the sweet vibrations roared through him in a cosmic release.

Her eyes had a dreamy light, and the corners of her slightly swollen lips lifted. "Why so serious?" Her voice was a husky murmur.

"I want to remember the way you look at this

moment." He brushed her cheek with his lips and patted her hip. "Good flight?"

"Amazing." When she looked up at him, her smile faded. "But I missed you."

He rolled off her and got to his feet. When she stood on her toes to kiss him, the tips of her breasts grazed his chest. If he didn't get his clothes on, they'd be naked here in the woods until sunset. He grabbed his shorts.

Chapter 28

"Mr. and Mrs. Sawyer."

The next morning, in the breakfast room, Steffi turned to regard the tall man standing at her shoulder. Seated beside her, Sawyer growled. Steffi rested a hand on his arm to keep his *loup-garou* from pouncing. The glow from their early morning lovemaking dimmed.

"May I join you?" Without waiting for an answer, the stranger pulled up a chair and set his coffee cup on their table. "That's better." He presented a business card from his jacket pocket and peered at Sawyer. "I like the blue eyes, brother. Nice idea."

Brother? This must be Roland. He was heavier than Sawyer, and his brown hair was thinning at the temples. Clad in a bespoke suit—did all Montaigne men use the same tailor?—he looked smoother and less weathered than Sawyer did. Clearly, he enjoyed a comfortable life.

Sawyer turned to Steffi. "My dear, may I present Roland Montaigne?"

"*Monsieur.*" She extended her hand. Roland's palm slid against hers as if it were waxed. "Pleased to meet you."

"Likewise, I'm sure." Both brothers behaved as if they were following an etiquette book. Roland glanced from Steffi to Sawyer. "The honeymoon is going well, eh?"

Sawyer glared at the other man. "Why are you

here?"

Roland sipped his coffee. "*Papa* wants me to review the books and negotiate with the owners."

"What?" Sawyer sat up as if struck by lightning. "He charged me—Steffi and me—"

"To explore a bit." Sawyer's brother lifted a hand. "He has read your reports and thinks you've been distracted. I can see why." He directed a smirk in Steffi's direction. "He told me to take over."

Sawyer's face darkened.

Steffi covered Sawyer's fingertips to hide the tips of his claws, which threatened to break through. "Not here."

Sawyer glanced at the Simple Human diners, who watched their table. "You're right." He turned to his brother. "But—"

"You and…Mrs. Sawyer…will check out today. My car will take you back to Montreal. I'll handle your rental." He turned to Steffi. "One of our planes will fly you to Chicago. Everything you left in Montreal is being sent to your residence."

When she opened her mouth in a mixture of surprise and protest, Sawyer thundered, "No!" and leaped to his feet. He loomed over his brother. "We weren't scheduled to leave until tomorrow, and even then," his eyes met hers as he spoke, "we're not done."

The boulder in Steffi's throat melted, and she could breathe again.

"I suppose a few more hours won't matter." Roland finished his coffee with a leisurely swallow. "I'll settle your bill, and someone will be waiting for you in the lobby when you're ready to leave." He stood. "Oh, and *mademoiselle*—Mrs. Sawyer, my father wants you to have this." He pulled an envelope from his jacket pocket and set it by Steffi's plate. "I'll see you back in Montreal, brother." With a nod, he turned on his heel.

"Brother." Sawyer uttered the word as if it were a curse. He sank back in his chair. "I should have known." He snarled. "My father never misses a chance to remind us that we're all pawns in his game."

"I didn't know you cared so much about his approval."

"I try not to, but when he gives me a job, I want to do it well and see it through to the end. That he has pushed me aside this way—it's an insult." His fist slammed the table. "I'm sorry, Steffi."

"Your father's a jerk, and your brother evidently a jerk-in-training, but you're not like them." She stroked his hands. "I've had a wonderful time here with you. I will not let them ruin it."

The twitch in Sawyer's cheek disappeared. "You're absolutely right." His lips brushed her cheek. "This is our time."

"Our time." The words sounded lovely, but what would happen when the day ended?

She was about to ask when Sawyer gestured at the large white envelope. "What's that?"

She eyed the engraved return address. "The Montaigne Foundation?"

"Another of *Papa*'s tentacles. Check for anthrax."

She shook her head but heeded Sawyer's warning. The flap lifted easily. She unfolded the thick paper and read slowly.

"Well?" Sawyer gestured at the letter. "What does he want now?"

She shook her head. "He asked The Foundation to

review my academic background…the research I've been involved with. Because of my 'significant contribution to knowledge'—their words—they are awarding me—" She held up the enclosed check. The number of zeroes made her head spin. "This can't be right."

She offered the letter to Sawyer. He whistled. "Looks like you can develop your own research project. Or support another scholar you want to work with. Researchers will be itching to have you on their team."

When Sawyer folded the letter and handed it to her, she set it on the table. "I don't want someone to hire me because I come with money attached."

"It's not the money alone, Steffi. This adds something extra to everything else you bring to your work." He pushed his chair back and stood.

"A lot of something extras." She put the check between the folds of the heavy paper and slipped the whole package into the envelope, which she rested against the pepper mill.

"What are you doing?"

She gestured at the envelope. "Your father wants to get me out of your life. He thinks he can wave a little money—okay, a lot of money—in front of me to make me disappear." She slapped her napkin on the table, got to her feet, and folded her arms. "If he were here, I'd tell him what he can do with that check."

Sawyer grinned. "That's something I'd pay to see." When she turned to leave, he took her arm. "Look, I understand your position." He picked up the envelope. "Don't throw this away." She opened her mouth to object, but he lifted a finger. "Hear me out. First, although *Papa* no doubt influenced the Foundation—

heavily, I'm sure—they wouldn't have given you this award if they didn't think you deserve it. Second, it's yours—no strings attached. You can use it whenever you choose...or you can lock it away and never look at it again. Eventually, someone from the Foundation would contact you about your intentions, but you can take your time. Speaking of which," as he spoke, he glanced at his watch, "we should go, or we'll miss our tee time."

Steffi frowned. So Sawyer wanted to follow their original plan to spend part of their last day evaluating the golf course. At least, the kitchen was supplying a picnic lunch. On the ridge, she could spread her—she glanced at Sawyer's scarred wrist. Not today. Even if she hadn't hurt him, she should rest her wings. She looked up at the disconcerting blue eyes. "Now that your brother's here, we no longer need disguises. Why don't you lose the padding, the beard, and those silly contacts?"

"Good idea. What about the mustache?" He stroked his upper lip and gave a villainous chortle.

She laughed. "It tickles. Which is kind of fun."

"Maybe I'll grow a real one. What do you think?"

Her response stuck in her throat. With that new mustache, he might be tickling his mate. "It's up to you."

"RIP Tom and Abigail." He cradled her chin in his hand. "Today belongs to Steffi and Sawyer."

Steffi and Sawyer. "I like the sound of that." For today, at least. After that?

His mouth met hers in a short, sweet kiss.

****

With a flourish, Sawyer putted out for the fourth time.

After her next three attempts missed the hole, Steffi swore.

"Don't be so upset." Sawyer used his most soothing voice. Steffi hadn't wanted to golf, but if they'd stayed close to the lodge, his father's minions would be pushing them to leave, and he'd have to watch Roland's pathetic attempt to imitate *Papa*'s take-charge manner.

She crossed her arms. "You're so much better than I am. If you'd kept your belly pads, this would be a fairer competition."

"Sorry. If it's any consolation, Tom Sawyer's clothes still get in the way." He hitched up the droopy drawers and turned so she wouldn't see his smile. She could roar. She could fly. She had orgasms that pulled them both into the heart of ecstasy. At least, he was a better golfer.

"Not enough."

"Maybe I should have worn the contact lenses."

"No!"

When she rolled up on her toes to kiss him, he flashed a grin, but it didn't change her sour expression. He stroked her arm. "Remember, *chérie*, I've been playing since I could hold a club. Golf is part of the business world. I'm sure that when it comes to esoteric information about world geography or human societies, you'd win, hands down."

"No one keeps score on that." When her next ball plunged into the rough, she whacked the head of the club against the manicured lawn and cursed again. "I hate this dumb game."

"I can see that." He patted her tense shoulder. "Once we're done, we'll reward ourselves with the picnic up on that nice ridge."

Gold and green sparks lit her dark eyes. "We've played enough. Let's head for the hills."

"Don't tempt me."

When she turned, her body pressed into his, and her hands caressed his temples before sliding into his hair to massage his skull. The sensuous rhythm flowed from his head to his toes. "Do you really want to waste time on this golf course?" Her husky whisper tickled his ear. "Aren't there more interesting things you'd rather do?"

As one of her hands left his nape to meander down his chest, he groaned. All-American girl, seductress, temptress—Steffi had as many forms as a woman as she had as a Shape-shifter, and he'd never discover them all. "Indeed there are." *And all with you. Only with you.*

On the ridge overlooking the resort, they devoured their picnic meal in record time. Polishing off the last of the strawberries, Steffi reclined on their tablecloth. "Delicious," she murmured.

Yes, she was.

"What a glorious day!"

"Glorious," he agreed. Joining her on the tablecloth, he kissed away the juice that stained her luscious mouth until the taste of Steffi herself remained.

She burrowed into his shoulder. "I wish this day would last forever."

Emotions knotted in his gut. Releasing her, he stood. "All things end." He walked to a far corner of the tablecloth.

She followed him. "You said I needed a vacation. I haven't had it yet."

When a tremor moved across her face, he clamped his hands to his sides so he wouldn't reach for her. "I was wrong." About so many things. "All you needed was a little time."

She laid one hand against his cheek. "You gave me

that."

Her fingers were unbearably soft. With the slightest turn of his head, he could kiss her palm. Then her wrist. Her arm. Her whole beautiful body. Every time they were together felt like the first time, that moment of surprise and rapture, because she was always so much more than he expected.

All things must end. The truth stiffened his bones. He would always be *loup-garou*, and she would always be so much more. At some point, she would want more. Without looking at her, he removed her hand and stepped back. "As flattering as it would be for me to believe that I helped, you healed on your own. You didn't need me."

She grabbed the front of his shirt and pulled him toward her. "I do now."

You silly, wonderful female. When his hands covered hers, the warmth of her fingers seeped through the shirt fabric to his skin. "You want me." *As I want you.* "You don't need me. Once you return to your normal life, you'll see how true that is."

She shook her head.

"I know how much you enjoy your work. The variety…the travel…the challenges. I can see it in your eyes and hear it in your voice when you talk about it. And you love your shifting. Especially the flying. When you came back from your bird shift, you glowed."

"Yes, but…you were waiting for me. Being with you has changed everything."

Turning, he moved away. "We've always known that this would end."

"Not so soon." He sensed without looking that she stood with legs apart, hands on her hips.

"Maybe we should take my brother's interference as

a sign that this is the right time to say goodbye."

"Why are you being like this?"

He did his best to sound as if he didn't know what she meant. "Like what?"

"So cool. Detached. As if nothing has happened between us."

He drew a deep breath. "I never said that." She was watching, waiting. "I didn't mean...I don't think...I didn't know..." He finally faced her. "Steffi, you are like no one else I've ever known. Looking at you takes my breath away."

Her slight frown eased, but her hands remained on her hips. "That's a good thing, right?"

"No. No. It is not." The harsh denial deepened her frown. "I should have known better. I should never have let things go this far. I am so sorry." But not for what they'd shared. He'd treasure those moments for as long as he lived.

A drop of blood appeared on her lower lip. He clenched his hands to keep from treating the wound. "I don't understand."

"You were my client. I took advantage of you."

"Hardly. I've been an enthusiastic participant every step of the way." She crossed her arms. "I'm not ready to fold up my tent and fly away because your brother and your father and anyone else in your family—everyone else in your family—tells me to." She lifted her chin. "Unless—is that what you want? Your last, big fling and all that."

My last—mon dieu! "No!"

"Good." She was beside him in a heartbeat. "Because I don't want this to end."

He cleared his throat. "But a time will

285

come…you're already thinking about Australia." *And Oh-Alex.*

When she wrapped her arms around his torso, her fresh-meadow scent filled his head. "You're planning to choose a mate."

His hands settled on the curve of her hips. "My family and my pack expect me to."

"I know they're important to you. So do it." Steffi drew a deep breath. "Take a mate but keep a mistress."

"No!" His voice boomed across the clearing. He cradled her face and kissed her with an intensity that rocked his body from core to skin. "I would never—"

"What else can we do? I don't want to lose you." The anguish in her gaze seared his bones.

"I don't think you could if you tried." He held her close as a plan took shape. "I have a cabin in Alberta. Small, but with the basic conveniences—washroom, hot shower, electricity."

Her breath stirred the hair on his collarbone. "Sounds nice."

"It's a start. I didn't want to build a proper house until I—" *Until I found my mate. Until I found you.* He paused. "My *loup-garou* will always need a pack, but I can transfer to one out there."

"You'll have to teach me—"

"No. You can never belong."

She pushed away. "Why not? I can be a *loup-garou.*"

"Someone could report you to OASIS for breaking the Covenant."

"Won't the members of your new pack demand that you mate?"

He hooked an arm around her waist. "I'll let them

know I already have. Some *loups-garous* do mate with Simple Humans or with other Shifters."

"But we can never shift together."

"Not with the pack. But I have enough land that we can do whatever we want on it." As he drew her closer, he could already imagine her body changing. She would be a spectacular *loup-garou*. *Mine*. The growl of his beast punctured his fantasy.

When he stiffened, she turned. "What's wrong?"

Mine. Until she tires of me. Of us. He clasped her hands and met her concerned eyes. "I should warn you. Alberta won't be like Quebec. I have enough in savings and investments for us to be comfortable, but nothing lavish. No private jets." And no future income from OASIS.

"I can live with that. Can you?" She fingered the cotton of his Tom Sawyer tee shirt. "No more tailored suits."

"They wear well, and I may be able to afford one occasionally if I need it." He scratched his jaw. "The real problem is that you, my darling, are much more than I will ever be. You have not only your amazing shifting ability but also other powers. You love traveling the world and studying its inhabitants. Alberta is a tiny slice of that world, and I am a *loup-garou*. Nothing more. What will happen when that's no longer enough?"

"What are you talking about?"

He hated to crush that confident smile. "You've never been in a relationship. I have." *But none like this.* "In time, the excitement fades." That had been true with Simple Humans and other females, but the day would never dawn when Steffi's smile failed to light up his world.

Her fingers dug into his shoulders. "I want to build a life with you, and I will do my best to keep it interesting."

"How long will that life be interesting for you? For instance, you won't be able to hang out in the Outback with your friend Alex."

Steffi laughed. "I love the way your eyes squinch up when you say his name."

His upper lip curled. "I hate the way your mouth softens when you say it." He grasped his fingers and rolled his eyes. "Oh-Ow…lex!"

She swatted his arm. "I don't sound like that!"

He massaged his biceps. "I may have exaggerated. A bit."

"Since it bothers you so much, I'll never say it again."

"Good." His lips brushed hers and returned for a more thorough engagement. The next time he could form coherent sentences, they lay sprawled on the tablecloth while their clothes littered the grass.

"We can do this," Steffi murmured, kissing his shoulder.

Sawyer sat up and brushed his disheveled hair back from his forehead. "I hope we can, but we have to figure out how you can meet your needs." He tossed her a few garments and pulled on his tee shirt.

While she put on her bra, he stepped back to keep his hands off her. He tightened the belt on Tom Sawyer's saggy golf pants. "My *loup-garou* needs a pack. What do you…and all your shapes…need? You can swim, leap, and soar."

"I can do that in Alberta."

"Yes, but if you want to be a seal or a pelican or even

a jaguar, you need the right habitat. You could be away for days…months."

"I don't think I can do long shifts." She kneaded her aching shoulder. "My wing tired after a short flight, and I needed to return to base. I don't want to wander too much anyway." She petted his jaw as if it were his muzzle. He dipped his forehead to brush hers. "Not when you're waiting at home."

"That could present another problem." He turned his hand to display the talon marks on his wrist. "I don't want to be the guy on the ground with the glove. The one who's always left behind. Hell, if we had children, you could all go traipsing off to Timbuktu, but I could never—"

She pressed her fingers against his mouth. "My ability comes from a genetic accident. I don't know if I'll pass anything along. My genes might be so messed up that I can't even have kids."

"I hope we can. My nieces and nephews are great."

"I'll take some tests. If it turns out I can't and not having children is a deal-breaker—"

"No, no." He gripped her hands. "I want to be with you."

"And I want to be with you."

"It's settled then. We belong together. We stay together." The truest words he'd ever spoken. He basked in the warmth of her kiss. "I'll arrange my pack transfer with the Elders and submit my resignation to the board." He gritted his teeth. "I should also tell my mother."

"That will be hard."

"Uncomfortable? Yes. Hard? I don't think so." Every cell in his body vibrated with joy. "I've spent much of my life fighting what I didn't want. You have no idea how liberating it feels to fight for something—someone—I do want."

"I can help you settle things here."

"I'd love that, but there's something else you need to do." Sawyer brought his hands together at his chin as if praying. "Now that you can shift again, you need to stabilize your ability."

"What? When were you planning to tell me?"

"I was waiting until you'd fully recovered. OASIS has drugs—"

"No! They're likely to give me something like X-Ting, something that suppresses my ability."

"I doubt that they'd be so blatant, but I understand your position."

"What happens if I don't take the pills?"

"I've never had a client who didn't, but records suggest that the ability may weaken until…it goes away."

"Vanishes?" Her horrified whisper hovered in the air.

"Or the ability remains, but the Shifter returns to the base shape without intending to do so."

"So I could become human while I was flying?"

"I suppose."

"That would be messy."

To say the least. "This stability thing applies to regular Shifters. With you and your sisters, who knows? You might never need it."

"Or I could lose everything tomorrow. Again." She groaned.

"There is an alternative that Shifters used before we had the drugs. It's harder."

"Of course. Does it work?"

"Older Shifters attested to its effectiveness." He paused. "You must visit The Seer."

Steffi burst out laughing. "You're kidding, right?" When her gaze locked with his, the merriment drained from her features. "There really is a Seer?"

He nodded.

"I thought that was someone our Mentors made up. Like the Tooth Fairy or the Boogey Man." She wiggled her fingers in fake fear.

"The Seer is very real and, from what I've heard, doesn't suffer fools. You'd best be respectful."

"All right. Where do I find this Seer?"

"The Seer finds you. Favors sites with high spiritual energy."

"High spiritual energy." Steffi brought both hands to her temples. "That narrows things not at all. The world is full of churches, temples, shrines. I could wander for years."

He took her hands. "In North America, The Seer often appears at Devils Tower."

She brightened. "Wyoming. We can stop on our way to Alberta."

"You must go alone." He kissed her forehead. "Once I've settled matters with my family, I'll join you there."

She linked her hands behind his neck and kissed him.

Chapter 29

Sawyer's hands rested on Steffi's hips, and his lips stirred the hair at her temple. "This calls for a celebration." He looked up. "Great day for a run."

"In broad daylight?" Steffi surveyed the cloudless sky. "I thought you wolves only shifted under the full moon."

Sawyer laughed. "You've watched too many old horror movies. The full moon is special. That's when we make our first shifts and choose our mates."

When he stepped back and stretched, Steffi visualized his long legs bending, his hands changing into paws and his nose becoming a snout on which platinum fur sprouted. She gestured toward the thicket. "Have fun. I'll keep watch while you shift."

Instead of leaving, he reached out. "Come with me, Steffi." His gray gaze implored her. "Run with me." His growl throbbed with urgency.

She rolled her shoulder. Strong enough, especially with support from three other legs. The green of the golf course unrolled below the ridge. "I don't want to violate the Covenant."

"Covenant be damned." He brought his mouth close to her ear. "I won't tell if you don't." His voice was smoother than silk. "We've been humans together, and we've experienced each other's shapes. Let's shift together."

His excited breath against her neck quickened her pulse. Everything he said made sense. If she became a *loup-garou* today, who else would ever know? Sawyer's face shone with expectation. If a threat did appear, Sawyer would protect her. "Let's!"

They packed up the picnic stuff, stripped, and hid the basket with their clothes in the hollow at the base of a large maple tree. Sawyer transformed swiftly as if he were donning a second skin, and in a sense, he was.

Steffi closed her eyes and visualized a wolf. When nothing happened, she opened her eyes. Sawyer, resplendent in his thick, silver fur, but with the same gray eyes, sat waiting. She was about to give up—perhaps her ability wasn't as stable as it should be, or it might be too soon to try a new shape—when her haunches lengthened. Her pelvis tilted to accommodate the change from biped to quadruped. Her heartbeat quickened, and the shift accelerated. She shook her furry head and stretched, glorying in the muscle and power of this new body. No wonder *loups-garous* refused to share it.

She had little time to contemplate her new shape because Sawyer leaped toward her. His tongue swiped across her jaw. His teeth flashed in a ferocious grin, and he was off, racing down the nearest hill. Although he was fast, he slowed until she caught up. They ran together, side by side, across a wide meadow on the other side of the thicket. When they could run no more, they paused to drink from a nearby creek before lying down.

Steffi groomed Sawyer's majestic head and curled beside his muscular frame. His love for his *loup-garou* surrounded him like a wall she could never breach. He would make friends in his new pack. Running and hunting together would strengthen their bonds. The parents, siblings, mates, and offspring of his friends would belong to the pack, but he would have no one except their children, assuming she could have them. How long before he began to regret his isolation?

A nip behind her ear interrupted her reflections. Preening and pawing, Sawyer did a little dance. His invitation chased her thoughts into the shadows. Time to play!

Steffi obliged by leaping at him and then racing away. He gave chase. When he caught her, they tumbled in the tall, sweet grass on the edge of a large forest. This was Sawyer's world. Sawyer's life. She could never be the mate who ran with his pack.

When sharp teeth clamped onto the fold at the back of her neck, she stiffened. *Damn.* She'd heard that growl before. In the plane to Montreal. The first time Sawyer's *loup-garou* had expressed his need to mate. She tried to shake him off, but his teeth tightened. Steffi closed her eyes.

This couldn't be happening. Didn't the female have to be in heat? Evidently not, because Sawyer's big body covered hers, not like her human lover, whose lovemaking seasoned passion with tenderness, but like a beast bent on satisfaction. Of course, she too was a beast, and her *loup-garou* reveled in Sawyer's musky scent and the big furry body that surrounded her. She ached to feel him inside her.

No! No! Stop! Her *loup-garou* seemed to be seeing fireworks instead of her human's alarm flares. Humans could walk away if their agreements failed. But *loups-garous* mated for life. Which would be fine if she were a pure *loup-garou* instead of an Anomaly. What if Sawyer mated with her today but later found his true *loup-garou* mate?

Go! Her human roared with authority that shot fear through her *loup-garou*. The need to escape wiped out physical desire.

Sawyer was bigger and stronger, but she was fast and flexible. With a snarl that startled her, she broke away and streaked toward the forest.

She bounded into the woods with Sawyer in pursuit. She couldn't outrun him, but once she caught her breath, she could become a bird and fly back to their picnic spot. Sawyer would be unhappy, irritated, but after she shared her fears, he would understand.

A twinge in her left front leg slowed her. Behind her, Sawyer howled. His paws thumped faster, faster. He was gaining on her. Time to fly. But she couldn't shift on the run.

Something slammed into her right hip and knocked her sideways. What the—

Metal snapped with a deadly crunch. An agonizing shriek shredded the quiet air. Steffi stumbled to her feet and looked over her shoulder.

Sawyer. Was. Down.

Keeping her eyes on the fallen wolf, she shifted with agonizing slowness, as if every cell opposed the change from *loup-garou* to human. Then she edged toward her lover. Evil-looking blades bit into one of his furry legs. The blood loss didn't look critical, but the pain must have been excruciating because his powerful body shook with moans.

"Sawyer."

He gave a whiney growl, but she brought her head close to his ears. He was still Sawyer. Always Sawyer. He would never hurt her. "My sweet *loup-garou*." She stroked his fur. "I'm sorry…so sorry." She edged toward the steel jaws. "I'm going to free you. This could hurt." When she triggered the release, Sawyer snarled. Dragging the wounded leg, he tried to stand, but collapsed.

She took his massive head between her hands and looked into pain-glazed eyes. "Rest. I'm going for help. I'll be back soon." She kissed the fur above his nose.

Retracing their path by foot would waste valuable time. When she visualized her falcon, her body swiftly adopted the familiar shape.

The first flow of air over her wings ordinarily made her pulse race, but anxiety diminished that momentary pleasure. Her left wing was weak. Fortunately, she didn't have far to fly. Aloft, she soon found the current that led to their picnic spot. Her feet barely hit the ground before she became human.

The Emergency key on Sawyer's phone provided no help, but she found his brother's business card in his wallet and used her own phone to e-mail, text, and message.

—*Sawyer hurt. HELP!!!*—

Her overheated brain repeated the message as she dressed. She packed the golf cart and checked her phone again. Nothing.

Turning toward the lodge, she slammed her arms against her ribs, clenched her fingers into fists, and squeezed her eyes shut. *ROLAND!!! COME!!!* Power drained, she leaned against the nearest tree trunk.

"How the devil did you do that?"

Her eyes flew open. Shaking his wet hands, Sawyer's brother stood in front of her. "One minute I'm in the washroom, and the next—" He tucked in his shirttail and checked his zipper.

"Sawyer's had an accident. He's hurt."

Roland looked around. "Where is he?"

She gestured toward the woods. "Do you need to shift?"

Roland sniffed. "His scent is on the wind." He leaped into the golf cart and scowled at Steffi when she joined him.

As they covered the terrain, she provided an edited version of the accident that omitted her shift.

Roland called for an air ambulance. "Antoine's good at sensing obstacles. He must have been distracted."

The blame landed like a weight upon her shoulders. She could still hear Sawyer's rapid breath and feel that bump on her hip. He must have fallen or stumbled into the trap when he pushed her away. Once again, he had saved her, but this time, the rescue had a price.

Her heart shattered at the sight of Sawyer's human shape stretched on the leafy ground. The damaged foot remained a nasty blend of blood, bone, claws, and fur. His breathing mixed with low sobs. She ached to hold him as he'd held her after the attack in the park, but Roland sprang from the cart and went down on one knee beside his brother. He said something in French. Then he lifted Sawyer's head and slipped something between his lips.

"What are you giving him?"

"Something that may help with the pain." Roland frowned. "Don't stand there. Get whatever you packed that can cover him."

Thankful that Roland knew what he was doing, she scrambled to obey.

Working in swift silence, Roland cleaned the wound and wrapped the mangled leg. "You've made a mess of it this time, brother."

Watching, Steffi rolled her shoulder and bit her lip. "I can become a gorilla, and we can lift him into the cart."

"The less he's moved, the better. Help should be here soon. They're following my GPS."

When he hovered at her shoulder and sniffed, Steffi tensed.

"Take the cart back to the lodge."

She shook her head. "No." She started toward Sawyer, who was beginning to stir, but Roland blocked her.

"Go. Now. You broke the Covenant."

She clutched her collar. "You have no proof." A chugging noise filled the air above the trees.

"You reek of *loup-garou,* and there's something…off…about your scent. I've no interest in reporting you, but someone on the medical team will surely do so."

She hesitated. Under normal circumstances, she might have been able to mask the telltale aroma, but multiple shifts and transporting Roland had exhausted her power. She planted her feet and crossed her arms. "I'll take my chances. I'm staying with Sawyer."

"Think of my brother." Roland's jaw tightened. "He shifted with you…perhaps even encouraged you. OASIS will punish you both."

Steffi gasped. "But he's a Montaigne. Surely, your family's influence—"

"Important families have important enemies. Ours would take great pleasure in our disgrace."

When Steffi turned toward Sawyer, Roland grabbed her arm. "If you care about my brother, you must go. He may lose his leg, but if you stay, he could also lose his shifting ability and a significant part of his intelligence. Is that what you want?"

"No. Of course not." Sawyer's tormented wail echoed in her mind. She yearned to comfort him, but Roland had a point. OASIS wouldn't hesitate to destroy her for defying the Covenant. Sawyer would be collateral damage. She gripped Roland's arm. "Please take care of him."

Roland patted her hand and gave her a thin-lipped smile. "Of course, I will. He's my brother." He turned her toward the golf cart. "Your ride to the airport will be waiting at the lodge. Have a safe trip."

Blinking back tears of frustration, she drove the golf cart out of the forest and over the rolling hills. Every tiny bump shot up her spine. As she approached the clearing where they'd picnicked—where they'd planned a life together—people in scrubs and white jackets were hauling equipment from a helicopter bearing a medical insignia along with the ubiquitous Montaigne logo.

Help is coming. Be well, my love. She stifled her tears.

As Roland had promised, car and driver waited in front of The Snow Angel. Feeling lightheaded, she swayed back and forth. Not only had she violated the Covenant, she'd relished the transgression. She'd loved the feral energy, the lean sinews and strong jaws of her *loup-garou*. Most of all, she'd loved being with Sawyer in a pure, animal state as much as she'd loved being with him as a human. She loved being with Sawyer.

Hell, she simply loved Sawyer. Today, she'd even

dared to believe that they could share a future. Then, their dreams came crashing down. How much would he remember of the accident? Of this day? What would happen to his leg?

She scanned the sky. By now, the helicopter would be carrying him back to Montreal, to his family. They would do everything in their considerable power to help him recover so he could take his place. As much as it hurt, she hoped he would find his true mate.

When she squeezed her hands to keep from shrieking, Abigail Sawyer's extravagant diamond glared at her. "I'll be right back," she told the driver. From the concierge, she obtained an envelope on which she printed Roland's name. She started to pull off the jewelry but stopped. Sawyer's hand had been warm when he'd slipped the rings on her finger. *"Keep the rings."* She crumpled the envelope.

She sank into the leather upholstery of the car. Her head hurt. Her chin dropped, and her bones felt as if they'd turned to toothpicks. Moving Roland with her mind had sapped her energy. She squeezed her eyes shut. She would be strong. No matter how bad she felt, she would not cry. Sawyer had encouraged her to open up to her emotions, but she could still maintain control. She would go on. Someday, she might even forget. But right now—

She sat up.

"Take me to Devils Tower."

Chapter 30

From a distance, the top of the butte seemed to float above the clouds. The quiet grandeur of the vision eased the turmoil in Steffi's soul. The closer she came, the more the spirit of the site surrounded her, along with many other visitors. For the first few days, she studied the faces of those who followed the trails around the monument, but none of the bright-eyed tourists and steel-jawed climbers looked like a seer. Not that she had any idea what The Seer would look like. Her Mentors had never provided a description.

At least, speculating about The Seer pulled her away from Sawyer's pain. Deep and savage. Cutting through every inch of his body. That bloody human calf barely connected to his mangled *loup-garou* foot. His moans and shrieks shredded her dreams and haunted her waking hours. Her stomach churned, and tears stung her eyes. She tried to send positive thoughts, but her mental messages of encouragement and support met barriers stronger than the block on his phone. Sawyer was where he belonged. Receiving top-notch medical care with the support of his family and his pack.

How long did she wander in the shadow of Devils Tower? Beneath the tides of faces and voices flowed a calm as awesome as the monument itself, but that steadying influence eluded her. She had lost Sawyer. If she failed to find The Seer, she might lose her restored ability. Even if she did make contact, The Seer might not grant her request. Perhaps The Seer, like OASIS, thought Anomaly was synonymous with Abomination. Maybe she should go back to Chicago and get on with her life. She would shift for as long as she could. "No," she muttered. *I won't give up.*

She eyed the steep stone tower. A popular legend described how girls fleeing a giant bear had reached this place. The ground rose beneath the girls to lift them away from their pursuer, whose claws left the long marks down the sides of the structure. Taken into the sky, the girls became stars.

Steffi sighed. The closest she had come to heaven had been in Sawyer's arms. Instead of claw marks pulling the tower toward the earth, might the lines be the paths of hopes and prayers moving up? Steffi fixed her gaze on the summit, and everything else faded away. *I will stay.*

"You follow a tangled path."

The voice was so soft it might have come from inside her head.

Steffi caught her breath. Every cell in her body stilled. When the voice remained silent, she spoke. "I left the man I love in pain. Horrible pain."

"That suffering belongs to him. Some paths we must travel alone."

"Like this one?" When Steffi turned, she nearly fell on her face in front of the statuesque golden-haired figure clad in a long white gown. "You look just like I imagined you would when our Mentors told us about you."

The figure brushed a hand through the shimmering rainbow that encircled her. "I am what you expected."

"I had no…but we are told you have many powers." Other travelers on the path jostled past but took no notice. Steffi massaged her right temple. "Am I dreaming? Hallucinating?"

The Seer's lilting laughter was like a song. "No."

Steffi glanced at the people scurrying by. "Why don't they stop and look?" If she was talking to herself, wouldn't the passersby regard her as if she were a lunatic?

"We are here but not here." As if turning on a lamp, The Seer's hand—she seemed to have the normal human appendages—revealed a transparent wall separating them from the oblivious stream of tourists.

"So I can see them, but they can't see us. We're in sort of a bubble. Interesting." Steffi faced The Seer. "Sorry. That's not why you're here." She gestured at the wall. "But this is fascinating." Wait until Libby and Dayzee—a chill stilled her excitement. "Can I tell my sisters about this?" She slapped a hand against her mouth. Duh! Next, she'd be wanting a selfie!

The Seer's fingers barely moved, and the walls became opaque. "Your picture would fade…as will your memory, once we have finished."

Steffi tilted her head. "You can read minds."

Another enchanting laugh. "You are not the first human-based Shifter I've met."

Steffi's cheeks heated. How could she be such a moron? "I know that many of us seek your help. I don't want to waste your time."

"All time is my time. But thank you. What is your request?"

Steffi dropped to her knees. She opened her mouth, but the entreaty that emerged was not the one she'd mentally rehearsed. "Heal him. Please!"

The Seer's soft features grew solemn. "Like the pain...and the path...that request...belongs to him." Regret weighted her words.

Steffi gazed down at her clasped hands. "I'm sorry. I didn't know." *But I would have if I'd listened to my Mentors.* "Is it possible..." The question died in her throat. Although her Mentors had been vague about The Seer's appearance, they'd been unanimous on one item: With millions of supplicants, The Seer responded to only one request per Shifter.

Steffi blinked back her tears of disappointment. She'd had her chance, and she'd blown it. "Thank you for seeing me. It has been an honor." She looked down and waited for The Seer to vanish.

Instead, the musical voice chanted in something that might have been Gaelic. The fleshy center of a thumb pressed the middle of Steffi's forehead. "Goodbye, my child."

"My child." Steffi closed her eyes. A wave of peace spread from the center of her forehead across the crown of her head and down the sides of her face to her neck. The feeling flowed across her collarbones, down her arms to her fingertips. Serenity filled her heart and overflowed into her core, her hips, her legs, her toes.

When Steffi opened her eyes, she was sitting by the table in her Chicago apartment. Familiar photographs surrounded her. The spot in the center of her forehead was still warm. The Seer might not have stabilized her ability but had given her a blessing. *Thank you.*

Chapter 31

In his dreams, Sawyer ran, as far and free as the wind, over rolling meadows, up forest trails, through winding caverns, always returning to the hills in the shadow of Mount Tremblant.

In his dreams, Steffi was always with him, as dark as midnight with that silver blaze down the middle of her *loup-garou* forehead.

In his dreams, they played, hiding and hunting in the woods, romping in the sun-kissed fields, until the need to mate possessed him.

In his dreams, he covered her quickly, his teeth at her neck to steady her. Her back fur rubbed against his belly as she lifted her hindquarters to receive him, and he took her hard and fast with pure animal abandon. Then, she looked over her shoulder, and they were humans on that round red bed. Breathing his name, she drew him deeper and deeper into her heat. When the golden shimmer began, she disappeared.

Be well, my love.

"Steffi…" In the dark room that had been his adolescent lair, he still whispered her name when he awoke. On the helicopter, he'd cried for her.

"She's gone." Roland stated the obvious.

If his leg hadn't hurt so much, if he'd been able to stand, he would have shaken the full story from his brother. As it was, he'd flailed so violently that the

305

attendants had threatened to knock him out again if he didn't calm down. Everyone had celebrated Roland's coming to his rescue.

Steffi... Tears glistened in her eyes, and her hands were gentle but firm when she caressed his head. If he'd been stronger, his wounded *loup-garou* might have lashed out. But Steffi had no fear. The haze of his pain blurred her words. Her lips pressed above his nose. *She kissed me.* The air stirred, every flutter piercing his leg like an arrow. Then she was gone.

In the hospital, when he questioned Roland, his brother said, "Didn't see her. Maybe she tried to find a doctor in town. Or maybe she heard that help was on the way and decided to leave. After all, she had no reason to stay, eh?"

And every reason to leave. A Shifter with Steffi's skills wouldn't want to play nursemaid to a cripple. She'd been willing to limit her freedom when he and his *loup-garou* were healthy and whole. Now, he couldn't stroll in *Maman*'s garden without stopping to rest.

The damaged nerves in his *loup-garou* foot transmitted few pain signals, but his calf still throbbed like a kettledrum beaten by a demon. When he complained, the doctors reminded him that without prompt medical attention, infection might have claimed his leg. He might have died. Some days, he wished he had.

According to his father, the proprietors of The Snow Angel apologized profusely. They had set traps along the property line several years earlier after a guest grumbled about wolves. Rather than face a lawsuit and adverse publicity likely to trash the desirability of the property, the owners had surrendered the land to Montaigne

Enterprises at a bargain price. When his father razed the resort, Sawyer planned to sprinkle salt in the furrows.

"*Attention, Giselle!*"

His baby sister, Marie, alerted her five-year-old not to launch herself at her ailing uncle. Gripping the carved handle of the cane Lucie had sent, Sawyer stood to greet Marie and Giselle on the garden path.

"*Bon jour, oncle Antoine.*" When the little girl hugged his thighs, he caught his breath at the pull on his wounded calf.

"*Bon jour, ma petite.*" He ruffled his niece's golden hair—almost as silky as Steffi's—and settled back on the bench.

The child joined him and folded her small hands in her lap. "How is your leg?" She mimicked her mother's most polite voice.

"*Giselle!*" His sister groaned.

Sawyer hushed his sister's objection with a warning hand. "Thank you for asking, Giselle. My leg is feeling much better." That was what the doctors told him, so it must be true. Over time, his leg might heal, but his heart? Never.

Giselle's fingers crept up to his forehead. "You look sad."

Clasping her hand, he smiled at her. "That would be a terrible way to greet you, *n'est-ce pas?*"

With a giggle almost as enchanting as Steffi's, the child nodded enthusiastic agreement.

"So," he addressed her with the utmost solemnity, "what shall we do that will make us both happy?" He glanced at one of the pockets in his jacket. "A treat, perhaps?"

His niece pulled a wrapped candy from the pocket

307

and did a merry little dance that brightened the garden.

His sister laughed. "I wish to talk with your uncle. Kitty and Jacqui are in the house. Why don't you run along to play with them?"

The little one obligingly departed.

Marie took her daughter's place. "You're so good with her."

Sawyer smiled. "It's easy. She's a sweet girl."

His sister's face grew serious. "You're good with all of them, Antoine. You are their favorite uncle."

"That's because I always have a little something here for them." He patted his pocket.

"No. You have something here." Marie patted his chest. "In your heart. You will be a wonderful father, my brother."

If only... "*Maman* has been giving you ideas."

"Don't be silly." Marie's hands fluttered. His sisters were terrible liars.

"What's her name?"

Marie blushed. "Rose Maxwell."

Sweet and simple. "Not from Quebec, eh?" Sawyer crossed his arms. "So your friend is seeking a mate?"

"Well, yes, but that's not why I—"

"Yes, it is. Give me her number, and I'll call her." When his sister reached for her phone, he stopped her. "Better yet, why don't we go to dinner with you and Nick?" He pulled out his phone as if he needed to consult his empty calendar. If he'd taken a picture of Steffi, he could have made it his screen saver. Not that he needed it. Her image was imprinted in his memory. "How does Wednesday sound?"

"I'll check with Nick." Marie gave him a quick hug. "We all want to help you make the right choice when the time comes."

When the time comes? Sawyer patted her cheek. "I may have lost the use of a foot, but my mind remains sound. I'm capable of choosing my own mate." He had done it, too, in that beautiful green field. *My mate.* If only she hadn't panicked. Whoever laid that trap had hidden it well, and she'd been heading straight for it. To get her out of the way, he'd run faster than he'd ever run before. Couldn't let those metal teeth chomp through Steffi's foot. With one bump, she was safe. Once again, he heard the thud and felt the steel bite. With a handkerchief, he wiped the sweat from his forehead.

"Antoine, are you all right?" His sister eyed him with concern.

"I will be." He checked his watch. "Now, please excuse me." He pulled on the neck of his tee shirt. "I have to change."

His sister's eyes widened. "You have a date?"

He gave her his most roguish grin. With luck, she'd spread the rumor that he was making his own moves in the mating game.

A short time later, Sawyer waved at the elegant woman seated in a discreet corner of the restaurant.

She popped to her feet and kissed his cheek. "It's so good to see you, cousin."

"Good to see you as well, Yvette."

She indicated his cane. "Your recovery is going well."

"That's what the doctors say." He settled into the seat beside her. "They restored the circulation in my foot, but the nerves are too damaged to shift." He shook his head. "OASIS has researchers working on the problem."

"That's promising."

"I suppose, but research could take years." He paused. "The doctors recommend amputation."

"No!"

"Don't look so horrified." He patted her hand. "With a prosthesis, I should be able to walk, even run." *But never far enough or fast enough to lead the pack.*

"What will happen when you shift?"

"I can change the settings."

"Why hurry? You're already walking."

"Not comfortably, and the longer I wait, the more difficult it may be for my body to handle the changes. More important, the more likely my boot might be torn or come loose. Simple Humans spying a *loup-garou* foot on a human body could expose and endanger us. Surgery's scheduled for October."

"After the cotillion."

"Don't want to disappoint the parents and the pack...although once my prospective mate sees this—" He tapped the boot. "—she may have second thoughts. Like *she* did." When the server appeared with the menus, he fell silent. After they placed their orders, he said, "She left me, Yvette. Alone in that forest. I could have died if Roland hadn't found me."

"I hear he seizes every opportunity to boast about saving you."

"He's earned the right."

"Interesting coincidence...that he happened to be in the woods."

"Not at all. He says he had a feeling something was wrong."

Yvette frowned. "Roland has never struck me as the intuitive type."

"He is my brother. We have a natural bond."

"Perhaps. Or maybe Steffi told him, but he's left that part out."

"Why would he do that?"

"To be more of a hero."

Sawyer considered objecting, but Roland did lap up the attention and praise, especially from *Papa*.

"You don't believe she abandoned you."

"I don't want to, but…she said something, but I don't remember what. The next thing I knew, she was gone. When I was in the hospital, I didn't hear from her."

"Your mother blocked my calls. I'm sure she did the same with Steffi's."

"I've tried to forget her—God knows, I've tried—but it's so… I still dream of her. When I can't sleep, I lie awake thinking." He looked at Yvette. "We were having the best day. Except for the golf." He smiled. "Steffi hates golf. She's learned to swear in a lot of languages, and she used them all."

Yvette laughed. "Must have been fun."

"It was. But there was more." He toyed with his silverware. "We worked everything out."

"Pardon?"

"We were going to stay together."

Yvette frowned. "She's not—"

"I know, I know." Sawyer waved off her objection. "But some *loups-garous* have chosen Simple Human mates, and Steffi's more than human or Shifter." His glorious mate. The haughty lift of her head. The wicked gleam in her eye.

"Cousin, are you all right?"

Yvette's question jerked him back to reality. "I'm fine."

"Are you sure? You looked…lost."

"Sorry. I was thinking."

"About Steffi?"

He nodded. "I want to tell you something, but you must swear never to share it with anyone else."

Yvette smiled. "Sounds serious."

"It is. Swear."

Yvette brought her hand to her heart. "Should I seal the oath with blood?"

"No." Her sense of drama elicited a smile. "Steffi and I were so happy we decided to celebrate." He paused. "This is the part you can never, ever tell."

Yvette crossed her heart.

"We shifted."

Yvette's eyes grew huge. "Together?"

Despite the pain, he smiled at the memory. "You should have seen her *loup-garou*. The perfect mate."

"Your perfect mate."

Yvette's words pierced his shrunken heart. "We played a bit, and everything felt so right. But when my *loup-garou* wanted her, she ran."

"Back up, cousin. You tried to mate with Steffi?"

"Well, yes." Beneath Yvette's probing gaze, he shifted position. "We'd already...as humans...so—"

"That's not the same as *loup-garou* mating, and you know it. So does Steffi." Finished with her meal, Yvette placed her serviette on the table. "Before you shifted, did you exchange vows?"

"No."

"When were you planning to do it?"

Sawyer looked down at the table. "The topic never came up."

"I thought you'd worked everything out. What did you say when you proposed?"

"I didn't—"

"Tell me that you at least said, 'I love you.'"

Sawyer's head came up. "Steffi knows I love her. I tell her that with every look…every touch."

"Antoine Sawyer Montaigne, how can you be so stupid? We want to hear those words. We need to hear them." Yvette's expression registered exasperation. "After all the women you've been with, how could you not know that?"

"It's not something…I never even thought of saying those words with any of the others. I do love Steffi, and I thought she loved me. But then she…left."

Yvette threw up her hands. "Put yourself in her place. You made an agreement. An agreement but no commitments, am I correct?"

Sawyer nodded.

"Then, you—whose idea was it to shift?" When Sawyer didn't reply, she shook her head. "Steffi violated the Covenant because you wanted…and then you tried to mate. All Shifters know that *loup-garou* mating creates a lifelong bond. You had made no vows, and yet—"

Sawyer slapped his forehead. "How could I have been so stupid?"

"Family trait." Yvette's affectionate smile was like sunshine peeking through the clouds. "Mostly shows up in the males."

Once, he would have argued the point, but his last day at The Snow Angel—that wonderful, horrible day— had turned his world upside down. "You know, my parents expect me to choose a mate at the fall cotillion."

Yvette nodded.

"They've been so good to me since the accident that

I don't want to disappoint them, but the closer it comes, the more I wonder how I can—I mean, when I made my original promise, I didn't know what it meant…how it felt…to find your true mate. I will never have that feeling with anyone but Steffi."

Yvette pointed the demitasse spoon at him. "Tell her."

"I've tried. As soon as I could communicate, I called, texted, e-mailed, used every social media I could think of. Nothing. I sent flowers, but they couldn't be delivered. I called a friend in Chicago to check on her. None of the other tenants had seen her. She travels a lot, so no one missed her." She'd gone to Australia. With Oh-Alex.

"Even before…I knew she would leave someday. That's why I didn't push for any commitment. Her ability and power are so much stronger than anything I could ever hope to have even if I were still whole." He stroked the pale scars on his wrist. "When we were together, sometimes—don't laugh!—when she looked at me, I felt like one of those Greek gods." Her dark eyes caressing every inch of his body. He groaned. "If she saw what I've become, she'd be repulsed."

"Not if she loves you."

"Don't you understand? She doesn't love me. She can't. She loves the man I *was*."

"But if she's your true mate—"

"I know that, but Steffi—she's not *loup-garou.* She doesn't feel the bond."

"How can I help?"

"I mean to keep my word to my parents and the pack. But first—" He met his cousin's sympathetic gaze.

"You're the sole member of my family who knows what I've lost. Will you help me grieve?"

Chapter 32

Like a fortune-teller reading tarot cards, Steffi turned over each of the papers on her kitchen table. Two weeks ago, the future had been clear. First, a flight to Seattle to see Alex. Now, the prospect of being squeezed into a metal tube with Simple Humans roiled her stomach. In the bathroom, the remains of lunch reappeared. No mouthwash could rinse away that yucky taste. Twice so far, but the day wasn't over.

When she returned to the table, Dayzee's ring chimed on her phone. Steffi fingered a strand of shaggy hair close to her cheek. What a mess! Good thing Dayzee'd never seen her Marcel cut. How different it felt to have a haircut that actually made you feel beautiful. It also helped when the man you loved looked at you as if he thought you were the most beautiful woman in the world. Sawyer had years of practice appreciating women. At the cotillion, he would look at his mate with love and devotion as well as desire. Composing her features, Steffi accepted the video call.

"Hey, Steff, it's about time I heard from you." Her sister was standing in California sunshine, with a lot of noise in the background. "Libby and I have been wondering what you were up to. Enjoying Paradise with Sawyer Montaigne?"

Her stomach flipped at his name. "Hardly."

"Didn't work out, huh? That's too bad."

"It was a fling." She sat up. "More important, I've recovered my ability."

"Great!" Dayzee applauded. "Have you told Libby?"

"Not yet. Since I got back, I've been busy."

"Right. And you're coming here to visit after your interview with the hot guy from Indonesia?"

Once Steffi would have agreed with Dayzee's description. Before Sawyer. "Alex isn't *from* Indonesia. His research—"

"Must have been good to the last drop." Before Steffi could object, her sister grinned. "I'm glad you're not wasting any time moping over the one that got away."

Dayzee's image of Sawyer as a fish slipping off the hook came uncomfortably close to how his unconscious body had looked in the forest that last day.

"Australia with Alex." Dayzee flashed a lascivious smile. "Yum."

Steffi would have rolled her eyes, but she was too busy suppressing another bathroom run. "About as much fun as being locked in a steam bath." Plumes of steam from the hot tub framed Sawyer's face. The silly beard. That outlandish mustache. Beneath the makeup and padding, still Sawyer. Always Sawyer.

"I'm looking forward to your visit. What's your ETA?"

"I'm sorry, Day. I've been meaning to call, but things have gotten away from me. I'm not taking the job." Steffi glanced at the table to be sure she hadn't left the tests where her sister could see them. She'd stared at those stupid lines for hours, but they wouldn't disappear.

"Why not? Sounds terrific."

317

"The research would be interesting, but the weather is insane. Like 120 degrees when Alex plans to be there. I don't want to put my recently recovered ability through that kind of stress too soon."

Dayzee's eyes narrowed. "You sure you're all right? You look a little green."

"Maybe the color's getting weird on your phone. I'm fine." Steffi swallowed. "But I do have to go. Talk to you soon."

"Call Libby!"

****

A few days later, Steffi sat at her table and reviewed the job that might have been. She'd have been working directly as Alex's assistant. In addition to handling her own contacts, she'd have kept records of everyone else's progress. She'd have helped draft the report and had her name on it. A solid academic job with no long, stressful shifts. An impressive addition to her resume. Once, she would have danced around her apartment at the prospect. Now, she stuffed the papers into their original envelope.

Oh, God! Another bathroom run.

Sawyer had joked about The Snow Angel staff's using pins to add the hearts that adorned their garish condoms. If he'd thought the protection defective, he would surely have resorted to his personal supply. He was too tied to his family...to his pack...to take chances. Those galactic orgasms had changed everything else in her body. Why not the condoms? Not quite everything had changed. A speedy sperm could still penetrate a receptive egg.

Sawyer had looked wistful when they'd talked about children. What would he say if—no. He had enough to deal with. He didn't need a reminder of the glorious day that had become a gruesome nightmare.

Still, he had a right to know. What would happen then? Perhaps *loups-garous* didn't acknowledge offspring who came from illicit coupling. More likely, the packs accepted offspring who could become *loup-garou* but rejected the alien parent. Sawyer would never allow them to take her child away, but Antoine would obey the law of the pack.

When she visualized a barricade of Montaigne *loups-garous*, a chill scraped her heart. They would dare her, tongues dangling from the open mouths that exposed their long sharp teeth in sinister grins. When she tried to breach their wall, they would advance, slowly, to give her a chance to back off, to leave her child with them. If she kept her human shape, they could easily overwhelm her. If she shifted to something more menacing—a dragon perhaps—they would scatter, but many would perish in flames. Sawyer and their child might be among them.

No! She could never let that happen. If only he hadn't tried to mate. If only he hadn't pursued her. If only he hadn't bumped her. *If only, if only, if only.* She pressed her hands to her ears as if that could shut out the clang of the metal, Sawyer's howl bleeding into her bones as if she, too, had been impaled.

She shouldn't have run from him. She should have let him take her. No one else would ever have known, and they would now be on their way to his cabin.

When her door buzzer sounded, she frowned. None of her friends in Chicago knew she had returned. Who could...Sawyer! *Don't be silly.* Her heart began to pound as if she were training for a marathon. She punched the intercom button. "Yes?" She held her breath, half-hoping, half-fearing. This visitor wanted someone else in the building.

"Steffi, it's—"

"Yvette." The soft voice surprised her. Steffi surveyed her messy apartment.

"I must see you."

Oh, dear. Had Sawyer's cousin decided to strike out on her own? Why now? "It's good to hear your voice. I'm sorry, but I…I'm not feeling well." Steffi's cough sounded fake. "Some kind of flu that won't quit." She paused. When the other woman didn't respond, she added, "It could be contagious."

"It's about Sawyer."

Sawyer! With her heart pounding in her throat, Steffi mashed the door release. Yvette had come all the way from Montreal. She must have bad news. Steffi ran a hand through her disheveled hair and composed her features. *Whatever has happened, control.*

When Yvette knocked, Steffi opened the door and stepped back.

"How good to see you again!" Sawyer's cousin swept into the room. In her tailored pants, shirt, and patterned jacket, she was as stylishly put together as ever. Bright colors. No hint of black. Her makeup was polished, and her hair looked as if she'd just left Marcel's chair. She opened her arms, but Steffi stepped farther back and held up both hands.

"Best keep your distance." She pointed to her throat. "Flu."

When Yvette gave her a quick once-over, Steffi started to cover her torso with her arms, but refrained. Nothing was showing yet. "You've come a long way. Would you like something?" She hurried to the breakfast nook. "Coffee? Tea? Soda? Milk?" She sounded like an overworked flight attendant. *Let's get this over with.*

"I'm fine, thanks."

She must not want to stay any longer than necessary, another sign of disaster.

Yvette gestured at one of the kitchen chairs. "May I?"

"Oh, yes, please do!" Steffi took the opposite seat. "About…" She couldn't say his name, couldn't ask. Instead, she pulled the papers from the envelope. "I'm getting ready to leave for a new job. In Australia." She lied with surprising ease.

"Oh." Both of Yvette's impeccable eyebrows lifted slightly.

"It's better this way." Steffi paused. "I appreciate your coming here. How…when did he…when did…it…happen?"

Yvette squeezed Steffi's hands. "Sawyer isn't—I can't say he's fine, but he is healing, after a fashion."

"Thank God!" Pulling away, Steffi sat back in her chair and took a deep breath.

"He misses you."

"I tried to get in touch with him but could never get through."

"His family blocked calls. Including mine."

Steffi's lips twisted. "When I couldn't talk to him or get any news on his condition, I tried other—I have these new, psychic abilities."

When she described moving Roland at The Snow Angel, Yvette cried, "I knew he was lying! He's such a sooky baby. Wants everyone to believe he was the hero."

"He did call for help."

"After you summoned him."

321

Steffi dismissed the objection. "He saved Sawyer. That's what matters."

"How did you use this new ability to reach Sawyer?"

"I tried sending words of encouragement." *Be well, my love*. Closing her eyes, she laced her fingers. "At first, I felt darkness and pain. Pain gave way to anger at himself...and at me. After that, a flood of incredible sadness. The last time, nothing." She opened her eyes. "He shut me out."

"He's tried to contact you but with no success."

Steffi drew a sharp breath. "When I went to Devils Tower to meet The Seer about stabilizing my ability, I wanted to quiet my mind, so I turned off everything. I must have a million unread messages." She looked at Yvette. "Poor Sawyer!" As if he hadn't endured enough.

"He thinks you've moved on." Yvette gestured at the papers on the table. "I suppose that's true."

"What about him? Has he...moved on?"

"Not yet. But in three weeks, he plans to take a mate at the fall cotillion."

Three weeks? "That's a good thing, isn't it? He belongs with his family, his pack."

"Does he?" Yvette put her elbow on the small table and rested her chin in her palm. "You ran with him."

Steffi gasped. "How do you—Roland promised..."

"Sawyer told me." Yvette's features relaxed. "So Roland saw you."

"No. He smelled me." Steffi slapped the table for emphasis as she recalled how Roland's gaze bored into her skin.

"And threatened to expose you."

Steffi nibbled on her lower lip. "I think he did what he thought was best for Sawyer...for the family."

"And for Roland."

Steffi stood and walked to the opposite wall before turning back. "When we ran, at first, being together was exhilarating. I loved being *loup-garou!*" She opened her arms. "Almost as much as I loved... Remembering how he looked still makes my blood sing."

Yvette tilted her head. "I've seen more *loups-garous* than you have, but I admit my cousin was a handsome specimen."

Was. The word slammed into Steffi's brain. She wasn't going to cry, was she? "He was so different in his *loup-garou.* Still Sawyer but he moved with such ease, such freedom, such joy." Now, movement brought him pain. Steffi sank back into her chair. "For the first time, I understood what he was giving up for me."

"Oh, Steffi." Yvette stared at her. "You misunderstood. My cousin loves his family and his pack, but that joy was not for them." Yvette reached for Steffi's hand. "It was for you."

Steffi pulled away. "How can you be so sure? You weren't there."

"Because I saw it in his face and heard it in his voice when he talked about that day. My cousin has been with many females but has loved only one." She gazed directly into Steffi's eyes. "You are true mates."

"He wanted...but I couldn't...I didn't want him to lose...I ruined everything." Steffi buried her face in her hands.

"Sawyer loves you."

Steffi looked up. "How can he? Whenever he looks at his leg, he must remember that I—if I hadn't—it was my fault."

"*Pas du tout.* Not at all. He remembers that you left

him. He believes you are repulsed by his condition."

"That's ridiculous."

"Is it? Be honest. His appearance matters to you, and he knows it. When you talk about the strength and beauty of his *loup-garou*, your voice warms and your face lights up."

Steffi flushed. "He has a beautiful body, and I *do* admire it, yes, but Sawyer is so much more, as a human and as a *loup-garou*."

"He needs to hear that from you."

Steffi blinked back the tears that clouded her vision. "I do love him, Yvette, but I can never be his true mate without violating the Pack Covenant."

"Then OASIS should modify the Covenant."

"The *loups-garous* would never agree."

"All packs and other alliances vote on Family-wide policy changes, but OASIS can institute changes on a pack level. That gives individual packs the choice."

"Sawyer's father is the Montaigne alpha. He will never agree."

"Under ordinary circumstances, that's true, but your situation is not ordinary." Yvette grinned. "If he balks, you could do a bit of mind-bending as you did with Roland. Even better, you can tell him about your 'flu,' eh?" She winked. "*Oncle* César dotes on his 'flus'."

So much for secrets. Steffi hugged her midsection. "Three weeks isn't much time. First, we have to get OASIS to make the change. They think my sisters and I are nothing but trouble. I don't think they'd agree to meet with me."

"Of course, they will see you. You bear The Seer's Mark."

The spot on Steffi's forehead warmed. "So?"

"Didn't your Mentors tell you what it means?"

"Probably." Steffi shrugged. "I didn't pay much attention, didn't think The Seer stuff was real."

"And now?"

"Oh, yes. Even though I don't remember anything about our encounter except that I blew the chance to stabilize my ability." Her index finger found the mark. "I thought she touched me out of pity."

"Hardly." Yvette scoffed. "The Mark identifies you as a possible successor."

"What?"

"The Seer is ancient but not immortal."

Steffi smacked the table. "No! I want a life with Sawyer and our family, not floating around and talking to strangers. Anyway, I can't—I don't know anything about being The Seer."

Yvette laughed. "Relax. This is not an imminent appointment. Or a certain one. But a day will come, probably far in the future, when you will be called to learn what you need to know, along with other candidates who carry the Mark. From that group, the new Seer will emerge."

"It better be very far in the future." Steffi took a deep breath and scrolled through her Contacts. "We should talk with my sister Libby's Mentor, Ellyn. She knows OASIS policy backwards and forwards. I bet she'll help us frame the proposal." Steffi put her phone on the table. "What if OASIS refuses?"

"They will respect The Seer's Mark."

But they don't respect me or my sisters.

Yvette brought her hands together beneath her chin. "If all else fails, true mates belong together."

"Three weeks," Steffi murmured. "Not much time."

Yvette pointed to the phone. "Make the call."

Chapter 33

"Watch what you're zipping!" Steffi swatted the hands that were sealing her into the floor-length gown.

"Be still, or you'll mess up your shoulder wrap." Dayzee glanced at Yvette, who watched with the concentration of a general preparing for battle. "This silk feels gorgeous. Where did you find it?"

"*Madame* Berceuse." Yvette bowed her head. "I'd be happy to introduce you."

"Yes, please! We're up for three special effects awards, and this fabric would make a fantastic red-carpet gown, don't you think, Steff?"

"Sure," Steffi muttered, studying her reflection in the full-length mirror. Marcel had threaded white jasmine through her upswept hair, and Yvette's makeup magic had transformed her into a dark-eyed beauty. Her gown was a frothy mixture of silk and chiffon in shades of red, with black velvet trim that drew attention to her bosom. Perfect for dazzling her mate.

"Steffi!" Yvette was at her side. "Hands off the hair."

"Yes, ma'am." Bending her knee exposed more bosom. "Oh, dear."

"What's wrong?" Yvette asked.

Libby's gaze moved from her sister's face to the bodice. "It's the cleavage, isn't it?" She turned to Yvette. "Steff got the best breasts, and she's always tried to hide them."

"Not tonight." Yvette drew herself up. "My cousin admires your bosom."

Steffi laughed. Sawyer thought all breasts were beautiful.

Dayzee snickered. "Flaunt it if you've got it, and, sister, you've got it."

"But it's all anyone will notice."

When Steffi folded her palms over her heart, Libby cried, "Don't you dare!"

Dayzee sidled up. "Look at it this way, Sis. If people are eyeing those babies, no one will notice the real one." Dayzee and Libby exchanged high fives.

Smoothing her skirt over the slight bulge, Steffi looked from one amused sister to the other. "I'm glad someone's having a good time." She turned again to the mirror. The gown looked graceful from all angles. Everyone agreed she would make a breath-taking entrance.

Yvette clapped. "Let me see. One last time." Circling Steffi, she murmured and made minor changes. At last, she stepped back. "You're ready."

Steffi hesitated. "Suppose he can't bear to look at me?"

"Kiss him as if his life depended on it." Although Yvette's voice was light, her expression was solemn. "It does."

****

Sawyer viewed the crowded ballroom. The only thing in life more boring than a board meeting had to be these cotillions. For centuries, *loups-garous* had established their bond by mating in the forest beneath the full moon. In recent decades, mating had become more about putting on a show of prosperity. On the positive side, the cotillion gave females an opportunity to dress up in their human shapes, and they looked splendid.

Sawyer smiled at another candidate parading past on her father's arm. Like her peers, she had the beauty of youth but little character. *Maman* encouraged him to choose a mate he could mold to his tastes as well as one likely to breed on first mating. His sister Marie's friend Rose had a hearty laugh, but she seemed more interested in dancing with other prospects than talking with him. An O'Shaugnessy from Vancouver had charm but little else, and she smelled like watermelon. The more he spoke with these innocent girls and beautiful women, the more he ached for the mate he'd lost. The longer their separation, the more deeply the memory of Steffi's *loup-garou* rooted itself in his heart.

His good foot tapped the rhythm of the dance, and his body recalled the movement, but his damaged foot merely shuffled. Although the prosthesis would improve his mobility, never again would he dance on his own two feet. Not that it mattered. Now, he danced only in dreams. With the support of his cane, he thumped around the ballroom.

At the far end of the hall, couples were lining up to enter the Commitment Room, where the Elders heard and recorded their vows. Younger mates received a blessing and a gift. Older mates, congratulations and a handshake. Smiling, whispering, and holding their partners close, everyone in the line looked happy, and why not? They'd found their hearts' desire whereas he—he'd never love the female he mated with tonight, but he would give her everything he could. Except his heart.

As he circulated on the edge of the dance floor, he

forced himself to converse with every fourth eligible female. Some were beautiful. Some were bright. A few were both. All were clearly delighted by his attention. In the busy ballroom, Montaigne power and privilege outweighed physical deformity, but how would these women respond if he removed the boot and exposed his damaged *loup-garou* foot?

He returned to his original station.

"Antoine." From tiara to toe box, his mother glittered.

He offered a slight bow.

She gestured at the assembly. "What are you waiting for?"

Good question. "There are so many lovely women, *Maman*. It's hard—"

His mother lifted her chin. "Choose."

With a grunt, he gripped his cane and prepared to make another circuit, this time counterclockwise. Surely, someone—

An excited buzz filled the air. Sawyer glanced across the ballroom at the grand staircase. A flash of red made his heartbeat stutter. Could it be? No. But it was.

"Steffi." He breathed her name.

The band must have continued to play, but as he took in the figure at the top of the stair, the music faded, and everyone else in the room became shadows. White blossoms entwined in her dark hair. Her creamy bosom rose above the bodice of her gown. She looked more beautiful than he remembered.

I must be dreaming...or hallucinating.

No, it's me.

His jaw dropped. *Steffi! I can hear you?*

Another weird ability. Her hands clutched her small

330

bag. *You're alone?*

Not anymore.

Her shocked gasp was like a slap. *You have chosen. You. Only you.*

Her smile brightened the ballroom.

She descended at a speed that belied her regal appearance, her shapely thigh flickering through a slit in the long skirt.

Not so fast! Muscles tensing, he gripped his cane. If she stumbled and he raced to the steps to catch her, he'd trip and fall flat on his face, the textbook image for what he was feeling and a humiliating reminder of what he'd become. *Slow down! Please!*

Steffi stopped. With a nod in his direction, she resumed her descent at a more dignified pace.

When his cane tapped the boot, he froze. He should leave before she saw his foot, but he couldn't take his eyes off her.

On the last step, she turned toward him, and the soft light around her deepened. *Sawyer.*

Her thought caressed his spirit.

"*Mademoiselle* Anbruzzen." Scarred hand jammed into his pocket, his father stepped forward.

The music died. Everyone else in the room drew closer to the stairs to watch the Montaigne family drama unfold.

With a groan, Sawyer shifted position until he could see Steffi's face over *Papa*'s shoulder. *You remember my father.*

Her lips quirked. *Who could forget?* Laughter danced in her words. The smile she offered *Papa* could have melted a glacier.

His father's shoulders set like steel rods. "This event

requires an invitation. Please leave."

Steffi lifted her chin. "I understand that Shape-shifters come here to choose their mates." When she looked over his father's shoulder and dipped one set of extravagant eyelashes in a wink, Sawyer's heart nearly leaped from his chest. Although she spoke in halting French, she had a clear and commanding voice. Other, more suitable males looked ready to leap to her side. Sawyer growled and tightened his grip on his cane as if he could beat them away.

Jewel-encrusted gown rustling with every step, his mother joined his father. "*Loups-garous* are here to choose their mates. You are an Anomaly." His mother spat the word.

The corners of Steffi's mouth twitched at the insult.

His mother gestured to the security guards. "Remove her."

"Now, now, let's not be hasty." Beneath his mother's glare, Steffi's smile broadened. She extracted several folded papers from her bag. "OASIS has amended the Pack Covenant regarding those of us who are born without Family affiliation."

Pushing through the crowd, Sawyer paused to stare at Steffi. She had negotiated with OASIS? What a female! And she wanted *him*! Maybe not. His aching leg brought him back to reality. Steffi didn't know how he'd changed.

"Anomalies." His mother sneered.

"Yes." Steffi tapped the page. "OASIS has agreed that we may join a werewolf or *loup-garou* pack so long as the pack alpha consents." She indicated a spot. "Please sign here." When she offered the papers to *Papa*, he took them but kept his fingers far from Steffi's.

"What is this foolishness?" His mother appealed to the onlookers before turning to his father. "César, you will not—"

"A moment, please." His father perused the document. Then, he regarded Steffi. "This appears to be in order. But you should have submitted it before the cotillion so that I could have conferred with the Elders and verified the authenticity of the form with OASIS."

Steffi sighed. "I received my official copy two days ago. You can see the OASIS seal, and I'm sure you recognize the signatures. If you wish to confer with your Elders, please do." She smiled at Sawyer. "We can wait."

Gripping his cane so tightly his fingers cramped, he thumped his way through the crowd to join her.

What had Yvette told him? Women needed to hear the words. "Steffi, I was a fool. I should have told you I loved you, but I didn't. I'm sorry."

Eyes widening, she drew back. "You…didn't…love me?"

The catch in her voice stabbed his heart, but before he could respond, his mother spoke up. "Of course, he didn't. How could he? You're the one who—"

When she pointed at Sawyer's foot, he growled. Clutching the diamonds at her throat, his mother recoiled.

"Sawyer." Tears glistened in Steffi's eyes. "I am so sorry."

His soul shriveled beneath her pity. "You've nothing to be sorry for. I was the one who kept wanting more and more until—" He lifted the ugly boot so she couldn't avoid it. "I got what I deserved."

"No. You saved me—again—and I left you."

Reaching out, he helped her step down to the floor.

If only he could pull off her glove and kiss her warm palm! "I thought you had abandoned me, but through the worst of it, you were with me. In here." He touched his temple. *Be well, my love.* "I didn't know that until I heard you tonight. When I talked about the voice, the doctors said I was hallucinating and gave me drugs to make it…your voice…go away." He cleared his throat. "I loved you then. I love you now. I think I will always— but everything has changed. I've—"

"Not everything." When she slipped off her long gloves and cradled his face in her hands, her fresh scent surrounded him, and that outrageous diamond dug into his cheek.

"You kept the rings!"

"They made me feel close to you. I love you, Sawyer Montaigne. I love who you were. I love who you are. I love who you will be." The honey in her voice soothed his troubled soul.

"I am so much less than I was, and you—you are so much more."

"I am your true mate, and you are mine." The fire in her eyes dared him to disagree.

Maman cleared her throat. "It's not quite that simple."

Sawyer swore under his breath.

"To join a pack, one must be able shift to the *loup-garou* shape. Where is your proof?"

Steffi opened her mouth, but Sawyer spoke first. "OASIS has certified that Steffi and her sisters can take a myriad of shapes from elephant to worm."

"We have no interest in worms or elephants." His mother spoke with icy patience. "Show us your *loup-garou.*"

Worry gnawed at Sawyer's gut. At The Snow Angel, Steffi shifted as smoothly as a natural *loup-garou*, but stress might disrupt her restored ability. "You don't need to do this."

"Yes," his mother insisted, "she does. Everyone in this room shifted to become a pack member." A murmur of agreement rippled through their audience. "The Anomaly has already requested one exception to our laws. Must we grant another?"

When Steffi drew a deep breath, her breasts almost popped out of her gown. They looked fuller than he remembered. The onlookers seemed restless.

"Silence!" Sawyer shouted. "Let her speak."

Steffi clutched her bag. "I would be delighted to shift, but my doctor has advised against it at this time."

Doctor? Sawyer studied her serene face. The scar on her forehead where she'd stored her video implant had changed. "Are you ill?"

"No, thank goodness." She pressed one of his hands against her belly. "Just pregnant."

His pulse stuttered as he found the swelling. Her scar glittered like a small starburst. "*Enceinte? Pregnant? Vraiment? How long?*"

"About four months."

Four months? We're having a— He opened his mouth, but no words emerged. He felt as if he'd swallowed a balloon that threatened to carry him away.

She pulled something else from her bag. "Here's their first picture."

Their? He consulted the photo and met her amused gaze. "Twins?"

Steffi nodded.

Dropping his cane, he caught her up in his arms. His

good foot lifted to waltz her around the room, but his *loup-garou* paw was like a lead weight.

"Don't be too excited, Antoine." *Maman*'s tart voice rang out. "They may not be yours."

"Mind your tongue, madam." Releasing Steffi and retrieving his cane, he stepped between his mother and his mate. "If you were a man, I'd wipe the floor with you."

His mother made a scornful gesture at his ruined foot.

Steffi's grip on his arm tightened. *If you have any doubt—*

None whatsoever. When he kissed her, the rest of the world disappeared.

"So the Anomaly can breed." *Maman*'s words cut into the lovely moment. "Your offspring may not qualify for pack membership."

Linking her arm with Sawyer's, Steffi faced his parents. "They will be half *loup-garou*. If they are Anomalies, we will train them to accept the *loup-garou* as their primary animal shape." She turned to his father. "*Monsieur* Montaigne, if you wish to keep your son and his offspring in the Montaigne pack, all you need do is sign."

Papa hesitated.

When the starburst scar on Steffi's forehead grew brighter, his father's eyes widened, and his mother grabbed his father's arm. "Seer," she whispered.

With a flourish, his father wrote his name. He regarded Steffi. "For this agreement to take effect, you must now make a public declaration never again to shift to any shape except *loup-garou*. You must renounce all other shapes."

"No!" Sawyer's protest rattled the chandeliers. He looked at Steffi. "If you agree, you will surrender your lioness, your jaguar, your owl, your falcon…and shapes you haven't yet explored."

"OASIS said that to get something, I had to give something."

"Not pieces of who you are."

Steffi glanced at his boot. "We've both changed. My shifting has limitations." She indicated her left shoulder. "This limb tires more quickly than the others. I cannot fly as far or as long as I did. And I failed to stabilize my ability."

"All the more reason you should use it as fully as you can for as long as you can." Sawyer addressed his parents. "If the Montaigne pack does not wish to accept my mate as she is, then I relinquish my membership." His mother gasped, and his father drew back as if Sawyer had punched him.

Steffi gripped his arm. "You don't have to do this."

He kissed The Seer's Mark on her forehead. "I choose *you*." He took the document from his father's unresisting hands and tore it until the shreds fell like snowfall. "We can go to Alberta as we planned. We'll start our own pack." He patted Steffi's cheek. "The Anomalies Pack, eh?"

Steffi beamed. When he offered his arm, she took it.

As they moved toward the staircase, an anguished cry rang out. "You promised!"

He turned. Misery dissected *Maman*'s composed face. "I promised to take a mate." He draped an arm across Steffi's shoulders. "I have done so."

"*Antoine!*" His mother stamped like a petulant child.

"My name is Sawyer." He turned to Steffi. "*Allons.*"

"One moment." Steffi slipped beneath his arm. When she approached his mother, the pain on *Maman*'s face turned to fear. The older woman stepped back, and Steffi paused. "I mean you no harm." She pressed her hands together at her heart and lowered her chin. "A few words."

The tightness at the edges of *Maman*'s mouth softened, but her gaze remained wary.

Steffi spoke to his mother, but the band was tuning up, so he couldn't hear what she said. Steffi's radiance surrounded both women. When the light disappeared, the angles in *Maman*'s body softened into curves. She looked pleasantly surprised.

Joining him, Steffi smiled.

"What did you tell her?"

"That I will do my best to be a good mate…and that we look forward to seeing her at the christenings, where she will have a place of honor."

Smart, sexy, and kind? Would his marvelous mate ever cease to surprise him? The joy in his heart threatened to overflow. "Thank you." When he lifted his booted foot, Steffi glanced at the stairs. "Don't worry, *chérie*." He hooked the cane on his wrist, rested his hand on the banister, and offered his free arm. "I can do it."

She slipped her fingers into the crook of his elbow. "We can do it."

He kept his back straight, his head high as he willed his damaged leg to ascend the steep stair. Although the band had started to play, he sensed that many were still watching, waiting to see a Montaigne fall. He wouldn't give them the satisfaction. It was a stairway, not Mount Everest. As a boy, he'd bounded up and down it more times than he could count. Tonight, however, he'd entered through a back door. Now, every step up took longer than he recalled. As he hoisted his leaden foot, he silently blessed the physical therapists who'd goaded him into resuming his exercise program. He'd reach the top if he had to crawl. Sweat slid down his nose.

"Almost there." Steffi's voice steadied him. She moved her hand from inside his arm to his elbow and squeezed. "Yvette and my sisters are waiting outside."

Chapter 34

"Yvette, eh?" At the top of the staircase, Sawyer stopped and drew a deep breath. "I wondered why she was avoiding me."

Guilt prickled in Steffi's throat. "She wasn't avoiding you. She was in Chicago helping me."

"I should have guessed. What did she tell you?"

Steffi toyed with the snap on her purse. "Enough to make me hope that if I came here tonight, you might love me again."

"Steffi, my love, I thought I'd already made that clear." He placed his hands on her hips, and his gaze reached into her soul. "I never stopped loving you."

Silver glistened in his dark hair, and the angles of his cheekbones and jaw stood out in a thinner face, but he was still her Sawyer. "Nor I you."

Before they could kiss, someone at her shoulder grumbled something in French about their moving along.

With a nod at the security guard, Sawyer released her. His wistful glance toward the swirling dancers on the ballroom floor lowered her high spirits. She gripped her bag to keep from clutching his arm and pulling him away. "It's not too late. You can go back."

He stared at her. "Why in the world would I do that?"

"The way you were looking…" She gestured at the ballroom.

"I was wishing that I could dance with you tonight." His lips brushed her temple. "I hope those dancers will know this happiness."

The guard harrumphed.

Sawyer slapped the man on the shoulder. "We're leaving."

When they moved into a large reception room, the guard closed the door to the ballroom. "For years, my mother led the cotillion planning committee. When she came here for meetings, she brought Roland and me. We 'fenced' on the staircase, and we 'skated' across the foyer." Sawyer gestured at the smooth, gleaming floor that led to the double doors of the entrance.

"Must have been fun."

"Yes, but we earned our share of bruises." He held up his cane to display the pronged tip. "I can manage the floor with this, but you—" He pointed at the ridiculous stilettos.

Steffi laughed. "I'll take them off. That's what I did when I came in. Put them back on before I came down the stairs." She grasped his lapels. "Don't tell Yvette."

"Your secret's safe with me." He patted her hands. "Go easy on the jacket, eh? I won't be buying a new one anytime soon."

"This should see you through my sisters' weddings. Libby and Tommy may be next in line." She smoothed the fabric, but her hand lingered on his broad shoulder.

When she took off her shoes, she shivered. "On the way in, I was in such a hurry I didn't notice how cold this floor is. I was so afraid I'd be too late. Then I saw you with that little redhead."

Sawyer shook his head. "I don't—"

"She was standing right beside you and looking up

at you as if she'd found the man of her dreams."

"We may have exchanged a few words, but the moment you appeared, I saw only you."

Steffi smiled. "Good."

By the time they were halfway across the room, Sawyer paused with every step. Steffi stopped by a spot with end tables and chairs. "Whew!" She wiped invisible sweat from her forehead. "I need to use one of the restrooms they hid in that far corner." She gestured toward the opposite side of the large room. "I won't be long." She patted the back of a chair. "Why don't you wait here?"

A few extra minutes playing with her hair gave Sawyer a longer break. She returned with cups containing water from the fountain outside the lavatories.

Standing, Sawyer drained his cup in a gulp. "Thanks. I needed that."

"I can see why. That ballroom is so hot. I didn't spend much time in there while you—"

"It did feel like years." He turned to look at her. "Until you walked in."

His embrace felt like a homecoming. The slow, sweet kiss sent ripples of longing from the crown of her head to her toes. When she rested her cheek against his chest, his steady heartbeat boomed in her brain. She could stay here with him forever if the security people would let them.

As if he were reading her mind, Sawyer kissed her shoulder. "We'd best be going." He moved his injured foot.

"Is it bothering you?"

"No more than usual."

Her fingers tingled. She gathered her skirts and

dropped to her knees in front of him. "May I see it?"

The corners of Sawyer's mouth tightened. "It's no different than it was in the forest. Aside from being washed and shaved so it fits in the boot. I should have showed it to you before we—you can still...walk away." His hand hovered above the boot. "It's ugly. Grotesque."

"Sawyer! It's a part of you."

"Not for long." His laugh came out like a bark. "In three days, the doctors are cutting it off."

He seemed resigned, and yet... Power stirred in her core. "You were planning to hide it from me for three days? Please!"

With a grunt, he returned to his chair. After he undid the buckle and loosened the ties, she slipped off the boot to reveal the bare *loup-garou* foot. When she touched it, he started to pull away. "I love all of you, Sawyer—every inch." She massaged the foot.

"Thank you." He leaned forward in his chair. "I think this is the first time I've looked at it...that I haven't wanted to chew it off and be done with it.

"I hope you won't mind, but we can't go straight to Alberta. I have to stay in Montreal while I learn to use the new foot. By then, it will be winter—never the best time to set up housekeeping in that area—and you'll be..." He drew a semicircle in the air.

"Not that big, I hope!" Steffi laughed. "So we'll wait till spring. Our first family trip!"

Sawyer tilted his head toward the ballroom. "They're playing a tango. Can you hear it?"

"It's loud enough to hear in Montreal."

He shifted position. "The new foot's supposed to work almost as well as the real one. Once I'm comfortable, maybe we can give the babies their first taste of ballroom dancing, eh? Our babies!" He grinned. "It's still hard to believe."

"That's because you missed the first three months."

"Bad?"

"The pits."

His knuckle lifted her chin. "You should have told me."

"At first, I couldn't get hold of you and…I didn't believe…didn't want to believe… Then, so much was happening. Negotiating with OASIS. Preparing for the cotillion. And you had other things to deal with."

He gripped her hands. "Nothing as important as this. If you'd told me, I'd have come—well, not running—but as fast as I could hobble."

"You're here now. That's what matters." Her index finger traced the deep line where his human ankle would have been. "So many scars."

"Doctors poked around a bit when they tried to fix the damaged nerves."

Suffering lingered beneath his matter-of-fact voice. She closed her eyes and wrapped her fingers around his ankle. "I'd like to try something. Tell me if anything hurts, and I'll stop."

"If I feel anything, I'll let you know."

Power joined with emotion, the light spread from his ankle to his four toes and the tips of his claws. Sawyer steadied his amazed breath but remained silent. The glow deepened, and her power moved beneath his skin, across muscles, into connective tissues. Her energy brushed the dead nerves. A few tips responded, but most did not.

The light went out. Steffi sank to the floor, buried her face in her useless hands, and sobbed.

"Steffi, sweetheart, please don't cry."

Sawyer's arms were around her. He was sitting beside her on the floor. How much had it hurt to move down here from the chair? "I'm so sorry."

He pulled out his handkerchief and blotted her tears with the same gentleness he would use to comfort their children. "It's all right."

"No, it's not." Her lips twisted. She stared at her hands. "Why does my power harm but not heal?"

He cradled her chin. "Your power doesn't harm—it protects you. In time, you may become a healer, but not yet. You've already given me one miracle tonight—when you glided down those stairs. No, two miracles. Three, I suppose. Twins!" His mouth met hers in a kiss that left her aching for more.

He returned to the chair and pulled on his boot. Balancing with his cane, he rested one knee on the floor and reached for her hand. "Would you do me the honor of exchanging vows beneath the full moon to seal our mating?"

Steffi clapped. "Yes! Oh, yes." That golden aura surrounded her.

Standing, Sawyer helped her to her feet. "Your sisters can serve as our witnesses." Steffi hugged him.

"Don't forget Yvette."

"Ah, yes. I have a few words for her. Starting with 'thank you' and including 'godmother' if that's all right with you."

Outside, moonlight splashed across the open lawn. In the surrounding wood where pack members mated, candles flickered. Howls filled the air.

"Steffers! Over here!" Waves and whistles emanated from a figure standing on the far edge of the parking area.

"Dayzee, I presume."

"She's never been subtle."

As they wove between the parked vehicles, they talked about the days ahead. Sawyer slowed and rested against a fender. "You know, I used to avoid thinking about the future."

Steffi regarded him. "Why would you? Everything was planned. You were going to take a mate, settle down, lead the pack, and manage Montaigne Enterprises."

"Then you walked into that lobby."

"And demolished everything."

"Hardly. I didn't realize it until I met you, but I never thought about the future because I didn't want to think about it."

"It would have been secure and comfortable."

"Like a padded cell. Or a coffin." He stroked her cheek. "You and I are on a journey, a path filled with promise and surprise."

"It won't be easy."

"We'll have our share of trials, I'm sure, but we will face them together, eh?" He kissed her. "Steffi, *ma bien-aimée*."

"What does that mean?"

"Beloved."

"*Bien-aimée*. Rather pretty. Sounds like Ben and Amy." She lifted her chin as inspiration struck. "One of the twins is a boy. If the other's a girl, we could name them Ben and Amy."

Sawyer gave an emphatic nod. "I like that."

On a small rise by the rental car, three women waited. Libby stood with arms crossed. Dayzee bounced from one foot to the other. Yvette approached. "You were in there for so long. Did you have to use your persuasive powers on *oncle* César?"

Steffi laughed. "Sawyer didn't give him a chance."

"Pardon?" A frown creased Yvette's brow.

Steffi exchanged a glance with Sawyer before she spoke. "We're going to start our own pack. In Alberta."

Yvette stared at her cousin. "She's joking."

Sawyer chuckled. "Not at all. Of course, I understand if you want to stay with the Montaignes."

Yvette's smile dimmed. "After all that's happened, I don't think that would be wise." She gestured at Steffi's sister. "Dayzee says she can help me find work in California, so I'm going back with her."

"That's great!" Sawyer hugged his cousin.

"You can all be founding members of the Anomalies Pack," Steffi informed her sisters. "Isn't that right, Sawyer?"

"Yes, but let's talk about that tomorrow. Tonight, we have more important business." Sawyer's smile shone like a candle in the dark. "Mating." He turned to Yvette. "*Madame* Grillant, as a pack matron, would you be willing to officiate?"

His cousin beamed. "I would be honored. Let me see." For a moment, she surveyed the area. Then, with a nod, she indicated a nearby clearing. "You and Steffi will please stand there facing each other."

Together in the center of the clearing, Sawyer clasped Steffi's hands. In the moonlight, his solemn face glowed with joy.

Joining them, Yvette rested her phone on the low branch of a tree. "We can record the ceremony and register it with OASIS." She extended her arms. "Libby, Dayzee, come here. We're going to make a circle." The three women joined hands. "We surround you with a circle of love."

As their emotion added to the love that bound her to Sawyer, Steffi whispered, "Thank you."

Drawing herself up, Yvette released her grip on the other women's hands and signaled for them to separate as well. "Let us begin." She spoke in a low, serious voice, clearly in awe of what she was about to do.

When Steffi met Sawyer's warm gray gaze, her heart gave an enraptured bounce.

Yvette said, "Antoine Sawyer Montaigne, please begin."

Sawyer took a deep breath and squared his shoulders. "I, Antoine—" He stopped and began again, "I, Sawyer Montaigne, choose thee, Stefanie Lorraine Anbruzzen, to be my mate."

Yvette nodded at Steffi. "Now you, Stefanie Lorraine Anbruzzen."

Steffi took in the rugged contours of Sawyer's face. He was walking away from his entire life, yet he looked like he'd won the lottery. "I, Stefanie Lorraine Anbruzzen, choose thee, Sawyer Montaigne, to be my mate."

"Please repeat after me, once again starting with the male." Yvette's sharp gaze stopped any feminist objections on Steffi's part. "Thought of my thought."

Sawyer lifted Steffi's palms to his forehead and recited the phrase.

Shifting his palms to her forehead, Steffi followed him. *So far, so good.*

"Light of my light." The words seemed to dance on the forest breeze.

Sawyer moved her hands to his eyes and spoke.

Copying his gesture on her side, Steffi echoed the

words.

"Breath of my breath." Every phrase bound them more closely.

Sawyer murmured the words into her fingers, which rested against his mouth.

Steffi whispered her response. When she kissed his thumb, Sawyer's brows lifted. *I can't help it if you're irresistible.*

Don't make me laugh! When he coughed, Yvette almost smiled.

"Now, please speak together."

Sawyer rested Steffi's hand against his chest while she brought his to her bosom.

"Heart of my heart," Yvette intoned.

Their voices chimed in unison.

Sawyer lowered his palms to her navel, and she imitated the move on his body.

"Life of my life."

Sawyer's boom covered her softer voice. Dropping to his knees, he wrapped his arms around her and kissed her belly. *Bonsoir, mes petits. You will love growing up on the prairie.*

Steffi stroked his hair. "They will love having you as a father. Almost as much as I love having you as my mate."

Yvette cleared her throat. "We are not yet finished. You will both please kneel."

Trying not to fuss while adjusting her dress, Steffi joined Sawyer, who kissed her hands. For a second, Yvette looked as if she might swat Sawyer, but she drew a deep breath and recovered her dignity.

"Let us conclude." Yvette extended her arms and lifted them so her hands rested above Steffi's and

Sawyer's heads. "Under the laws of this province and the regulations of the Organization to Assist, Serve, and Inform Shape-shifters, I, Yvette Montaigne Grillant, declare that Antoine—" Sawyer coughed. "—*Sawyer* and Stefanie, having made their vows, are mated till the end of life. May you have a long, happy union." She brought her hands together and dipped her chin. "You may now enter the woods and mate."

"Not tonight," said Sawyer, helping Steffi to her feet. "The doctor doesn't want Steffi to shift."

Steffi cocked an ear. "Too noisy out here anyway with all those other mates. I know they're celebrating, but they really are loud."

"Wolves," Sawyer reminded her.

Yvette laughed, her bubbly spirit replacing the stiffness of her pack matron. She retrieved her phone from the tree. "I'll submit this and send you a copy, too."

Dayzee and Libby rushed up to congratulate the new mates.

After her sisters took selfies and photos, Steffi turned to Yvette. "Thank you for this…and for everything. I can't tell you how much…how grateful…" When she sniffled, Sawyer offered his handkerchief.

Dayzee said, "Don't cry! This is a happy time."

"Relax, Day." Libby put a hand on her younger sister's shoulder. "These are happy tears, right, Steff?"

Steffi wiped her eyes and nodded. Then she reached out to Sawyer's cousin. "Thanks to Yvette."

Yvette's blue eyes sparkled. "I couldn't let my favorite cousin take the wrong mate, now, could I?"

Steffi hugged her.

Libby eyed the building that housed the ballroom. "With all the howling that's going on, I bet this get-together's ready to break up. Let's move our celebration to the hotel."

"Champagne for everyone!" Dayzee pointed at Steffi. "Except you." Dayzee turned to Sawyer. "She always was the party-pooper."

Steffi threw up her hands. "AKA designated driver."

Sawyer held Steffi close. "Good thing I've hung up my party hat, eh?" The fatigue in his voice dulled the joke.

From the warm circle of Sawyer's arm, Steffi regarded her sisters and Yvette. "As much as I love you all and appreciate everything you did tonight, I am beat." She faked a yawn. "See you at breakfast."

****

When Sawyer closed the door behind them, the relief on his face was obvious. "Thanks for begging off the festivities. I don't think I could have lasted much longer. Sorry I can't carry you across the threshold."

Steffi caressed his arms. "All that matters is that we're here now. Together. Mated until the end of life."

"Welcome home." Sawyer's knuckle lifted her chin so their mouths could meet in a gentle kiss.

When they separated, Steffi looked around. "I didn't know you had a house in town."

"I didn't. Until a few weeks ago. I was recuperating at the family home, in my old room. I could hardly bring a mate there. This isn't quite in town. I wanted privacy."

Steffi surveyed the living room. "Could use more furniture."

"I did buy a bed, and my sisters gave me some things they didn't need. They said I shouldn't do too much because my mate would want to make it our home."

"Wise women." Steffi smiled at him. "I haven't

even met them, and I already like them." She worried her lower lip. "I hope they will like—"

"If they want to stay close to me, they will love you. Not as much as I do, but…like a sister."

Steffi wandered through the house but stopped at one room. "It looks like you bought a toy store."

"When my sisters visit, my nieces and nephews will need a place to play."

Steffi squeezed one of the plush bears that occupied a child-sized rocking chair. "You're going to spoil our kids, aren't you?"

"I'm going to love them. As I love you." He took her arm. "Come see my favorite spot."

French doors on the back wall of the kitchen opened onto a garden ringed with trees and surrounded by high stone walls. As Steffi breathed in the cool night air, Sawyer drew her back to his solid chest.

"A magical moon. A beautiful night." His kiss grazed her temple. "Too bad we can't mate as *loups-garous*."

She turned and met those watchful gray eyes. He might look tired, but the erection that poked her hip suggested otherwise. "Oh, but we can."

"You said the doctor—"

"I exaggerated. I wasn't about to be bullied into breaking the Covenant in a roomful of witnesses. The doctor did say I could shift safely until the third trimester. I shouldn't keep a shape more than a few hours, and I should restrict my shifting to mammals of roughly human size. So no birds, fish, whales, or elephants. But *loup-garou*? No problem."

He ran a finger down her nose. "Clever mate."

She loosened his bowtie and began to unbutton his

stiff shirt. "Now, if you'll unzip me…"

"With pleasure."

Moments later, their *loups-garous* stood, fur glistening in the moonlight. When Sawyer threw back his head, a triumphant howl rang out. Steffi's soft, strong call blended with her mate's. Together, they faced the future.

A word about the author...

People like to quote F. Scott Fitzgerald on there being no second acts in American lives. Born in Baltimore, Maryland, in 1944, I am entering my fifth act. I began to write at age ten when I received a portable Smith-Corona typewriter for Christmas. I was a staff writer with Maryland Public Broadcasting in its infancy (1969-1972) but left to go "back to the land" AKA my hippie days, when freelancing and contractual work with MPB kept us financially afloat. I started writing romance in the late 1980s but paused to earn a PhD in English and teach. Upon retiring, I returned to romance.

Thank you for purchasing
this publication of The Wild Rose Press, Inc.

For questions or more information
contact us at
info@thewildrosepress.com.

The Wild Rose Press, Inc.
www.thewildrosepress.com

CPSIA information can be obtained
at www.ICGtesting.com
Printed in the USA
JSHW050508130323
38852JS00002B/29